Out of the Ashes

ALICIA BUCK

Out of the Ashes

SWEETWATER
BOOKS
an imprint of Cedar Fort, Inc.
Springville, Utah

ISBN 13: 978-1-4621-1727-7

Published by Sweetwater Books, an imprint of Cedar Fort, Inc.
2373 W. 700 S., Springville, UT 84663
Distributed by Cedar Fort, Inc., www.cedarfort.com

LIBRARY OF CONGRESS CATALOGING-IN-PUBLICATION DATA

Buck, Alicia, author.
Out of the ashes / Alicia Buck.
    pages cm
    Summary: When Ashelandra's widowered father dies, rather than risk discovery of her magic studies by an autocratic uncle, she flees and enlists her fledgling magical skills to help the prince search for his kidnapped fiancée.
    ISBN 978-1-4621-1727-7 (perfect : alk. paper)
    1. Fantasy fiction. 2. Adventure stories. [1. Orphans--Fiction. 2. Princes--Fiction. 3. Voyages and travels--Fiction. 4. Magic--Fiction.] I. Title.
    PZ7.1.B82Ou 2015
    [Fic]--dc23

                                    2015011168

Cover design by Michelle May
Cover design © 2015 by Lyle Mortimer
Edited and typeset by Justin Greer

Printed in the United States of America

10 9 8 7 6 5 4 3 2 1

Printed on acid-free paper

To my amazing writing group, Chelsi, Sarah, and Alyssa, who pushed me to finish and lovingly pointed out the problems that needed to be improved. And to my husband, who is always willing to listen to my story ideas, no matter how crazy or impractical they may be.

Also by Alicia Buck
Flecks of Gold

Chapter One

"Ashelandra, you little minx, get into the house this instant!" Baron Fredrick Camery's yell floated across from the manor all the way to the stables where Ash stretched to tie a knot, securing the hay suspended above.

Ash paused at the sound of his voice before surveying her contraption to make sure everything was in working order. Her eyes traveled to the door of her horse's stall where a ball sat precariously balanced at the tip of a ramp. Once the stall was opened, it would roll from its resting place down that ramp, drop off the edge, and strike a lever below, triggering the rope that held a sack of hay suspended above. The sack would then slip open to dump the hay into Windrunner's feeder. It was highly likely that when the stable boy, Bill, opened the stall he would acquire a layer of hay on his face and shoulders as well, but she felt sure he wouldn't mind a little grass in his hair in exchange for one less thing to do. She couldn't wait to see him jump in surprise.

The two stable boys, Teddy and Bill, were in the middle of a fight. Both fourteen-year-olds were sulking, and Ash wanted to do something to shake them from their depression. Because she was three years older than the two boys, and because of her status as the Baron's daughter, neither felt comfortable adventuring with Ash anymore. Ash found it frustrating and boring. When Ash found life too dull, she felt duty-bound to liven it up.

She rubbed her hands together and looked around for a good viewing spot that would keep her out of Bill's sight. The sun slanted in through small gaps in the boards, illuminating the dust floating in the air. They were tiny glowing beads dancing and whirling through the warm stable musk. Windrunner whickered, shifting to the edge of her stall to peer over at her mistress. Ash reached out an absentminded hand to rub Windrunner's nose as she scanned the stable.

"I mean it, young lady." Her father's shout sounded deceptively soft

1

because of the distance. Her head twitched toward his voice, unwilling to miss the imminent show, but reluctant to make her father irritated. He was a jovial man, difficult to faze. He might bluster a bit but he rarely became angry without cause. The problem was that it was likely that she'd given him cause. She considered for a moment.

Could Cook have complained about the missing pepper? She hadn't even gotten the chance to experiment with it yet. Her jokes were always harmless and, she liked to think, even helpful every once in a while. Still . . . Ash cocked her head in thought. She couldn't think of any recent pranks that merited a reprimand. She spotted a good hiding spot and inched forward.

"If you don't show yourself by the time I get to five, you won't be allowed to ride Windrunner for a week." This was one of the worst threats her father could possibly pronounce. Also, did his voice sound closer than before?

Ash abandoned her potentially perfect hiding place in the next empty stall, and rushed out the doors of the stables, skirts catching in her legs as she crossed the pebbled driveway past the carriage house. She rushed around the southwest corner of the manor, keeping to the graveled drive that circled behind the miniature maze of trimmed rose bushes situated in front of the manor, to the front door, where her father, Baron Fredrick Camery of Trebruk, waited with a small smirk on his face.

"Drat," Ash exclaimed upon seeing the smile. It meant that he'd fooled her into coming when she wasn't really in trouble. It also meant that he probably wanted her to do something tedious.

"Watch your language, young lady." The Baron sighed and for an instant, Ash was distracted from her pique. Her father's face looked haggard, his once firm skin sagging, as if lacking the energy to hold itself up any longer. Had he always been so pale?

"Go and put on one of your day dresses. The Marchioness is coming for a visit." He winked, and his features transformed, the fatigue replaced by his usual good humor.

"Lady Amelia?" Ash wasn't sure if she was happy about the prospect of seeing the Marchioness or not.

"She's bringing a young lady with her as well, to make your acquaintance. I believe it is one of her cousin's children who is staying with her at the moment. She thought it would benefit you both to socialize together, considering that you are both seventeen and still need practice before you are unleashed onto society."

Ash scrunched her face in a very unrefined manner. "Is this really necessary?"

"I'm sorry to tell you, my dear, but you need all the practice you can get. I've done you a disservice by keeping you so isolated despite being but a stone's throw from the king's city. It's my own fault for wanting to avoid the stupidity of society, but I've prevented you from learning how to deal patiently with the tedious rules of decorum. Try not to shock her too much, please. She isn't used to young ladies acting like preadolescent hooligans."

"Really, father, I'm hurt." She straightened her back, puffing out her chest and lifting her chin dramatically. "I can't imagine why you'd doubt my ability to behave in a respectable and mature manner." She tried not to smirk and ruin the effect of her pose as her mind flashed to the mortified dandy she'd accidentally-on-purpose unseated from his horse the other day during her daily ride. She had no idea who the man had been, but he'd still felt it was his business to reprimand Ash for not riding sidesaddle. She'd decided to prove how much more practical maneuvering while riding astride could be. Ash's supercilious expression wavered. Had her father somehow heard of the incident?

The Baron arched an eyebrow, and she thought he probably had.

Though she was tempted to stick out her tongue to tease him, that would only further prove his point. Instead, she took languorously slow steps toward her room upstairs, keeping an ear out for any interesting noises. At the base of the stairs, she heard a yelp come from the direction of the stables and grinned.

"You can't imagine, can you? What have you been up to now?" her father asked. She switched from her slow plod to hurdling the stairs two at a time, so he quickly added, "And don't try to get away with not wearing a corset. As understanding as Lady Amelia is, she would still never stand for it." It was a comment that, if said by a father to any other refined young lady, would instill instant mortification.

Ash merely looked back at him from the top step noting that his blue and silver waistcoat was looking unusually crumpled and loose. He leaned against the wall in a slump, as if her antics had made it difficult for him to find the energy to stand without support. For a moment her breath caught in worry, until he took a pretend threatening step away from the wall toward the stairs. "I'll send Jenny if I have to," he warned.

She felt the tension in her shoulders relax and winked, a devilish glint in her eye that she knew would make him worry about whether or not she would obey.

***

In the parlor, Ash sat stiffly in her rich golden day dress, regretting that she'd obeyed her father's request to wear a corset. Miss Penelope Squire kept prattling away about lace: needle lace, bobbin lace, crocheted lace . . . It was a topic so dull that if it were a knife, Ash couldn't even use it to slit her corset strings to free herself for escape. Ash wasn't sure if the girl talked so much because she was nervous, or if a constant stream of chatter was her usual state of being. But really, who wanted to waste so much time on something so meaningless? She tried to pay attention so the young woman would feel more at ease, but it was as difficult as keeping awake through deportment lessons.

Every so often, Miss Penelope darted scandalized glances at Ash's gown, as if the girl couldn't quite make herself believe that a young maiden not yet into society would be so bold, much less allowed, to wear such a flamboyant color. Young women were supposed to wear pastels. Ash forced a courtesy smile, and Miss Penelope looked away quickly to ask the Marchioness Lady Amelia Langrove of Lanraven about what her coming out gown had looked like.

Lady Amelia was a striking woman with small laugh lines around her eyes. She wore her light brown hair in a halo of loosely pinned waves that pulled into a twisted bun at the back. The style softened the size of her nose so one hardly noticed that the appendage was just a little too big for her oval face. The loose bun also helped soften the harsh line of her jaw and made her seem more inviting. She was one of the few gentry that ever visited Trebruk manor. She could be too formal for Ash's taste, but she could also sometimes be persuaded to relate fascinating travel stories and veer from appropriate, ladylike conversation to more intriguing subjects if Ash approached her in the right way.

Despite what her father had said earlier about needing to practice socializing, Ash didn't think deadly, dull chitchat was anything but a waste of time, and Miss Penelope's continuous prattle about fashion was keeping the conversation from being anything but mind-numbing.

The young girl seemed invested in appearances. Miss Penelope's dress was a suitable soft pink with fluffs of lace sprouting from the skirt like feathers on a ruffled bird. The color worked well with her pale skin, rosy cheeks, and contrasting dark brown hair. If Ash were to wear such a thing, however, the effect would not be so striking. Ash's skin was unfashionably tan, her hair neither blonde nor brown, but rather a sort of undecided combination. The gold of her gown helped her hair seem like gilded wheat with twisting brown streaks but when she wore pale colors the effect was muted, transforming it to an unremarkable muddied blonde. Ash's rich gown not only accented her hair, but it also brought out the butter-toffee flecks in her sage-green eyes.

Not that she cared a great deal. If the truth were known, it hadn't really been Ash's intention to choose a color that would flatter her. She just hated pastels. When the seamstress came to outfit her in the clothes she would wear for her presentation into society this coming season, she'd just chosen the bold fabrics she liked best and let the seamstress choose the styles, pleading only that they not be frilly and that they be as comfortable as fashion would permit. As a result, Ash ended up with a collection of dresses that looked much more sophisticated than usual for a young lady's coming out, gowns free of ruffles with long lines and dropped waistlines that flattered her figure. Ash's father commented wryly that he thought the sophisticated effect was rather ironic given Ash's penchant for pranks.

"Your name is so unusual, Miss Ashelandra," Miss Penelope gushed, distracting Ash from her thoughts. "However did your parents think of it?" There was a slight whine to Miss Penelope's tone, like mockery, but the girl's eyes were unreadable, her smile polite, if small. Had Ash's inattention been too obvious?

"My mother was a sorceress. She gave me a sorceress's name," Ash said.

Miss Penelope's smile dropped as her mouth fell open. Lady Amelia shot Ash an exasperated glance, and her lips turned down in a warning frown. A twitch at Ash's lips threatened to curve into a smirk, but the thought of her mother using her last dying breath to give Ash the name Ashelandra Enando Camery of Trebruk stole the enjoyment from shocking Miss Penelope Squire.

"She was a performer?" Miss Penelope asked, sounding scandalized.

Ash scowled, and Lady Amelia broke in hastily before Ash had a chance to replay, "No dear, she was a lady who could do actual magic. I hear King Ferdinand has a young new sorcerer just a little older than you two, though he is out of the country at the moment on some errand for the king," Lady Amelia added in an obvious ploy to stop Miss Penelope from offending Ash further.

Ash wasn't too surprised by Miss Penelope's response, however. People usually had one of four reactions when hearing anything about magic. The first was the most common, and that was for their attention to turn away from the subject, as though the thought of magic was hard to remember. Though the country had been full of magical creatures, plants, and sorcerers thirty years ago, to some people the reality of that past had faded from their minds until they'd slowly transformed their perception of all things magical from fact to fairy tale, not something to dwell on or think about overmuch.

The second type of reaction was wary distrust. This group of individuals did not forget the reality of their country's history, but because the details of that history had also faded from their minds, they felt a fearful suspicion of magic's mysteries.

Some simply accepted magic as something that existed but was no longer connected with them one way or the other. They might consider it an amusing curiosity but weren't concerned overmuch with it.

The last group was the smallest; those who, like Ash, wanted to know everything they could about magic and all that had been lost in the great ban thirty years ago.

Because of Miss Penelope's comment about her mother being a performer, Ash reasoned that she belonged to the first group, so when her head tilted with an unreadable look and she asked Lady Amelia to tell her more of the new sorcerer, Ash was surprised that the subject hadn't been slid over and forgotten as she'd expected would happen.

Lady Amelia waved her hand dismissively. "Oh, he's about twenty or so. I hear he and Prince Phillip are good friends. His name is Sorcerer Tioroso or some such nonsense. Really, Miss Ashelandra, you have to admit that sorcerer names can be a mouthful. Though I did hear him cast a spell once, and his name is nothing compared to the strange clicking and popping sounds he emitted with a few consonants and vowels stuck in between. I don't know how anyone without a beak could make such strange noises."

Ash curved her lips in wry understanding. Mastering the language of sorcery was a monumental undertaking.

"What did he do?" Miss Penelope asked, her slit gaze indicating that she still doubted whether he truly could do real magic or not.

"He created an illusion of one of the creatures that used to run around wild before the king gathered the fourteen sorcerers to banish all magical beings. It was the most curiously hideous thing I've ever seen, at least six and a half feet tall with bumpy gray skin, a huge hooked nose, and eyes the color of swamp moss."

Ash sat forward in her seat. "What was it called?" she asked.

Lady Amelia's nose scrunched in concentration, as if having a hard time recalling the name. "I think it was an okret, or something similar to that." She brushed her hand through the air. "The name doesn't really matter, but the creature was one of the main reasons the king finally decided that he needed to banish all magical beings. One okret could destroy an entire village in a night, and the king was finding it difficult to defend all of the people against this and other magical creatures."

"If magic was banned, why does the king have a sorcerer?" Miss Penelope asked. Was that wrinkle at her nose a sign of contempt? Ash couldn't say for sure.

Lady Amelia gave her the stern look of a teacher to a pupil who had said something daft, and Miss Penelope's face flushed. "The king didn't forbid the practice of magic. In fact, he needed the sorcerers to banish the magical creatures. It took fourteen of them to cast the spell. If not for the sorcerers' magic, dangerous beings would still run wild in our land, wreaking all sorts of havoc. For some reason, however, sorcerers became harder and harder to find, disappearing almost as thoroughly as the creatures. An unfortunate side effect of banishing magical plants and animals and such, I suppose. No one knows why. The king was delighted to discover one of the last sorcerers left, and one so young too." Lady Amelia smiled indulgently, as if the king were a child who'd done something amusing.

A chill rushed to replace the hot confinement under Ash's corset. She knew that sorcerers had been declining, but tucked away in her manor, she hadn't fully realized the extent.

"What do you mean 'one of the last sorcerers left?'" Ash asked, trying to make her voice sound casual rather than anxious.

"I don't know if he really is. There could be sorcerers in other kingdoms, but for a long while no one seemed to have any use for magic. I was surprised when casting spells fell out of favor so quickly. Maybe as the number of those able to perform spells decreased, people began to forget. They failed to remember the great asset sorcerers have been to the kingdom. The young Sorcerer Tioroso's teacher recently passed away as well. I know of no others."

Ash felt sick. The possibility that she and the sorcerer at the palace might be the only magic workers left anywhere frightened her. Soon it might be lost forever without anyone even realizing that an integral piece of the world was missing like a peach without a pit. The peach would be easier to eat, but without the chance of future trees, more peaches would be impossible.

"I've never really understood why the king banished magical creatures. Were all the magical creatures really so horrible? Was it really necessary to banish everything?" Ash murmured, the words slipping out before she considered whether they should.

Ash's comment flirted close to criticizing the king, and Miss Penelope looked horrified. She glanced around nervously as if expecting the king's soldiers to pop out from the behind the curtains and drag Ash away for treason.

"It will be hard for you to imagine, since the land is so peaceful now, but there had been an increase in the usual activity of magical beings. All the sorcerers of the land were not enough to counter the problems that arose, so the king did what was necessary to protect the kingdom." Lady Amelia's eyes locked on Ash's repressively.

Ash ignored the warning, a reckless heat infusing her words. "But he didn't have to confiscate all the magical classification books. Surely there is no harm in learning about what is now lost."

"Ah, now that, I can tell you, is only a rumor. I have it from the king himself that he never banished the classification books. Like the sorcerers, however, the books started disappearing, until there are very few left now. Magic is incomprehensible." Lady Amelia huffed, as if she wished she could teach magic proper behavior.

"But where did everything go?" Miss Penelope asked with a slight clip of skepticism singing through her tone. Ash thought she asked the question to point out how unlikely it was that anything strange had ever really existed, despite Lady Amelia's own experience with the matter.

Lady Amelia ignored Miss Penelope's tone and shrugged delicately. "There are rumors that a hidden land exists somewhere in our country where all the magical creatures retreated. Perhaps the sorcerers also went there and took the books with them. The Sorcerer Tioroso might know more about the matter."

Lady Amelia flicked her hand in a dismissive gesture. "As interesting as this subject is, we are here to improve your general conversation. I think we should leave the past in the past and change the subject," Lady Amelia said.

There was a moment of silence. Miss Penelope fluffed her pink lace–laden skirts with gloved hands, Then, as if reminded, she stole a look at Ash's ensemble. Ash watched Miss Penelope with interest and felt the edges of her lips curl up as she waited to see if Miss Penelope would meet Ash's expectations. Miss Penelope opened her mouth, closed it, and Ash thought the young woman might decide to stay silent. But no, silence didn't seem to be in her nature.

"That is an unusual dress you are wearing, Miss Ashelandra. I don't believe I've seen a style quite like it in the fashion sketches my seamstress showed me when we were discussing what would be most fitting for a young lady newly out into society." Miss Penelope smiled sweetly, but her voice still held that hint of disdainful whine.

"I imagine not." Ash smiled back, not baited in the least.

"It is a good color for you, even if it isn't 'the thing,' " Miss Penelope continued.

When Ash just smiled in thanks, Miss Penelope became obviously irked. "Perhaps your choice had something to do with your heritage? But is it really wise to publicize who your mother was? Everyone I know thinks as I do"—she slid a hasty glance at Lady Amelia and corrected herself—"*did* that sorcerers are really just performers. It might lessen your chances for a desirable match." Miss Penelope's eyes were wide and guileless, but her mouth twitched at the corner and Ash's eyes narrowed.

"Really, Miss Penelope," Lady Amelia reproved.

Miss Penelope lowered her head, hiding her expression but not the flush of her cheeks.

Ash wasn't sure if Miss Penelope was really trying to be malicious, or if she was just tactless, but she'd gone too far for Ash to just let the matter lie. Those in the past who had dared malign her mother later found themselves embarrassed by an ungraceful stumble at the most inopportune moment. Sometimes the offender might be humiliated to discover that she'd been walking around with something brown and viscous stuck to the back of her skirts. The slime always washed out without any trouble, however. And no one ever suffered permanent mortification from a little stumble now and then.

Mischief crept into Ash's thoughts. Her father said he always knew when she was up to something. He said the butter toffee flecks in her eyes almost glowed. Her licked lips flattened in a lazy smile that transformed her face from ordinary to stunning. He told her once in a moment of weakness that he could never bring himself to fully curb her impishness for fear of killing that enchanting metamorphosis. Ash tried to keep her face expressionless, lest she give herself away, but couldn't seem to stop her lips from sneaking upwards, for Ash had a secret, something that made her most brilliant pranks possible. Ash wondered what Lady Amelia and Miss Penelope would think if they knew she studied her mother's sorcery texts daily with more fervor than she ever gave to etiquette lessons. Sorcerer Tioroso might be the best sorcerer in the country, but he was not the last.

She caught Miss Penelope's eye, and the girl winced and shifted in her chair.

Lady Amelia began talking of her recent encounter with a foreign ambassador while at court. The words washed over Ash, understood but unheeded. Her focus was on Miss Penelope. Lifting her hand to cover her mouth, Ash quietly popped a spell so simple she'd discovered it by accident as a toddler. A puff of breeze tapped the back of Miss Penelope's head, mussing the curling loops of the hair left loose from the half bun at the crown of her head.

Miss Penelope's head twitched. She lifted her hand to check her coiffure and glanced behind her, looking toward the closed window before turning back. Ash waited a moment, then popped the spell again. The breeze separated a few strands from the curls to brush against her neck like the fingers of a ghost. The young woman scratched with sharp, annoyed fingertips before glancing around to identify the source. Ash kept her gaze fixed steadily on Lady Amelia, so she noticed when Lady Amelia caught sight of Miss Penelope's scratching.

Pop, and a larger breeze stirred Miss Penelope's hair, freeing a strand from its pins. It whirled playfully before the floating coils fell. Miss Penelope slapped her hand to her head to stop more locks from falling. Her skirts bunched as she pivoted, searching the parlor intently.

"Would you please stop fidgeting?" Lady Amelia snapped. Ash tried not to grin. It was nice to have someone else reprimanded for restlessness for a change.

Before Miss Penelope could explain her unrefined restlessness, one of the maids rushed into the room without even knocking.

"Miss Ash," she said out of breath. Miss Penelope's eyes widened, her blush of embarrassment vanishing upon hearing the scandalous nickname all the servants used. Ash reflected ruefully that her father's attempt to get the servants to stop calling her by her nickname and, instead, refer to her with her full name had failed miserably. When she was little, Ash had been a constant ball of energy and motion. The servants found using her full name to call her took too long. By the time they completed it, she was already out the door and crouching through the fields, pretending to be a wolf sneaking up on its prey. It wasn't long before formality had been dropped in favor of expediency.

"What is it, Jenny?" Ash ignored Penelope's scandalized expression. The young maid was breathing heavily, and even her freckles looked pale.

"Lord Fredrick has collapsed, Miss," she said.

Ash found herself standing. "Send for the doctor," she ordered, following on Jenny's heels.

"What about us?" Miss Penelope asked. Ash half turned in the doorway and regarded the girl with the first hint of real dislike.

"Go. We'll visit again when the Baron is recovered." Lady Amelia brushed her hands forward encouragingly, but Ash didn't see. She was already out the door and up the stairs at a dead run.

The handyman, Tom, and the cook's son were in the upstairs hallway carrying her father to his bedroom. Ash kept pace with them. The corset's tight confinement combined with her mad dash up the stairs made breathing a struggle. Her breath came in short, staccato puffs.

All she could do was pant for a few moments before she was able to ask, "How is he?"

"Can't say, Miss Ash. Jenny was just bringing him his tea when he collapsed. We thought it'd be best to bring him up to his room."

"Good thinking, Tom," Ash said, puffing as she helped Tom and Henry place her father's limp form onto the bed. Tucking his hands under the sheets, she noticed for the first time the blue staining the tips of his fingers and the dark hue to his swollen hands. She dragged the chair from the writing desk to the bed, perched on its edge for a moment, then jumped up to adjust his covers. She lowered herself again, only to prop his head with more pillows when she saw how difficult it was for him to breathe lying prone.

By the time the doctor arrived, her father was awake, but pale, his breathing irregular. Ash paced at the foot of his bed, chair forgotten. Her father's bloodshot eyes tracked her progress back and forth with an expression Ash could not bring herself to look at directly.

Dr. Joyce shook his head at the Baron as if in reprimand. He tried to make Ash leave the room, but she ignored his demand by marching back to the forgotten chair and sitting with heavy finality, taking her father's hand.

"I've hidden the symptoms for as long as I could, but I don't think it's possible any longer," Lord Fredrick said to the doctor. His eyes shifted to Ash, eyebrows scrunched in apology. "I didn't want you to worry but you need to know. I'm dying, Ashelandra."

"What?" Ash, jumped up, snatching her hand from her father's feeble grasp. "I don't believe you. Who told you that? Doctor Joyce? We'll find a better doctor—one who knows how to heal you."

Dr. Joyce huffed, but Ash didn't care. She only cared about fixing whatever was wrong with her father.

"Dr. Joyce is not the only doctor I've consulted about my illness. A virus infected my heart, affecting its ability to function properly. Nothing can be done about it," Baron Fredrick said.

"By doctors, but what about magic?" Ash's voice was a whisper of desperation.

"Ashelandra." The warning in her father's voice was sharp as he looked from her to Dr. Joyce beside her. He blanched and panted, worn from that one word, and Ash felt guilty, no matter how silly he was for warning her to stay silent about the possibility that she could look for a spell that would heal him. Lady Amelia had just talked about how magic wasn't forbidden, but her father probably worried the doctor was, like Miss Penelope, skeptical of magic's existence. He could even be one of the superstitious types, but she didn't care.

She decided to let Dr. Joyce finish his examination while she retreated to the hidden closet where she kept her magical texts to search for a solution. She found several spells of healing, but no matter how hard she squinted and twisted her mouth to experiment with making just the right blend of sound, the best she could master was a spell that bestowed only partial healing.

As Lady Amelia had said, the language of sorcery was a tricky thing to master and not many had the inclination nor the gift to attempt it. Most of the books that Ashelandra owned had set phrases for different spells that must be memorized, but she also had one book that contained a dictionary and showed several ways the verb conjugations might change depending on what type of spell she was trying to work. Ash had tried to just learn the words so she could string together her own spells, but the attempt had failed more often than not.

Sometimes different types of spells were so varied in their wording and composition that it seemed to Ash as if the language of sorcery was not just one language after all, but several hobbled together, making it impossible to ever learn how to speak it fluently on her own,

The spell of healing was one of the trickiest Ash had tried so far. The book seemed to indicate that another phrase with a certain pitch needed to be added to complete the spell, but such a feat was physically impossible for her alone. Roughly translated, the phrase she finally worked her mouth around was similar in meaning to a transformation spell, but instead of trying to transform one form to another, like water to glass, she was changing a broken substance and making it whole again.

She tried it on a cut she gave herself with a kitchen knife, and determined that it only gave about a week's worth of healing. The spell didn't work on her body twice to make the cut disappear entirely, and Ash wondered if that was because the spell was still incomplete and therefore incapable of making a full transformation. She attempted it on her father anyway after the doctor left and he lay sleeping, but she could detect no improvement in the illness's insidious creep.

When she was small, her father had often sat her on his knee to recount how her mother could turn a bowl of water into a delicate crystal bird, move two-hundred-pound masonry slabs through the air, or create elaborate illusions of butterflies swirling in a colorful frenzy. Ashelandra had wanted nothing more than to be like her mother, a magnificent sorceress. But making that dream a reality had been a long, hard, struggle—one she was still striving to attain. She felt so helpless and inadequate.

As soon as Ash could read, she snuck into the history section of the library where the tall shelf of heavy boring tomes pulled away to reveal the recessed shelf behind containing her mother's magical texts. She'd squirreled away the books and spent hours tucked from sight, a book in her lap, trying to puzzle out the cryptic lessons scribbled within the dusty pages. At six, she couldn't make sense of much, but by ten she had mastered a few little spells, such as making a puff of breeze and lighting a candle.

Now, at seventeen, she could move fist-sized rocks from one place to another (she couldn't yet handle anything heavier) and transform water to ice. She felt, too, that she was on the verge of getting the change from liquid to glass right. These were tricky spells, requiring memorization and recitation in the clicky language of sorcerers that Lady Amelia found so odd. For Ash to have gotten so far at seventeen without a tutor was quite a testament to her determination and willpower, but it wasn't enough. Other than through her books, she had no way of learning what could be done for her father—no way of hearing the correct pronunciations. She was like a canary in a cage hung in a vast forest. Though the trees were just beyond the cage's wires, there was no way to reach them.

Days passed. The sickness sapped the strength out of Lord Fredrick as his fatigued heart struggled to beat until he couldn't even sit unaided in bed but had to be propped up with dozens of pillows. Ash haunted her father's room, magical texts spread in a jumble over the floor as she clicked and popped the sounds of spells that might help him. The bothersome noises, combined with Ash's constant fidgeting, eroded her father's patience until he weakly snapped that she was to stop her magical attempts and sit still or go away.

She sat still, but had to concentrate very hard on not moving.

Baron Fredrick smiled at her then, a tired saggy smile filled with little energy, but much love.

"I never thought I would see the day when my little girl would rest so quietly beside me. You can't even read a book without kicking your feet around." His words came out in jolts and pauses as he gathered the breath to continue. "You remind me of your mother. Not the fact that you can't sit for two seconds without squirming." Ash stilled her hands as Baron Fredrick's breath wheezed in. "But she had the same unbound enthusiasm for the fun in life. It seeped off her like nectar and people gathered to her like bees to a flower. Swains left and right vowed their unconditioned love. One even became a priest when he realized she'd chosen me for some inexplicable reason. Don't know how I got so lucky. She and you sprinkle exuberance like liquid sunshine. Don't lose that when I go away."

"You're not going anywhere, Father. You'll get better," Ash said, tears obscuring her vision as they ran down her face.

"No, I won't. It's better to get used to that fact now, dear." The rasping of her father's breathing and her sniffling echoed through the stone chamber. "I'm so sorry for letting you down this way. With you only seventeen, your uncle will become your guardian and the caretaker of this estate until you turn twenty-one. I wish it weren't so, that there was someone else, but he is all the family I have left. The guardianship goes to him by default, as much as I would like to prevent it."

Ash didn't want her father to tire himself by talking too much, but she couldn't help asking, "Why? Is he very dreadful? Is that why you never introduced him to me?"

"We became estranged from each other long before you were born. I hope he won't hold that against you, but even if he does, he has very different ideas about how a daughter should and should not act. I fear you will exasperate his patience beyond what he can endure," he wheezed. Despite the pallor of his face, his lips crooked up at this, as if the idea of his brother's discomfort was not so very bad a thought.

"You make me sound like the devil himself." She laughed weakly with a hint of her old humor.

"Of course not, my dear. Did I not just say how much I love your vivacious spirit? Your uncle, however, frowns on independence in a woman, as well as the study of magic. Do not let him beat the brilliance out of your world." Fredrick closed his eyes and panted, beyond the ability to speak more. By this time, Ash felt frantic. She longed to throw herself across his chest and beg him to live, but she knew to say anything would help nothing, would only tax her father further.

That night as her father slept, Ash sat thinking of what he had said about her uncle. Though many people didn't care about magic one way or another, her father's comment made Ash think that her uncle's dislike might be even more pointed than usual. She decided to err on the side of safety.

Gathering all the magic books littering her father's chamber, Ash carried them to the hallway on the way to her room. She checked both ways to see if anyone was around before pressing a tiny carving on the baseboard. A section of seamless wall opened to reveal a small closet. She'd found the hiding place by accident when she'd been a little girl pretending to be an intelligence officer in the king's army tasked to discover clues to the disappearance of the royal jewels. Actually detecting the hiding place had given her quite a thrill at the time, and she'd spent weeks going over every inch of the manor for more hidden chambers. She discovered three passageways, another small storage space, and a little cubbyhole no bigger than a letterbox or a five-hundred-page book.

One passage led from the kitchen to the dining chamber. Another, accessed from the sitting room, had a ladder in a shaft going straight up to the attic. The third was from one of the lesser bedrooms that led to the armory, of all places. As soon as Ash was old enough to qualify for a room other than the nursery, she begged her father for the chamber with the secret passageway, despite the fact that it was much less grand than the rooms the family of the house traditionally chose in the main hallway.

She never discovered why her ancestral home had hidden rooms and hallways, because no one else seemed to know they existed, and she was careful to couch any inquiries about them in such a way that she could keep their existence to herself. They'd made some of her best pranks possible.

The books she referenced the least went into the closet. She placed the rest within the passage in her room, and then raced back to her father to plant herself firmly by his side. He was still sleeping, his breath ragged and shallow.

Servants came to entice her to sleep if only for an hour but were abruptly sent away again in a manner they had never before encountered from Ash.

Chapter Two

The Baron slipped away from the world three days later, Ash clutching his hand desperately as if she could hold in his life if she just concentrated hard enough. At her failure, she felt the color of her world fade with his passing. The rich green brocade of the bed sheets turned gray, the golden raised patterns blurred and phased to nothing.

The servants didn't discover the Baron's death until hours later and were afraid to approach at first, but when Ash didn't respond to anything said to her, they finally just helped her to her feet and directed her out of the room. She moved from one necessary task to the next like a puppet and passed through the days leading up to her father's funeral in a listless daze. Ash vaguely recalled Lady Amelia's brisk commands to the servants reducing the number of tasks required. Though noted, she wasn't able to appreciate Lady Amelia's presence. Instead, Ash blanketed herself behind a wall of forgetfulness that padded pain, even as she went through the motions of preparing the funeral and fulfilling the million little tasks that needed to be done.

**

The day of the funeral dawned vibrant and glorious. Ash dimly resented the birds' cheerful chirping. The breeze wafting pleasantly across Ash's brow batted her with cat paw taps, trying to nudge her out of her muted cage of protection.

At the small family cemetery, the Trebruk servants ushered the visiting gentry to the seats arranged neatly before the coffin where the priest waited to address the mourners. The visiting gentry, dressed in stiff black dresses and suits, shuffled quietly to their seats, as unrecognizable to Ash as a veiled painting.

The priest's words echoed through her head as meaningless sounds, a sibilant spell of grief. Then, like a blow of an ax, her defenses were breached as she watched the crowd standing like irrelevant statues, surrounding her, surrounding the hole as it swallowed her father's coffin whole. She would never see his dear, loving face again. It was forever sealed. Tears rained down her cheeks and the great aching pain of her loss struck like a spear to her very core. Her breath hitched in loud gasping sobs that rang out over the quiet crowd like a saw ripping back and forth through a tender tree trunk.

Someone close to her cleared his throat.

He coughed and then poked her side. She was barely aware of the sting.

"Control yourself," said a deep voice, its grumbling bearlike growl almost inaudible.

The words were finally enough to get Ash's attention. Her gasping faltered as she looked over and then up into a stern angular face weathered by time with severe lines around the eyes and mouth. He was a large man with a broad chest, and only a slight widening of girth around the middle despite his age, which seemed to be about forty-five or so.

For a moment, Ash believed she'd heard incorrectly, and so stared stupidly up at the man through blurred eyes, sucking in painful jagged breaths.

He leaned closer to whisper, "You are in a public place."

She found it difficult to take in enough air to answer. When she did, her response was much louder than the man's hushed reprimand. "My father is dead. We are at his grave."

The man blew out a sharp hiss of air as if to shush her. "Yes, where it is your duty to comport yourself with grace and dignity for your father's sake."

Through the haze of grief wafting around her like a dark shroud, Ash felt a stab of annoyance. She managed a deep ragged breath.

"He wouldn't mind." Turning toward the lowered grave, she dismissed the man.

"Of course not. He never did care about what was respectable. It doesn't surprise me that he wouldn't teach you the proper way to behave."

The spark of annoyance bothered her fog of grief like a fly transformed into a buzzing wasps' nest of anger.

"How dare you, a stranger, order me to hide my sorrow for the loss of my father. What kind of vindictive cad would then proceed to insult the memory of the Baron at his very funeral? I don't know who you are, sir, but you are not welcome here. Please leave." Ash's voice rose in volume until all the subdued mourners' eyes were drawn to the unexpected conflict.

The man looked shocked for a moment, his cheeks colored before he shook his head, pulled down the edge of his black double-breasted waistcoat to straighten it, and narrowed his eyes. "How dare you address me so—I, who have come all this way as a favor to your father to watch over you. I am Lord Richard Camery of Durbinshire, Regent of Trebruk, and as such I am perfectly entitled to tell you how you must and must not act. Nor do you have the authority to order me to leave," he growled, forgetting to keep his volume low.

Ash's eyes widened, aghast. This was the horror she would have to face daily until her twenty-first birthday? Her heart ached in angry dread. She should have clamped her mouth shut and sat on her anger right then, but heartache and anguish at the picture of a bleak future spent in the company of such an ogre combined to fan the flames of her wrath to even greater heights.

"My father did not want you here, and neither do I. Consider your obligation fulfilled. I do not need you, as I am perfectly able to run the estate on my own. Go back to your home and leave us who loved my father to mourn in peace," Ash spat.

"You have no choice in the matter," Lord Richard hissed. He glanced around at the audience surrounding them, adjusted his already perfectly straight coat collar, and leaned in toward Ash so that his menacing expression was only inches from her face. In a low snarl too quiet for any but Ash to hear, he said, "You'll do well to remember that for the next four years I am in charge of this household. Unfit behavior as you have just displayed will not go unpunished." He straightened and nodded confidently as he pulled at the extended white frill of the undershirt, making sure it fell perfectly to the beginning of his palm past his coat sleeves.

Ash wanted to grab his coat and scrunch it in her fist, ruining his constant efforts to keep it looking crisp, but she was finally realizing through her pain and anger that she may have acted rashly and made her situation worse than it otherwise could have been. Her father had warned her that her uncle might be antagonistic and she would need to be careful. As much as she wanted to rip apart Lord Richard's belief in his own importance, for her father's sake, she would resist her natural inclination. She jerked around, determined to ignore her uncle from then on as much as possible.

The mourning gentry alighted carriages to travel the mile distance back to the manor where food would be served and conversation spattered about like dried paint drips, unwanted and hard to remove. Ash waited for Lord Richard to climb into an open carriage driven by Bill so that she could avoid another confrontation, then walked back to the manor.

***

As soon as Ash had sent off the last guest, feeling finally freed from the weight of giving all of them the expected polite attention while they expressed their condolences—some sincere, some obviously not—Ash turned to find her uncle suddenly before her. He stood too close. Ash suspected he used his extra height as a tool to make her feel small. She took a careful step back so she wouldn't do something foolish.

"I've decided to overlook your behavior from this afternoon. I suppose the pain of losing a parent could make even the most respectable individuals become temporarily unhinged. You are female, after all. I will not extend such leniency in the future, however, so take care that you modify your behavior from now on," Lord Richard rumbled.

Ash bit her bottom lip to stop herself from commenting.

"Now, in all the business of the day, you have not yet been able to meet my children." Lord Richard moved his broad body to the side, revealing two individuals standing behind him. "This is my eldest, Jane. She's eighteen, and my son, James, who is nearly seventeen."

Jane glanced over shyly at her cousin before dropping her eyes modestly to the floor. She was a striking creature with pale blonde hair pulled up softly, completed by a bouquet of ringlets gathered at the back of her head and a few artfully curling tendrils hanging free, framing skin of purest porcelain. Her eyes were large amber brown, her lips full. She wore a black silk mourning gown of the finest cut, the corset accentuating her slim waist and the skirt trailing in perfect folds to the floor. Jane lowered herself in a graceful curtsy. Ash stumbled a graceless curtsy in reply.

James wore a suit exactly like his father's, accenting the resemblance between father and son. He was an inch or two shorter than Lord Richard, his shoulders less broad. His waist was trim with youth, but his jaw curved sharply in the same manner as his sire, and his dark brown eyes were a youthful duplicate. His light brown hair was different from Lord Richard's only in that it held no trace of gray at the temples. As James bowed shallowly toward Ash, she noted that another difference was the way James's slightly faded waistcoat and overcoat showed wrinkles where his father's had none. She curtsied with as little depth as he, and with formalities finished, the silence stretched awkwardly.

"Come with me upstairs. We need to get the sleeping arrangements in order. I will want my children close to the master bedroom so that they can be near me. If you stayed next door to your father's room, we'll get the maids to move your things."

Ash felt her cheeks burn, but she kept the expression on her face smooth. "You will not need to trouble the maids. My room is in a different hall entirely."

Lord Richard looked surprised, and a little guilty, as if the revelation that he would not be displacing her from her room exposed the pettiness of the demand. "It is? Well, I will wish to see it."

Ash's lip was starting to get bruised from all the tense pinching. Her uncle raised his brow in question when she led them all to the lesser hallway where her room was located, but after grunting noncommittally when he saw how much less luxurious her room was from those of the greater hallway, he let her retire without any further comment.

As soon as Lord Richard turned the corner, Jane handed Ash a handkerchief with roses embroidered around the edge. Jane's lips curved slightly, though her eyes were sad. She turned and followed after her father. Ash locked the door and listened for her cousin's retreat. Jane's actions distracted her from her despair for a moment, but the horror of her uncle was too much to bear on today of all days. She flung herself on her bed and hit her pillows over and over, tears soaking the blankets. Finally, exhausted, she fell asleep.

***

Ash retreated to her room as much as possible in the days following her uncle's arrival, wishing to avoid more conflict, and needing the time to massage out the terrible ache of loss lodged in her chest. She couldn't always stay there, however. Though Lord Richard was happy to ignore her most of the time, he made it quite clear that Ashelandra's presence was required daily for the evening meal in the dining room.

The meals were quiet affairs. Lord Richard sat stiffly at the head of the table with Jane to his left and James on his right. Ash sat further down beside Jane. No one spoke, though Jane flashed a few tentative smiles toward her drooping cousin. Ash was grateful for Jane's encouraging glances, but they were over before Ash could summon the energy to respond.

Soon, however, the promise Ash made to her father to continue to find joy in life gently fluttered against her sorrow and soothed some of the ache. She began to notice the song of the bird's melodic trills scaling through the branches. Her naturally curious spirit and a desire to go adventuring in the forest beckoned her to leave off her mourning. She peeled off the stiff formal mourning gown of silken ebony with its bothersome wide hoopskirt and stiff, confining waist. Technically, she'd been allowed to dress in other colors for several weeks now anyway. The official mourning period was only two months on account of a past king who, it was rumored, had cared more for how sallow black made him look than he did for his lost wife.

Hanging the mourning gown carefully in the wardrobe, she dressed in one of her hardier sky blue cotton dresses. It didn't require a hoop or a corset, granting her glorious freedom. Slipping through the secret passage in her room, she glided out the armory, through the chapel that connected to the manor on the east side, and toward the great outdoors without anyone the wiser.

Catching sight of movement across the walking garden, Ash paused behind a bush to watch her uncle and cousin practicing with rapiers in the small grassy clearing by the apple tree that she and her father used to practice next to whenever she could convince him to put propriety aside and teach her sword fighting and shooting.

Ash smiled sadly at the memory. He often bowed to her wishes despite the disapproving headshakes of the servants, and she thought he secretly enjoyed teaching her something she wasn't really supposed to know. Sometimes she wondered if he'd gifted her with her mischievous nature rather than her mother, despite his constant insistence that it was all her mother's fault.

James was clearly struggling to breathe normally as his father attacked with swift, merciless blows that James barely managed to block in time. As they ranged across the grass, Ash could tell by the swift and precise swish of his rapier that Lord Richard was holding back. He seemed barely winded as he pushed his son back mercilessly.

They were both dressed in white practice shirts, waistcoats, and breeches. A silly sort of uniform to use while fighting outside, in Ash's mind, considering how much harder white was to clean.

Even as she watched, Lord Richard slipped past James's defenses. Her cousin slipped, his knee hitting the ground in a grass-staining slide. Lord Richard's rapier caught the sunlight as it swept in to thwack James on the arm in a bruising blow while James struggled to recover his balance. Ash hoped for her cousin's sake that they were practicing with dull blades, but couldn't be sure from where she stood.

"You're too slow," her uncle yelled loud enough for Ash to hear, though she was half a house length away. Ash couldn't make out what he said after that as James got to his feet. He flicked his sword around in an arc and twist that Ash had a hard time following with her eyes, and James copied the movement more slowly.

"Again. Faster," he yelled loud enough for Ash to hear, and James tried to copy his father's movements more quickly as Lord Richard switched from one training form to the next.

Ash shuddered. Lord Richard was an excellent swordsman, but Ash would take her father's instructions over her uncle's any day. Poor James. Losing interest now that they were merely practicing drills, Ash headed into the forest.

The earth smelled of rich loam and wet leaves. Sunlight filtered through the trees in a bright lacy pattern. Ash ran down a small deer trail that led to her favorite large pond. A group of ducks squawked at each other as they floated on the surface, and Ash murmured the click and pop that would cause a small breeze to ruffle the feathers of the nearest duck. It quacked in surprise and turned in confusion.

A small giggle bubbled to the surface for the first time since her father's death, and Ash settled down near the bank, heedless of the mud staining her skirts. She felt a whisper of life flutter in her chest as she teased the birds. The possibility of happiness stirred, despite the deep hole her father's absence had left in her heart.

She made the mistake of losing track of the hour. By the time Ash got back to the manor, she'd missed the evening meal. She tried to slip in through the servant's door and sneak to her room unnoticed, but the whole house was a frenzy of activity. There was no way she could slip by everyone, and no point in trying, since it was obvious from their calling her name that they were looking for her. It was too late to pretend she'd been home the whole day, so she turned from the servants' door and instead walked boldly through the front entrance to Lord Richard, who was striding through the hall with a scowl on his face, fists clenched at his sides.

Catching sight of Ash, he jerked to a halt. "Where have you been all day?" For a moment Ash wondered if he'd been worried. "And what are you wearing? You look like a servant." He sniffed disdainfully. "Make that a peasant. No servant would be caught looking so filthy." He closed in on Ash, invading her space, towering over her, and the illusion of concern vanished.

"I went for a walk in the woods and lost track of the hour. I'm sorry, Uncle," Ash said as contritely as she could. It took quite an effort of concentration to keep her face from broadcasting the disappointment she felt.

"You are not to go walking alone in the woods ever again."

"There is no need to be concerned. There has never been any problem of banditry in our woods. They are well protected by the king's guard." She studied Lord Richard's face, wondering again whether his demand could possibly stem from a desire to keep her safe.

"I'm not worried. I'm astonished. That you would assume I was merely concerned about your safety only shows how irresponsibly my brother has raised you. It's unfit for a young lady to go out alone, and I will not have it. You are as mannered as a savage. I will not allow such wanton behavior while I am your guardian. Now go to your room." He'd begun his speech in a normal tone of voice, but by the end his breathing was hard, and his voice echoed loudly through the hall.

Ash clenched her fists, her short nails biting into her palms. She pivoted fiercely and marched to her bedchamber.

She did try to heed her uncle's rules as much as she could stand, but it seemed she was always doing something wrong. His rules were like the tide—constantly shifting. Ash suspected he sometimes made them up at the moment of her supposed infraction.

The next day, she ran across the pebbled road leading to the front door and jumped the steps two at a time to where Lord Richard's personal servant, David, stood. He was the only servant brought in by her uncle to Trebruk Manor, and already he'd made himself disliked by all of the household staff. Lord Richard immediately placed him in the position of most power as butler, and David did not hesitate to prove to the other servants how that made him their social superior.

David had just taken Jane's hat and gloves and was about to close the door when Ash rushed through. David seemed more nettled by Ash than anyone else in the household. She thought it was probably because though she didn't adhere to his precious rules of social protocol, he couldn't reprimand her as he could the other servants. Lord Richard and David were the perfect lord/servant combination. It made Ash sorry for the man, though she knew he would neither understand nor welcome her pity.

David's practiced aloof façade broke as she bounded past, and he glared at her. Later, she was forced to stand quietly in the parlor as her uncle reprimanded her for her unladylike behavior. Ash saw David peeking in through the open doorway, a small smirk on his face.

When her uncle turned away, she caught David's eyes and raised her brows with a long unwavering look of promise. His smirk faltered, and he ducked out of sight.

The next day, as David helped Lord Richard into his riding coat, Ash was watching expectantly out of sight, the corner of her mouth sneaking upward.

"What's going on here, David?" Lord Richard asked when he noticed the sleeves of his jacket were hemmed four inches above his wrist. "When I asked you to fix my loose sleeve, I didn't mean that you should make my coat over for a child."

David flushed and bowed. "I'm sorry, sir. I'm not sure what happened. I must have gotten the measurements wrong. I'll be sure an' fix it right away." David was so flustered his carefully cultivated upper class accent slipped slightly near the end.

"Perhaps two weeks without pay will convince you to never let it happen again, because if it does, you'll find yourself out of a job." He took his coat off and flung it at David. "I can't go riding now. Bring some tea to my study. You can handle that at least, can't you?"

"Of course, sir." He bowed several more times to Richard's back, looking stricken.

Ash felt a prick of conscience. She should have realized that her uncle's reaction to imperfect clothes might be disproportionately severe. The man never stopped straightening his jackets, after all. She should have just made David look clumsy in front of the servants. He would have been embarrassed, but nothing direr would have resulted from the stumble. As much as she disliked the man, she would admit her prank to her uncle rather than let David be dismissed.

She need not have worried.

A couple of days later, Ash was in her room when she heard movement outside, then the bang of a hammer. Curious, she opened the door to find her uncle supervising Tom as he nailed in a metal bolt to the door. The handyman's cheeks flushed, and he gave her a glance of what she interpreted to be embarrassed apology.

"What are you doing?" she asked, bewildered.

Her uncle's expression was grim. "You must learn your place, and if that means that I must lock you there, then so be it. Now get back into your room so the man can finish," Lord Richard said grimly.

"What could I possibly have done to deserve imprisonment?"

"David informed me that you were out in the woods again, after I specifically forbade you. If you will not obey my rules, you will suffer the consequences."

"David did, did he?" she said thoughtfully. Ash noted wryly that though she'd made his position precarious a few days ago, David hadn't hesitated to use her insubordination to place himself firmly in Lord Richard's good graces once more. She supposed it was only fair, considering her ill-thought-out prank the other day. Also, a bolt on the door, though unjust, would not stop her from leaving whenever she wanted. Even if the door was guarded, making it impossible to open the door with magic, she still had the passage to the armory, though she supposed she would have to be careful to listen at the hidden door before emerging, considering how often her uncle and cousin entered the room to retrieve the practice swords.

"He was right to tell me. It may be too late to save you from your father's inadequate teaching and the bad blood of *that woman*," he spat as if something foul were coating his tongue, "but I will do my duty, and at least try."

"What woman?" Ash felt the first flare of real anger toward her uncle. "You wouldn't, by chance, be referring to my mother, would you?"

"You will never speak of being *that woman's* daughter. The only reason there might be hope for you is because she died when you were born." He paused, watching Ash as she felt her face flush with angry heat.

"You have her eyes," he accused before he shoved her back through the door and slammed it shut. Ash struck her fist against the door, imagining it to be her uncle's back. How she wanted to show Lord Richard just how much she was like her mother. She wished she could sweep his feet from under him and drive him mad with visions of bugs crawling on his skin, nibbling holes in his precious clothes.

***

The next day Ash discovered that simply being locked in her room was not the end of her punishment. The bolt was thrown back in the early morning followed by a loud staccato rap at the door demanding immediate entry. Ash deliberately took her time to answer, despite the fact that she was already dressed in her best silk burgundy gown. The hoop skirt was small for current fashion, but acceptable, and her corset stays held her back uncomfortably rigid.

When her uncle saw that she was respectably clad, her hair pulled off her face, the back of it hanging free, as was proper for a girl under eighteen, he humphed. "I have decided that you will take lessons in etiquette with Madam Delany. She is downstairs now, so don't keep her waiting."

"As you wish, Uncle," Ash said, her voice sugary sweet. She suppressed a smirk when she saw her uncle's suspicious glare and sailed smoothly past. He was forced to follow her down the stairs. As Lord Richard reached the last step, Ash clicked softly. One of Lord Richard's feet caught on the stair's lip. Unbalanced, he stumbled, and was forced to cling unflatteringly to the rail, making his tall, intimidating form look suddenly ridiculous. Ash was barely able to contain the amusement from her eyes.

"Oh, Uncle, are you well? That last step is a bit tricky at times," Ash cooed. Lord Richard straightened in a hurry and growled that he was perfectly all right and that Ash should stop dawdling and get to her lesson. She went, but she worried the twitch at the corner of her mouth was dangerously close to growing into something her uncle would recognize.

Ash was not above playing a part when required, and Madam Delany wasn't a bad sort of person, though Ash thought her a little too formal and dull. Ash had been through deportment lessons before and had learned everything required as quickly as possible so that she could get rid of her teacher and go back to doing what she pleased. This time was no different. She was the model student, anticipating Madam Delany's every wish so that after only four days Madam Delany declared to Lord Richard that Ashelandra had no need for a teacher of etiquette.

"Lady Ashelandra is truly an angel. She is well-behaved and knowledgeable. I feel that my services would be better spent elsewhere," she pointed out to Lord Richard.

He looked at Ash in blatant disbelief, but Madam Delany was dismissed, and Ash was again free for the time being.

Chapter Three

Ash's door was bolted from the outside for a week, despite Madam Delany's decree. Breakfast and lunch were taken to her room. Attendance at dinner was the only time she was let out, and her uncle watched her closely for signs of wilting submissiveness.

Ash felt his regard like a boa constrictor—his ever-tightening grip desperate to squeeze her into obedience. She warred with herself on whether or not she should satisfy his fantasy and play the part of desperate prisoner when at the table. On the one hand, it would irk her uncle delightfully if she revealed her unconcern; on the other hand, it might lengthen her sentence. She didn't mind sneaking out to the forest every day, but she missed talking to the servants. In the end, she decided to adopt an air of slight depression, and Lord Richard seemed satisfied.

To keep herself entertained, she used her free time puzzling out spells or spying on the new additions to Trebruk manor. She was free to set up as many pranks as she wished while still staying free of suspicion—she was always very careful to remain unseen from even the servants—but she found that the urge to set up elaborate tricks had dimmed with the death of her father.

Ash did not watch Jane very much. The poor girl did little but take short walks in the garden and sew needlepoint. Ash felt a prick of sympathy for her elegantly-coiffed cousin. James was another matter. A massive tree near the stables had a limb almost directly above the stable yard where Ash sat to observe James like a child gazing at a particularly interesting insect.

His treatment of the servants was typical for an upper class gentleman secure in the knowledge of his superiority as he ordered them to get "his mount" ready. "His mount" was really Ash's favorite silver gray mare, Windrunner. Watching helplessly as her horse was readied, she wished she could snatch the mare from James and gallop away. When Windrunner really flew across the ground, Ash could almost imagine she was flying, gloriously soaring through wispy clouds. She longed for such an escape. Instead she contented herself with watching Bill and Teddy wrestle playfully as they waited for James to return.

James brought Windrunner back foaming at the mouth and jumping nervously at sudden movements. As James barked for servants to come, Ash's lips pursed and a spark of mischief resurfaced. Ash clicked a spell, slipping the stirrup from his foot. Caught mid-swing to the ground, he tumbled to the dirt with a satisfying thud at Windrunner's feet. The horse shied, great hooves stomping down near James's fingers. He snatched his hand away and rolled, adding another layer of dirt to his clothes. The servants tittered quietly, smart enough not to let James hear. They were also careful to appear ignorant of his fall when James jumped to his feet and glared menacing at all around, face smudged, hair sticking straight up at his crown. He snapped for someone to take his horse and stomped to the house. Only when he was safely out of hearing did the two boys guffaw audibly. Ash chuckled as she slithered down the tree and back to her room.

***

Lord Richard made a big production of opening Ashelandra's room at week's end. The bolt slid back from the door with a loud snick, and Ash, who was just about to slip out the hidden passage, had to scramble back through and shove the false wall shut before her uncle barged into the room without so much as a courtesy knock.

An insincere benevolent smile curved her uncle's lips, which slipped back to a thin straight line when he noticed Ash's practical blue dress.

"Why are you dressed so? You should be properly attired in your mourning clothes. It has only been three months since my brother's death. I should have known your flamboyant act of grieving during his funeral was simply that—an act."

Anger burned through her. There he went changing his rules again.

He knew as well as she did the proper mourning period was past.

When she'd had lessons with Madame Delany he'd had no problem with her colorful dresses, but he seemed suddenly on a mission to prove her an unfaithful and unfeeling daughter.

She looked out the window at the leaves slashing in the cool morning breeze like knives nicking the air and wished she could do some rending of her own. Ash forced herself to take a deep, calming breath. Her hand scuffed the gray stone of the deep windowsill, the rough surface chafing her skin and distracting her from her anger.

"Since no one can see me when I'm locked in my room, it is of little consequence what I wear. It does not reflect in any way on the depth of my feelings. I doubt anyone obsessed with inconsequential trappings would understand," Ash couldn't help but snap back. She'd never before known a man so infatuated with clothes.

Lord Richard's hand, still on the doorknob, went white as he squeezed the brass knob so tight that Ash expected to find finger impressions in the metal when he let go. "It is not inconsequential. It shows a lack of respect for my brother's memory. I imagine it's something *she* would do."

Ash scraped her hand harder.

For a moment she was sure he would leave, slamming the door behind him, but after several seconds of silence where Lord Richard and Ash stared wordlessly at each other, he loosened his fingers from the doorknob one by one as if carefully releasing them from a newly formed hand mold.

"I'll overlook your attire and your impertinence. Once. Get dressed in something presentable and you may come down and join your cousin in the sitting room." Lord Richard finished with the air of one who feels he is bequeathing a great favor and expects his due gratitude.

"Thank you, Lord Richard," Ash said through gritted teeth.

He swept from the room. As the door clicked shut, Ash's palm hit the granite hard before she moved to her wardrobe and retrieved her red and gray riding gear. Anger boiled under her skin. To be "freed" from her bedroom simply to be confined to another room was too much to bear, and Ash wanted to soothe her poor mare before James ruined Windrunner for good.

She took her secret passage downstairs to avoid detection, slipped outside, and walked quickly for the stables. Nodding to the stable boys, she went to Windrunner's stall and began putting on her horse's tack. The stable boys knew better than to do it for her, and she was left alone.

The only sound was the crackle of hooves shifting hay, and the snuffle of resting horses. Windrunner turned her nose into Ash's chest and sighed wetly into her bodice as if divulging to Ash the great burden she'd had to bear for the past week in the company of James.

"I know, dear. I saw," Ash whispered soothingly into the horse's ear. "I just wish there was something I could do to spare you." Dust motes floated through the slats of sunshine coming through the stable door like sparkling petals. The smell of hay permeated the building, a cloak of comforting familiarity.

"What are you doing in here?" someone growled. For a moment, Ash was afraid that her uncle had already routed her out, but when she turned she saw that the intruder was James. Ash's hand tightened on the mare's lead rope.

"And what are you doing with my horse?" he demanded. Windrunner sidled sideways at the sound of James's voice. Ash distracted the mare and herself by whispering calming nonsense into Windrunner's ear before turning back to James.

"I am taking *my horse* for a ride, and I do not want you riding Windrunner ever again. She has a sweet disposition and it is obvious from her reaction to you that you have treated her ill." Ash tried to keep her voice level.

Her cousin's fair skin darkened as the blood rushed to his face.

"She may have been your horse before, but she isn't any longer. She's mine now, and I will ride her whenever I please. I'll have to tell Father that your punishment was not quite long enough." The superior nasal sound to James's voice grated on Ash's nerves. "You obviously intended to take Wind-twitcher out without an escort. He will be very displeased." James turned from Ash to yell out the door, "Hello there! Stable boy! Come take care of this horse as I take my cousin back to the house."

Bill popped his head in the door nervously. Ash could see that he was not sure what to do. She assumed he had heard the whole of the conversation while out of sight. The look in Bill's eyes said he guessed what Ash's reaction would be even if her cousin did not.

"Don't bother, Bill," Ash said to the lad. She shot James a scathing look. *Wind-twitcher!* She snorted. He probably couldn't recall the mare's real name because the best he could coax out of the animal was a jolting and uneven trot.

"I am taking Wind*runner* out now whether my cousin likes it or not. If you feel I should have an escort, perhaps you can try to catch up," she said to James, and with one swift motion she threw herself up onto the horse, staying astride in the sidesaddle position despite the fact that she'd saddled the mare with a man's saddle. She might as well avoid adding more fuel to James's tattle-telling if she could. She swiftly maneuvered the mare out the door to the trees. James made a grab for her horse's reins, but when that failed he yelled at Bill to saddle another horse quickly.

As soon as Ash was safely under the cover of the trees she threw one leg to the other side of the horse and urged Windrunner to a full gallop. The wind whipped her face and ripped away the chains of her unhappiness. Windrunner floated across the terrain as if winged. Ash wanted to yip in relief, but stayed silent, soaking in the feeling of freedom. She knew she was doing something reckless and that her uncle would be furious, but she didn't care. His words about her father and mother burned in her mind like kindling in a fire, and she wanted to escape the suppressive pressure surrounding the manor now that Lord Richard was there, tainting her refuge.

In the distance the sound of pursuit reached her ears, and for a moment apprehension dulled her giddiness. A punishment for her rash act was sure to follow. She slowed the mare and veered from the road onto an almost invisible trail in the woods. James passed by without even pausing. Ash urged Windrunner a resigned step forward in order to meet him, but then flicked the reins to the right so the mare would turn. She couldn't do it. The thought of returning with James was more dreadful than the certainty of punishment, and the joy of riding unfettered through the trees seemed worth the ineffectual imprisonment her uncle could mete out.

Near the end of the day, she rode Windrunner back to the stable. At the sight of her, one of the stable boys ran like wildfire toward the manor. Ash sighed as she took off her horse's saddle, began brushing her down, and waited to be arrested. Windrunner's sides quivered in delight, and short hairs flew through the air, mingling with the dust motes in a time-honored dance.

"Since Madam Delany was profuse in her praise of your manners, I can only assume that your behavior does not spring from ignorance, but from willful disobedience," Lord Richard said from behind Ash. His voice was quiet, devoid of emotion. A shiver shot through her.

Ash reluctantly turned to face her uncle. She could think of nothing to say, and her uncle's expression made her decide that silence was perhaps her best course of action.

"You will be confined to your room for a month. Apparently, one week was not enough time for you to evaluate the consequence of rebellious behavior," he growled, his anger finally breaking through. His eyes narrowed further, and Ash realized that she forgot to look devastated by his punishment. It was too late to pretend, so she simply strode past him to her room, his heavy steps stalking her progress.

***

The time passed quickly, and Ash found the only disadvantage to being "confined to her room" was that she had to be careful no one saw her roaming free. She missed the company of people, but was distracted from her solitude by her magic books, which she snuck from the hidden cubby and toted outside where she spent many hours trying to master the tick-click snap of new spells. She also stalked the wood life of the forest, and observed the habits of the creatures while sitting as perfectly still as possible.

As the days passed, the pain of her father's loss eased more, and she found she enjoyed her secret freedom. Sneaking out and escaping any expectations for proper behavior was a relief rather than a burden. She searched her magic books for illusion spells and dreaded the day of release when she would be expected to perform her maidenly duties of sewing pointless pillow covers and making deadly dull social calls to neighbors—allowed only the briefest of jaunts on her horse while accompanied by an escort.

Ash's attitude during dinner was clearly never depressed enough to satisfy Lord Richard. His scowl became deeper and deeper every evening he observed her. The stilted conversation was never pleasant, and it was painful to see Lord Richard sitting at the head of the dining room's large oak table where her father used to sit, but he apparently still deemed her demeanor as too unaffected.

After the first week, he charged into her room when lunch was delivered, and scoured her chamber, taking all the books Ash had scattered about. Ash blessed the foresight that had made her store her magic books within the hidden passage.

On the second week, he returned and confiscated all her art supplies. The loss of her sketches renewed a spark of anger, but she had already learned from her uncle's previous theft and had hidden away all the things truly valuable to her.

Her uncle succeeded in stirring her anger, but she refused to bow to his desire, so after the theft of her possessions, she made an extra effort to engage Jane in conversation at dinner, striving to keep her topics light and her expression peaceful.

When her room had been locked for nearly four weeks, she was almost discovered outside by a group of nobles on a morning ride and picnic. Ash lay flat in the tall grasses by her favorite pond, observing a mother quail with her hatchlings. Though the pond was technically still on her father's land, it bordered the king's vast swath of forest kept undeveloped for the game. Despite that, Ash had felt the possibility of visitors coming from the king's forest was highly unlikely, so when the pounding hooves, neighing horses, and tinkling laughter of people startled the mother quail, Ash also shivered in momentary fear. The frightened bird fled from the bushes, her children following on her heels as if connected by string. Ash lay very still, hoping the grass was tall enough to conceal her while they passed.

"Oh, this is a lovely spot, Prince Phillip. I confess I had not imagined we would ride quite so far. Let's stop here for tea," a high-pitched voice squealed in delight. She failed to completely hide her out of breath pant. Ash winced and looked through a gap in the broad grass leaves to see a group of three nobles accompanied by five servants. Each horse sported the country's livery of royal cobalt blue with a golden rearing unicorn on each side. The servants, two women and three men, were simply dressed in muted blue with brass buttons at the waistcoats for the men, and practical riding skirts for the two women.

They were already dismounting, spreading out blankets, setting out china, and making a small fire for the teapot so that the nobles could have their beverage piping hot. No one else seemed out of breath, and Ash concluded that they must have taken the road from the palace through the city and only turned in to the woods recently. If they'd ridden from the palace through the king's woods, the trip would have been too arduous—the trails too narrow and overgrown for a simple picnicking party. Ash groaned softly and resigned herself to wait.

"Don't you think this is a delightful little pond, Prince Phillip?" the squealer added, fluttering her arms as she sat sidesaddle atop her horse like a turkey fluffing its feathers.

"Yes, Lady Vivian, it's quite nice," Prince Phillip responded dutifully. Looking at his glazed green eyes, Ash had to stuff a chuckle back down her throat. Ash had never seen the prince in person before, and she took a moment to compare the reality of him to what she'd heard. It was well known that the prince had just celebrated his eighteenth birthday. She had to admit that he was as handsome as rumored.

He had a trim face and a well-defined jaw. His straight nose gave him a regal look, and his clear, emerald-green eyes were framed by thick red-gold eyebrows. Bright hair reflected the sun like a copper helmet, but a brush of light freckles on his face contrasted with the image of unapproachable royal, making him look slightly impish. His dark-green coat lay across the pommel of his saddle, abandoned. The long sleeves of his white shirt wavered in the slight breeze, and his glossy green waistcoat and breeches hugged his trim form flatteringly.

The lady with Prince Phillip waved her lacy, gloved hands feebly at a servant to help her down. Her jade green dress was so stiff, her corset so tight, Ash wondered how she managed to breath at all, much less sit. She had dark brown hair, topped by a plumed riding hat, which she checked quickly once she'd dismounted. Ash wondered if the lady was always so fussy about her looks, or if having the prince near made her extra conscious of her appearance.

Next to her, a man dismounted quietly. His suit was well tailored, but dull in appearance, a sort of faded brown. His breeches fit well, with simple brass pins holding up the white stockings just below his knees. Though he joined the prince and lady on the spread blanket, he remained quiet unless asked a direct question. Lady Vivian fluttered her hand at Prince Phillip. He helped her sit on the blanket and the food was served on delicate porcelain plates. Prince Phillip held his food in a bored confident manner, the Lady Vivian in as artful a position as possible, but the third man held his own dish only briefly, nervously, before setting the plate down on the blanket.

"Come, Sorcerer Tioroso, do some magic for us. It is so thrilling to witness real magic," Lady Vivian simpered. Prince Phillip's lips turned down slightly, but the lady didn't notice. She was too busy watching the sorcerer's cheeks color. Ash's interest plucked up, and she looked at the third member of the party more closely. So this was the young sorcerer Lady Amelia had mentioned. He had light brown hair, brown eyes shaded by long lashes, and lips almost too full for a man. But his crooked nose, which looked to have been broken then set improperly, dispelled any femininity to his features.

"Lady Vivian, please don't tease Sorcerer Tioroso. He is not a toy for your amusement."

"Oh, pish posh. All I'm asking him for is a small something to add to the enjoyment of our outing. He would not deny us such an inno-cent distraction now, would he?" she asked. She giggled nervously as if doubting her own statement. Her high voice grated on Ash's nerves, and she wondered why the lady addressed her question to the prince rather than the sorcerer. Ash noticed that despite Lady Vivian's attempt at nonchalance, she darted a glance at the woods around her as if afraid someone other than the prince she wanted to impress would hear her request. Ash thought she must be one of the types of people who were more suspicious than interested in magic and was only pretending to Prince Phillip's ease in order to ingratiate herself with him.

"No, My Lady," answered Sorcerer Tioroso.

He spread his hands wide, showing Ash that the shy young man had a small flare for theatrics after all. Hand movement wasn't really required to work spells. He click-whistled under his breath a complicated phrase too quiet for Ash to hear. She strained to discern all the words and their sounds, but he was too far from her.

Ash watched as a miniature castle bloomed from the ground in front of the picnicking party. Turrets burst from the ground and expanded, then linked together by brick walls complete with battlements. A small drawbridge lowered toward where Lady Vivian sat. Behind the illusion, a long duck feather lifted from its resting place at the edge of the pond and floated through the back wall of the castle, over the drawbridge, to Lady Vivian. It hovered before the stunned lady, a small puff of breeze making the down feathers ripple at the base of the shaft. Sorcerer Tioroso clicked a new spell, and the upper veined feathers sprouted red petals as the shaft transformed into a thorned stem. The down elongated and uncurled into leaves. A partially blooming rose dropped gracefully onto Lady Vivian's lap as the illusion of the turreted castle faded. Her eyes reflected a combination of amazement and panicked horror. Her hands lifted, as if to swipe the flower far from her lap before a glance at the prince's calm, pleased expression recalled her to her situation.

She gobbled a laugh like a high-pitched turkey and changed the shooing motion of her hands into clapping. They slapped together in an offbeat staccato as her eyes skittered from her lap to the surrounding area and back.

Prince Phillip's clap was heartfelt as he smiled at the sorcerer. "That was impressive, Sorcerer Tioroso. I've only ever seen that kind of castle in books before."

Sorcerer Tioroso ducked his head shyly in acknowledgment. "There was a castle like that in the kingdom to the north where my teacher and I lived when I was young."

Ash was so full of curiosity that she could hardly keep herself still. She wished she could ask Sorcerer Tioroso to teach *her* the phrases he had used. She could think of quite a few more useful ways of using those spells on James and Lord Richard. The illusion's detail was impressive. She'd only managed to project blurry shapes so far. Ash resolved to go back to her books and work on perfecting her illusions' sharpness. It almost sounded like he'd used more than the set phrases she knew in her books, or had he used the slightly different dialect that seemed to be required for different types of illusions? Ash ached to run out of her hiding place to ask.

Also, she hadn't yet mastered a transformation as dense as that of a feather to a rose. That would be really useful. She fell short of converting denser material because the phrases were longer and the verb conjugation too complicated. So much seemed possible with an actual teacher. The grass surrounding Ash wavered at her sigh.

After her body was stiff from sitting still too long, and Ash was ready to gag Lady Vivian so she would no longer have to hear her high-pitched simpering, servants began repacking the food and dishes. Soon Ash was again alone. She stood and stretched aching limbs before running full speed back to the manor in order to reach her bedroom before the servant who delivered her lunch found her gone.

***

"I will not stand for it!" her uncle burst out that evening at supper. His face was flushed, his hands clenched into fists. Ash looked up, jolted from her thoughts on the amusing encounter with the prince, the sorcerer, and the lady in the woods. She was envisioning all the delightful things she could do to her uncle if she could somehow find and convince Sorcerer Tioroso to properly train her.

"Your behavior is insupportable," he steamed.

"But I haven't done anything," Ash protested.

"That is exactly my point. You have been confined to your room for nearly four weeks now, and yet you sit at this table smiling!"

Ash debated and discarded the idea of baiting her uncle further. He sat waiting for an explanation so she said mildly, "I have a very good imagination."

Lord Richard's brows drew down. Across the table, James tried to parrot his father's stern glare, and Ash returned his look with one of contempt. Red spread from James's neck up to stain his face. Jane sat with her head bent next to Ash, hands pulling nervously in her lap.

"Imagination? That sounds perilously close to something a sorcerer would say. It must be rooted out for your own good. I am trying to save you, Ashelandra." Richard's face was a confusing mask of impassioned fervency. He set his fork on his plate firmly, the metal making a sharp clink on the porcelain.

"Perhaps your creature comforts have clouded the severity of your punishment and made it seem less substantial than it is. If you are comfortable enough to imagine fantastical things, it is my duty to rectify that." Lord Richard clapped his hands and a servant arrived. "I want Ashelandra's room stripped. Replace her bed with a cot. There is to be nothing else present but her clothes, is that clear?" The maid, Jenny, stole a swift look Ash's way, concern evident on her young freckled face, but she curtsied to Lord Richard and hurried away to do his bidding.

When she returned to her room, Ash found the old granite stonework bare, her paintings gone and her large rug, which had cushioned the stark cold of the floor, removed. The servants had dismantled her four-poster bed and carted off the pieces along with her down mattress. In its place sat a small cot made of a thin wooden frame and canvas stretched tautly across the top. The armoire containing her clothing remained, but all other possessions had vanished.

Ash viewed the scene with her uncle looming behind her. Her face felt tight, and she gouged her nails into her palm rather than give her uncle the satisfaction of seeing her cry. Without turning she stepped into the room, snagged the door and shut it in his face. She heard the bolt clunk shut and her uncle's heavy footsteps walk away. Then the angry tears swept over her in a rush like a tidal wave sweeping destruction in its wake. She plotted her revenge.

***

The next day, her uncle took a long ride on his favorite stallion. When he returned and dismounted, the stable boys discovered that his black breeches were stained light brown where he'd sat upon the saddle. The stain perfectly matched the color of the leather, and the stable boys looked on in horror, too afraid of a whipping should they tell the fierce lord of his condition as he strode back to the manor.

Lord Richard tramped through the house for a full hour with no one saying a thing until his son pointed out what everyone else had already seen but been too terrified to make known. Lord Richard stomped to his chamber, his face the burnt umber of mortification.

41

Her uncle's torture didn't end there though. That evening, Ash imagined the scene of the maid turning down Lord Richard's covers. She anticipated his slide into bed only to feel something smooth brush over his foot. Right on cue, Ash heard the roar of an angered grizzly echo through the manor. The patter of servants' feet rushed past her door to his chamber to see what was amiss. After much yelling and confusion, Ash surmised that someone, probably Jenny, had finally pulled off the covers completely to find the slithering garden snake Ash had placed there.

Lord Richard demanded the disgusting creature be killed immediately and threatened to dismiss the maid who had made up his bed, but Jenny managed to convince him that the snake had gotten into the bed on its own, looking for warmth.

Ash heard the roaring even from her lesser hallway and she smiled in delight until a quiet knock at the door signaled someone's presence.

"Who is it?" she queried.

"Well, ma'am, it's Jenny. May I come in, miss?"

"Of course." Ash rose to unlock her door from the inside as Jenny slid the bolt open from the outside. She quickly ushered the maid into her room and closed the door.

"Am I allowed visitors now?" Ash asked with a raised brow, and a mischievous smile.

"No, an' I shouldn't be here, but I've come to ask ye to stop pulling pranks on yer uncle, Lord Richard. Heaven knows he deserves it, but he near fired poor Mary for the snake trick, and he lashed Bill five times for what happened to his pants."

Ash winced, and all the fun she'd derived from her revenge sapped away.

"How could I have had anything to do with these events? I've been locked in my room," Ash said cautiously. She'd always liked Jenny, but Ash wasn't sure how far their mutual regard would extend now that Jenny was dependent upon her uncle for her employ.

"Ach, all the servants know that a little bolt on the door couldn't hold ye if'n you truly wanted out—what with yer sorcery an' all. And we've witnessed many a prank pulled by ye in the past. We have no wish to betray ye to yer uncle, but neither do we wish to be the ones to pay for yer prankin'," Jenny said, her stern expression sitting strangely on her young, usually pleasant countenance.

Ash was shocked. Though she'd never actively tried to hide her magic study before her father's death, none of the servants had ever commented on it before, so she assumed that they were like those who did not seem to care or notice anything related to magic. That the servants all knew of her skill made her realize that they hadn't been as oblivious as she'd thought.

"Everyone knows I study magic?" Ash asked.

"Well, an' everyone but the new man, David, and no one would ever be tellin' the likes of him," Jenny scoffed, her pretty freckled face scrunched in contempt.

Ash felt like she'd eaten an apple only to learn it wasn't an apple after all, but a cucumber instead. How long had everyone known? Why had no one said anything? She felt as if she'd spit in their face, acting so childish by pulling pranks that might get the very people in trouble who had kept her sorcery quiet from her superstitious uncle.

"I'm terribly sorry, Jenny. I didn't think of the consequences to you. After all everyone has done for me I can't believe I was so selfish. From now on, I will try to think of ways to torment my uncle that won't have repercussions to any of the servants. If you'll allow me, I recently mastered a small spell that will help Bill's healing. It won't heal him completely, but it speeds up the process a bit," Ash offered.

Ash watched Jenny's reaction carefully for the suspicious look that sometimes marked the faces of those hearing about using magic, but Jenny just nodded.

"Well, an' that's fine. I'll send him up quiet like."

"Oh, good. That's good." Ash found she was a little nervous about performing a spell on someone other than herself. She'd done the healing spell on her father, but it had made no difference to his health.

"Oh, and Jenny, better tell Cook to remake the special blueberry muffins my uncle likes to have in the morning else he'll be locked in the privy all day long. I don't know if he could trace that back to the food, but he might."

There was a reflective twinkle in Jenny's eye, but then she reluctantly nodded and cracked the door to peek out before slipping through, silently shutting it behind her. Ash stood in the bare room, musing gloomily and kicking herself for not considering the consequence of her tricks to the staff of Trebruk manor. When her father had been alive, there would've been no talk of a beating or of dismissing someone for such things, and Ash belatedly realized that this was probably because her father knew who the true culprit was.

Bill tapped mildly on the wood outside Ash's room and she pulled the youth in quickly. They stared uncertainly at each other for a moment.

"Are you sure you're willing to let me perform a spell on you?" she asked him.

"I've watched ye practice. Ye know what yer doin'," Bill said confidently. Ash could detect no trace of hesitancy in his large blue eyes.

"All right." Ash moved behind Bill, and he lifted his shirt. Her breath hissed in at the sight of the puffy red ridges, several of which had split and bled.

"I'm terribly sorry, Bill," Ash muttered meekly after whistle-click-snapping the sorcery words to the spell that would speed the healing to the welts on Bill's back. "You should have told my uncle that it was my fault. I should have been punished, not you."

Bill blushed as he pulled down his shirt and looked around at the stark gray granite of her chamber containing only the little uncomfortable cot in the corner and her armoire of clothes. "Well, an' miss, but I understand why ye did it, an' it t'aint half of what he deserves for the way he's treated ye," he mumbled. He looked up shyly but with a little smile. "I really liked the trick ye pulled on yer cousin t'other day with the stirrup. He could blame no one for that. Mayhap you could think of some more things like that."

"An excellent suggestion. Thank you, Bill." Ash grinned wickedly in a manner that invited Bill to join. It also happened to light up her features in a way that was unaccountably stunning. The gap-toothed fourteen-year-old blushed deeply and regarded Ash with wide worshipful eyes. She shooed him discreetly out the door and perched on her cot, shifting from one spot to another as she tried to find a comfortable position. Finally, she gave up and sat on the floor, back against the wall, to ponder over the revelations and events of the day.

Chapter Four

SEPTEMBER 11, 1747

Lord Richard was suddenly plagued with poor coordination as he stumbled on nothing more than air on the stairs, or while pompously striding away from a servant recently upbraided. Ash knew he told no one about the billowy form he sometimes saw floating past his second story window at night, but he became suddenly adamant about keeping the curtains closed in the evenings.

During an unexpected visit from Lady Amelia, who'd come to inquire after Ash's health, his foot slipped from under him just as he was bowing politely to the lady. He pitched forward and caught himself on her skirts, ripping the seam at the waist. Ash was surprised when Lord Richard apologized repeatedly, even following her out the door.

Lady Amelia did not demand Ash's presence before she left. Even the unflappable Lady Amelia was too irritated to remember her original purpose in coming, much to Ash's chagrin. Though the show had been amusing, Ash hadn't meant to make her uncle trip that spectacularly, nor had she wished to embarrass Lady Amelia. The consequence to her crime was to miss the reprieve that Lady Amelia's presence would have given her.

After a week, Lord Richard released Ash from her hollowed-out bedroom cell. He did not allow Ash any freedom of movement, however. He just marched her straight to the sitting room where her cousin Jane perched gracefully on her chair sewing a needlepoint picture of forget-me-nots and robins.

She lifted her golden head from her work to flash a sincere, if tentative, smile. Ash returned her greeting with a rueful grin of her own, before seating herself primly as close to her cousin as her voluminous peach bow-bespeckled skirt would allow. Ash thought most people ought to rethink bows on dresses, but Jane's peach bodice was open in the front showing a decorative cream stomacher with several small bows in a row down the front that didn't detract from the elegant lines of the dress. The sleeves were tight until the elbow, where a bow marked the switch to bell-shaped cream lace.

"Jane, please keep an eye on your cousin." He turned to Ash. "I would advise you to check with Jane before acting on any of your barbaric impulses. Her manners are always above reproach. If you wish to avoid further isolation, it would be wise to emulate her."

Ash stifled a surge of resentment toward her cousin. After all, she'd been the only member of the household to show Ash any kindness, even if she was too timid to talk much. Several times at the evening meals Jane had looked like she was about to say something to Ash, but after catching sight of her father's imposing frown, would close her mouth. Jane's situation struck Ash as even more pitiable than her own. After all, Ash had lived seventeen years with a father who loved her and doted on her. Jane had been squashed under the suppressive thumb of Lord Richard her entire life.

As soon as her uncle was gone, Ash turned to Jane. "Let's go outside."

"If you like," she said accommodatingly and tied off her thread.

When Ash began to head for the stables, however, Jane held back and nervously plucked at the cream lace of her full sleeve.

"Wait, please. We haven't permission for a ride. Let's walk through the garden." She tugged at her dress in distress and half turned as if searching for help. "Please," she said again in a plaintive, helpless sort of way.

It was impossible to be defiant in the face of Jane's panic. The girl had probably never misbehaved in her entire life. If imprisonment and purloining of belongings was Lord Richard's usual punishment, and Jane had no way to escape, Ash could understand why Jane might be reluctant to disobey her father's wishes.

Ash relented and walked with her to the garden. She had to admit that this time her uncle had been cleverer in his planning than previously. Ash would not willfully rebel if it meant that her sweet cousin would be punished as well. But after several rounds about the garden and back into the sitting room where Ash found the needle more likely to prick her fingers than the fabric, she knew that day after day of this existence would drive her insane. Jane was no help. As kind as she seemed to be, she was also frustratingly quiet. Every attempt at conversation ended quickly when Jane answered questions in a word or two.

The pin pricked her again. Sucking her fingers, Ash put the cloth down and headed for the library. Jane looked up in concern. "I'll return in an instant. I simply wish to get a book to read," Ash assured her.

Jane scrunched her beautifully arched eyebrows uncertainly. "Would you like me to go with you?"

"Nonsense. I'll be right back." Before Jane could protest further, Ash slipped out the door and escaped to the library. She retrieved her favorite novel and returned to the sitting room to find Jane standing uncertainly, eyes vacillating between the door and her seat.

"See, I did not abandon you." Ash bounced back to her chair, and Jane gratefully lowered herself back to her own seat, taking up her embroidery again. As Ash read, she could see Jane glance now and again at Ash's book. She opened her mouth as if to speak, but Lord Richard passed by the open door. Her eyes dropped back to her needlepoint, and she made no comment.

***

After four days of doing nothing but reading, Ash was ready to snatch Jane's pointless needlepoint and fling it against the wall. The few languid strolls Jane and she had taken around the garden were not good enough for someone so unaccustomed to inactivity.

"I asked father if we could go riding today," Jane announced. She eyed Ash's legs twitching rapidly up and down. "Father says a lady must never fidget." Ash scowled, not feeling quite so sympathetic toward her cousin, but she stilled her legs.

"Since we have permission, let's go." The word *permission* tasted bitter in Ash's mouth, but she was more interested in leaving than causing more trouble at the moment. Ash jumped out of her seat as if propelled by a spring.

"We'll have to change and send for James first," Jane said apologetically as she snipped the thread from her dandelion. Ash's face flashed a betraying look of distaste and annoyance before she schooled her expression into one of calm acceptance. James was fetched quickly, proper riding outfits donned, and Ash was forced to let the stable lads saddle a bay mare while James had Windrunner prepared for him.

"This will need to be a short ride. I've business to attend to," James announced loftily to the girls. Ash suppressed a fresh surge of irritation, transforming the feeling into something more useful—desire to make mischief.

"What sort of business? I must confess that I hadn't even thought until now about what sort of work my uncle . . . and cousin do. Have you a profession? Accounting perhaps? No, you don't quite seem the type for numbers. Ah, I know. You deal with horses. You certainly have an excellent eye for good horse stock. I would enjoy hearing about your business," Ash spoke a bit too sweetly. James's face colored. Windrunner shied beneath James's seat as he spurred her forward to the road. The trees canopied the path like a gigantic umbrella, making Ash wish furtively that she could tear off her confounded riding hat.

"I am a gentleman," he snapped.

"I am simply trying to make conversation." Ash studied James's face as it retained the hue of a tomato, wondered idly what part he resented most; the fact that Ash had subtly accused him of being a thief or her implication that Lord Richard and he were poor gentlemen and, therefore, required to work.

"I doubt that you would understand if I did speak of a gentleman's duties, but I am already aware that you are out of the usual way when it comes to gently-bred women, so, if you must know, my father and I make investments here and there which require my attention." James regarded Ash with a challenging lift to his brow.

She shifted her position on the saddle to hide her irritation and relieve her bottom from the discomfort of sitting with her legs draped to one side. Her stays jabbed at her abdomen, forcing her to sit straight in order to breathe properly. Such vexation in spirit could prompt only one kind of response from Ash—mischief.

"I'm sure you are correct, dear cousin. I only managed a small portion of my father's investment before letting my solicitor take it over. My father worried I would not be allowed to continue overseeing the businesses once my guardian arrived. I must say that was a lucky bit of foresight on my father's part. I thought him overcautious, but he once again proved to be a veritable wizard in matters of business and the human character." Ash's tone was matter-of-fact as her eyes slid sideways to observe James's reaction.

James's jaw clenched, and his legs were tight on Windrunner. The horse fidgeted and shied forcefully to the side. "Oh" he raised his eyebrows skeptically—"and what sort of *investments* did you deal with, cousin?" he drawled, a faint note of disdain coloring his tone.

Ash didn't want to be too specific about what she'd dealt with in case he and her uncle tried to figure out a way to steal it from her. She knew part of James's anger stemmed from the belief, instilled by his father, that all of Trebruk's assets should be under Lord Richard's control. She decided to play on James's aristocratic prejudices to help ensure that he and his father would not think her business investments worth acquiring.

"This and that. Cotton, inventions, those sorts of things. Father dealt with most of the inventions himself, however. He loved discovering and supporting new useful creations such as the steam carriage." Ash felt a ping in her heart as she reflected on her father and forgot momentarily her purpose: to needle her cousin.

"Steam carriages! Bah!" James's rude snort snapped Ash out of her reverie with a jerk. "The things are a nuisance and require a horrible amount of work just to keep the blasted machines running. And when they do run, they go so slowly a horse in trot can outpace them. What a foolhardy investment." Even if it had been her plan to make James think her investments not worth seizing, his scorn was irritating.

"And cotton! What a waste for your father to invest in something so coarse, so common. Only servants and peasants wear such drivel," James continued blithely. Though he spoke with much vigor, Ash had the impression that James was parroting someone else's opinion rather than voicing something he truly believed. It was stupid, but she couldn't resist revealing to James how foolish he was.

"Why, James, I thought you were a supporter, seeing how your shirt is made from cotton," Ash imbued her voice with amused sarcasm. "Perhaps you were unaware. There are many different fabrics made from cotton, such as muslin, organdy, oxford, and so on. It's understandable that you would be unaware of your clothes' composition."

"This from a girl whose needlepoint looks like something that comes out of the back end of a horse. You're mistaken. My shirt is made from . . ." James cleared his throat. "I make sure my attire is from the very best of sources, as would any person of true noble birth." To compensate for his ignorance, his eyes roamed slowly up and down Ash's body as if to remind Ash of her own tainted origins. It was a good effort, but Ash still felt that his act fell slightly short of having any true impact.

At this point Ash was surprised to hear Jane utter, "Please, James, let us change the subject. You are being unforgivably rude and ruining the pleasure of our ride."

"Of course, Jane dear. I am bored of this subject as well. Shall we talk of the weather?" he asked his sister solicitously.

Ash was tired of James's condescending words despite the amusement his poor execution afforded. She wanted very much to rebut his witless parroting. She imagined first flaying then flaming his blindly held misconceptions to cinders. However, Jane looked distressed, and to prove him wrong would defeat her goal anyway. It seemed the littlest bit of discord put Jane in a state of acute suffering, so Ash stayed silent as brother and sister discussed the most harmless and innocuous of subjects: the sky's clear pale hue and whether those little clouds in the distance would spell a shower later in the day.

Ash switched positions on her saddle again so her derrière would not go numb, and tried to spare Jane from censure by pushing aside the temptation to throw one leg over her saddle to the other side and leave her two cousins in the dust of her horse's wake. The ride seemed interminable. Ash wondered why James had even mentioned wanting to get back quickly. He seemed in no hurry to do so now.

She was impressed with how long a pointless conversation about weather could continue, and between siblings no less. Surely family would have something better to talk about to each other. Ash shook her head in bafflement and was relieved when they finally turned back. The wispy distant clouds that had looked no bigger than a cotton ball rushed over the sky and multiplied, darkening into an ominous gray that heralded rain.

***

They reached the stables still dry, but the rain began later that evening and continued into the next morning. That did not stop Ash from rising early and escaping the manor before she was emotionally blackmailed into good behavior by being chained to her guileless cousin's side. She couldn't do it anymore. The monotony was slowly driving her insane. To shake off the shackles of boredom was a need too intense to be ignored. She slipped to the stable, saddled her horse, and was out the door into the storm without even waking the stable boys.

The rain soaked through her sturdy cotton dress in an instant, but Ash hardly felt the chill of the water as she urged Windrunner into a gallop and drove through a meadow in the woods feeling gloriously free. Her wheat hair whipped wetly behind her like streamers. Though her hands were white from cold, her cheeks were flushed with the joy of the moment until Windrunner's piercing neigh was unexpectedly answered.

Ash swiveled her head to find where the whinny had come from and finally spotted a horse and rider emerging close to her from the woods. It was too late to head for cover and avoid the encounter, so Ash reigned in her mount and waited, back straight, chin held defiantly high.

She had expected her uncle or James, and so sat ready for battle. When the rider approached, however, she was shocked to see the rider was a person she'd never formally met. At least, he'd never seen *her* before. She'd had hours to observe him as her muscles stiffened from holding still in the grasses.

He wore plain brown riding breeches with a dark brown vest and overcoat, but the material was cut to fit his trim form perfectly. The fabric had turned darker from the rain, and even Prince Phillip's bright copper hair was subdued from the damp gloom of the day.

Though Ash was curious as to why the prince would ride alone on such a tempestuous morning, her curiosity was overshadowed by an unexpected feeling of apprehension. Sitting astride in her soaked cotton dress, her hair free and tangled about her shoulders, she knew she looked unorthodox, wild even. It was not the best way to first meet one's future king.

He came within calling range and shouted out, "Hello there. Are you in distress? Have you need of assistance?"

Ash searched the meadow frantically for the answer of what to do. If the prince was anything like her uncle, there was no telling what would happen to her if he found out she was riding against her guardian's wishes. The punishments that her uncle had meted out so far for her disobedience would pale in comparison to what a royal could do, or even what her uncle would do after the humiliation of having her defiance revealed to someone of such import.

She wrenched Windrunner around, and with a last panicked glance over her shoulder at Prince Phillip, urged her mount into a gallop.

"Wait," he sputtered before pushing his own horse to chase hers.

She had a head start, but the prince's mount was equal to Ash's lovely mare. She could not outpace him. Windrunner was hot and sweating from exertion despite the chill of the day. The trees covered them, and Ash jumped Windrunner over a large fallen trunk, hoping the prince would not be able to follow. She looked behind again to see his horse sail smoothly over the dead wood and land with light grace on the other side.

"Bother," she blurted unintentionally, and Prince Phillip was so close that his head jerked up at the sound, an expression of confusion filling his face. He sat up straighter on the saddle, as if unsure of whether or not to continue following.

"Please, Lady, stop. Why do you run from me?" he yelled as she wove Windrunner through a twisting path of thorny bushes and dense young trees. Unscathed passage required precision and speed. His horse fell slightly behind, but he was still far too close for Ash's peace of mind.

"Why do you chase me?" Ash yelled back in exasperation after a particularly difficult maneuver over a stream lined closely with more thorn bushes. She had to turn Windrunner quickly at the edge of the water so the mare would not ram her chest into the unforgiving undergrowth.

"I'm just trying to help. You shouldn't be alone out here!" he shouted after executing the jump without a break in stride. Ash really hoped that the prince didn't share her uncle's views on what a proper lady should and should not do, but his words were hinting that he might agree with Lord Richard's attitude.

"Thank you, but I am in no need of assistance, so please stop following me," she hurled back over her shoulder, feeling another twinge of apprehension.

"I can't just leave you unattended in the woods."

After this grim pronouncement further confirming her fears, Ash spurred her mount to even greater speed. She was forced to slow again to weave Windrunner through a meadow where boulders jutted from the ground as if dropped randomly by a giant.

"Please, let me at least see you safely to wherever you're going," came Prince Phillip's voice. He was hidden from view by the boulders, his words dropping on Ash's ears as soft as the filtered rain dripping through the trees.

She hopped the stream and twisted to determine how far behind the prince was. He burst from a rock directly across the water like a pheasant flushed from the bushes and stopped at the edge, his horse's hooves churning the mud on the bank as they lifted up and dropped back down in the same place. The stallion sank lower with each step.

Ash jumped when he appeared, and Windrunner shied, turning nervously in a tight circle to face Prince Phillip's horse across the stream. Then Windrunner stilled, a frozen reverse reflection to the black mount facing her. Ash shot an alarmed look straight into Prince Phillip's exasperated gaze and then flicked her eyes downward at his horse's hooves, which had worked themselves five inches deep in mud.

Furrowed brows lifted to a devilish arch, and her lips curved up impishly. She could see the prince's knit brows and pinched lips relax. His mouth dropped open, and his eyes slowly opened wide in an expression she thought close to surprise, but with a light in his eyes that hinted at something else she didn't recognize.

"I thank you for your concern, but I know these woods well, and I prefer solitude." She sounded a quick click-brrr-snap before turning Windrunner and jumping back under the trees and out of sight. Behind her, she heard the prince urge his mount forward, but Ash's spell thrust a bucket's worth of water from the stream onto the prince and his horse.

He was already wet, but she hoped it would befuddle the prince and further soak the ground at his horse's feet, turning the already sucking mud at the horse's hooves even stickier. It would take Prince Phillip time to get his horse free. Using that reprieve to the best of her ability, Ash found a direct trail to the road and galloped as fast as she could away from her dogged pursuer toward home.

***

Lord Richard was waiting for her in the stables. Ash wondered ruefully as she led a soaked and winded Windrunner into the warmth of the musty building if her uncle had been waiting long. Did he have nothing better to do? Before she got too near, Ash snagged the stable boy lurking near the door. Bill shifted his feet as if wishing to flee, so she gave him an escape.

"Windrunner needs to be given a cool down and rubbed well. She's had a hard ride." Ash handed the reins to a grateful Bill, who then quickly led Windrunner back outside to be walked. She watched him slip out the door and wished she could do likewise. Instead, Ash turned back slowly to face her uncle. He advanced from the far side of the stable to his favorite position of looming over her. She hoped he would confine her to her room quickly, and without too much fuss.

"I see you are dressed as a servant again. It seems locking you in your room is not enough motivation, nor has Jane's influence had any effect on you," he said in a low growl that somehow seemed more menacing than roaring. "If you wish to dress and act like a low-class whelp, then I will not stop you any longer. Come with me," he ground out. He grabbed her by the arm and propelled her out of the stable. The wet gravel slid and spit from her feet as he dragged her over the drive, past the rose garden, and into the house entryway.

David, who popped his head into the room only seconds after the door banged open, raised his eyebrows in surprise but made no other indication that he found Lord Richard hauling his niece painfully by the arm at all shocking. Only his eyes betrayed a hint of satisfaction.

"David, gather all the servants into the ballroom. I have an announcement to make." Lord Richard's hand on Ash's arm was branding her through the fabric. She was sure that when he finally let go there would be a large red band ringing her flesh that would later blossom into all the colors of the rainbow. He tugged her toward the ballroom. She stumbled, managing to throw her foot out into the path of her uncle's long stride so that he tripped and staggered as well. She smiled grimly, before flattening her lips as she contemplated what new punishment her uncle had concocted for her this time.

Lord Richard held her in the center of the room as servants flowed inward in ominous silence. Ash noticed they kept their heads' lowered and filed into the room in an orderly line. There had never been such gloomy structure to a servant gathering when her father lived, and Ash was surprised that Lord Richard could affect so much change in the servants so quickly. It sobered her even more to realize that she was not the only one to be affected by her uncle's hard handling.

Ash's hair hung wet and limp down her back with several moist tendrils stuck uncomfortably to her face. A small puddle started to form on the marble floor at her feet. She shivered, beginning to feel the effects of her jaunt in the rain, and she was aware that she smelled of damp horse. Most of the servants huddled close together in their lines, eyes averted toward the floor. A few glanced up nervously toward Ash and Lord Richard.

When David had indicated by a stiff nod toward Lord Richard that all the servants had arrived, her uncle said, "I've brought you all together this afternoon so that there will be no confusion in the future. Lady Ashelandra of Trebruk is to be addressed as 'lady' no more. She obviously does not desire to be one, and so I am inclined to grant her wish and give her the station she deserves.

"From this day forth she will work as a servant alongside all of you. If she does not work, she does not eat. All expensive clothes are to be taken from her room." He looked derisively at Ash's attire. "She does not wear them often anyway and will, I am sure, not miss them. If anyone treats her as a lady rather than a fellow worker, they will be dismissed. If anyone tries to do the chores assigned to her, they will be dismissed. Do you understand?"

"Ye can't do that!" yelled a young voice. The servants shuffled nervously. Ash recognized Bill's accent and hoped her uncle had not. Anger surged in her like lava in a volcano about to explode. Her uncle searched determinedly through the house help, trying to identify who'd spoken.

"Who said that? Identify yourself at once!" he roared, and Ash's molten anger shot forth.

"It does not matter who spoke. It's the truth. You cannot make me a slave in my own household. You may be my guardian, but you are a temporary fixture. This is my house, and I will evict you from it the very day I turn twenty-one," Ash spat, so hot from anger she could feel the water on her dress turning to steam.

"You are not twenty-one yet, and until then I decide what you do and what you are." His lips curved in a sharp hook of triumph. A drop of icy rainwater crawled down Ash's neck. She shivered.

She pushed the chill away. "A guardian is not a jailor, nor does your guardianship give you unlimited power. Are you so egotistical that you think yourself a god?"

Lord Richard laughed, and Ash felt shock freeze her cold limbs as she watched her uncle's shoulders shake with mirth.

Pain burst across her cheek. The sound of a loud clap echoed through the large ballroom followed by a combined gasp from the watching help. Ash's head whipped backward from the force of the blow. She stumbled and fell to the floor in a heap.

"To you, I am God. Remember that and there may be redemption for you. Forget it, and God's punishments will seem as nothing to mine." His eyes were wide with glorified glee. Ash looked away quickly as if insanity were contagious, spread by a hot, fevered stare.

"Since you are already on the ground, your first task will be to wash all the floors of the manor. You"—he pointed at Jenny—"take her with you to get what she needs to start." He then turned his enraged glare onto the rest of the servants.

"Remember what I told you. If anyone acts in defiance of my will concerning Ashelandra, he or she will no longer have a position within Trebruk Manor. Now be off about your business." His boots clicked loudly in the silence as he stalked across the floor and out of the room.

Ash stayed on the floor while the servants shuffled out after him. Stunned and angry, she didn't want to see the look on the servants' faces and dreaded meeting anyone's eyes. A quiet cough made her finally glance up to find Jenny standing above her. She couldn't help but glance toward Jenny's face, but the young maid would not meet her eyes.

"Come along with me, my La . . . Miss . . . uh . . . Ashelandra," Jenny said, searching the floor studiously as she spoke. She lifted her eyes to meet Ash's for a fleeting moment, and Ash saw pity and indecision warring with guilt across Jenny's freckled features.

"It's all right, Jenny. This is not your fault. Show me where to go." Ash stood slowly, gingerly touching the flaming skin on her cheek and temple. She was shivering. Jenny noticed and detoured to Ash's bedroom to allow her to change into something dry before leading her down to a closet near the kitchen, which held mops, bristled floor brushes, rags, buckets, dusters, and soap, as well as other cleaning supplies that Ash couldn't name.

Jenny gathered what Ash would need and then helped her understand how to dip the mop into the bucket and ring the excess water off before pushing it vigorously around the floor. Watching Jenny demonstrate, the job seemed to be fairly straightforward and easy, but after Jenny left, Ash found that it took a certain knack she did not possess to wring out the water efficiently. Dipping the mop into the bucket was not difficult, but to brace the handle while twisting the cloth mop end was awkward, and her weak grip never seemed to be tight enough to wring out much water. After only a few minutes of pushing and pulling the mop across the floor, Ash's back and arms ached.

It took her five hours to finish cleaning the marble and wood floors. It would have taken less time, for most rooms were clean already and no one would have noticed her skip over a few areas, except that her uncle sent David to spy on her as she worked to make sure she covered every space. He crept to the archways of the rooms she was cleaning every few minutes. His presence made the pain in Ash's cheek flare and flamed her anger. The mop moved in sharp hard strokes across the floor until David went away again. Then it slowed to a stop as Ash planned what to do.

She felt adrift, like a sailor cast from the mother ship to the middle of the ocean in a row boat not meant for deep waters, with no supplies and no way of knowing which way to row to find land. Only a few months of life with another captain and the Trebruk servants cowered, more subservient than they ever had been before. How could she allow herself to bow down to her uncle's demands if it meant increasing his stranglehold on her household? How could she not, if her refusal to do Lord Richard's wishes destroyed the lives of the servants she loved like family?

She went to bed exhausted. The chase through the woods followed by so much unfamiliar physical labor had sucked her energy so that she lay on the bed, unable to move, but unable to sleep as her tired muscles twitched from fatigue and her weary brain mulled in useless circles over how she could liberate herself from her insupportable situation.

***

Ash wasn't sure when she drifted into an uneasy sleep, but no time at all seemed to pass when she was woken before dawn by Jenny.

"I'm sorry, Miss Ash, but Lord Richard insisted that ye get up to work when the rest of us servants do," she said, her face flushing.

"It's all right, Jenny. I'll be down in a minute after dressing." Ash pulled herself slowly into a sitting position. Her sore muscles shouted at her. Jenny colored a deeper shade of red, making her freckles stand out like island clusters on a map.

"Beggin' yer pardon, but he insisted that someone keep ye in sight at all times today. I'm real sorry, but I can't afford to lose me job, Miss. I gotta support me ma and pa. They're too old to do much for themselves these days, and I'm the only child they've got."

Ash knew that. Of course she did. She often visited Jenny's parents to bring them food or to help with little chores that were too difficult for the aging couple. Ash sat very still on her cot, picturing the weathered faces of Jenny's parents and struggled to master her emotions. It would be cruel to direct her rage against Jenny when her uncle was the culprit.

After three deep breaths while Jenny stood in tormented silence Ash said, "You should probably stop calling me Miss, then, Jenny. My uncle will most likely take exception to any sort of formal address, no matter how minor."

Ash stood quickly, ignoring the scream of her muscles as she dressed in another of her serviceable gowns she used for adventuring. Jenny handed her the crisp white apron that all women servants wore over their dresses, and Ash lowered it over her head and tied the strings behind her back. The ribbon felt tight and heavy like chains. Ash noticed that all of her formal wear had been removed. She clenched her teeth but swallowed down the curses she wanted to spit forth. It would serve no purpose. It occurred to her that her father's solicitor would know what to do about her situation and might even be able to help rid her of her uncle somehow. If she was to be under constant surveillance then she would need to focus her energies on finding a way to slip past her jailers and escape to the king's city to see him.

The day blurred from one exhausting unfamiliar chore to the next, and Ash found it increasingly difficult to muster the energy to keep a sharp eye out for a way to escape to the city. She was always surrounded by servants and frequently checked on by David, James, or her uncle. Ash did not see Jane, but since her uncle kept her working mostly in the less public areas of the house, Ash didn't find Jane's absence astonishing. It wouldn't surprise Ash if Jane didn't even know what had happened.

No opportunity for escape presented itself to Ash all day long. She found that she was no longer expected to dine with her cousins and uncle, and she thanked heaven for small favors. After eating some bread, cheese, and two apples, Ash was escorted to her room. The bolt slid shut on the outside of the door.

Ash stood for a moment, looking toward the hidden door. She was so tired, and if she left now, her escape might be blamed on the servants. She didn't want to get those who depended on their jobs fired. Her knees buckled, ending her inner debate. She fell toward her cot and didn't get up again until the next morning.

Each day Ash was worked like a slave. Her chores were assigned by her uncle rather than the staff. Ash thought that if the servants had been the ones making the assignments, her labor each day would be greatly reduced. She did twice the work of a paid maid, and if her uncle was hoping to wear her past the point of exhaustion, he succeeded.

Ash took as many shortcuts in her chores as she could, but her uncle had hired a new manservant whose job seemed to be solely to watch Ash and make sure she worked. Willie was a slimy-looking fellow with yellowed teeth and greasy brown hair that hung thin and lank to his shoulders. He wiped his constantly dripping nose with a handkerchief as he sat comfortably watching Ash. A little leering half smile appeared when Ash bent to rinse out a rag or stretched to dust an upper shelf. She shivered and sought to keep turned away from him as much as possible.

***

Ash didn't see Jane until the third day of Ash's sentence to servitude. Jane came upon Ash in the upper hallway as Ash stretched to dust the tops of the doorframes. Willie stood ogling Ash where the hall turned a corner, but he quickly bowed as Jane approached.

Jane stopped, nodding uncertainly at Willie. "What are you doing, Ashelandra?"

Ash lowered her aching arms and turned to Jane. "It's been three days now, Jane. You cannot be so isolated as to not have heard." Ash's fatigue made her words sound stern and unforgiving.

Jane's cheeks bloomed red. She shook her head, though the movement didn't convey denial.

"I'm sorry. I wish . . ." Jane glanced quickly at Willie, who was watching the exchange avidly, and the red flooding her cheeks drained to white as if her embarrassment had been sucked away by fear.

"I'm sorry," she said again before continuing down the hall past Ash, eyes to the floor, disconnecting herself from the situation.

Chapter Five

The bruises on her arm and face blossomed into full color and faded away again before Ash found a chance to carry out her escape plans without involving anyone innocent. The sun was just peeking beyond the trees, and the air was cool still, not yet enveloped by the sun's thin blanket of heat. She was weeding the garden, one of the more pleasant chores, when Willie was confronted by an angry David.

"You, Willie, I've gone to complain to the master about you and he wants to see you right away," said David, his lips quivering with suppressed rage.

Willie tilted back his head to look up at David, scratching his greasy hair in apparent indifference. "What for?" he drawled.

"Some of the silverware has gone missing, and I saw you slip the Chinese mother of pearl music box under your shirt just this morning when the servant girl was turned away and you thought yourself unseen." David's chest was puffed in righteous indignation, but Ash didn't fail to notice his smirk when he referred to her as "the servant girl."

Willie's face paled and his eyes flicked around nervously before he regained his expression of unconcerned boredom. "Yer lying just to get me bagged. Ye can't prove nuffin'. I've a mind to ask him to dismiss ye, for slanderin' folks' good names." His voice rose as he heaved himself up from his sprawl on the ground.

"Let's go talk to the master, and we'll just see who ends up getting 'bagged,'" continued David, his voice raised now to a condescending tone. David marched past Willie toward the house, and Willie hurried to catch up so that the butler would not have the tactical advantage of being in the lead.

As soon as the two men were out of sight, Ash dropped her trowel and ran toward the stables. She hid around the corner from the door, picked up a large stone, and hurled it at the corral's wooden fence. It hit the wood with a loud thwack. After a few moments, the stable doors opened and Bill's face appeared. He glanced about for a moment and Ash ducked back out of sight mumbling a series of click-shush-snap phrases.

"Teddy, come help me. One of the horses is runnin' past the corral's fence," Bill cried in alarm. Ash saw the two boys run frantically past the corral toward the forest where her hazy illusion of a horse disappeared into the trees. She ran into the stables to saddle Windrunner with frantic speed, her fingers fumbling in her haste. The translucent illusion would not fool the two boys for long. A twinge of worry hit as she made Windrunner let out her breath so Ash could tighten the saddle's girth. She wished she could do something to make sure the stable lads would not be punished.

Ash threw herself onto her horse and burst out of the stable, galloping at full speed toward the king's city and her father's solicitor, Mr. Thursley. She would just have to resolve this matter as soon as possible so that Richard would no longer have power to affect anything in her household.

She reached the city two hours later. The sun flared hot in the sky. Windrunner was breathing hard, and Ash dismounted to walk her horse through the crowded city streets to more easily cool her horse and maneuver through the press of people.

She had been to Mr. Thursley's a few times before, but she still had difficulty winding her way through the twisting streets of the outer district. Once, she had to ask for directions to the business quarter. The vendor she asked eyed her suspiciously, taking in her dirty cotton dress and fine horse. She straightened her shoulders and assumed an air of haughty entitlement. The attitude seemed to confuse the squat man enough to comply with her request and give her directions, but she hurried away from him as quickly as she could just in case he decided to call a city guard to check on her. A lower-class woman traveling alone was common, but no lower-class woman would have a horse so fine, and an upper-class woman would not be alone. She sighed when she made it unquestioned to the business quarter where her father's, now *her* solicitor's, office was located.

The long connected buildings gave her pause for a moment, and she had to count doors before finally recognizing the sixth entrance as the one bearing the small plaque stating *Mr. Robin Thursley Esq., Solicitor.* She wrapped Windrunner's reins around a posting pole and bounded up the steps. The door tapped a little bell hanging above as it swung open. There was a rustle of papers before a young man popped his head out from a desk placed next to the entrance. She didn't recognize him from previous visits, and Ash realized with a pang that Mr. Thursley must have hired him after her father's death.

"Can I help you, miss?" he asked, looking dubiously at Ash's dirty attire and mussed appearance. Ash self-consciously smoothed her hair.

"I need to speak with Mr. Thursley."

"Mr. Thursley is much occupied and isn't receiving new clients at this time." He began to turn back into his room with a last dismissive flick of the eyes.

"I am not a new client. Tell him that Baroness Ashelandra Enando Camery of Trebruk must speak with him immediately," Ash said, her voice ringing with command. His back jolted to a stop and he spun quickly to face her.

"I'm terribly sorry. I'll fetch him right away, My Lady." He looked at Ash and flinched, though Ash wasn't really sure why.

"Lady Ashelandra, I was not expecting you," Mr. Thursley said, appearing in the door of his office. The young man's head jerked toward Mr. Thursley, then turned bright red. Ash looked away from his discomfort and concentrated on her solicitor.

"I had no chance to send word of my visit, but I need to speak with you without delay." Ash smoothed her skirt as Mr. Thursley swept a comprehensive glance over her worn and dirty dress. He nodded and held the door. His office was elegant and organized with only a few piles of papers across his desk. She regarded the deep blue plush chair set across the desk for visitors, tugged at her dirty skirt, and decided to remain standing.

The door clicked softly shut, and Ash turned to see Mr. Thursley regarding her with narrowed eyes. Emotion did not often play across the older man's thin face, and his expression was the closest to concern she'd ever seen.

"What has happened to warrant this visit, Lady Ashelandra?" he asked, his voice smooth and enigmatic.

"I'll come straight to the point. My uncle has made me a slave in my own home. At first he simply locked me in my room, but when I continued to fall short of his expectations, he announced to the household staff that I was to work as a servant and was no longer to be regarded as a lady of the house. I am watched constantly by a goon my uncle hired specifically for that purpose and am worked harder than any of the other servants. Surely Lord Richard cannot do this. There must be something you can do to stop him," Ash finished, only then realizing that she'd been pacing back and forth the short distance between desk and visitor's chair.

"Surely not." Mr. Thursley's voice rose in pitch, an abnormality from his usually calm and cultivated tone. His words expressed doubt, but his lowered brows and parted lips conveyed absolute belief in Ash's accusation.

Ash halted and met his eyes squarely. "It's been weeks now, and only chance allowed me to flee to you for aide. This must stop. The law will support and protect me from such twisted *guardianship*. It must."

Mr. Thursley's lips tightened, a small sign of distress. "In cases such as these, the guardian would be evaluated and, if found wanting, replaced by a different relative until you were of age. You, however, have no other family. Your mother was the last of a dwindling line of great sorcerers, and Lord Richard and his children are all that is left of your father's kin." Ash loved the way Mr. Thursley stated the fact of her mother's sorcery without hesitation or nervousness. His refusal to shy from speaking of magic had been one of the things that had drawn Ash's father to him.

"Must my guardian be related to me?"

"Until recently, many of our laws were quite archaic, in my opinion, but with the banishment of magical creatures, some revisions have begun to take shape. No progress has been made in the matter of guardianship as yet, however. As things stand now, you must be related to your guardian unless you have no relations. I will see what I can do. We may be the vehicle for reformation in guardianship law. But, currently, the law is against you until you reach your majority."

Dirty frock forgotten, Ash sank to the chair in defeat. "I can't go back there. Who knows what my uncle will do to me for coming here." To her utter mortification, she felt tears sliding quickly down her face. "Forgive me." She turned away slightly to hide her weakness.

"No, no." Mr. Thursley rose and came around his desk to her chair, offering her a handkerchief. His thin features were wrinkled in concern. "I'll do all that I can to stop this barbarism, and I will prevent your uncle from abusing your estate in any way. When you reach your majority, we will take swift action to be rid of him entirely."

The tears had stopped, leaving Ash drained and empty. "Four years is a long time. What if I can't last? What if he . . . if I . . . ?" She couldn't bring herself to voice her worst fear—that she would be broken, ground down to a mere shadow as her uncle wished.

Mr. Thursley grasped her hands, his knuckles white, painfully tight, and looked her earnestly in the face. Ash was struck by the expressiveness of his usually remote features. "You won't be. You are strong of heart like your father and as crafty as your mother. I've seen your potential. You will find a way to survive and even grow stronger. I will file a petition today and push for a review as soon as possible. I know it will be hard, but your case will have more potency if you can show that you are doing what your uncle has demanded despite how unreasonable it is."

She took a deep breath and nodded before rising from her chair. "I should get back. It would probably be best if my uncle didn't know I came here. Do what you can, Mr. Thursley. I am very grateful for your help." She gave him a tremulous smile and left the office, riding as slowly as she could back to Trebruk manor.

***

Her reception at the house late that evening was much as she had expected. The servants ran around like ants in a dither, but her uncle stood still, a silent menace positioned at the manor's front door. Bill took her horse silently from Ash and then retreated quickly to the safety of the stables. She noticed a limp to his step and winced in guilt. Ash kept her steps even, solid and unhurried, but her heart was jumping with an erratic tapping, betraying her fear. She stopped at the bottom of the steps, unwilling to come any closer.

"Why did you bother coming back?" Lord Richard asked, his voice a low growl of outrage.

"This is my home. You are the trespasser. I will not allow you to drive me off my own land. Nor will I be treated as a slave." Ash climbed the far side of the steps and swept past her uncle, but her movement was jarred to a halt as Lord Richard whipped his hand up and manacled her arm in his vicelike grip. She could not stop a small yelp from escaping before she clamped her mouth shut and bit her teeth against the pain.

"Until you are twenty-one, I may treat you any way I like. You will do as I say, or you will be punished," he hissed in her ear, and then he slapped her so hard her vision went black and she sagged against his stone grip. When her eyes cleared, she looked into the hallway to see James standing perfectly still, his hands white fists at his sides, his eyes strangely unnerved. He caught her glance and his expression turned flat and unreadable.

Lord Richard raised his hand to strike again, but Jane entered the foyer to stand by her brother, her doe eyes wide with concern.

"Father?" The tentative word stilled Lord Richard's swing, and he lowered his hand slowly.

"No need to worry, dear. Why don't you go up to your room? It's late," Lord Richard said. His voice softened to something almost kind.

"Of course, Father. But what is wrong with Ashelandra? She looks unwell. Since I'm headed that direction, perhaps I should help her to her room." Ash looked over to see her uncle's clenched jaw release. The blood vessel at his temple faded back to invisibility.

"You're a good girl, Jane. Take her along with you. It will give her time for reflection. I will be by shortly to bid you good night."

Jane glided forward and took Ash's other arm in a delicate touch of support. Her hand on Ash's arm was ice cold. Richard's grip released, and Ash felt the blood rush back to her fingers. James stepped aside to let the two girls through to the main curving staircase reserved for family and guests. Ash hadn't used it for weeks. She'd grown accustomed to climbing the servant's stairwell, and fancied the wide marbled steps had grown higher and fatter than before.

Jane walked beside Ash in silence until they were at the top of the stairs. "You must understand. My father is not always so vexed. He can be kind, but he is easily aggravated. If you could just see your way to acting more demure, things would go easier."

"I doubt there is much that I could do at this point to ease my situation, but thank you for your concern," Ash replied, unsure of how to feel about Jane's advice, and wondering how much of herself Jane hid in order to stay in her father's favor.

At her room, Ash said a courteous good night to Jane and then bolted the door. She did not want any more unpleasant encounters.

***

The next morning, Ash woke to Jenny's soft knock and inquiry. Ash's face throbbed, and she lay for a moment on her cot trying to decide what to do. She could take Jane's advice and meekly work all day, every day for the next four years. Even Mr. Thursley had advised her to act the part of obedient ward in order to strengthen her petition. If she refused to work, she might also be struck again. Her uncle might decide to beat her, even if she scrubbed and scoured the manor. That might help her case against him, but it wasn't worth the risk to her well-being.

Jenny knocked again, and Ash rose to her feet to let her enter.

"Lord Richard has given the servants the day off. He wishes you to complete all the staff's work for the day while we are away. I'm sorry. What he asks is impossible. I would stay, but . . ."

"I know, Jenny. I wouldn't ask you to jeopardize your position. I think the impossibility of the task is the point my uncle wishes to make. Go have a good day. Tell your parents I said hello." Jenny hesitated for a moment at the door before turning quickly and scurrying down the hall out of sight. Ash watched her disappear, considering again if she should make the effort to complete an impossible task or not. It was likely she would be beaten either way, but Jane's words and Mr. Thursley's advice echoed in her mind. It occurred to her that if she could get beyond this initial punishment and make herself more invisible to her uncle, he might begin to forget about her enough for her to find a few moments of freedom.

The day was grueling, and as she had predicted, she didn't finish everything. She didn't even know everything that she should do. Her uncle rebuked her for a full fifteen minutes about the unacceptable food she'd prepared. Ash didn't know how to cook and so had arranged bread and cold cuts on a plate for her cousins and uncle for breakfast, lunch, and dinner. Dinner had been the breaking point for Lord Richard. Ash could no longer stay silent.

"I've done everything you asked of me today that I possibly could. If you wanted better food, you should not have sent Cook away. You can shout and hit me till I'm as colorful as a blueberry, but it will not change the fact that I can't cook," Ash replied, trying to keep her voice sounding as demure as possible. Lord Richard looked slightly startled by Ash's subdued tone, even if her words fell a little short of diffident.

"Very well then. Get back to work," he huffed, searching for some sign of rebellion so he could punish her. Ash kept her eyes lowered and went back to work.

When Ash continued to work diligently for the next few days, Lord Richard seemed to lose interest in her, only checking on her every once in a while personally. David, however, often hovered around Ash and her guard dog, Willie. He watched Willie suspiciously, and Willie scowled back resentfully. Ash suspected that David also enjoyed watching her work at menial tasks below his station.

***

The next week, Mr. Thursley showed up at the manor demanding to speak with the Baroness. Richard refused to let him, until Mr. Thursley explained that he had filed a petition to have Lord Richard removed as Ashelandra's guardian, and his refusal to let Ash's legal adviser see his client would certainly help his petition be granted. Lord Richard's generous allowance as Ash's guardian would then cease.

Lord Richard fetched Ash but then sent for his own lawyer, who filed a counter petition that argued that Ash's rebellious nature had forced her uncle into necessary disciplinary action in order to curb her destructive tendencies.

A legal war ensued that resulted in the court ruling in her uncle's favor under the condition that Mr. Thursley visit every week in order to ensure that the disciplinary measures did not negatively affect Ash's health.

When Ash heard the ruling, she wanted to scream with frustration. She contemplated running away until her twenty-first birthday. But she was cautioned by Mr. Thursley that if she did so, and was found and brought back again, the court might allow her uncle even more power over her. They might even take away the meager protection that Mr. Thursley's visits afforded.

She was glad, at least, that her guard dog, Willie, was eventually given tasks that kept him away from the house and its valuables. Though Richard knew that a constant guard was no longer needed to keep Ash working, as she had too much to lose if she ran away, he seemed reluctant to dismiss the oily man. Every so often, when Willie was free of the mysterious errands her uncle sent him on, he watched Ash with a steady reptilian intensity as she scrubbed the floors or rinsed the laundry.

All she could do was grit her teeth, a sour taste in her mouth, as she ignored him and kept working.

Chapter Six

Ash wiped her forearm across her brow and looked up from scrubbing the floor to the clock on the mantel. It was nearly two. She would need to get out of sight quickly before any visitors came calling. Lord Richard had specifically instructed that she remain unseen at this time of day. Not that any of her few old acquaintances would recognize her anymore, Ashelandra thought ruefully as she gathered up the bucket and scrub brush before heading to the kitchen.

Three years of manual labor had changed Ash. Her hands were rough, calloused. Her knees were perpetually bruised from continuous kneeling. She'd lost weight, though the servants were very kind about making sure Ash didn't completely starve when her uncle was in a temper and decided to vent his anger by denying her food. Her dress was a hand-me-down from Jenny. Every night Ash had to spend time sewing the frayed seams of her skirt so that it wouldn't fall to pieces.

Outwardly, she took Jane's long-ago advice and worked to hide any sign of rebelliousness from her uncle so that after several months Lord Richard seemed to begin to forget that Ash wasn't just another servant of the house. But she couldn't resist pulling brilliant jokes every now and then that would embarrass her uncle and sometimes James. She was careful to always hide any magical elements in her planning and didn't mind the subsequent punishment of withheld food. The look on her uncle's face was always worth the price.

Mr. Thursley's visit once a week to check on Ashelandra's health kept Lord Richard from ever hitting her again. Ash could tell, however, that despite his obvious legal victory, the visual reminder of his limitations still rankled her uncle. She was careful to refrain from pranks right after a visit from Mr. Thursley. The end of April was a time for caution as well. Her birthday fell on April twenty-second, and the reminder of her creeping independency chaffed her uncle's nerves like sandpaper on skin. Even David and Willie tiptoed through the manor to avoid his notice on her birthday. It was not a good time to tempt his temper.

Though it was difficult to find time, Ash studied her magic books whenever the opportunity arose. She was getting much better at discerning the meaning and sounds of the sorcery language, and had become better at guessing when the dialect or verb usage needed to be different for certain types of spells.

The servants helped her here as well. They found small ways to aid her that Lord Richard, David, and Willie wouldn't notice. This left her more time to study, although not much. She was able to squeeze in an hour here and there a few times a week. But despite their kind interference, Ash felt that she hadn't been able to progress as much in her studies as she would have wished had she enjoyed more leisure.

As she put away her cleaning supplies, she noticed a carriage arriving. Probably one of Jane's many admirers. Since Jane came out into society shortly after arriving at the manor, she'd had a bevy of men asking for her hand, but Lord Richard had refused to allow her to marry any of them. He apparently had bigger fish in mind for his only daughter than the many equal-ranking minor lords that had set their cap for her.

Despite the fact that her dowry was unappealingly meager, he schemed as avidly as any matchmaking mother for a duke, or at least a marquis. The result was that though Jane was still popular, she was also still single. Ash often felt sorry for her reticent cousin. Jane may not have been reduced to servitude, but she was as much a prisoner to her father's whims as Ash was.

Ash waited until she was sure all three of her relatives were safely ensconced in the receiving room, with David waiting obediently just outside, before she hung her apron on the peg by the kitchen door. With a wink at Cook and his son Henry, she scrambled out the door, retrieved her books from their hiding place next to the stable, and disappeared into the forest to practice magic. She didn't go far, knowing that if there was trouble, Cook would loudly bang twice on his pan so she could hear and run back before she was discovered gone.

To loosen her mouth, she started by reviewing her illusion spells. After she'd gotten the hang of it, she found illusions were the easiest kind of magic. The words flowed more easily for illusions. Also, because they didn't deal with any tangible mass, even complicated images didn't take the amount of careful concentration that a spell to change something from one form to another did. Her once hazy shapes had improved so much she could now make illusions complicated enough to be smelled and lightly felt, so long as the person didn't push too hard.

Next, she practiced moving objects around. She was to the point where she could move objects of at least forty pounds, but no more than that, and not very far. Though there was only the slightest variation in tone and wording between the spell to move something the size of a pebble and that of the spell to move a boulder, Ash found those almost imperceptible changes in the tone of a click or dip of a snap, combined with her focus of will, made a big difference in the spell's difficulty.

The area of magical study that gave her the most difficulty, however, was transformations. It was not just a matter of memorizing the text and speaking the words correctly. It was also a matter of focus and perfect inflection. If levitation took a firm resolve, transformation required iron determination. The denser a material, the harder the spell was to speak, like the difference between saying the word "hard" and the word "problematic." Though similar in meaning, the connotation of "hard" and "problematic" differed, just as the transformation spell's words could be comparable, while at the same time diverging in its denotation. No matter how hard she tried, she hadn't been able to master changes more complicated than water to glass, or a feather to a flower.

Grabbing a thin stick, she began to practice the spell that would change it into bone. She repeated the spell over and over, changing a sound here, a pause there, until her tongue and cheeks went numb from all the contorted snap clicking. Each failure ate at her confidence and made success that much more difficult until she finally threw the stick down in disgust.

The sound of a pan being struck reached her. She cast an illusion spell of invisibility on herself. After her uncle made her a servant, she'd practiced persistently until she could walk through the manor unseen any time she wished. After stashing her books by the pond, she sprinted to see which code Cook had left. A sprig of rosemary hung from the frame of the kitchen door, Cook's signal that she was to go to the gardens. She raced around the corner and through the gate into the garden, diving down among the plants where she released the spell of invisibility and began to pick weeds in a zone of singular concentration as if she'd been at the chore for hours.

The gate banged, but Ash kept her head bowed, her hands moving methodically among the plants. She heard the rustle of satin, and her shoulders relaxed infinitesimally.

"Hello, Ashelandra." Jane's voice was timid. Ash squinted up. Jane's back was to the sun, and the lowering rays framed her face and golden hair in a halo of light. Ash sighed and glanced down to her work-roughened hands. It was sometimes quite a bother to Ash that she couldn't just hate Jane, but Jane was too confoundedly nice for any emotion more negative than mild annoyance.

Swiping her arm across her brow to brush a ratty strand of hair out of her face, Ash said, "This is an unexpected surprise. Did your swains already depart for the day? They're usually more persistent."

Jane blushed, making her even more pretty.

"I had no callers today, and I'm glad," Jane said with unusual passion. Embarrassed, she looked around as if searching for something.

"There's a stool over there if you wish to sit," Ash said, guessing what Jane searched for, and felt a little smile quirking at the corner of her mouth.

Jane looked down at her silvery blue dress with tiny pearls sewn into the embroidery of the skirt, then at the weathered wooden stool longingly, but remained standing.

"I'd better not, but thank you. I came to tell you that we received a visit from Marchioness Amelia Langrove today. I believe she was a particular friend of your father's. She inquired after your health, wanting to know why you were still at school and hadn't been presented into society yet."

Ash felt a surge of gratitude to Lady Amelia for remembering her. It was comforting to know that someone besides Mr. Thursley hadn't completely forgotten her. For a while Ash had feared that her uncle ripping Lady Amelia's dress would stop her from visiting Trebruk Manor ever again, and it did for several months. By the time the Marchioness had finally come to call again to enquire after Ash, Lord Richard claimed Ash had gone away to finishing school. Ash had been outside as Lord Richard spoke with Lady Amelia and didn't even know she'd missed disproving her uncle's lie until the lady had already departed.

Lady Amelia had not called again until now.

"You'd better marry soon, Jane. It will be a blow to Lord Richard's plans for you when people find out what sort of guardian he really is."

"Some won't care. They may even applaud him."

Ash squinted up at Jane. She put her hand up to shield her eyes so she could better read her cousin's expression. Jane looked tired.

"Do you fear that is the sort of person you'll have to marry?"

Jane shrugged elegantly.

Ash bent back to the ground, pulling weeds as she thought. There would be no legal consequences to Lord Richard if others discovered where she'd been and what she'd been subjected to under her uncle's care. But socially, Lord Richard would have a harder time convincing the world that he was an elegant, genteel sort of man with a son and daughter worthy of any prince or princess.

Lady Amelia's visit must have been an unhappy reminder that others knew of Ash and would be wondering when she would be coming "home" from school. She was twenty years old. It was already an unstable fabrication to claim Ash was away to studying when most other girls didn't stay at school past eighteen.

"What did my uncle say when Lady Amelia enquired after me?" Ash asked cautiously. Jane's cheeks bloomed a becoming pink.

"He implied that you'd gotten unladylike notions in your head about book learning and refused to come home."

Ash laughed, startling Jane.

"I wager that didn't go over very well with Lady Amelia. She's quite learned herself."

"She did seem displeased." A soft laugh escaped before Jane continued. "She put father down quite forcefully before she returned to the subject of you. She said learning was all very well, but that you were almost to your majority now, and needed to be presented at court. She demanded he give her the address to your school so that she could write you herself and insist that you come home."

"How did Lord Richard respond to that?"

"He said he would write again immediately and demand that you come home, citing Lady Amelia's superior reasoning."

"I see." Ash kept her eyes to the ground, pulling up weeds so that Jane would not see the emotions on her face.

"Lady Amelia said she expected to see you at the ball for the prince in a fortnight. It's a masque, but Lady Amelia informed my father that she would be a peacock, and if he wanted her continued support he'd better bring you along. She wishes to see how you've turned out."

Ash sat back on her heels and stared up at Jane incredulously. "Did he agree?"

"Lady Amelia did not give him the chance to disagree. She left immediately after pronouncing her demand," Jane said with a serene smile. The smile surprised Ash. Though her cousin had always been quietly kind, they did not often get a chance to speak to each other. Ash was usually busy with work, and Jane's father had commanded her not to talk to Ash.

"Does your father know you're here?" Ash asked, suddenly curious.

Jane looked away, "No. I must go, but I thought I should inform you of Lady Amelia's visit since it is unlikely that my father will do so."

"I didn't mean to frighten you off. Thank you for telling me, but will it really come to anything? Will your father really dress me up and take me to the ball when there is the chance that I could pronounce to the whole court where I've really been these past three years?"

"I suppose not," Jane said brushing self-consciously at her cream satin skirt. Her hands stilled, and she looked directly at Ash. "But Lady Amelia will be waiting to see you. If you do not come, she will be displeased. The last thing Father wants is to alienate us from the society to which she could introduce us. Without her support, Father's plans of a successful marriage would be unlikely. Everyone listens to and heeds Lady Amelia's opinions."

"I hadn't realized she was so influential. But you are forgetting how easy it would be to evade Lady Amelia's command. He could simply say that I became sick and couldn't make the journey in time."

"Oh, I hadn't thought of that," Jane said with a pretty frown.

"Though I do appreciate that you came to see me, it would be unpleasant for you if your father found you in my company. Don't trouble yourself over me, Jane. I'll be fine," she assured the girl, who stood like a sad silver-clad angel looking down on the kneeling muddy supplicant.

"I'm sorry, Ashelandra," Jane said with feeling before she turned and gracefully glided out of the garden through the gate, back to her sphere of lonely luxury.

Ash watched the gate swing closed with mixed feelings. She still wasn't sure how to feel about the prospect of going to a ball. It had been so long since she'd acted the part of a baroness in training that she didn't know if she could anymore. For the rest of the day, Ash went through her assigned tasks with her ears half-cocked, listening for the approach of her uncle. She hadn't missed wearing a corset, but to wear one might be worth the bother in order to feel the smooth brush of satin against her skin. She looked down at her rough cracked fingers and cringed. She'd have to wear gloves.

Her stomach twisted in hunger, and she let herself dream of the succulent food that would be served at a royal ball. She could eat her fill of sweet meats, candied fruits, cakes, and exotic juices. Well, she could eat as much as a stifling corset would allow anyway. Still, it would be worth the discomfort.

Lord Richard didn't appear that day. Nor did he speak to her in the week that followed.

***

Three days before the ball, it was obvious that Lord Richard planned to use some form of excuse to explain Ash's absence. Ash had felt insecure and excited about the possibility of joining the ball the first day she had heard of it. The day after that, when she still didn't see Lord Richard, her worry at remembering how to behave like a genteel lady eroded into suspicion. The third day without any word of a ball from her uncle, Ash bypassed misgiving and ran straight to anger. It simmered like stew left too long in the pot.

Again she felt the injustice of her situation burn in her chest. It seemed insufferable that her uncle should get away with treating her like a slave and not even have to pay the consequence of social disapprobation. Mr. Thursley would have published Lord Richard's behavior to all if it would have done any good, but he was not a peer and did not move in the same sphere. Lord Fredrick had chosen Mr. Thursley because of his marked interest toward all things magical and had been Mr. Thursley's only titled client.

What would Lord Richard do when Ashelandra reached her majority and kicked him out of her house? A chill ran through her at the thought. Would he try to do something to Ash to stop that from happening? Would he hide her permanently in a cell, poison her so it would appear she died of sickness, or arrange an accident while traveling?

But then common sense quieted her momentary fear. She shook herself from her wild musings. Lord Richard could not do anything to Ash, not with Mr. Thursley aware of her situation and checking on her to make sure she was well. But he would put off the moment of truth for as long as possible.

A slow smile crept up her face as she thought of this. The idea for a most brilliant and satisfying prank bloomed to life inside her head. Had anyone been passing by, they would have known immediately that Ash was up to something, but Ash was alone in the garden gathering vegetables. None of the help were there to know that they should try to persuade her from another rash course of action that would most likely get her punished, and Ash was glad of it. She didn't want any of the other servants trying to dissuade her, tainting the pure enjoyment of the chance for mischief.

***

The night of the ball, Ash watched carefully as Jane alighted into the coach followed by Lord Richard and James. The men wore rich, well-tailored clothes, each holding a mask in their hand that they would put on when they reached the palace. Lord Richard wore forest-green, his mask an imitation of leafy greenery. James's clothes were sky-blue with a simple white mask in the shape of a cloud. Ash did her best to memorize the masks and fit of the clothes for later reference. She looked longest at Jane. Jane's mask was already in place in order to avoid mussing her carefully up-swept hair. It was painted to look like a butterfly with purple, green, and yellow wings. Her dress mimicked the look of the butterfly in a more subtle and flattering way. It was mostly purple, with green embroidery and golden hems.

As soon as the coach was out of sight, Ash ran to find Annette, Jane's maid. With her mistress gone, Annette was enjoying herself in the kitchen, flirting with Cook's son, Henry. Ash could tell immediately that Annette didn't look upon Ash's interruption with favor. Ash would have to tread carefully.

"Oh, Annette, you really are amazing. I just watched Jane leave and her hair looked as if it had been styled by a team of royal maids. Isn't Annette talented, Henry?" Ash gushed. Henry, who dealt with Ash more often than Annette, narrowed his eyes at her, but smiled warmly at Annette, who blushed and appeared much more pleased with Ash's entrance than a moment ago.

"Sometimes I wish . . ." Ash trailed off and then put an excited look on her face. "Annette, do you think you could do my hair like Jane's just this once while they're gone? I wish to feel like a lady again for just awhile. I'll owe you a favor later. What do you think?" Ash leaned forward, looking eager. Annette gazed longingly at Henry, and Ash could tell she would much rather stay, but no one had forgotten who Ash really was despite her uncle's decree.

"Certainly, Ash. You don't owe me anything, either," Annette said with a parting glance at Henry. Henry smiled at her and then gave Ash one last suspicious glance before the two women left the kitchen to make Ashelandra's hair exactly like Jane's in style, if not in color.

Ash's next stop was at the stables. No one was in sight, so she quickly saddled Windrunner. She was just tightening the girth when Bill walked in the stable door. He'd shot up at fifteen, and now, at seventeen, was taller than Ash by a good five inches. He stopped just inside the door, obviously surprised to see Ash about to take the horse.

"Ye look nice," he said and then blushed a beet red. Ash reached a self-conscious hand up to her hair. She looked down at her stained everyday work clothes. Her mouth quirked.

"Don't you mean, 'Where are you going?'" Ash teased as she secured a bag to the saddle. Bill, whose face was just starting to turn back to normal, reddened again. Then he smiled, a spark of curiosity lighting his brown eyes.

"What *are* ye doing? Ye're up to mischief, aren't ye?" he asked excitedly. Ash grinned at him and winked. Bill colored even more deeply.

"I'm off to snatch a whisker right off the lion's nose, and he won't even know it's gone." Ash felt her grin stretch a little too wide and tried to check herself. Bill's smile faltered.

"Ye're not going ta get in trouble, are ye? I'd hate to see ye punished again."

"Not to worry. I'm just after a bit of fun. I'll be very careful, and I'll return a little after midnight I should think, long before my uncle and cousins get back. Don't worry about waking to help me," Ash instructed as she mounted her mare.

"I'll be here to help ye," he muttered, his face still ruddy. Ash thought about arguing but decided against it as she urged her mount out the door at an easy trot.

Excitement hummed through her. Windrunner picked up her mood and tried to trot, but Ash held the horse back. She needed to preserve her hair even if she also found it difficult to maintain a sedate pace. Thinking of the coming adventure made her wish to urge Windrunner to fly over the roads, but she'd tricked Annette into copying Jane's style for a reason. It would be complicated enough to keep track of the color, feel, and design of Jane's attire without having to worry about the hairstyle's detail, though she'd still have to lighten the shade. Mimicking Jane's clothes might be dangerous, but easier than thinking up a complicated ensemble without any frame of reference, and if she stayed far away from her cousin all night there would be no reason for the nobles critical of fashion to think Jane's ensemble unoriginal because Ash would appear to be the same person.

During the hours it took her to ride to the palace, Ash kept herself occupied by practicing her illusion, making sure she had all the features firmly fixed in her mind so that there would be no flaw to her disguise. She was careful to stop casting spells when fellow travelers passed, though she did get an uncomfortably long appraisal from a man driving a cart of hay in the same direction. He took in her ragged clothing, thoroughbred mare, and immaculately styled hair with a suspicious scowl on his face. Ash decided to chance a trot in order to get well ahead of the farmer.

It was very late evening by the time she reached the city. The ball would have been going for hours already. Though there were people still out, it seemed a rougher sort ruled the streets at night. She decided to cast the spell of invisibility over herself and Windrunner as she rode quietly by the lit houses and darkened windows of the businesses. The people she passed cast their eyes about, searching for a horse they could not see.

Soon the palace's wrought-iron gates came into view. Even in the dim lantern light reflecting off the iron rods, Ash couldn't help admiring the workmanship of the twisting metal vines that sometimes led to blossoms while other times curled in on themselves. The gate and surrounding wall would never hold back anyone determined to get inside. Though the king posted two honor guards at both ends of the entrance, the country's geography—surrounded on all sides but one by nearly impassable mountain ranges—kept the kingdom protected from most foreign threats.

Both guards stood stiffly in position next to the entry. Their gold-striped blue uniforms accented their poise, making them look crisp and unapproachable. They lost some of their starch, however, when they heard the clopping of Ash's horse pass through the gate. After looking around and seeing nothing, one man made the sign warding against evil. He touched his closed fingers to his ears and eyes, and then above his head in a scooping gesture to throw the evil behind him. The other guard cleared his throat in reprimand, and his companion snapped back to attention, wincing in embarrassment.

Ash sniggered quietly as Windrunner trotted past the long lane lined with thick trees on either side. She stifled a gasp as the trees on either side gave way to reveal the palace ahead. Lights blazed through every window like shimmering mountains of gold.

Despite the veil of night enfolding a few portions of the palace in shadow, light shone through many of the three stories of windows that covered the palace. It lit up the building like sparkling facets of an intricately cut jewel. Balconies extended out from many of the rooms in graceful arching curves. Past a manicured garden, two sets of curving stone stairs led up to the main entrance, where the walls were a semi-circle until straightening and extending equally to connect with two square wings jutting from each end.

The path circled around a fountain of crystal birds frozen in the midst of launching into flight. They were also lit by lamps within the water, obviously spelled by Sorcerer Tioroso. Ash stopped a moment, wondering what spell he'd used. The light shone upward, making the water sparkle as it sprayed up from behind the crystal bird's spread wings. The birds' otherworldly beauty was mesmerizing. She shook herself and clicked for Windrunner to continue past.

Windrunner trotted smoothly around one side of the palace's enormous jutting wings. At a horse's meadow, Ash dismounted and left the mare to graze. Dropping the invisibility illusion, she retrieved the plain white mask she'd found in the attic. It hadn't been easy. Though Ash had remembered that there was a mask up there somewhere, it had taken illicit minutes stolen here and there that added up to hours wading through years of accumulated junk in the attic to find the mask. Ash circled around to the gardens where the revelers took in the evening air when overcome by the heat and stuffiness of the ballroom.

Behind the cover of an ornamental bush, Ash click-snapped the words to transform her hair from wheat to pale blonde. Another spell changed her plain work dress to an exact copy of Jane's exquisite ball gown. The detail was perfect, down to the long silky purple gloves. One more sentence of rounded vowels with a single snap and her white mask matched that of Jane's butterfly mask. She secured it to her face, careful not to damage her hair, then strode out from behind the bush into the crowded ballroom of the royal palace where revelers danced and laughed, and music filled the air with intoxicating gaiety.

Ash's eyes swept the room for her cousins and uncle. Though most of the male costumes were cut the same with the usual wide-sleeved coats showing the frilled edges of their undershirt, fitted waistcoats, and knee breeches with tight stockings, the men made up for the similarity by wearing a riot of colors. Ash could spot neither James's sky blue, nor Lord Richard's dark green among so many vibrant choices. She thought Jane would be somewhere among the dancers but couldn't see the butterfly dress anywhere. Ash caught sight of the buffet table filled with glittering golden platters full of food. Where once Ash might have simply enjoyed the sight of the artfully heaped dishes, now she couldn't help but think of the immense effort required by the staff to produce such wondrous dishes. Thoroughly impressed, her direction changed. She could look for her uncle while eating just as well.

A hand grabbed her arm, and Ash jumped.

"Sorry, dear. I didn't mean to frighten you, but I saw you were without a partner and thought I could help." Ash hadn't heard Lady Amelia's voice in years, but she recognized it instantly. "If you're looking for your father or your brother, they're over there, near the far doorway."

"Thank you," Ash said, trying to mimic Jane's slightly higher breathy voice.

"Don't bother with them at the moment. There's someone I want you to meet. I was sorry to hear about Ashelandra. I hope she recovers soon," Lady Amelia said as she led Ash through the crowd.

"Oh, I wouldn't worry too much. Circumstances might have prevented her from coming, but she was glad to hear that you thought of her," Ash said sincerely.

"Of course. I've missed the little minx. She was always doing something interesting."

Ash grinned. The thought occurred to her that she could tell Lady Amelia the truth. She could expose her uncle this very night and make his life much less comfortable. But even as the thought floated up, it sank again. What good would telling Lady Amelia do her right now? It would not stop Lord Richard having power over her. As his anger rose, so would the labor required of her. He might even assign Willie to be her watchdog again. The possibility made Ash shiver. It wasn't easy avoiding the oily man as it was, even with the power to make herself invisible.

"Ah, here he is," Lady Amelia interrupted. "You can't come to a royal ball and not dance with the prince. Though I know we are supposed to pretend not to know who everyone is, I think it would be much easier if I just introduce you properly." Prince Phillip smiled at Lady Amelia as she delivered this speech.

Ash panicked. She hadn't danced in years, and to do so pretending to be Jane could have devastating consequences to her cousin. Even if she did want to sabotage her uncle, she didn't want to harm Jane in any way.

"Dear lady, whatever could you mean? My identity is well concealed behind this mask," the prince said sweeping his hand up to indicate the golden unicorn mask that did little to conceal his face, and nothing to cover the coppery hair that blazed like armor in the light. Using the royal symbol of the unicorn settled any lingering doubts of the prince's identity.

Lady Amelia glared at him, and the prince's grin shrank, though it looked more like he was trying to look repentant than actually feeling that way.

"Prince Phillip, I'd like to introduce you to Lady Jane Camery of Durbinshire. She is a very becoming creature, and you'd be the luckiest of men if she accepted your offer of a dance."

Ash felt heat rush to her face. She looked around for some way to escape, but the masked prince was already bowing.

"I would be honored if you'd dance with me, Lady Jane," he said dutifully as Lady Amelia moved off.

"It's really not necessary. I had no idea that Lady Amelia was bringing me over to force me upon you," Ash said, backing away, trying to keep Lady Amelia in sight.

"I'm a perfectly willing victim, I assure you."

Ash paused, her mouth quirking against her better judgment.

"But perhaps it is you who wishes to be freed of the obligation," he added.

Ash smiled wider. "Perhaps. I fear my feet may not be up to the challenge when in the presence of such an imposing individual."

She looked around again, but Lady Amelia had disappeared into the crowd.

"I, My Lady? Surely you've heard of my reputation as being the most unprincely of princes."

Her attention caught, she looked back at the prince and tilted her head in challenge. "Is it possible for a prince to be unprince-like?"

"Most definitely. Dance with me and I'll tell you all about it," he said, offering his arm. Ash laughed. She hesitated, still worried about how she would perform, but the prince had caught her curiosity. She wanted to know more than what she'd learned by spying from the grasses as he'd picnicked or running away on a horse as he'd chased her.

"Well, I certainly can't refuse now. There's nothing more compelling than a mystery," she said, feeling a grin stretch upward.

As Prince Phillip took Ash's arm to escort her to the floor, she inquired, "So, Your Majesty, what could possibly be considered behavior unbecoming of a prince?"

"Well, I'm no longer sure that I should tell you. That would make me less of a mystery, and therefore less intriguing," Prince Phillip said as he spun her through the waltz.

"Are you suggesting that this is the only mystery you possess? Are you so easily deciphered then? You would tell me one thing about yourself, and I would know all?"

Prince Phillip laughed. "I certainly hope not."

"Very well then. Let's put it to the test. Tell me one thing about yourself, and I'll then proceed to unmask your whole character," Ash challenged.

"That is quite a task you have set yourself, and on so little information. What if I were to only reveal that I like cake?" Prince Phillip's lips curved in a teasing smile, and Ash answered in kind.

"Ah, but that would make you more like a prince rather than less like one, wouldn't it? You mustn't back out of your promise. Tell me one reason you are considered less princely than is usual."

"Very well. I often go riding alone, leaving the escort my father would wish me to have behind at the palace with no one the wiser." Ash felt a distinct disappointment. It must have shown in the slight frown of her lips. "Was my answer displeasing somehow, My Lady?" he asked.

Ash was going to deny it, but decided against dissembling.

"Well, yes. I suppose I was expecting something more radical. Wishing for time to one's self, while a hard commodity to come by, is hardly surprising, especially since you are a prince. I should think it would be more rare to you and, therefore, more like a forbidden activity. To seek after it seems a natural thing for a prince to do."

"You wound me, My Lady. Is this, then your assessment of my character: that I am nothing more than a very princely prince who only wishes he weren't?" Despite the levity of his voice, Ash felt that her words may have pricked him.

"Not at all. To seek for freedom and solitude when it is so often denied is not a light matter, nor does it reflect a shallowness of character. We all seek for freedom from our own prisons. I am glad that you are able to break free of yours once in awhile and be as unprincely as you desire." Ash's voice turned sad. The orchestra struck the last chord of the waltz, and Prince Phillip looked down on the butterfly mask she wore with a slight frown of his own.

"This will not do. I've enjoyed our conversation, but to end it on such a melancholy note is insupportable," Prince Phillip said. Ash grinned.

"Then I shall end with an assessment of your character. I think you a splendid prince with a hint of fun that all the boring politics of court have failed to stamp out, and with a sense of adventure that would have you on a horse and riding to slay a dragon at a moment's notice if only you weren't tied to obligations here. How did I do?"

"I like that picture of myself very much. If only it were true," he said, moaning dramatically. They laughed together as he led her off the dance floor, but the prince's laugh died quickly, his face sinking into a brooding half frown. "I wish that were true more than you can guess, but the pressure of politics cannot always be avoided." He glanced around at the masked assembly without really seeing them until his eyes landed on another red-headed man. Only a dunce would fail to realize that the matching golden unicorn mask artfully resting on high cheekbones and extending above the man's forehead in a spiraling horn was King Ferdinand John Cornwall. The king caught his son's stare and nodded with the weight of command, though Ash couldn't be sure what he was directing his son to do.

Ash was intrigued, but she sighed. It had been so natural, so easy to dance with Prince Phillip, but it was late. Ash started to retract her arm from his hold. He gripped her tighter.

"Would you care to dance again? It's almost time for the unmasking, and I confess, that I would very much like to see the face of such a charming and politic reader of men's characters."

Ash hesitated. She'd enjoyed the prince's company, but if it was nearly time to unmask, it was later than she'd realized, and she would have to leave soon to make sure she returned before her uncle. The food beckoned her like a siren to a sailor. It would be satisfying to irk her uncle in some way as well. Still she found herself surprised to realize that staying a little longer next to the prince was more enticing than both food and mischief.

"Is that truly your wish, or are you bowing to the pressure of politics?" Ash asked, tilting her head in the king's direction.

Prince Phillip's lips curled ruefully. "Yes and no. My father is insisting it's time I showed interest in marital prospects. Spending a longer interval with you will help soothe his mind, while at the same time granting me the luxury of pleasant company. You don't mind, do you?"

"If I granted you a reprieve, you'd owe me a favor in return." Ash's mouth curved up cheekily.

The flash of a dress exactly like her illusion caught the corner of Ash's eye. Jane was near. She had to disappear before she created a double identity disaster.

The real Jane moved perilously close behind the prince. Ash didn't have time for more than a mumbled, "Sorry, would you excuse me for a moment?" before she slipped out of Prince Phillip's grasp straight through a crowd of masked revelers behind a potted plant. She studied the dress of a lady near her with hurried intensity before stringing the spell together to changed her disguise to match that of the lady's feathered angel frock.

Ash stepped out just in time to see Prince Phillip intercept the real Jane. She moved closer to hear what was said, feeling a momentary pang to see her cousin where she wished to be herself.

"There you are. Is anything the matter?" Prince Phillip asked.

Jane looked around and finally seemed to decide that Prince Phillip was, in fact, talking to her. "No, I'm well. Thank you," she replied timidly.

"Well, what do you say? will you help me fend off my father's keen eye by dancing with me, Lady Jane?" Prince Phillip asked.

Jane started, looked behind her as if searching for something, but replied, "Certainly, Your Majesty." Proving to Ash that though most of the revelers liked to pretend to not recognize each other, Jane did not dare deny addressing the prince properly.

Below the mask, his lips formed a little frown. "I could have sworn your eyes were green, but now they look more amber. I'm sorry, I suppose that just proves I'm not as observant as I thought. Shall we?" he asked, extending his arm for Jane to take.

A few feet away Ash winced and began to regret the whole expedition. She would hate to get Jane in trouble in any way. All she could do was hope that Prince Phillip didn't wonder why Jane knew nothing of what he and Ash were just discussing.

She watched as Prince Phillip escorted Jane to the dance floor. From her vantage point, Ash could see that Jane said very little. The little frown of confusion rarely left the prince's half-hidden face throughout the dance. Ash knew she should leave, but she couldn't stop herself from watching. Surely Jane would do or say something that would reveal to Prince Phillip that he was now dancing with someone different. As the music hit its final vibrant chord, Ash matched the prince's path, moving to stand close enough to hear the conversation between Prince Phillip and her cousin.

The room was heavy with heat. People pressed closely together, waiting for the announcement from the herald that they could finally remove the hot masks making their faces perspire. Ash watched the prince gaze at her masked cousin before he flicked annoyed, squinting eyes toward the herald, who stepped forward as if summoned by his impatient glance.

The herald thrust a large bronze staff to the ground three times. Its boom rang through the ballroom, silencing the roar of voluminous whispers. "It is time for the unmasking," he intoned in a resonant voice that carried through the brief silence. A cheer arose from the revelers, and masks were ripped off heads by fed up men and thrown into the air, or in the case of most of the ladies, carefully removed so as not to ruin delicate hairstyles.

Prince Phillip took his mask off in one fluid motion. He then watched Jane closely as she daintily undid the laces holding her mask in place. Ash observed them both, a strange weight that felt like inevitability settling on her chest as Jane's mask fell away and Prince Phillip's mouth dropped open a moment before he caught himself and shut it with a snap. Ash turned on her heel and pushed rudely through revelers rather than trying to move with the crowd's flow.

As she wedged her way past people to the buffet table to grab as much food as she could carry on her way to the garden doors, someone ran into her. The food in her hands fumbled to the floor, and she scowled at the man. Her glare faltered when she realized that the man was Sorcerer Tioroso.

He didn't even glance her way after colliding into her but kept staring at something beyond Ash's shoulder. Curious, she glanced back again to see what was so riveting and saw that the sorcerer, like the prince, was staring intently at Jane. She spared a sympathetic thought for the drably dressed sorcerer, before making her way once again out of the ballroom. Ash was sorry now that she'd come, couldn't even think why she'd thought it would be a good idea. She didn't even have time to push her way back through the crowd for more food.

She chided herself for lingering near the prince to see what would happen, and for reacting so strongly to the look she'd seen cross Prince Phillip's face as he beheld Jane. They'd had an intriguing interlude, but that was all. It didn't matter that the memory of her first meeting with the prince in the woods had floated through her thoughts over the intervening years more frequently than she wished.

She should simply take comfort in the thought that she may have helped her cousin in securing for herself the most desirable of husbands, one even her uncle would approve. If Jane married Prince Phillip, then perhaps Lord Richard would be satisfied with living in the palace and leave Ash to her manor without Ash having to worry about any scheme he might concoct to wrench her inheritance from her.

These were all very fine sentiments, but they sat in her stomach like lead.

At the door, she noticed a man in a familiar forest-green suit. His back was to her, but she would recognize her uncle's detestable shoulders anywhere. He was holding a plate with a palm-sized apricot and toasted pecan tart. Ash's cheeks pinched into the mask she still wore as her grin spread wide.

Clicking the spell for a wind to brush his arm, she swiped the tart from his plate as Lord Richard turned to see who'd touched his precious clothes.

"What the devil!" Ash heard him exclaim, but she was already beyond the door, out of sight, savoring the nutty sweet taste of triumph.

Ash found Bill waiting for her in the stable. She put on a smile for his benefit but wasn't able to completely hide her fatigue. Her clothes were back to their normal stained state, and she'd pulled the pins from her hair as she rode back so that she wouldn't have to feel them jabbing into her skull any longer. It fell free in waves to mid back, ruffled by the wind.

Bill stared. "Ye look like a wood sprite," he breathed before his eyes widened as if realizing he's spoken aloud. He looked away, blushing.

Ash smiled wryly as she dismounted, unable to agree with his assessment. She felt merely wild with no hint of mystical to soften the image. Bill took Windrunner's reins, still keeping his face slightly averted.

"You don't need to help me, Bill. I can take care of Windrunner myself," she said but then couldn't keep a yawn from emerging. Bill finally met her eyes and grinned a little.

"Ye've worked all day and had a long night. I think ye best get to bed. Let me handle the mare for ye."

"Thank you, Bill. You're very kind," Ash said sincerely. His cheeks flushed, but his gaze was firm as he smiled.

Chapter Seven

The household was in a frenzy the next morning. The servants had been ordered to clean the manor from top to bottom on the chance that Prince Phillip might come to visit. Ash finished cleaning the ballroom and sitting room quickly, passing a duster here, swishing a halfhearted sweep there. She'd cleaned the rooms the day before and felt no great need to labor diligently over something that was already done. When she was sure everyone's attention was focused elsewhere, she took herself off to the woods to practice sorcery.

As she stood at the pond where she'd been trapped long ago watching Prince Phillip, Sorcerer Tioroso, and the lady, she couldn't help reliving her experience of the previous night. Her last-minute prank on her uncle seemed very insignificant in the light of day. The prince had distracted her from accomplishing anything more complicated. Still, she didn't mind as much as she might have.

She sighed and loosed her hair from its taut braid. She'd wound it too tightly this morning and didn't want to be distracted from her spells by a sore head. Next, she enunciated the shush and click in the words of the spell to raise a sphere of water about the size of her cupped hands. It floated in front of her. She squinted at it in consideration. Today she would try to shape the water as she turned it into glass. Deciding that simplicity was probably best, she looked around her to get ideas. Her eyes fell on a stick, but she shook her head. Too simple. The leaves were a possibility, but she wanted something with a few more dips and curves. She looked down at her feet to consider and noticed her frayed work shoes. Though the laces made copying the worn shoes too complicated, a dancing slipper would have the dips and curves she was hoping to practice while still staying simple enough for her to handle.

Sweat beaded her forehead as she slowly snapped the water into the shape of a basic slipper before quickly clicking the sounds that would make the water turn to glass. At the last slap of her tongue against her teeth, the sound of an indrawn breath behind her made her heart leap to her throat. She whirled around. The glass fell to the ground and shattered behind her.

"You!" accused a male voice from atop a black stallion. Ash craned her neck up to behold Prince Phillip staring down at her. "I remember you. You used magic to soak me. You gave my horse quite a fright before he was finally able to pull his hooves from the mud."

Ash forced herself to straighten from her defensive crouch and lower her arms to her side. She felt a twinge of fear ping through her. The prince might have a sorcerer, but she still didn't know how he felt about others practicing magic.

"I? It was raining. The downpour must have worsened," Ash said cautiously.

"I think I can tell the difference between the feel of rain and that of a solid mass of water thrown on my person."

She backed away a step.

Prince Phillip held up a placating hand. "You need not fear. I am not against the practice of magic. The sorcerer at the palace is a good friend of mine."

Ash relaxed a fraction. She took comfort from the fact that he still didn't know who she was and if she was careful, would never see her, even if he called on Jane. That way he would have no way of exposing her use of magic to her uncle.

"Forgive me, Your Majesty, but you would not stop following me. I had to take drastic measures, and adding a little more water didn't make you any wetter than you already were. I would have thought that one such as you would understand the desire for privacy." Ash arched her brows and directed a pointed glance around the prince indicating his lack of escort.

"Ah, yes," he said, and Ash saw his cheeks rouge. He straightened up self-consciously. "It appears you have the advantage of me. You know who I am, but I don't know your name."

"Perhaps I prefer it that way, Your Majesty," she replied, relaxing enough to flash a mischievous smile before clicking the illusion spell that would make her invisible. The prince might not mind magic practitioners, but she didn't want to chance exposure.

"Drat. Why is she always disappearing before . . . Miss," he said in a louder voice. "Please don't go. I didn't mean to scare you." His breath came out in a huff, and Ash watched as he turned his mount toward the manor. She almost didn't hear the mutter that followed. "Of course she would appear again now."

This comment spiked Ash's curiosity. Walking while robed in invisibility, she followed the prince. Being on horse, he arrived at the manor well before Ash, so she slipped in the open kitchen door and lithely avoided the bustle of the servants as she made her way to the sitting room. She slid quickly through the door behind Jenny as the serving woman brought in the tea and sandwiches cut in dainty squares. Jenny left the door ajar when she left. The room was shrouded in an uncomfortable silence.

Jane sat at a chair near the window, her eyes locked on the hands clasped in her lap.

"Are you feeling well this morning, My Lady?" the prince asked, shifting slightly.

"Quite well, Your Highness," Jane replied without looking up.

"I don't know if you noticed, but I left my escort well behind. They should be arriving shortly. I hope it's not too much of an inconvenience to your household. I suppose I should have just stayed with them, but as I said before, I can never pass up an opportunity for a moment of freedom." Prince Phillip grinned. Ash noticed Jane's brow wrinkle at Prince Phillip's mention of "before," but when he spoke of freedom it was as if she couldn't help herself from looking up to meet his eyes. She smiled shyly back.

"Yes, freedom is a rare thing for many people, but I would imagine that you have a degree more than most, Your Majesty," she said quickly before lowering her eyes again to her lap.

"I beg to differ. I am but a slave to my country," he said dramatically. Ash suspected he was trying to get her to look up again, but she just smiled demurely into her hands.

"I'm sure you are correct, Your Highness," she responded softly.

Prince Phillip frowned.

"You're just going to agree with me? That's not very sporting of you. Come, you said I was more free than most. You must defend your position."

Jane glanced up in surprise, before flicking her eyes back to her lap. "I suppose I assumed that you have more freedom to do as you wish. If you want something, there are not many who would dare deny you."

"You'd be surprised at how many there actually are." Prince Phillip's tone was dry. Jane looked up and gave a sincere smile. Ash watched Prince Phillip's reaction to that smile and began to feel distinctly uncomfortable about listening in on a private conversation. She quietly backed out of the room and headed to the garden where it was unlikely anyone would come looking for her, but where she would not get into trouble for being found if she happened to be missed.

Ash heard the arrival of more horses and assumed the prince's retinue had scurried to catch up with the prince. How frustrating he must be to his guards. She felt a momentary twinge of guilt that she wasn't helping the other servants get everyone settled, but then she pushed it aside. She wanted to stay out of sight of anyone connected to the prince so that she couldn't be identified to him later.

Finally, after every weed in the garden was long since pulled, Ash heard the sounds of horses being prepared for departure and the slow progress of the prince's retinue leaving. Ash stood and brushed off her skirt before dropping a look in on Cook to see if it was all right for her to be gone for a while. Cook's big hands engulfed the small paring knife as he cut a radish into the shape of a flower. His muscled arms reminded Ash more of a blacksmith's than those of a cook's. They looked out of place doing such a delicate task.

"Leave. Lord Richard is in such a state of bliss, I doubt he'd be noticin' much of anything for a few hours," Cook assured Ash when she asked what he thought. She grinned, noticing with affection Cook's perpetually flushed cheeks and the crow's feet around his eyes from smiling. He set the radish flower on a plate of salad and turned to a basket of apples. Ash snatched the apple he was reaching for before he could grab it and dodged his playful swat on her way out.

Wanting to try the transformation spell that had been interrupted before, Ash went back to the pond and began again. Just as she got to the part that would solidify the water and turn it into glass, the crack of a branch startled her and made her lose her concentration. Water splashed to the ground, ricocheting onto her dress's hem and shoes.

"Bother!" she shouted half in fear as she turned to see what had made the sound.

"I'm sorry," said Prince Phillip.

"You again!" Ash cast an annoyed glance at her dirty hem, even as she edged away. "That is the second time you've distracted me. What are you doing here anyway?" Ash asked. She tried to be cross rather than worried. She'd been ambushed twice in one day, and by Prince Phillip of all people. Ash noticed that he was without his horse and briefly wondered why.

"I was curious to see if you would return here," he said simply.

Ash grimaced, a knot of alarm lodged in her chest. "It will be the last time."

"Why?" Prince Phillip stepped closer. There was only a few feet separating them now, and Ash took an uncomfortable step back, heels sinking into the mud at the pond's edge.

She opened her mouth to respond but couldn't think of a reply that would sound very rational. "I have to go," she said instead, preparing to don the illusion of invisibility again. Prince Phillip took three quick steps toward her and grasped her arm gently, but firmly.

"Don't disappear again."

Ash felt her nervousness transform into a more comfortable anger.

"You may be a prince, Your Highness, but that does not give you the right to manhandle me. I am not without defenses," Ash retorted hotly to the face inches from hers.

Prince Phillip blushed and released her arm, though he didn't back away. "Forgive me. I acted without thinking. I just wanted to stop you from vanishing again before I had a chance to talk to you."

"Why?" Ash demanded, confused. To her further astonishment, Prince Phillip blushed again.

"I wanted to make sure you were real and not a figment of my imagination." His voice was soft, embarrassed.

"Are you convinced yet?" Ash asked with a touch of her old humor. Prince Phillip saw the quirk at her mouth and smiled hesitantly in return.

"You feel real enough, but I only ever see you in the woods, and you always manage to disappear without a trace. You give no name and will say nothing about yourself. I'd feel much better if you would at least tell me something that would ground you more firmly into reality."

"Ah, I see. I have become a mystery to be solved, and there is nothing more compelling than a mystery," Ash said, noticing the prince's jerk at the words that so closely paralleled their conversation from the previous evening. She smiled more widely, a bit of mischief creeping into her thoughts. "Very well. I will give you answers that will put your mind at ease so that you can move on to more fascinating pursuits. My name is Ash. For now, I am a servant who escapes her leash once in a while to study sorcery. Nothing very interesting about that."

"Nothing interesting! You practice magic. That in itself is a mystery not so easily brushed over. Also, if you are a servant, why do you speak like a noble? The only sorcerers I ever heard of were from noble families," Prince Phillip retorted.

Ash hesitated. She could tell the prince the truth, but what would that accomplish really? Like Lady Amelia, he might be able to defame her uncle. But he was interested in courting Jane. Ash doubted that he would do anything that would jeopardize his courtship. If he was looking to marry her cousin, then he would be that much more willing to hush up any scandal that might prevent his marriage. He could make Ash's situation even worse than it was now. She'd rather not chance it.

"I am an excellent mimic, Your Majesty," Ash said. Prince Phillip's copper eyebrow rose, making him look a little fey, while eloquently accenting his doubt. Ash pressed on quickly, as if spewing more words would make her story more believable.

"As for the magic, I inherited some old magic books and wanted to try my hand at it. My life contains little luxury. I wanted to do something to distract myself from my everyday drudgery. I'm not sure if you'd understand that, being a prince, and I'm aware that studying magic is not as popular these days, but I have to do it to stay sane." She hadn't meant to say so much and felt her cheeks heat up in embarrassment.

Ash lifted her chin loftily to hide her discomposure. "Now, if I have answered all of your questions, I really should be getting back."

She moved to pass him but paused as he half raised his hand. When he made no further move to stop her, however, she walked by him and out of sight into the shelter of the woods. Ash thought she'd done a credible job of making an enigma into something unremarkable, or at least understandable, and not something a prince would care about. She hoped. Maybe she wouldn't have to avoid the pond from now on after all. Strangely, the thought did not cheer her as much as she'd supposed it would.

Chapter Eight

AUGUST 31, 1750

The day was getting dark. Ashelandra knew she'd missed dinner, but also knew that Cook would keep something warm for her. He really was the nicest man, Ash thought affectionately. Lord Richard and James were most likely in the study at this time, and Jane had probably already retired to her room. Ash glanced up at Jane's window to see if the light was on and was startled to see a man's figure silhouetted by the light from Jane's room. James must be visiting his sister.

Inside, Cook gestured furiously for Ash to come closer. "I'm sorry, m'girl. I tried to signal ye to come back, but ye musen' a heard. Lord Richard came searching for ye after dinner and was in a terrible state when ye could na' be found."

"He didn't punish anyone, did he?" Ash's stomach clenched.

"Nay, but he wanted ye to go straight to his study as soon as ye was found," Cook replied.

Ash scowled but began walking toward the study. "Wait. Take a roll at least. I dunna think you'll be eating much else tonight," Cook said. His thick brown brows furrowed sympathetically.

"Thank you, Cook."

Ash paused to savor the roll fully before heading toward her uncle's displeasure. He would not beat her very much; at least he would not leave any visible bruises, but he had a whole arsenal of unpleasant punishments that he could mete out. Ash briefly considered sneaking past the study to her room, but that would help nothing and would only delay a worse punishment later. With a sigh she knocked on the partially open study door to announce her presence.

"Enter." The deep voice of her uncle drilled through the crack of the wooden door. Ash stepped into the lamp-lit study and noticed that James was also inside, his visit to Jane apparently over. Her eyes strayed to the book-lined shelves and comfortable red velvet upholstered sitting chairs where she and her father used to sit in the evening; sometimes in silence while reading, sometimes in deep discussion. A wash of sad regret pulled at her before her uncle's voice brought her back to reality with a thud.

"Where have you been?" he demanded.

"I thought you would want me to stay out of sight of the prince or any of his men, so I stayed in the garden until there was nothing else there for me to do, and then I kept myself out of sight until I was sure they were gone," Ash said as meekly as she could.

"That's nonsense. No one would recognize you even if they once knew you in the past. I'm surprised you still misbehave, knowing the consequences." Lord Richard's fingertips were white from the pressure of his grip pinching the wooden stem of his quill.

"They may not recognize me, but if I spoke to anyone they would be able to detect that my accent is not that of a servant." Ash knew she should stop herself, but the words kept tumbling out. "And really, Uncle, wouldn't you rather have me stay out of sight than spreading my 'tale of woe' through the ranks of the prince's men? I had your utmost consideration in mind. Even if I said nothing and someone were to recognize me again when I inherit, there would certainly be questions then."

Ash restrained herself from adding that no matter what her uncle did to her now, it was only a matter of months before he would have no more power to do anything. But even hinting at how close her time of independence was had been a mistake. Ash could see her uncle's expression redden, his scowl deepen into a look that, if Ash were honest with herself, never failed to frighten her.

"You will mention nothing of your situation ever or you will discover that my punishments in the past have been but a mild irritation to what you will then suffer," he said quietly, but with a look in his eyes so terrible, Ash had to force herself to stay still rather than recoil. Would he really go so far as to murder her after all? After seeing his intent expression, she wasn't sure if she should easily dismiss the idea as she had before.

"Mr. Thursley knows of my situation, and if you kill me, he will make sure that you inherit nothing," Ash said, her hands gripped tightly into fists.

"My dear girl, who said anything about killing? That certainly wouldn't help me get what I want. But if something should happen to make you unable to care for yourself? You will need a guardian to watch over the estate for the rest of your life."

Ash gaped in horror at her uncle, but the look in his eyes was too calm to bear so she rested her gaze on her cousin's face. James looked a little pale. His eyes slid quickly away from hers.

"The terms of your guardianship hang upon the condition of my good health." Much to her annoyance, Ash's voice wobbled.

"Oh, calm down," her uncle said, eyeing with a calculative expression Ash's hand on the doorknob from behind his desk. "I'm not going to do anything to you. But you are right about one thing. The prince will, I hope, be visiting quite often from now on, and I can't have you in the way while he is here. You are to be confined to your room for the next few weeks until Jane has charmed the prince into a proposal. I wouldn't want you to get bored like you seemed to earlier today when you wandered off, however. I will have all the mending sent to your room. See that it gets finished before the good news is announced. James, see her to her room," Lord Richard directed before turning dismissively to his papers on the desk. "Be sure to bolt the door."

Ash's hands shook as she left the study. She tucked them around her ragged skirts so that James would not notice as he followed her up the stairs.

James hesitated at the door. "I'm sorry," he said unexpectedly before closing her door. She heard the familiar sound of the bolt being shot into place, but even knowing she could escape did not quite overcome the feeling of being trapped.

***

Ash forced herself to remain in her room for the next few days so that she could learn the pattern of who delivered her meals and at what time. Also, despite Jenny keeping the most complicated mending, there were still a lot of sheets and simple clothes to sew. She tried to hurry through the piles, so she would be free to roam.

On the third day, when Ash realized that her uncle had delegated the task to servants and decided to ignore her, she had a quick word with Jenny to request that the servants leave the food tray and any new mending inside the door if Ash didn't respond to a knock. This way Ash could be outdoors for the whole day without having to return for every meal.

Leaving the manor by donning the invisibility illusion, she slipped through her hidden door down the inner stone steps to the armory exit, which opened behind a large draping banner. Ash tugged at David's tailcoat as she passed him in the back hallway leading to the kitchen's always open door to the outside, and he jumped, brushing frantically at his clothes trying to dislodge an imaginary bug. She held back a snicker and maneuvered around Cook and out the door with a light heart. It was the first time in years she'd had so little work. It was a heady feeling.

Ash meant to avoid the pond. She fully intended to study somewhere safe from accidental discovery, but that was where she'd hidden her books, and somehow she found herself too lazy to carry them somewhere else. She passed the rocky shoreline where nothing grew, to the reeds that clustered a narrow curve of the pond. Shoving past the thick growth, she sat in a mashed down nest in the middle. Still at the water's edge, she had a clear view of the ducks dipping their heads into the murky wet in search of food, but was hidden from view to all except someone directly across the water.

It had been three days since last she saw the prince. Ash reasoned that, if he'd come before, he'd surely given up by now, and wouldn't easily see her even if he did. On that comforting thought, Ash settled down on her stomach, elbows dug into the flattened reeds, fists propping her head as she studied the book lying on the ground. She was determined to master changing wood into bone and needed to decipher the pronunciation better, always a tricky task when consulting nothing but a sorcery book's dictionary. For a moment Ash allowed herself to long for a tutor. The thought of Sorcerer Tioroso sprang up, but how was she to even see him again? She chided herself for not talking to the sorcerer at the ball.

There was a snap in the woods behind her, and Ash spun quickly to see if someone approached. She felt an odd leap in her heart, but was confused to see the very sorcerer who had recently occupied her thoughts pass by Ash on the path leading to the manor. He didn't see her. Ash glanced at the sun to see if it was the usual visiting time of Prince Phillip. Did Sorcerer Tioroso have business so urgent he must interrupt the prince's visit?

Curiosity tickling the need for action, she clicked the spell for illusion and followed the sorcerer until he had reached the back door to the manor. He glanced back when a twig snapped under Ash's feet, and she dropped back a little. To her surprise, he clicked the illusion of invisibility for himself. She quickly snapped the words to a counter spell that allowed her to see him. Sorcerer Tioroso stepped toward the open back door to the kitchen. Ash slipped. The bushes she hid behind rustled. Sorcerer Tioroso looked up, narrowed his eyes, and moved to investigate.

She held very still, but he was walking straight at her, and she had to step back or be knocked back. She misjudged his speed. Sorcerer Tioroso's knee knocked into her retreating leg, and his hand brushed fabric.

"What!" He stopped stunned. It didn't last long. Ash heard the click-burr-snap of the invisibility counter spell, and Sorcerer Tioroso's eye widened when he saw Ash.

"Hello." Ash grinned ruefully, trying to project harmless innocence.

"Who are you? I've never seen you before. Who's your mentor?" Sorcerer Tioroso asked, the astonishment overpowering the wariness in his voice.

"I don't have one. I learn on my own."

The sorcerer's mouth gaped. "That would be very difficult. How much have you mastered?"

Suddenly, Ash didn't feel so willing to discuss her studies with a stranger, even if he was a fellow sorcerer. She shrugged, "I'm no master. What business do you have with the prince that would require sneaking into the household?"

Sorcerer Tioroso looked down. "If it was something I could declare to strangers, then I wouldn't have been so secretive."

His answer struck Ashelandra as probable, but odd. If it were an urgent matter, why didn't he dismiss himself from Ash quickly and fulfill his purpose in coming here? Instead, he lingered next to Ash, as if he was afraid if he left her, she would go and announce his presence to others.

"What brings you to this manor?" he asked, tinting his voice with threat.

Ash tried not to bristle. "I saw you in the woods and was curious, so I followed." It was the truth, if incomplete.

"Do you live far from here?"

"No. If your message is so urgent, why do you stay here with me? Why not go and deliver it?" Ash pried.

"Certainly, I will," he said, turning red. Ash thought it was from embarrassment, but then his voice turned hard. "I think you should go home. It isn't safe for young girls to linger in the woods alone."

Ash raised her eyebrows in credulous question.

Sorcerer Tioroso's feet shifted, but his eyes locked with hers, uncompromising. "I'm merely concerned for your welfare."

A brush of fear prickled her skin, even as annoyance bit. Though the man was young, he was a full sorcerer, and she was not. Perhaps it was in her best interest to retreat for now.

"Of course. I'm keeping you too long from your task." Ash backed away as Sorcerer Tioroso nodded a farewell. She circled around through the woods so that she could view the kitchen from the shelter of the trees near the stables.

Sorcerer Tioroso was already disappearing through the door, unnoticed by all but Ash. She didn't dare follow. What a strange encounter. It seemed as though he had wanted her out of sight before entering the building, but why? He'd skirted the question of why he had to enter so stealthily. Ash couldn't see why her nearness would matter when she already knew he was there. The prince would most likely leave as soon as he'd gotten the message anyway. Odd. She shook off her thoughts and went back to the pond to study, a small part of her hoping that a different man would soon interrupt her.

After an hour, she decided that the prince must have gone back another way. If the sorcerer's business was as urgent as he'd claimed, then it was more likely the prince had taken the main road as soon as he received Sorcerer Tioroso's message. Ash sighed and flopped to her back, book open above her as she tried to get her mouth to correctly click the passage she was reading.

Four hours later, her mouth numb, jaw exhausted, she'd given up on that particular passage and was trying her hand at weaving grass together into a crown. The grass had other ideas. A sound in the woods distracted her. The crown fell to pieces and Ash looked up to see Sorcerer Tioroso taking the same path back to the palace that he'd taken earlier to the manor. She was hidden in the reeds, so he again failed to see her as he passed. Ash thought it strange that he was only now returning to the palace. Surely he would have gone back with the prince long ago.

The tree shadows stretched and grew as evening approached. Ash shrugged off the question of the odd sorcerer and headed home.

In the following weeks, Ash sometimes caught glimpses of the sorcerer headed to and fro on the forest path and often wondered what business led him past her household. He couldn't always be seeking the prince, she decided, because Prince Phillip wasn't usually visiting during the times Ashelandra saw the sorcerer walking toward the manor. Nor was she ever able to follow him to his destination again. Somehow she always lost him at the edge of the forest even if she clicked the spell to see through the invisibility illusion.

It was almost as if he used a spell specifically directed at Ash to keep her from finding where he went. She supposed that made sense. He didn't know her and had probably been sent on secret assignments by the king or prince. Still, she couldn't help but start searching through her sorcery books to discover what spell he was using to thwart her efforts, and if there was a counter spell. She didn't look to interfere in the king's business. She searched because, as she'd told the prince, there was nothing more compelling than a mystery, and she was long overdue for a little mischief.

When she finally found the possible spell, she was annoyed by how simple it was. Sorcerer Tioroso seemed to be using a double illusion spell that hid him even when she spoke the illusion's counter spell. She wasn't sure how to negate the second illusion, but she found something that might help even if she couldn't see the sorcerer. Connected with the spells to move objects, it was a spell that essentially translated to mean "Where is Tioroso?" The only requirement a sorcerer must have to make it work was the person's name.

After finding the tracking spell, she lay in wait for the sorcerer, hidden among the reeds. Using the double invisibility spell had proved difficult to master, and her invisibility spell didn't seem to help much with hiding from him, so she didn't bother with either. He passed at his customary time, and Ash tried to stay far enough behind that she could keep him in sight without being discovered. She was so intent on being unnoticed while staying on his trail that when a form loomed up before her from a fork in the path, her heart kicked in fear and she screamed.

Her body's attempt to jump back was thwarted by a rock at her heels. She felt herself tip backwards. Strong hands reached out and clutched her arms, stopping the fall.

"It seems I am constantly startling you, Miss Ash." Ash looked up to see Prince Phillip smiling down at her, green eyes hinting at barely controlled laughter.

For a moment she stood dumbly, held in his secure grip. "I wasn't, that is to say, you needn't . . ." She extracted her arms from his long, slender fingers, straightening and regaining her balance. If not for the callouses catching on the fabric of her dress, Ash thought his hands would be too pretty for a man. "I'm fine. Thank you for preventing my fall." She finally recalled what Prince Phillip had interrupted. "Oh bother." Craning her neck, she peeked past the prince, wondering if the spell would track Sorcerer Tioroso even out of sight.

"Were you looking for someone?" Prince Phillip's copper red eyebrows furrowed, and he turned to look behind him where Ash searched.

Too late, Ash remembered to watch her words. "Yes, uh . . . well, it's not important. Are you returning from visiting Lady Jane?" she asked to distract him.

He turned back. "I have just come from Lady Jane's. How did you know?"

"I thought it common knowledge that you court her. Do you plan to propose soon?"

A blush spread across Prince Phillip's cheeks. His smile spread wide, but there was a spark of uncertainty in his green eyes. Ash felt a pang but banished it. "I just did, and she accepted. I left my horse in Lord Richard's stables so I could walk through the forest for a while to let it sink in."

"And why aren't you enjoying the moment with your bride to be?"

Concern shadowed the prince's happy expression. "She said that she felt unwell and needed rest. If I'd known beforehand that she wasn't well, I would have waited to ask on a better day."

"I'm sure she is just as happy now, even if she doesn't feel her best. It isn't every day a prince proposes. My u . . . Lord Richard is most likely deliriously happy as well." The thought of Ash's uncle basking in his victory gave her pause. He might just want to boast to Ash. She needed to go back to her room immediately. She could only hope she wasn't already too late.

"I hope that she is marrying me for a better reason than that." Prince Phillip laughed, but the chuckle sounded unsure. "I am sure that after we spend time together away from Lord Richard, she will feel more at ease," he added, as if he weren't quite aware he was speaking aloud.

She started edging around the prince toward the path to the manor. "I'm sure you are right. I have to go now."

"Don't go yet . . .," Prince Phillip began, but it was already too late, Ash had disappeared. She looked one last time at him as he stared in her direction unseeing and then ran for the manor as fast as she could.

Chapter Nine

As the hidden door in her room snicked shut, she heard the bolt to her bedroom door slide back. She lunged for the lunch tray by the door and slid it under her cot. Making a supreme effort to calm her breathing, she hurried to the window, grabbed the sheet and needle she'd prepared for quick camouflage, and pulled the already threaded needle through a tear with quiet grace.

Lord Richard strode in; his features arranged in a look the closest to exuberance Ash had ever seen on the austere man.

"Why, Uncle, you look positively giddy. Am I to assume that the prince has finally proposed?" Ash enjoyed watching her uncle's smug happiness fade as she robbed him of the announcement's impact.

"He has."

"Congratulations. Now you and my cousins can go live in the palace and leave me in peace." The moment she said the words she regretted them. Lord Richard's eyes narrowed in a way that made Ash take an involuntary step back, digging her hip into the sharp edge of the windowsill.

"To marry royalty, we must at least have a holding of our own." Lord Richard stepped forward.

"That is easily overcome. The prince could gift you a holding in order to make this marriage possible. I'm sure he loves Jane enough to be willing to overlook or at least circumvent an outdated law."

Lord Richard stopped moving, and Ash relaxed a fraction.

"That may be true, but in order for him to do that I would have to correct his assumption that this manor isn't, in fact, mine. It should be. It should never have been able to pass to you." Her uncle's eyes gleamed unnaturally bright. Ash shifted her weight to her other foot, edging herself away from Lord Richard along the windowsill's lip.

"The lie would be discovered sooner or later. We even took the matter of your guardianship to court. There's no way you can hide who the true owner is no matter what you do."

106

"I wouldn't speak so soon. Did you think I would sit in a useless stupor these past three years? If you recall, our court hearing was in the lower courtroom most often used by commoners. There was one ancient judge, a witness to take notes, our lawyers, you, and me. The judge, poor man, died last year. The record of the trial has been tragically lost, and no one has seen the man who took the notes for years." Richard shrugged. Ash felt fear begin to seep like frigid water through her veins.

"Mr. Thursley has a copy of everything."

"You've had so much time for contemplation lately, I thought you would've noticed that more than three weeks have passed without a single visit from Mr. Thursley."

"What did you do to him?" A tickle of sweat slid from the left side of her hairline down her temple to her cheek.

"I did nothing. There was an unfortunate fire in his office one night while he was staying late, however. He was rescued from the flames, but is still in the hospital. The doctors aren't sure if he will ever fully recover. All of his documents were lost in the fire."

"Why?" The word burst forth in a gasp of horrified disbelief.

"You are a boil, a filthy pustule beget by the last vestiges of a disease that should have been wiped out when all the other magical things were. Even if you were to mysteriously disappear, my treacherous brother still didn't repent of his mistake and make sure that the manor would pass to its rightful owner. How could he do that to me? To me, his only family?" As he spoke, he took slow steps toward Ash until she was trapped in the room's corner with nowhere else to go.

"Willie, get in here," Lord Richard called.

A stab of panic rocked her. She took a shaky breath, realizing for the first time how frail her assumption of safety had been. At Lord Richard's order, Willie appeared, leaning against the door. His suit was well made but was an obvious cast off of Lord Richard's. Willie's limbs were too lanky to fit the material as it had been intended, and it hung on him like the dressings for a scarecrow. His oily hair was slicked back into a ponytail at the nape of his neck, and a sinister smirk curled on his lips as he examined Ash from the door's frame like a cat eyeing a grounded bird.

Though Lord Richard was often harsh, she'd never before seen the hint of something dark that now swirled in his eyes. They were a bottomless pit that she might fall into and be lost. He'd practically admitted to murder, most likely with Willie's help. She felt the petrifying power of fear as she never had before.

"If that's the case, then it does you no good to hurt me." Her voice cracked. Her gaze darted to the blocked door where Willie eyed her hungrily from behind her uncle's approaching form.

"Not true. It does no good to kill you. We've discussed this, Ashelandra. I'm surprised you haven't yet figured out your role in this family. One might refer to you as a cog in a clock. The little clock piece is necessary to keep the clock working, but it serves its purpose out of sight. I need you here alive. But that's all."

"You can't have destroyed everything. Someone will find out." Ash felt her heart banging in her chest and a quivering in her throat.

Her uncle's broad shoulders shrugged off the threat as if it were nothing more substantial than a fallen leaf. "I've been very busy making sure that isn't a possibility. I may not have been able to remove you from inheriting, but everything else related to your situation is as if it never existed. Without your precious lawyer around, should you have an unfortunate accident that leaves you alive but sadly damaged in the mind, I will be appointed guardian over you for the rest of your pitiable life." He was too close. If Lord Richard grabbed Ash, she wasn't sure she would be able to break free. Even if she did burst past her uncle, Willie stood waiting, and the look in Willie's eyes made Ash think he hoped she would try to get past him.

"Even if I'm injured, you won't get anything." Ash had thought the clause father made in his will strange when Mr. Thursley first read it to her, but he must have been more worried about leaving Ash in her uncle's care than she'd thought. The will stated that if Ash were to have an accident that either killed or made her incapable of running the estate, the manor and all of Baron Fredrick's other assets would then revert to the crown, with the exception of the sum needed for Ash's comfortable care. Ash edged as far from the corner as she could without bringing herself closer to her uncle. She was only inches from the hidden door.

"Not if you are married."

"To James?" Her mouth fell open. "The law requires that I give my consent to such a union, and I never will."

"The law. The law," he mocked. "How is the law to ever know consent wasn't truly given if you are married and incapable of denying it?" Lord Richard lunged, but Ash was ready. She invoked the strongest moving spell she knew. It was only enough to make her uncle stagger, but it gave her enough time to reach behind her and press one of the roses carved in the stone that ringed the room in a dividing border. The camouflaged lever to the secret door sank in enough to make a handle. She wrenched it open. Lord Richard let out an inarticulate shocked roar and moved to follow, but she slammed the door in his face. Her uncle barely had time to save his fingers from the sliding stone. The lock snicked shut. She hoped it would take him time to find the hidden latch. Even if he ran out of her room and down the stairs, he still didn't know where in the house the passage led, giving Ash a few precious moments of lead.

She raced down the inner passage, feet barely catching every third of the narrow stone steps as she rushed downward toward the armory. Heart pounding, Ash paused behind the tapestry for the barest of moments to make sure no one stood in wait within the armory. The room echoed with silence. She grabbed a belt and saber with fumbling fingers and broke the glass display case holding her father's pistol. Jamming the gun into the belt, she snatched up the bag of balls and powder and ran out the door through the back hallway toward the front entrance. It was closer and Lord Richard would not expect her to take that exit. David watched her in offended surprise but didn't attempt to stop her as she flung the door open and jumped down the stairs.

"Catch her, you fool!" Lord Richard bellowed in rage from above as he stood at the top of the main staircase. His voice spiked ice through Ash's veins and shocked her feet into more speed. She could hear David fumble clumsily after her, but his movements were slow and confused. He did not worry her as much as the horror crashing down the stairs behind David.

"Bill!" Ash yelled across the yard as she ran. She sucked in a gasping breath and shouted desperately for the stable lad once more.

"Bill . . . get . . . Windrunner . . . Quick!"

Bill popped his head out of the stables, eyes widening as he saw her with the saber slapping her thigh, the pistol in her belt and the bag in her hands. Then he looked beyond her. His face paled, and he winked out of Ash's view. Ash didn't look back. Her feet spit out the gravel under her feet as she sprinted.

She grabbed the edge of the stable's doorway, using it as a lever to change direction and swing into the building without losing momentum, then pelted toward Windrunner's stall. Bill already had the horse out with a bridle on, but no saddle.

"Bill, I'm sorry," she gasped as she neared. "Go hide . . . so he doesn't know you helped."

Bill shook his head. "Ye yelled me name. He knows already."

Ash gasped. "Oh no. I didn't think."

Bill thrust the reins in Ash's hands when she stood hesitating and quickly lifted her onto Windrunner's bare back before she could protest.

"Go. I will try to delay him as long as I can."

"No. Willie's helping him. You don't know what he's capable of. Just hide or I can't leave." Ash held Windrunner still despite her panic.

His gaze swept over her rigid body, stopping at her eyes. She tried to meet his steadily, but she couldn't help her eyes from flicking to the stable's door.

"I'll hide. I promise. Be safe." He slapped Windrunner's flank, startling the mare into a jump toward the wide stable doors opposite where Ash had entered.

With a last worried look toward Bill to make sure he was getting out of sight, Ash turned away, struggling to remain seated on the mare's bare back.

As soon as the road reached a little way in the woods Ash sighed, her body slumping. She turned Windrunner onto one of the many small trails that she knew, heading deeper into the thick trees away from the main road. She slowed Windrunner to a walk. By this time she'd gotten her breath back enough to cast the spell of invisibility over Windrunner and herself, though it was hardly necessary once she was in the forest. Her uncle was not much of a woodsman, and Willie was city bred. They wouldn't be able to track her. The only other people he could safely order to look for her were the staff at the manor. David would search, but everyone else would only pretend to in order to keep their jobs.

The question that concerned Ashelandra now was where she could safely live until her birthday still more than half a year away. Lord Richard had threatened her today, but without evidence and Mr. Thursley's documents and testimony, no one would have the power to remove him as her guardian. A young woman's testimony would not hold as much sway as that of a man.

Her father and she had lived such isolated lives. The only noble who really knew her at all was Lady Amelia. Would the lady consent to hide her until her birthday? Ash had no proof that her uncle was trying to hurt her. If Lady Amelia sheltered her, and Ash was discovered in Lady Amelia's house, the Lady could be accused of kidnapping. It really *was* a stupid law, Ash thought bitterly. Maybe an inattentive king had let the law slip through as he was signing royal decrees long ago, unaware or uncaring of its ramifications to the affected children.

At the meadow where she'd once been chased by Prince Phillip, Ash slid off Windrunner. She hobbled the mare to a log. Windrunner could drag the wood, but it was heavy enough to keep her from roaming too far. Ash let the horse graze while she thought. The afternoon sun was sliding toward the trees. Dark would come soon, and though Ash wouldn't mind sleeping outside, she had no idea what to do about food. The warm weather was leaching away as summer slid to autumn. She'd need shelter when the nights turned bitter.

The jitter of adrenaline began to ebb, leaving her body limp. She shifted her weight, feeling hopeless and too tired to search for a solution to her situation. The drying grass crackled beneath her as she lay down and the scent of crushed weeds tickled her nose as she drifted to sleep.

***

Hoofbeats thumping through the ground that pillowed her ear woke Ash the next morning. She jumped to her feet, worried that Windrunner had broken free of the log. Instead, she saw her mare placidly chewing grass twenty feet away. A tall stallion loped toward her, Prince Phillip on its back.

She took one step toward her mare before deciding evasion was impossible. Stilling, she waited for the inevitable.

"Your Highness, so eager to visit your fiancé you couldn't even wait for the sun to fully rise?"

Prince Phillip dismounted and scrutinized Ash silently. Ash shifted her feet and then jumped as he reached forward and plucked a blade of grass from her mussed hair. She reached her hand up to smooth the unkempt strands back into place.

"From the looks of that crease on the side of your face, you came here much earlier than I. Heading into battle, are you?" He gestured toward the saber and pistol at her belt. Her face heated.

"I'm in retreat, actually. The advantage is all on the enemy's side at the moment." She carefully stepped away, weight on the balls of her feet, ready to sprint toward Windrunner if she must.

Prince Phillip's eyes tracked her movement. "So, you are out of a job."

"I would say, rather, that I have been liberated from slavery."

"I hope no one was injured during the escape." Prince Phillip stood perfectly still as he asked this, as if afraid any movement would startle her, and she would flee. She noticed his careful posture and laughed.

"I assure you, the one person who was in any danger of harm is standing before you." She grinned at him, a sly, slow smile full of mischief. "Before you try to tactfully ask, I will also tell you that I didn't steal anything as I left either. These things are mine," she said indicating the weapons and mare.

Prince Phillip began to shake his head.

"Don't bother to deny it. I saw your dubious expression," Ash asserted.

"You must admit someone in possession of a saddleless thoroughbred, a saber, and a pistol with no other discernible baggage does seem very suspect."

Ash's smile faded.

"I suppose it does. I own more. I just wasn't able to bring anything else."

"But does it do you any good?" One red brow rose doubtfully.

Ash hooked her thumbs in her belt and cocked her hip, recovering her smile. "It would be foolish to escape with only these belongings if all I could use them for was decoration."

Prince Phillip's eyebrow remained lifted in disbelief.

"Would you like a demonstration to prove my claim?" Ash asked.

"Please." Prince Phillip extended his arm out in invitation as he moved in line with Ash. "Can you hit that rock over there in the middle of the meadow?"

She squinted at the boulder about thirty feet away. "It's a large boulder." Ash took out the pistol and loaded the powder and ball. "Why don't we make the target the clump of moss growing near the top?"

"That's a very small target." He turned to her, eyes traveling from the loaded pistol to her face.

She shrugged, feeling her mouth turn up wryly. It had been several years since she'd last shot a pistol. Prince Phillip was right to question her skill. "It can't hurt to try."

Taking aim, she sighted down the gun and fired. The blast of the gunshot startled a pheasant from the meadow's grass. The two watched it rise above the trees before Ash turned to Phillip with an excited smile. "I haven't shot in ages. Let's go see how well I did."

Prince Phillip's face lit in a matching boyish grin. "Let's," he agreed.

They walked quickly across the grass to the rock. Even several feet away, Ash could tell that she'd hit the center on the boulder's patch of moss. "Ha! There you see." She pointed as they leaned in together to examine the bullet's score mark.

"Well done. You're a fine marksman." He turned his head to Ash in acknowledgment and Ash found that their two faces, crowded low to see the rock, were suddenly very close. She felt an unaccustomed flutter of nerves take flight in her stomach.

Ash cleared her throat and straightened quickly. The two stood in awkward silence.

A bird trilled in a tree at the meadow's edge. Ashelandra noticed the sun had risen fully above the branches. "Don't let me delay you. I'm sure you're anxious to see your fiancé." When Prince Phillip only looked at her, worry wormed its way into Ash's thoughts. "Unless you wish to waste your time taking me to a marshal to make sure my story is true."

She tensed a little, her flippant joke reflecting real worry.

"No. I won't do that, but you're obviously in trouble. Let me help you." He caught her eye but then flicked his gaze to their horses as if uncomfortable or impatient. Ash couldn't read his expression.

"There's no need. I'm fine." She held up her hands before her as if to stop him from moving forward. He remained motionless, staring at the horses.

"Is your definition of fine sleeping in a meadow? What will you do when the weather turns cold? What will you eat?"

Ash felt decidedly uncomfortable listening to the prince ask the very questions she had asked herself the night before.

"I'll think of something. I'm a sorceress in training after all." Ash slapped her hand to her forehead. "My books! I forgot to get them."

"You won't have to go back into the enemy's camp to get them, will you?" Prince Phillip asked with an unsure grin.

"Oh no. I found a secure hiding place in the woods for them years ago. It should be safe to retrieve them."

"I can at least accompany you as you find your books, just to make sure you get them safely."

Ash regarded him curiously, wondering why he bothered with her at all. "Why? You're a prince. I'm . . ." Ash brushed a hand down her ragged clothes, to illustrate her humble status. "And you have an eager bride-to-be awaiting you."

Prince Phillip shifted his feet and looked down avoiding her eyes. "What proper gentleman would leave a lady"—he glanced at her dress briefly—"no matter what kind, in distress? I realize that you won't let me do much to help you, but let me at least do this one thing. You have to admit, it isn't much." He looked very sincere, and Ash couldn't see any harm in letting him play the hero if it would make him feel better. She'd take him to get her books and send him on his way. Then she would have to face the problem of what to do with herself for seven long, uncertain months.

"Very well, but then your obligation to the pitiable maiden in distress is done. Agreed?" She held out her hand for a shake, the poor man's method of binding an agreement.

***

The forest was loud with the sounds of wildlife before and behind the two horses, but Ash and Prince Phillip rode in a bubble of silence. Ash was still trying to dispel the embarrassment of being ungracefully boosted onto her mare's bare back by a prince. Bill's much broader form, and years as a stable hand had made his boost efficient and quick, with no improper contact. Prince Phillip was well muscled, but leaner, and wasn't in the practice of helping young ladies mount horses without saddles. He'd cupped his hand to act as her stirrup but had overbalanced and been forced to grab her legs and push on her bottom so they wouldn't fall backward to the ground.

If Ash wasn't quite so embarrassed herself, she would have laughed at Prince Phillip's mortified expression. Instead, they rode awkwardly next to each other, so quiet that when their path in the forest ran parallel to the road they both heard the wagon approaching. Ash reined in her horse and moved toward the trees.

"Prince Phillip?" It was a question and a request all at once. She didn't dare say more for fear he would believe her a thief after all.

He stopped his stallion, and the two sat their mounts quietly, watching through a patch of bush that hid them from sight of the road but gave them a clear view of who approached. The wagon's driver came into view. It was Sorcerer Tioroso. Behind him, the wagon's bed was covered by a canvas, hiding the contents. Ash looked over to see the prince's brows furrow.

When the sorcerer passed out of hearing Ash said, "You certainly keep him busy. What is it that he does for you so frequently?"

"You've seen him often?"

"He's passed through the forest toward Trebruk Manor many times. I talked to him once, and he said he was getting you, but then I saw him pass by so much that I got curious. I found and worked out the pronunciation for the spell to track him." Prince Phillip's brows rose, and Ash was quick to add, "I know I shouldn't have, and I never found him anyway. You bumped into me the first time I tried it yesterday, and I got distracted."

"That's why you were so vexed with me. But wait, yesterday I'm sure neither I nor my father gave any sort of task to Sorcerer Tioroso. In fact, there hasn't been a need for magical solutions to solve the problems we've faced of late."

"So if he wasn't sneaking around all this time for you, what was he doing?"

"I'm not sure, but I'll definitely ask him as soon as I get back to the palace." Prince Phillip's face was solemn, and Ash thought it made him look more royal than before. "We used to be close, but he's been really strange lately, avoiding my father and me. I tried to talk to him about his absence as of late, but he managed to dodge the question and slip away."

"You seemed close before," Ash said.

"Oh, and when were you able to observe this?" Prince Phillip turned to her with too much interest in his eyes.

"I just chanced to see you a few years ago in the forest. You seemed very easy with each other."

The light of curiosity in Prince Phillip's eyes waned. He shrugged. "That was years ago. We've grown apart since then, especially in the past few months."

Ash cleared her throat to dispel the silence that followed. "We're very near my hiding place now. We just need to cross inward to the pond where you've often interrupted me." Ash blew a raspberry sigh of feigned exasperation.

Prince Phillip's expression lightened. "I would hardly call two times often, and I'd think that you'd welcome an interruption every now and then."

"I suppose, *if* it was someone I wished to see," she said with a wicked grin.

"Who doesn't wish to personally meet a prince?" Prince Phillip gestured loftily, but Ash wasn't sure if his boast was all jest.

"Be careful, Your Highness. You may want to take the broader path over there. The trees through here are too close for such an august personage to squeeze through. Shall I lay flowers in your path to make it more presentable?" Ash felt her mouth quirking once again.

"With you here to chastise me, my royal bearing has shriveled until

I find I am quite content with plain dirt on a trail no wider than this large brute I am riding." Prince Phillip's eyes caught Ash's, and his mouth curved in wry defeat.

Ash laughed as the path opened up to the pond. She slid down reluctantly and retrieved the sealed metal box where she kept her magic books in a hollowed out log. Prince Phillip watched from atop his horse.

"Your duty is fulfilled," Ash said, looking up. She saw his face pucker, his mouth opening in what she had come to know as another demand that he help. She held up her hand to stop him.

"A bargain is a bargain, Prince Phillip. Congratulations again on your engagement. I hope you will be very happy." He looked for a moment like he would still argue, but then his faced relaxed.

"Thank you. Good luck, Ash. I hope we will meet again."

After Prince Phillip rode out of view, Ash remained sitting at the pond, watching the family of ducks that lived there without really seeing them. Prince Phillip had distracted her from her problems, but the fact was she was no closer to knowing what she should do with herself now than she had been before. If only there was someone who would aid her instead of feel it was his or her duty to put Ash right back into the hands she was fleeing.

Ash thought of Lady Amelia again, debating the viability of asking for the lady's help. The lady was more forward thinking than most, and she'd already demanded to see Ashelandra soon. Added to that, Lady Amelia didn't seem to feel much love toward Lord Richard. Ash still worried about bringing trouble to Lady Amelia's door, but it was better than her plan to build a hut and live in the forest all winter.

How would she even build a hut? Ash had no tools, no skill. Magic might work. She could levitate branches into place while she secured them. Ash trailed her finger in the pond as Windrunner lowered her head for a drink. There was no real urgency to go anywhere when she had nowhere to go, so she delayed moving, as if staying still would freeze time and free her from having to decide. Finally, the press of pebbles jabbing through the thin material of her skirts became uncomfortable enough to goad Ash into standing.

She stretched carefully to save straining seams from bursting, and led Windrunner to a log so she could have enough height to boost herself up while holding her box of books. She would have to hold them on her lap as she rode since there was no other way to secure them. A crashing noise grew in volume from the path leading to the manor. Fear squeezed her heart. Had her uncle's search extended so far into the woods after all?

Prince Phillip burst from the path into view, and relief washed over her. His horse was breathing hard, and the prince mimicked the stallion's panting breaths as he pulled the reins sharply, stopping the hulking creature a foot away from where Ash stood stupidly watching.

"You're still here. I'm so glad. She's gone!" he gasped. Sweat beaded Prince Phillip's brow. His broad frame curved over his horse toward Ash, tense in coiled expectancy, as if he wanted to stretch down and scoop Ash up. It was disconcerting, and for a moment, Ash's heart leaped in a sort of delighted anxiety, until the words he'd spoken sank in.

"What?" Confusion drowned her unexpected response and mixed with relief. She wasn't sure if she was relieved it wasn't her uncle confronting her or if the prince's bewildering reappearance could excuse any aberrant emotions.

The prince's next words brought her back to herself. "Jane. She's been taken."

Chapter Ten

SEPTEMBER 29, 1750

Taken?" she repeated stupidly.

"Yes. Quick, get on your horse. We have to go after him." Prince Phillip tensed, and Ash wondered if he really would haul her up on his horse, but he slid lithely off his own mount and took the step necessary to bring him to Ash. He was too close. She took an uncomfortable step back off the log and into Windrunner's flank.

"Him?" Ash was utterly confused and flustered.

Prince Phillip swore and closed the gap between them by hopping over the fallen wood. He grabbed her by the thighs, and boosted her ungracefully, but effectively, onto Windrunner. Ash barely had time to utter a startled cry before he'd turned back to swiftly remount his own horse.

"Sorry, there's no time for niceties. We have to go after him now before we lose the trail."

Ash sat back solidly on Windrunner's back, adjusting the box of books on her lap so they wouldn't slide. As if sensing her mistress's intent, Windrunner stopped digging a hole with her hoof and stood still.

"I'm not going anywhere until you tell me what happened, and why you are suddenly behaving as if I am required to go with you," she said.

He regarded her with impatient superciliousness. "I am the prince. If I ask it, you are required to go."

Ash's emotional disquiet settled into the hard steel of stubbornness. She said nothing, but Windrunner stood as if carved of wood, and Ash's head tilted up as she bit the inside of her cheeks.

Prince Phillip narrowed his eyes, his posture rigid with held breath. The air rushed out, and his position settled into impatient resignation. "I went to see Lady Jane, but when the servant went to fetch her, she was nowhere to be found. They searched everywhere. She's gone."

"What makes you think that she was taken rather than just

temporarily out of contact with the servants?" Even as Ash asked, she knew Jane would never walk alone in the woods. She was too obedient to her father's decrees. Still, one never knew.

"There was evidence of a struggle. Some toiletries were swept from her dresser to the floor, and a drawer was pulled from its hinges and lay overturned on the ground as well." Prince Phillip fidgeted, moving his horse two steps closer to Ash. Windrunner snorted a warning at the stallion. The restlessness was catching. As Prince Phillip spoke, Ash felt a desire well up inside her to do something, anything, to help her cousin. But she needed to know everything.

"You said that we needed to go after him. Did someone see Lady Jane's kidnapper?"

"No, but I know who it is."

Windrunner was forced back a step as the stallion lurched forward.

Ash's brows rose in sudden understanding. "You think it was Sorcerer Tioroso, don't you? You said you hadn't sent him on errands near here, yet I have seen him often in the past weeks. I never did find out where he was going other than the first time, and that was to the manor." As she spoke, Prince Phillip edged his horse to the trail leading to the road where Ash and he had spotted the sorcerer not more than two hours ago. His urgency to leave was overflowing. It seeped into her like steam hissing from a teapot, and she had all the pertinent details, so she followed Prince Phillip down the path.

"Yes," he confirmed. She matched his horse's increasing pace. "That's why I need you. You are the only sorcerer I know other than Sorcerer Tioroso. You said you know how to find him. You'll lead me to him."

Ash bristled again, but she was to the rear of the prince so he didn't see her scowl. "I never got to find out if it would let me continuously follow him despite the magic he uses to hide himself," she shouted over the pounding of their horses' gallop.

"Well, you're all I've got. You said you were out of a job. You'll help get Lady Jane back!" he yelled.

If Ash hadn't been just as worried about Jane as the prince was, she might have been annoyed at Prince Phillip's high-handed manner. But his condescension aside, she was glad that she wouldn't have to beg her way into the search party.

At the road, they reined in the horses to examine the ground. Ash click-shushed the spell she'd learned to track the sorcerer and was relieved to sense his direction and distance. He was moving quickly.

"I think he is still following the road, but he seems to be traveling much faster than possible if he's only driving a wagon." Ash wondered if he were traveling faster by some magical means that she'd didn't know, or if he'd just switched to horseback.

Prince Phillip looked down the road as if he would follow at a gallop, but he hesitated. "Is it harder to sense him as he gets further away?" he asked.

Ash concentrated a moment. "It doesn't seem to be. Not yet, anyway."

"That's good news. We'll meet up with the escort I left behind. I should go back to the palace to tell my father what I am doing . . ." He looked down the road, eyes unfocused as if he could see the palace through the trees. He shook his head. "But we don't have time. I'll send one of my men back to inform him. That will still leave us with twenty soldiers, which should be enough guards to keep my father happy."

Even as he finished speaking, Ash and Prince Phillip were forced to rein in their mounts as the royal banner of cobalt blue with a rearing unicorn crested the rise, revealing a group of royal soldiers beneath its shade. The man in the lead, sitting rigidly atop his horse, bowed low in his saddle toward Prince Phillip, his right fist at his heart, and the men behind him followed suit.

"Captain Forbs, I need you to send one of your men back to the king with a message. Lady Jane has been kidnapped, and I am follow-ing the trail of her abductor. We can't lose any ground, so the rest of us will continue after the kidnapper now and get supplies along the way."

Captain Forbs nodded, displaying no surprise, as stoic as if retriev-ing a hostage was an everyday occurrence. He signaled one of his men to leave with the message while he eyed Ash. She studied him back, noting that his stiff body was stocky from muscle rather than fat. He looked about forty and had a trim brown mustache that didn't quite succeed in hiding a thin scar on his upper lip.

Prince Phillip noticed the captain's evaluating gaze. "This is Ash. She has some skill in sorcery. I've hired her to help track Ti . . . uh, the kidnapper."

Interesting. Ash wondered why Prince Phillip chose not to mention who he believed the kidnapper to be.

Captain Forbs nodded again, but his eyes slid to her fraying dress, paused at her horse's saddleless back, and rose to stop at the saber and pistol on her waist. He frowned.

"You'll need to turn around." Ash pointed down and circled her finger. "He is heading west, but I think we can keep on this road for a while," Ash said to the captain, hoping to get the large body of men moving.

Prince Phillip smiled his thanks. He urged his horse through the soldiers but stopped when he noticed Ash staying in the rear.

"You'll have to lead," he called.

Ash nodded, wincing self-consciously as she trotted to the front, and then spurred her mount into a ground-eating gallop. The other men followed. Ash sat astride Windrunner so that she could match the men's speed and still keep her seat on Windrunner's bare back as well as keep a hold of her books. Sweat gathered. Windrunner became slippery, hard to grip even with Ash's legs squeezed tight. She lowered her body over her box of books and concentrated on staying on. Ash was only peripherally aware of the scandalized looks on the faces of the road's fellow travelers as a ragged woman, riding improperly, galloped through, followed by an intimidating group of crisply dressed soldiers.

When they reached the town of Fane, the group was forced to slow down. Carts and carriages rattled through the streets. People strolled in an ebbing and waning flow of sparse to thickly bunched groups. It made progress frustratingly slow, but it allowed Ash to sit up and loosen her legs slightly. They ached from the unaccustomed labor.

Once back on the country road, Captain Forbs suggested that they trot at a pace that would move them quickly without exhausting the horses. Ash found that harder to deal with than the smooth speed of a gallop. Every once in a while, Ash would recheck Sorcerer Tioroso's position, and she found him still moving steadily west toward the Aster Mountains. It was a curious direction for him to take. The only easy passage out of the country was to the northeast where the mountains turned to hills then beach, leaving a passage between mountains and sea from Prince Phillip's kingdom to the country beside it.

It was possible to travel through some of the mountain ranges, but not easy, and the Aster Mountains were particularly difficult. When Ash last checked, Sorcerer Tioroso was still moving in the direction of the tallest mountain of the Aster range, Spirit Mountain. The nearest passable area was many miles to the south through a low point between two smaller peaks.

Not only was there no passage through the mountains at that location, the land before the mountain was a wasteland of barren, rocky ground. Nothing grew there. Thick dark clouds in the sky never cleared enough to allow plants to survive. Without any direct sunlight, it was easy for men and animals to trip on the treacherous slippery shale. No one lived there, and though the terrain was jagged, with many caves to hide in, if Jane's abductor did not move through the miles and miles of dark rocky land to where the sun finally peeked out again at the foot of Spirit Mountain, he would soon find himself out of food with no place to replenish it. His direction of flight made no sense to Ash.

The company traveled two hours after Ash felt the sorcerer's movement stop, trying to close the gap, but they were still far behind, and Ash didn't understand why. Again she wondered if Sorcerer Tioroso knew a spell to help his speed. She would have to search her books this evening to see if she could find a reference to a travel spell, though she couldn't recall ever coming across one before. Prince Phillip finally stopped when they reached Hunnington, a town with an inn large enough to lodge all of his men.

A tall man, dressed in rich green tailored clothing ,came out of the inn and bowed low to the prince. His stomach strained a little at the waist. The innkeeper was prospering.

"We'll need the horses cooled and fed. My men and I require provisions as well. Oh, and a lady's saddle." His hand flicked Ash's way atop Windrunner. Ash tried not to wince as the innkeeper's eyes turned to her.

"I'd prefer a man's saddle," Ash said. She kept her voice quiet but firm.

Prince Phillip looked up to see Ash sitting astride her mare, her dress necessarily hiked up to above her ankles. She blushed, thinking he and the men had had ample opportunity to see quite a bit of her limbs all afternoon. Carefully, she slipped one sweaty leg across Windrunner's back so that she was sitting sidesaddle before slowly sliding to the ground. Once on her feet, she lifted her chin and stared back at him, daring him to comment.

Without moving his assessing gaze from hers, he told the innkeeper, "Very well, get her a man's saddle." Finally, he flicked his gaze back to the innkeeper as the man began ushering his stable boy to take care of the prince's horses. "Also, search for a woman who could act as a companion to Miss Ash. I need a good horsewoman. We'll be traveling swiftly."

The innkeeper nodded, taking Ash in with a thorough inspection before dismissing her. Prince Phillip's men glanced covertly at her as they shuffled indoors. Ash backed further away, feeling discomfited. She held Windrunner's reins in a tight grip, her fingers turning white, as she waited her turn for her mount to be taken. Windrunner's sweat was soaked through her clothes. The wet cloth had rubbed and chaffed her skin so that she now felt like a fire was raging on her sore thighs. She tried not to limp to the inn's door after the stable boy at last took Windrunner to brush and feed.

Looking down, she noticed that a seam had come unraveled on the bodice of her dress, near the waist. She pinched the fabric together, wondering if the prince even intended to pay her or not. Even if he hadn't planned on it, she would make sure he at least gave her money to purchase a needle and thread.

"Would you join Captain Forbs and me for dinner? I want to discuss how we should proceed." Ash jumped at hearing Prince Phillip's voice so near her. She clamped her hand firmly over the frayed fabric to hide the tear.

"Of course. Could I have a word with the innkeeper, and a moment to freshen up?" she asked, trying to angle herself so that the second tear she noticed in her skirt was facing away from the lamp hanging outside the inn's entrance. The ride had been unforgiving to her already worn clothes. Ash felt every bit the beggar. She was practically dressed in rags, the saber and pistol still jammed in her belt. Her hair was a simple braid, still mussed from a night sleeping out in a meadow.

"That would probably be a good idea. I'll see if he has any riding clothes on hand to buy since we've all left on this journey embarrassingly ill prepared." His eyes focused on her hand clutching one rip together before moving to the open tear she'd tried to hide in the shadows. Ash felt her face heat.

She nodded without meeting his eyes and stumbled past him up the two cream stone steps and through the inn's open door to the well lit room inside. The walls inside were papered with gold fleur de lis, adding elegance to the cream stone floor of the room. Simple, rectangular, but well-polished tables filled the room in an arrangement that made the area seem spacious while still accommodating numerous customers.

Ash hurried past the tables toward the hallway beyond where a young woman dressed in a crisp navy blue dress led her to a room with an already drawn bath in a deep brass tub. The tub had a guilloche pattern of interlaced curving lines circling the rim.

It felt good to soak in the steaming water. She spoke the rounded vowels and clicks of the spell to help heal her sore thighs, and slumped into the water. Uncomfortable with making the prince wait, however, Ash sat back up and scrubbed herself quickly. She washed her hair and was already patting it dry with a towel when the same young woman tapped politely on the door and entered holding a maroon riding habit that didn't flare too much and even had a split skirt.

The fit of the dress was snug, but the stitches were firm, the fabric smooth and finely woven. Ash ran her hands over her waist, enjoying the feel of her first new outfit in three years. Though she felt a twinge of embarrassment that the prince would have to provide something so basic for her, it warmed her that he had done so quickly, and without making her appear a beggar. She hurried out to the dining area after twisting her wet hair into a bun and securing it with the pins left next to the washbasin for her use. Prince Phillip and Captain Forbs waited at a table near the corner of the room with the soldiers spread out at the surrounding tables. Some of them gave her curious stares or awkward bobs of their heads as she passed, not sure of her rank.

Prince Phillip stood as she neared the table, his eyes widening as he took in the lines in the riding habit that clearly accented her trim figure. His gaze rose to her wetly shining hair, and his brows relaxed as his mouth curled up.

Captain Forbs remained seated. He glanced in question at the prince, and the prince's face drew down into a frown. After a curtsy to the prince, Ash sat opposite the two men. The captain was scowling, and Prince Phillip didn't look much happier as he settled back in his chair. Ashelandra regarded the two men warily, unsure of what to expect.

Prince Phillip caught her eyes traveling back and forth between them and smiled reassuringly. "The captain and I were just discussing Lady Jane's kidnapping. He didn't believe me when I told him that it was Sorcerer Tioroso." The corner of Prince Phillip's mouth turned down in frustration.

"Forgive me, Your Majesty, if I fail to trust an assumption based on the information of an unknown source." The last was said with dripping disbelief as Captain Forbs eyed Ash, unimpressed with her new clothes and neatly pinned hair.

The corner of Prince Phillip's mouth pulled down further. "I told you. I did not reach this conclusion based solely on Ash's words."

"Then please tell me, Your Majesty, what leads you to believe that the sorcerer, a man I thought you called friend, has done something so outrageous and out of character?" His voice was calm, but Ash still felt that the drawl of his words bordered on disrespectful.

Prince Phillip chose to ignore it. "He's been disappearing a lot lately where no one can find him. You yourself remarked that his recent unavailability has forced my father to resort to more costly methods of addressing kingdom problems. I believe he was spying on Lady Jane at her manor." Prince Phillip's eyes landed on Ash. "Tell Captain Forbs what you told me."

Ash felt one side of her mouth tighten in annoyance. She did not feel inclined to do as the prince asked, considering Captain Forbs's last insinuation. But she did want to find Jane and would do anything she could to make that happen. So Ash bit her tongue and followed his order. She'd certainly had enough practice over the years. Even if he disliked her for it, she'd convince the grumpy man that the dictatorial prince wasn't just on a wild goose chase.

"I first encountered the sorcerer in the woods near my . . . Lady Jane's manor when Prince Phillip began to court her. Though he went invisible, I cast a counter spell and followed him to her manor. I wasn't stealthy enough, however, and he discovered me, along with the fact that I could cast my own invisibility illusion and see through his. I asked what he was doing, and he said that he was sent to get the prince. After that, I saw him several times but couldn't ever follow him. He'd done something to hide himself that I hadn't learned yet. It took a bit of searching, but I finally found a spell to track his whereabouts. I didn't get to use it until today, but it appears to be working." She clacked the spell to find the sorcerer. It dispelled whenever she was distracted. "Right now he is camped west of here toward the Aster Mountains."

"So you are a sorceress?" Captain Forbs asked, a note of distaste flavoring his tone. Since the captain had been quick to defend Sorcerer Tioroso against Prince Phillip's accusation, Ash could only assume that Captain Forbs disapproved of her specifically rather than sorcerers in general.

"I suppose you'd call me a sorceress in training," she said simply, trying not to let the captain rile her.

"Prince Phillip mentioned your name is Ash. That's a very simple name for a sorceress." His brow rose, and Ash was impressed with how much contempt Captain Forbs could convey simply by lifting an eyebrow. Aggravated, she copied the gesture, careful to add her own measure of scorn.

Prince Phillip, too focused on his mission to even notice Ash, spoke. "Stop baiting the girl. Her name is not the issue right now. We need to go after Sorcerer Tioroso as soon as it's light enough to ride. Ash and I saw the sorcerer driving away on a cart a half an hour before I discovered Lady Jane missing. When Ash cast her spell later, he was moving much faster. With her help, we will be able to find him and bring Lady Jane back."

Attention back on the prince, the Captain frowned. "All you have are circumstantial events that connect the sorcerer to Lord Richard's forest. You still haven't shown any reason why Sorcerer Tioroso would steal the girl"—Captain Forbs checked himself after seeing the Prince's glare—"*lady* away. He's been your friend for years," the Captain added reasonably. "Why would you assume that he was the kidnapper?"

Prince Phillip scowled at the table as if it could answer the questions if he put enough force in the glare. "He hasn't been friendly for a while now. He's been moody, rude even. He all but mocked me at court the other day, though the reference was veiled. Still, I suppose all his odd behavior combined with my anxiety over Lady Jane's kidnapping could have made me more willing to leap to an incorrect assumption."

Into the silence that followed, Ash couldn't help but ask, "Then why is he going west so quickly?"

Both men turned to her, and Ash cleared her throat.

"There could be any number of reasons," Prince Phillip replied, brow bunched in frustration. "He's not required to report his every action to us. I think it's worth following Sorcerer Tioroso to see what he is doing. His behavior is strange whether he has Lady Jane or not."

"I suppose I could cast the spell to track Lady Jane rather than the sorcerer. I've been tracking only him until now. That was stupid of me, especially if Captain Forbs is right, and the kidnapper is someone completely different," Ash said, feeling like seven kinds of foolish for not thinking of this obvious test before.

Before the men could respond to her suggestion, she issued the sharp snapping-shush sound of the spell, changing the name in the spell to Jane's. "She is stopped west of us as well. It seems like the same distance as the sorcerer, but it could be coincidence." It seemed unlikely to Ash, and she couldn't help feeling a little prick of pleasure knowing her discovery would irk the captain.

"I wish I hadn't been right," Prince Phillip said, his eyes weighted with regret. Ash winced, feeling a stab of self-reproach.

"I'll still reserve judgment, if you don't mind, Your Majesty," Captain Forbs said, eyeing Ash distrustfully.

Ash felt her jaw clench. "Do you doubt my ability, Captain? Or is it my honesty that is in question?"

"I question everything, miss. It's my job. You do appear less credible than most," Captain Forbs added.

Ash forced herself to speak calmly, though she couldn't completely unclench her teeth. "I see. And what leads you to that conclusion?"

"You have an aristocratic accent but were dressed in rags, which could be explained if you were a lady of name whose family lost their fortune. However, you ride like a man, and carry a pistol and saber, something no lady of breeding would do. I'm not sure what you are, but you are not someone I trust."

"Captain, you go too far." Prince Phillip's eyes met that of the Captain's steadily. "I trust Ash, and that is good enough," he said, a note of finality resonating through his voice. Ash wondered for a moment why Prince Phillip trusted her so steadfastly when he hardly knew her. In fact, he'd seen her in a very suspicious state just this morning. If Ash were he, she didn't think she would be so quick to dismiss Captain Forbs's doubts, even though the accusations chafed like thistle caught under her clothes. She observed Prince Phillip quizzically as he regarded his captain.

"I want merely to protect you, Sire," the captain explained, "so I feel I must speak, even if you don't always agree. I still feel it would be best if she gave up her saber and pistol. I doubt very much she can use them, and she won't need them with soldiers around. We'll all be safer. Guns and swords in the hands of the inexperienced are more dangerous to innocent bystanders than they are to any perceived enemy." His bushy eyebrows showed no trace of doubt that the prince would agree.

Ash didn't give Prince Phillip a chance to respond. "You are contradicting yourself, Captain, and it begs the question if I give up my weapons, who will protect me from you?" She arched her eyebrows and felt her lips quirk, but she knew her smile cradled a touch of ire with the humor.

"I can't have civilians with delusions of competency running around my men armed, no matter how much the prince trusts you." He nodded to the prince as if in concession, though he was clearly disregarding the prince's order to let Ash be.

"Then it's a good thing that I am experienced, isn't it?"

"You are a woman." He shrugged as if that answered everything. She felt the corners of her mouth fall for a moment before curving back up into a wicked grin. If she'd been at the manor, the servants would have recognized the smile to mean trouble.

"Enough," Prince Phillip said, his voice loud enough to silence the soldiers sitting at the nearby tables. A chair scraped a fraction across the floor and its sound echoed in the sudden quiet. "I've already warned you once, Captain, and I've seen for myself that Ash is an excellent shot. This subject is closed."

The subdued rumble of the soldier's voices resumed as a serving woman arrived at the table with potato leek soup, pickled eggs, braised Cornish hen, and apple cider. The prince must have ordered the food as Ash bathed. As Prince Phillip and a moody Captain Forbs discussed the supplies they'd acquired, Ash focused on the hen, cider, and soup, noting that the inn's cook had been careful to wash all the sand from the leeks so that the broth was creamy and smooth without the worrisome crunch of sand. The only problem was her new dress's sleeves. They were too tight. To get the soup spoon to her mouth, she was forced to lower her elbows and twist her wrist unnaturally to keep the spoon level. It took an embarrassing amount of concentration and made her feel ridiculous. When all that was left on her plate were the two pickled eggs, Ash eyed them, wrinkling her nose in distaste.

Captain Forbs and Prince Phillip quieted and focused on their food. Ash looked over to Captain Forbs as he bit into his eggs. His mouth pinched, his eyes squinted, but he chewed quickly and swallowed first one egg, then the other, a soldier doing his duty. The clatter of cutlery and din of voices filled the room. When Captain Forbes's head was lowered to his soup, Ash turned her body away from him, and in the cover of the inns clamor, clicked a spell. Her eggs vanished. The tock snap of another spell flipped the invisible eggs to the Captain's plate. She dropped the illusion and the undesirable food appeared at the Captain's elbow.

Prince Phillip looked up from his hen. Ash made sure her smile stretched honey sweet.

"Finished already?" Prince Phillip asked.

"Yes, Sire." From the corner of her eye, Ash watched Captain Forbs notice the pickled eggs on his plate. He glanced at Ash's empty platter, then the prince's. His was also empty.

Prince Phillip turned to look for the innkeeper. The man hung at the edge of the room, shifting his feet and watching for the prince's glance. As soon as Prince Phillip's eyes met his, the innkeeper hurried over.

"Were you able to find a traveling companion?" Prince Phillip asked.

"Yes, Your Majesty. I'll fetch her right away," he said. His stomach strained his coat as he turned and scurried through a door. Several minutes later, as Prince Phillip and Captain Forbs finished their meal—Forbs consuming all but the eggs—the innkeeper returned with a young woman in tow. She had small eyes and a thin mouth. Her face was a canvas of faded freckled spatters. Though she looked down demurely as the innkeeper approached, her lips looked pinched in temper.

"This is my daughter, Molly." Molly's eyes flicked up and then down again. Looking closer, Ash could see that the innkeeper and his daughter shared the same curved brown brows and small bump in their nose ridge. The innkeeper looked down proudly on his daughter, oblivious to her displeasure. "She rides well and will inherit my inn someday, property of her own." Ash tried not to snicker hearing the innkeeper's obvious hint. A little land was all it took to be eligible for a prince. Why not take the chance that Prince Phillip might fall in love with his daughter as he traveled? It was an opportunity too beautiful to miss.

Both Prince Phillip and Molly caught Ash's smile. Molly scowled, and her eyes narrowed. Ash sighed. She'd muddied the floor now. No doubt she'd have to scour it later. Prince Phillip looked chagrined ,though his lips hinted at a curve.

Captain Forbs redirected everyone's attention when he asked, "Why in the world do we need to drag along another woman? One will be more than enough to deal with. She isn't a lady, so why bother?"

Molly smirked. The innkeeper shuffled his feet and puffed nervously. Prince Phillip's emerald eyes narrowed, darkening them a shade deeper.

"She is a sorceress. Have you known of any sorcerers not from noble families?" Prince Phillip asked, though his tone made it sound like his words weren't really a question.

Molly's small eyes widened, revealing Forget-Me-Not blue irises. She took a skittish step back, but her father looked unconcerned, his brows rising in interest as he regarded Ash more closely.

"I haven't met many other sorcerers aside from Sorcerer Tioroso," Captain Forbs muttered stubbornly.

Captain Forbs turned to Ash, jaw set accusingly. "Well? Do we need to waste our time for you, delaying us even further by adding another woman just to satisfy society's silly rules?"

Ash freely admitted to herself that if asked the question by anyone else, she would have agreed with him wholeheartedly. Adding a woman to their party with unknown riding ability was not necessary. Molly might slow them down. And as for propriety's sake, two women against twenty determined men would not be able to defend themselves much better than one. It was simply a societal decoration pretending to be armor. And like armor, Ash found the stricture awkward, heavy, and restrictive, prone to hinder rather than help.

However, it was Captain Forbs who had asked the question, and that made all the difference.

"Forgive me, Captain, but you've given me no reason to trust that by disregarding those rules I would be safe," Ash replied.

Red suffused the captain's face in angry blotchy clumps. His jaw clenched, and his hands seized the table as if he would break it.

"You have nothing to worry about, Ash, and I'm sure Molly will do well as a companion," Prince Phillip rushed to say before Captain Forbs could respond to Ash's barb. "Why don't you and Molly head to your room. She can take care of any other needs you might have," he said, looking at the innkeeper for confirmation. The man nodded, though his eyes darted worriedly toward Ash and back to his daughter, probably pondering the wisdom of what he'd thought would be a wonderful scheme.

Ash stood, and Captain Forbs opened his mouth to say something, but Prince Phillip beat him again. "Captain, eat your pickled eggs. It isn't like you to waste food." The Captain's mouth dropped a little more, his incredulity rendering him speechless.

Ash felt her face relax, and her lips quirk once again as she followed a hesitant Molly to Ash's room. Molly stayed by the door's edge when they entered.

"Do you need anything?" she asked, voice laced with obvious reluctance.

Ash took a moment to think. Remembering the difficulty she'd had at dinner, she tried to stretch upward. The sleeve restrained her. The maroon fabric had tight seams and flattering lines. Because of her hard work over the years, her figure had improved, and the dress's fit accentuated her frame in all the right places.

The only problem with the dress was the dratted sleeves. The tailor must have thought a woman had no need of raising her arms above her waist to do anything useful like actually ride a horse or eat food.

"Is there anything that can be done about this?" Ash tried to gesture with one arm toward the other but got stuck. The servant girl squinted, which made her already small eyes look like slits.

"Take it off. I can slit the armpit seams and add a strip of cloth to give you more freedom of movement," she said, beckoning her arm impatiently, nervousness fading in the comfort of command. She left and came back with a basket of fabric, needles, and thread as Ash took the bodice off.

As soon as Molly returned, the innkeeper's daughter snapped the garment from Ash's hands and got to work picking apart seams with brisk efficiency.

"I could do that myself," Ash offered.

"The prince told me to take care of your needs," the young woman retorted before bending back to her work. Ash watched with quiet annoyance as Molly added pink fabric to the dress. It clashed with the maroon dreadfully. Ash would look like a gypsy when she raised her arms.

"What are you doing? There is fabric in the basket that matches my dress perfectly," Ash snapped.

Molly didn't even pause. Her head stayed fixed on the needle

133

threading through maroon and pink fabric. "Can't use that. It's spoken for."

"I see." Ash's disbelief dripped from her voice like melting icicles. Molly knotted the thread and bit off the extra, turning the top right side out again and handing it to Ash before going to stand at the door.

Ash studied the girl as she slouched by the door's frame waiting for any more instructions. Molly scowled at the ground resentfully. Her shoulders hunched. Ash was torn. Should she pay the girl back for her ill-mannered behavior by running her ragged with demands or should she let it go? Ash had felt the sting of servitude for three years, and it would mirror her uncle disturbingly if she punished Molly for being unhappy with the prince's command. She shivered.

"I'm fine, Molly. I'll see you in the morning," Ash said with a sigh.

Molly twitched a nod of acknowledgment before she slipped out the door.

***

The next morning Prince Phillip directed his retinue-turned-rescue party to gather their mounts and supplies. Ash saddled Windrunner, waiting until the mare expelled her breath before tightening and buckling the girth. She stroked Windrunner's neck.

"That trick is so old. I'm sure you can think of some new ones," she murmured to her horse. Windrunner curved her head around to huff in Ashelandra's hair indignantly. Ash chuckled as she surveyed the groups' activity. Molly stood off to the side holding the reins to a gray mare a full hand shorter than Windrunner. Both mare and girl stood with one leg bent in sullen resignation, though Ash did catch the girl darting interested glances at Prince Phillip now and then as he consulted with Captain Forbs on the supplies' distribution.

Saddle buckles were tugged secure, and soldiers mounted their horses. A young blond soldier helped Molly mount her lady's saddle and nodded toward the prince. Ash grimaced. It would be hard for the girl to last the day sidesaddle at the pace the prince would likely set, but Molly had refused to ride astride. As she passed, Molly wrinkled her nose at Ash's visible new boots the prince acquired for her this morning. Though the top of the shoe hit mid-calf and was still fully covered by her split skirts, it made Ash want to tug the fabric higher. But she didn't. The embarrassment of the gesture outweighed any satisfaction Ash might get from needling the girl.

With a flick of his hand, Captain Forbs arranged the soldiers in a formation surrounding the prince and Molly. Ash urged Windrunner to join Prince Phillip, but Captain Forbs glared at her. He jerked his head forward. She was expected to lead again. At least this time, she wouldn't be afraid of slipping off her horse. Much to Ash's chagrin, Captain Forbs joined her in the lead, but his presence felt more supervisory than protective. The group rode at a quick pace out of the inn's yard and through the increasingly crowded streets. People were quick to move aside, however, when they noticed the royal banner of a golden unicorn rearing on a cobalt blue background. The standard was held aloft by the soldier behind Ash. He anchored the long pole in his stirrup through the town, but collapsed the rod into two parts and strapped it onto his saddlebags as soon as the group was back on open road and the party's pace increased to a trot.

At the end of the day, the horses' exhaustion and the difficulty of moving well in the dark forced the prince's party to make camp. Molly dismounted from her horse in a painful, slow slide. The young soldier who had helped her mount that morning steadied Molly when her knees wobbled as she hit the ground. Prince Phillip didn't offer assistance as he watched the scene with a slight frown. He was clearly not happy with the innkeeper's daughter. The search party was forced to an increasingly slower pace as the day wore on and Molly's energy flagged. Ash felt a mixture of pity and annoyance toward her. Molly had whined most of the day to Prince Phillip, and though he'd made an effort to cheer her, the slower pace and her unhappy attitude had finally sunk the prince into surly silence.

At their campsite the soldiers moved about with orderly speed, setting up tents, and making a fire. After Ash unsaddled Windrunner and brushed her down, she noticed Molly struggling to put up one of the plain khaki tents the soldiers had acquired from Hunnington.

"Would you like some help?" Ash asked and began stretching the thin waterproof material opposite Molly so it would pull tight. Molly tugged hard on her end, yanking the fabric from Ash's hands.

Ash put her fists on her hips, exasperated. "You may as well tell me." That startled Molly enough that she stopped spreading the fabric to look directly at Ash.

"What?" She seemed confused.

"What exactly is bothering you so much? You've been annoyed with me since we first met," Ash replied.

"I don't like traveling." Her small eyes squinted in accusation.

Ash tried not to let the glare bother her. "It was a long ride. I can cast a spell to help ease your pain if you like."

Molly drew back, her hand lifting in a defensive position. "No. Don't you dare magic me!" Molly's voice rose in pitch, fear reflecting in her small eyes. Ash sighed. She'd suspected Molly was one of those more fearful of magic than fascinated, but had hoped she'd been mistaken.

Ash held her hands up. "I won't do anything if you don't wish it. Look, I'm sorry that you were volunteered by your father to come on this expedition. I can't stand when someone tries to make decisions for me. But I still hope that we can become friends."

Ash began to pull out the tent corners again. She picked up one of the poles and looped it into a hole before lifting it to stand straight and hold the fabric high. She waited for Molly to copy the procedure for the other side so they could connect a rope and peg it into the ground letting the resistance hold the material up.

Molly paused before expelling a shaky breath and aligning her tent pole with Ash's. As soon as the last rope was secured to the ground, Molly strode away.

Molly headed for the campfire where Captain Forbs crouched near a pot of water placed over the flames. A bag of foodstuffs was placed to the side of the fire, far enough away to avoid any sparks. Forbs looked up as Molly approached.

"Well, come on. There are a lot of hungry men to feed," he said.

At first Ash thought he was talking only to Molly, but as Molly reached the fire and the Captain kept looking in Ash's direction, Ash's brow furrowed. "What?"

"It's time for you two women to get to work. Food doesn't cook itself." Molly turned to the bag with resigned slowness and began rummaging through it, looking for the ingredients she would need. Ash narrowed her eyes.

She was also surprised that she was still expected to act as a servant. Hadn't Prince Phillip hired her as a sorceress? They hadn't exactly covered what he expected from her, but she'd assumed she wouldn't be working as a maid. She'd hoped to be done with cleaning for others, and she'd never been good at cooking.

Captain Forbs straightened from his crouch, and Ash looked around for Prince Phillip. He wasn't anywhere in sight.

"Well, don't be useless. Bring over those fish." He pointed behind Ash to where eight fish were strung between two tents' poles.

She felt her brow spasm. She smiled and the stretch of it felt feral. "Certainly."

All the men knew she was a sorceress, but perhaps Captain Forbs needed a reminder that she had not been hired to be the maid. Snapping a spell in a vibrant staccato, the rope holding the fish broke free from the tent poles. Strung fish flew through the air toward the captain. Molly screamed before dropping to the ground, and Ash flinched. She'd momentarily forgotten about Molly's fear of magic in her irritation with the captain. Captain Forbs's mouth tightened in annoyance as he eyed the fish hovering a foot before his face.

Every man stopped what he was doing and stared at the floating line of fish. Out of the corner of her eye, Ash saw a few of the soldiers make a sign warding against evil. Ash cringed. She'd made another miscalculation, though she was happy to note that a few of the men looked fascinated rather than disturbed.

"Didn't you ask for the fish?" Ash widened her eyes innocently.

Captain Forbs snatched the fish from the air with a grunt of irritation.

Looking around at the still staring men, Ash began to regret her mischievous ire as she realized that her rash act might have negative consequences. Even with a sorcerer of their own, she guessed that not many of the soldiers had had a chance to see real magic performed. Her hasty act might have affected their opinion negatively since she hadn't thought to prepare them for the sight of floating fish. She should have eased the men into the image and presence of magic, but Captain Forbs had the ability to goad her into thoughtless action.

Prince Phillip appeared from out of the woods. Where he'd been, Ash had no idea, but he'd obviously missed her latest spectacle because when he noticed the stillness of the people around camp he paused. His green eyes flicked from man to man before landing on Ash.

"What's happened here?" Prince Phillip asked, still looking at Ash.

Ash spread her arms wide, a message of harmlessness and put a sheepish grin on her face. She met Prince Phillip's eyes and turning to include everyone, tried to undo the damage she'd done by letting Captain Forbs goad her. "Just a little magic show. Didn't Sorcerer Tioroso ever perform for anyone? A little levitation and I have a captive audience." She tried to invite others to smile with her.

After a heavy pause, Prince Phillip clapped. A few other soldiers joined in hesitantly, but the sound pattered pathetically like weak rain around the camp.

"This is a treat. Sorcerer Tioroso hardly ever performed, and even then it was only for the gentry. He felt that being a sorcerer and being a performer was not the same thing. It's kind of you to give a show to those who haven't had the chance to see magic before, but I think it might have caught them off guard." Prince Phillip's voice rang with forced cheer and sounded more like a command than commendation. The one or two Ash had noticed make the sign against evil shuffled their feet as if they wished they could leave.

"Well, perhaps I'll limit my shows from now on if no one is interested."

Prince Phillip nodded in silent command. Ash was relieved to note that at least one man looked disappointed by this decree.

"I suppose I'll help Molly with dinner. I'm starving." She walked to Molly by the fire, though she was still reluctant to surrender to Captain Forbes's definition of her duties for the expedition. "Though I have to warn you, I'm not very good at cooking. At home, Cook was always telling me that when it came to preparing food, I was a hopeless cause."

When Ash glanced covertly around, she saw that all the men had gone back to their tasks. Only Prince Phillip and Captain Forbs still watched her. Prince Phillip still looked worried, but to Ash's chagrin he did not state that cooking was not a part of her duties. Captain Forbs's expression froze Ash's hand on the food bag. His glare burned with anger. She'd have to watch out for that one. She'd thought he didn't care about using magic since he hadn't seemed to mind Sorcerer Tioroso, but maybe his dislike stemmed from the fact that she was a woman rather than that she was a sorceress. Whatever the reason, he seemed far too much like her uncle for Ash's peace of mind.

Chapter Eleven

The next day Ash consulted Prince Phillip's map to compare what her spell told her of distance and direction to the land's geography. Jane was still headed in the same direction, which would take her and her captor firmly into the barren wasteland of rocks before Spirit Mountain. When Ash told Prince Phillip this, his brows rose in surprise. Captain Forbs eyed Ash suspiciously as if he suspected she was leading them purposefully astray.

They set out early in the morning, but Jane was miles ahead. By the time they made it into the wasteland, Ash couldn't guess where Jane might be.

Ash was still worried enough about her fellow travelers' reaction toward magic that she didn't try any more pranks on Captain Forbs, even though she was sorely tempted. Though Ash wanted to do something to help Prince Phillip's men become more comfortable with the idea of magic, she found it difficult to talk to anyone since she was required to lead the way. She tried to fall back once or twice and engage Molly in conversation, but Molly wouldn't respond to any of the questions Ash posed throughout the day. Molly hadn't spoken last night as they prepared dinner together either.

Occasionally, Prince Phillip pushed through the guard surrounding him to ask her if Jane's direction had changed, but he never stayed to chat. Ash sighed and endured the swift, quiet travel.

That night they were able to stay at an inn. Ash didn't mind that she sat alone at a table to eat. There were musicians playing on a little stage in the corner of the room. It had been a long time since she'd been able to enjoy music, and so she soaked in the feeling of satisfaction she got from listening to the violin's sad clear notes soar through the air. Soon they twined with a cello and viola in harmony. Despite the melancholy melody, it wafted through her mind like a gallery of portraits portraying the beauty and happiness she'd once enjoyed. She thought of her father's instructions as he lay dying. She had to admit, she'd failed to keep her father's wish. Her uncle had beaten at least some of the brilliance out of her world. Years of work coupled with the yearning to run away had brewed an ironic bitter aftertaste in her soul of late that hadn't been there before. The music reminded her that lovely things still existed.

As she watched the mesmerizing movement of the bows back and forth across the stringed instruments, the edge of her eye caught movement. Someone sat across from her at the table.

"They play very well. I was thinking of inviting them to the palace for a performance after . . ." When Prince Phillip didn't continue, Ash reluctantly turned her eyes from the musicians to look at him.

"I know Lady Jane would like that very much. She is fond of music," Ash said.

"If we get her back." His eyes were on the musicians.

"We will. We gained ground today, and Sorcerer Tioroso is not doing himself any favors by going toward Spirit Mountain. He'll be trapped."

"Not if the rumors are to be believed."

"Rumors?" Ash asked. Prince Phillip finally looked away from the instruments to her.

"You're a sorceress and you don't know about the rumors of Spirit Mountain and the maze of Ketskatoret?" His eyebrows waggled teasingly.

Ash pursed her lips, feeling ignorant. "I never had a teacher other than my books."

"Truly? That's amazing. How did you ever manage to decipher the spells?"

"With a pronunciation chart." Ash waved this away, more interested in what Prince Phillip had said. "What are the rumors of Spirit Mountain?"

"It's said that when the sorcerers cast the great spell to banish all magical things from the land, all enchanted creatures that could crawl, walk, or fly fled to Spirit Mountain. A few people were still worried that the spell would fade and the creatures would come back. They crossed the rock wasteland to build a wall that would contain them on the mountain, but it proved unnecessary. Nothing was there."

Ash remembered the conversation from long ago with Lady Amelia. She'd said that all the creatures had disappeared into a land hidden somewhere in the country. She must have been speaking of Ketskatoret.

"Where could they have gone? There's no pass through Spirit Mountain." Ash leaned across the table toward Prince Phillip, eager for more. A flash of anticipation shivered through her. She'd often felt the same excitement when her father told stories. The thought of Ash's father strummed inside her in tune with the cello's minor whole note, coating her eagerness with a veil of nostalgia.

"The rumor claims that the passage to Ketskatoret is somewhere on Spirit Mountain's steep slopes. The maze's name is amazingly difficult to pronounce, probably because it originated from the language of sorcery. But the place, if it exists, is supposed to be the source of all magic." It was only when Prince Phillip sat back that Ash realized he had leaned forward as if telling a secret he didn't want anyone else to hear.

"If, for some unfathomable reason, it really is Sorcerer Tioroso who's taken Jane, then it's likely he knows where that entrance is and is planning to escape to Ketskatoret. Even if he is a sorcerer, it is still a dangerous place for humans to go. We would be mad to follow him." Prince Phillip stared unseeingly toward the string players, his shoulders slumped.

"There really isn't any doubt about who has taken Jane anymore. Both have traveled on the same path too long to dispute it." Ash tried to soften the words by touching his hand with her fingertips briefly.

Prince Phillip looked at the hand Ash had touched, straightened in his chair, and nodded to her. "I suppose there is very little room for doubt, but I hate to acknowledge it. There is another rumor about Spirit Mountain. I'm sure it just stemmed from fear, but it's said that one way a sorcerer could undo the banishment spell and overcome the requirement of thirteen sorcerers is to make a sacrifice."

Ash sat up as if someone had jabbed her in the back. "That can't be. I've never read anything about sacrifice in my books. That's not how spells work." Her speech started out impassioned with conviction, but became less sure by the end. In Ash's understanding of magic, sacrifice had nothing to do with spells. A spell's power and intricacy depended on specificity, diction, and concentration. Was there a different kind of magic that Ash didn't know about, a method not found in her mother's few books?

"Even if that was possible, I still can't credit Sorcerer Tioroso with such depravity. There must be another reason. He might have taken her for ransom." Prince Phillip sighed. "I know there are things he wants changed in our country that my father was unwilling to do before. It was part of the reason he started becoming so sullen and angry with us. With my fiancée as his captive, he has more bargaining power than before."

"Well, whatever the reason. It won't matter. When I compared the distance indicated in the tracking spell to the map, it showed that Lady Jane was still in the wasteland. If we hurry, we may be able to get to her at the foot of Spirit Mountain, before he has a chance to climb very far," Ash said. She wanted to reach out to him again but didn't.

Prince Phillip smiled wearily. "You're right. I'm not giving up. I hope you'll excuse my moment of melancholy."

Ash cleared her throat. "Certainly. Of course you'll have moments like that. She is your fiancée, after all," Ash said, to remind herself as much as to comfort him.

"How do you know Lady Jane likes music?" Prince Phillip asked suddenly, head cocked, green eyes staring inquisitively.

Ash didn't know how to respond. She'd spoken without thinking. Perhaps she should tell Prince Phillip who she really was. He didn't seem like the kind of person who would send her swiftly back to her uncle, especially since he needed her now to find Jane. But her position at Trebruk Manor could affect the prince's engagement and marriage to Jane once they got her back. It would be quite a scandal, one that Prince Phillip might not want to deal with and would rather sweep quietly under the rug.

"Tell me something, Your Majesty. How do you feel about the law that states a person of royal blood must marry someone whose family owns land? You obviously don't mind that she is from very low ranking aristocracy. Would you still marry her if her father had no land to his name as well?"

"It would be very difficult to do so. There would be a lot of opposition to the match. I've already slighted many nobles by choosing a lady of such low rank. If she had no land, it would be impossible. But she does, so that has helped smooth the way somewhat. You still haven't answered my question. How do you know Lady Jane?"

"Oh, we met several times in the past. She is not one to think herself above talking to a servant now and then." Ash decided it was safer to keep the truth to herself for now. Prince Phillip had already gone through a lot of trouble to make Jane his fiancée. He would probably not look on any further complications favorably.

"When she talks," Prince Phillip said.

Ash laughed. "That's true. I've never met someone so content with quiet as Lady Jane."

Prince Phillip and Ash shared a grin. After a conspiratorial moment, his expression wavered, turning uncertain.

"I should retire. This is our last chance to sleep in a soft bed. I want to take advantage of it," he said.

"Sleep well. I want to stay and listen to the music a little longer." Ash smiled, but she felt uneasy. Her situation was so precarious. So much depended on others.

***

As they left the inn in the morning, Prince Phillip sent a messenger pigeon to the palace to update the king on where they were going and how long their supplies would last without any complications. Prince Phillip explained to the group that he wanted to have support on the way if the need arose.

They entered the rock-strewn wasteland and kept their pace as fast as they could without hurting the animals. Despite their care, however, they had to stop several times to replace the horses' thrown shoes. One mare stumbled so badly on the slippery shale that she fell over. Her rider, the young man who often helped Molly, was able to throw his leg out of the way in time to avoid being crushed by the horse, but he sprained his wrist in the process. Ash hurried to be the first to him so she could wrap his wrist.

"What's your name?" she asked, watching his face closely as she gathered the bandage. His cheeks were free of a beard's stubble. Only his chin showed the shadow of blond hair. It seemed unlikely that he was older than seventeen.

"Brett Johnson, ma'am," he replied. His eyes flicked away.

"I'm no ma'am, Mr. Johnson." Ash laughed. At the sound of Ash's lighthearted chortle, Brett looked up and met Ash's eyes.

"No, miss," he corrected. Ash began wrapping the white cloth tightly.

She waited until he was lulled by the rhythm of the motion moving round and round before carefully speaking, her eyes on her work.

"Mr. Johnson, are you afraid of magic? Because if you are, I won't bother you further. But if you're not, I would like to offer a partial healing of your sprained wrist. I can't heal it all the way yet. I haven't mastered a spell of that level, but I can make a week's worth of healing happen in a day. I noticed that not everyone was pleased with my levitation display the other day, so if you would like to decline, I would understand."

She looked up to gauge his reaction. His eyes were wide. She thought he looked nervous but curious.

"Would it hurt?" he asked.

"No. It tingles a little, that's all. I've done it on myself countless times." She smiled conspiratorially. "I'm not always the most graceful person." His eyes lit at the sight of her smile, and his lips curved up shyly in response.

"All right. I'll give it a try." His voice wobbled a little, betraying the fact that he was still unsure.

Ash clicked the spell to heal his wrist, and the slight crease on Brett's forehead smoothed out.

"That's amazing," he whispered, a look of worshipful awe replacing the hint of fear that had been there before.

"See, magic's not such a bad thing, is it?" She patted the finished wrapping on his wrist. "I would keep this on for at least a day, just in case though. You can never be too careful." Standing, she walked over to Windrunner. A thorough check showed the mare that fell was no worse for the experience, and the soldiers were ready to depart. Ash eyed Windrunner's saddle with weary resignation before mounting and continuing on.

***

They gained ground on the sorcerer, but had still not caught up to him by the third day through the wasteland when they reached the foot of Spirit Mountain. Though the sunlight was weak, Ash wanted to spread her arms and soak it in joyfully despite the constant gnawing worry for Jane. Two days of moving at a frustrating careful trot through cloudy darkness and a landscape of desolate rock had depressed her. Few plants grew through the slippery shale, and what had managed to struggle through the layers of rock had pale whitish-yellow leaves reaching for a vanished sun with desperate sickly fingers. The green of the sporadic grass clinging tenaciously at the foot of the mountain was a balm to Ash's eyes, though the blades were still faded from the weak light.

There was a yell up ahead, and Ash looked to see a soldier leading two extra horses to Captain Forbs. The horses were still saddled, their blankets soaked with sweat. Their heads hung low and drying spit crusted the corner of their mouths around their bit, though they weren't breathing hard anymore.

"They can't be too far ahead." Prince Phillip urged his mount forward as if he would go immediately up the mountain but then reined his horse to a halt. "Unsaddle their horses and turn them loose. We'll have to leave them for now."

The soldier holding the horses' reins nodded and quickly got to work removing the gear. During the wait, Ash checked Jane's location as she looked up the slope. The incline started gradually, but Ash could see that the party would soon have to climb a steep rocky slope with sparse clinging bushes and stunted trees. Jane could only be a few miles higher, but the mountain's rugged outcroppings jumbled on top of each other like messily piled blocks hid her from view.

The slope was gradual enough at first that the group could ride mounted for half a mile, but soon they reached a point where the path became too steep. Captain Forbs ordered the party to dismount. The supplies were redistributed in packs made for the soldier's backs. Even Ash, Molly, and Prince Phillip were required to wear one to ensure there would be enough supplies for each person. Captain Forbs assigned one of the soldiers to take the horses back to the other two at the foot of the mountain where the sparse grass clusters were most abundant.

Ash saw him turn from the soldier and unfortunately caught his eyes as she removed some of the food rations from her pack to make room for her sorcery books.

"We only have a week's worth of supplies for each person. Food is more important than books. Leave them with your horse's packs." The scar on Captain Forbs' lip stretched with his frown.

"I need them." Ash tried to fit the food rations back around the books, but had no luck.

"You won't need books where we are going," he scoffed. Prince Phillip walked up behind Captain Forbs and looked down to where Ash still tried to rearrange things to make more food fit inside without bursting the bag's seams.

"I have to agree with Captain Forbs. We'll need all the food we can carry. By packing your books, you're wasting precious space."

Ash stopped fiddling with the bag and looked up. "I will need them. I tracked Sorcerer Tioroso's position just this morning and found him with Lady Jane further up the slope. I am not as knowledgeable as he is in sorcery. I sometimes need to consult them to make sure I am pronouncing words correctly. And if there is anything that I must do that is beyond what I currently know, I will need these books. Prince Phillip, you suggested that Sorcerer Tioroso is taking Lady Jane to Ketskatoret. If that's true, then we'll be entering a place steeped in magic. I hope I never have to take a single one of my books out of this bag, but if I don't know what to do, they are the only source of information on magic that we have." Ash closed her pack and stood. She shrugged the heavy uncomfortable straps onto her back.

"Carry them if you must, but it's still a loss of food that we can't ignore." Captain Forbs' bushy eyebrows drew down and he scowled.

Ash shrugged indifferently. "I'll eat less. I'm used to it." She turned slowly, adjusting to the weight on her back, and began climbing.

The rest of the party soon followed. Ash felt sorriest for Molly. Though Molly had kept her distance from Ash, she'd still noticed Molly's discomfort as the group traveled over the past few days. They took very few rests. Ash could tell that her father had exaggerated Molly's expertise. Though she could keep her seat, she was unused to riding for long periods of time. She walked gingerly every time she dismounted, and Ash often saw her wince when her mare trotted.

Ash tried to offer Molly a spell of healing again, but after the hovering fish incident, Molly had avoided Ash as often as she possibly could. Even in their shared tent at night, Molly made sure to turn away and feign sleep as soon as they laid down, so Ash left Molly alone.

As they climbed, Molly's winces turned to soft groans. Brett stayed close to her, helping her at difficult passages, but she still soon trailed far behind the rest of the party.

Since there was only one climbable path, Ash wasn't required to lead. She stayed in the middle of the soldiers between Prince Phillip in front, and Molly and Brett in the back. Her sorcery books in her pack weighed her down, and the thought of less food to replenish her energy was depressing. Her saber also slapped uncomfortably against her thigh as she climbed. It was almost enough to make her wish she'd relinquished her weapons to Captain Forbs when he'd asked. Still, Ash was willing to put up with a lot of discomfort before giving him the satisfaction.

When the group stopped for lunch, Ash waited for Molly to catch up. She staggered into the small clearing breathing hard. Looking around for a place to sit, Molly seemed to give up. She dropped to the ground. Brett gave her a little pat on her back before moving to join the rest of the soldiers.

Ash crouched down in front of Molly so that Molly couldn't avoid looking at her. Handing her a piece of the hard travel bread made up of nuts, oats, dried fruit, and honey, Ash said, "I didn't mean to scare you with the fish the other day. We got off to a bad start, and I didn't make it any better. I don't know if Brett told you, but I did help his wrist heal faster. I can help you as well, if you'll let me. I hate to see you suffering, especially when there is something I could do to prevent it."

"I don't like magic." Molly flinched away from Ash.

Ash took a calming breath. "I can understand that it might seem strange and a bit frightening, but I would never do anything to hurt you."

"How am I to know that? I don't know you. You just showed up with the prince one day, and everything's gone bad for me since." Molly's voice wheezed in a tired whine. Ash tried not to roll her eyes. She was attempting to be sympathetic, and showing her exasperation would not help convince Molly to trust her.

"I suppose that's true. But, Molly, if I did anything harmful to you, there are twenty other men with us here who would quickly punish me for it. Also, if you weren't present, I would be the only woman among many men. What would people say?" Ash widened her eyes dramatically, hoping she wasn't overacting.

"That's true. You need me." Molly sighed, closing her eyes as if the effort to keep them open was too difficult. The travel bread sat uneaten in her lap.

"We need each other. So isn't it in my best interest to help you?" Ash cajoled.

"Seems to be." Molly barely opened her lids to peer at Ash apathetically.

"There you go. Would you like me to speed your healing? I can't do anything about your fatigue, but at least you won't be so sore."

"Yes." Molly exhaled. Her small eyes showed relief and a little guilt. Ash snap-clicked the words to the spell and watched the girl's face relax.

"Finish eating. You'll need the energy. We still have a lot of climbing to do before we catch up to Lady Jane," Ash said.

Molly just nodded and focused her attention on the food before her. When Ash stood and turned, she saw Prince Phillip watching her from a rock where he sat eating. She wondered if he'd heard what had transpired. He didn't seem to have the same reservations about magic as the others did, probably because of how often he'd been around Sorcerer Tioroso. Still, the sorcerer had betrayed him. Had that betrayal stained his opinion of magic like a drop of black dye corrupting crystal pure water? Nervousness caught in her stomach, and a fluttering bounced around in her chest as she quickly turned away to eat her own small meal.

Lunch was over all too soon, and the soldiers quickly packed up and began climbing once more, leaving Ash to follow with Molly and the ever-compassionate Brett Johnson in the rear.

Ash was intent on lifting her pack on her back when the load suddenly lightened. Someone helped her position it more securely in place. She turned, surprised to find Prince Phillip.

"Thank you," she said.

"It's no problem. May I walk next to you for a while?" he asked.

Ash felt her face heat. "I suppose."

"I'd like to ask you about Lady Jane, get your advice on what we should do."

"Oh, of course." Ash reddened even more, feeling like an idiot for temporarily thinking he just wanted her company.

"How far ahead of us is she?" he asked.

"She's high above. The extreme angle of the slope is making it hard to tell distance." Ash looked up, as though she could see Jane if only she squinted hard enough.

"I suppose I understand the difficulty. I wonder, however. How is she climbing so well? And why would she?"

Ash considered his questions as she navigated over a boulder toward the smoother path.

"Sorcerer Tioroso could be floating her up the mountain," she told Prince Phillip after he'd rejoined her on the wider trail. "Do you know how much weight he can levitate?"

"I couldn't tell you for sure. I did see him lift a deer once. It had a thirty-four inch girth which would make it about 120 pounds. Though the deer only hovered a foot off the ground as we traveled back to the palace."

"Lady Jane is probably around one hundred twenty pounds. He could be floating her up the mountain as he climbs on foot. If he was able to levitate both of them, they would be further up the mountain by now," Ash said.

"Are we catching up at all?" Prince Phillip asked.

Ash looked back down the mountainside where Molly, with the help of Brett, was only then reaching the boulder that Ash and Prince Phillip had long since scaled.

"I don't think so."

Prince Phillip followed Ash's gaze. "Could you levitate Molly up the mountain just as Sorcerer Tioroso is doing for Lady Jane?"

Ash laughed, wiping the sweat from her forehead as she maneuvered around another large boulder blocking their way. "Sorcerer Tioroso is much more advanced than I. The most I can lift is around forty or fifty pounds. Miss Molly is slim, but not that small."

"There must be something we can do," Prince Phillip huffed. Ash looked over to see his copper eyebrows furrowed in frustration. Drops of sweat beaded his brow, and Ash felt a sudden flash of a strange sort of envy toward her cousin. She wondered what it would be like to have someone care so much about her well-being.

"I could float Molly's bag next to me up the mountain. I really wanted to do that for my own bag, but refrained because of my ill thought out prank the other day. If you think it wouldn't bother the men too badly, I don't think her pack is beyond my abilities."

"I'm sorry about the way some of the men acted when they saw you do magic. Not all of them are suspicious of it. You just caught them off guard. If we'd had time, I would have stopped at the palace to gather only those who aren't superstitious. We'll just have to help the wary ones come to terms with it as we travel."

Prince Phillip climbed in companionable silence for a while, and Ash thought he'd discarded the idea of helping with Molly's pack until he added, "I think it's less that they are afraid and more that they just aren't used to spells. When Sorcerer Tioroso deigned to perform at court, it was well attended. He was constantly hounded by demands for performances. It might help the men better prepare for what may come later within Ketskatoret if they are exposed to a small thing like a bag floating up the mountain now."

Ash stopped to wait for Molly to catch up. She was surprised to see Prince Phillip stay with her rather than going to the lead to warn the others of what she was about to do. Molly was grateful to free herself from her load. The spell of healing had helped the girl, but Ash wasn't aware of a spell to increase Molly's endurance. After the bag was floating next to Ash on the trail, they resumed climbing. There was a marked difference in Molly's speed, but Molly was still exhausted. She soon fell behind. Brett dropped back to keep pace with her.

Ash looked back briefly to see Brett boost Molly so she could reach a handhold and climb over an impeding boulder. "Mr. Johnson is a really nice boy."

Prince Phillip looked back as well. He laughed. "Boy? He's nineteen. I doubt you are much older."

"Really? He looks younger than that. You're right, I suppose I can't really call him a boy then," Ash conceded.

Prince Phillip continued to look at her. "Well?" he asked finally.

"Well what?"

"How old are you?" Prince Phillip's eyes caught hers in question.

Ash gasped dramatically and raised her hand to her heart. "Your Majesty, what a thing to ask a lady."

He laughed again, his eyes crinkling. "I thought it was only offensive to ask if the lady in question was over thirty."

"That's only if the lady in question is married. If she is unmarried, society's definition of old suddenly becomes much younger," Ash quipped.

Prince Phillip stayed stubbornly silent as they climbed.

"Oh, very well, I'm twenty. Too young to be free, but still edging past the tender age of eligibility."

"As a year older, I consider myself to be well within the range of acceptable bachelorhood." He flashed Ash a jocular smile.

As Ash paused to rub an ache in her leg, she regarded Prince Phillip with one dubiously arched brow.

"I refuse to believe you are unaware of the unequal standard for men and women regarding what is deemed an acceptable age to remain unmarried." She straightened and continued climbing.

Prince Phillip let her catch up before he matched her pace. "I know there is for the gentry. I didn't think it mattered so much for commoners." Ash jerked, her heavy pack almost unbalancing her. She'd forgotten briefly that Prince Phillip thought her a maid. She quickened her climb, passing Prince Phillip while she composed herself.

"It still matters, just not for the same reasons," she said over her shoulder.

"Oh? What's different?" he asked, coming even with her again.

"Most of the time, a genteel lady does not have any other option but marriage. Her beauty and ability to charm are therefore linked to her age. The longer she must search for a husband, the more her desirability drops, so the age considered past prime approaches much more quickly than a gentleman since he is not dependent upon marriage to survive. A common woman, however, is free to earn her way in the world, but at a price. The work is often taxing, wearing her down years before her time."

Ash studied her hands, noticing anew the calluses and swollen joints. Even if she never scrubbed a floor again, they would never be as graceful as they had once been. She looked up to see Prince Phillip regarding her. Her arms dropped.

"A common girl has a small window of opportunity before the constant grind of work eats at her vitality and drains her optimism, as well as any beauty she might possess. Some seem to think that if they can marry and move away from working for the gentry to work their own land it would make life better. I am not sure if I agree, but I hope some find fulfillment in independence."

"Is that why you quit?" Prince Phillip asked.

"To marry and escape to a farm with my handsome beau?" Ash laughed. "If I had someone waiting for me when I ran away, why would I bother climbing this mountain?" Though the air was crisp, sweat soaked her clothes. She raised her arms slightly to let the cool air flow under her armpits.

Prince Phillip's smile made his green eyes seem brighter. "You enjoy the exercise?"

Ash glared. "Amusing."

That night the group crowded close together under an overhang. The tents were too heavy and cumbersome, so they'd left them far below with the horses, only strapping the tightly bound bed rolls to the top of their packs. Despite the fire, Ash felt the chill of the high mountain air creep into her bones. The waterproof bedding seemed as thin as tissue paper. Ash slept next to Molly and a soldier whose name she didn't know. Molly rolled away from her as she usually did, but Ash thought it was probably more from habit than a wish to avoid her. The soldier was careful to stay as far from her as the limited space would permit. She hoped he did it for propriety's sake, but the wary look on his face before he lay down suggested that he may have been remembering Molly's bag levitating up the mountain and into the camp before Ash finally cut the spell and let it drop to the ground. She smiled at him tentatively and was relieved to see an answering nod before he closed his eyes to sleep.

Chapter Twelve

The cold clung to her the next day even as sweat beaded her brow from the effort of climbing with a fifty-pound pack and maintaining the spell to levitate Molly's bag beside her. Mid-morning, Ash decided to check Jane and Sorcerer Tioroso's position, hoping they had stopped their upward progress. She halted in surprise. Molly's bag dropped to the edge of the path on the brink of tipping over and rolling down the mountain. Brett, who was not far behind, jogged forward to drag the bag more firmly away from the edge. Molly soon drew even, her panting breath making a visible white cloud in the chill morning air.

"What's wrong?" Brett asked.

Ash didn't hear. She snapped the spell to check on Jane and Sorcerer Tioroso again. "I don't understand," she said to herself.

"What don't you understand?" Molly's breathy annoyed tone recalled Ash to her surroundings. She focused her eyes distractedly on Brett and Molly beside her. Molly's freckles stood out from the heat of her face like brown speckles on a crimson egg. Brett shivered, his brown eyes opened wide in question. Ash turned, looking up the trail to see how far behind they were from everyone else.

"I need to talk to Prince Phillip. Mr. Johnson, would you try to catch up to him and tell him . . . tell him . . . just say I need to speak with him." Brett nodded and moved ahead while Ash clicked the spell to lift Molly's bag. "Let's go," she said to Molly.

Molly glared but seemed too tired to argue. Instead, she turned back to the steep incline with weary resignation. Ash sighed and followed. She tried to stay behind, but was too anxious, and soon passed Molly.

Ash maneuvered over a rocky rise and a turn in the path before she saw Prince Phillip and Brett resting on a rock, waiting. The prince sat straight, despite the heavy weight on his shoulders. One leg was propped on the stone, with his arm draped gracefully at rest on his knee. The pose emphasized the curve of his biceps and the sculpted line of his torso and leg. It was beautiful. Ash's breath caught for a moment before she forced herself to exhale, to meet his eyes.

"Jane isn't on the mountain anymore," Ash said as soon as she was close enough to be heard.

Molly's monotonous crunch-crunch of steps behind Ash halted.

Prince Phillip stood, a marble statue come to life. "That isn't possible," he said.

"I haven't even told you the impossible part yet." Ash pointed to a large group of thick dark clouds that the traveling party would soon come even with. "They're over there where those clouds are."

"Are you telling me Jane and Sorcerer Tioroso are in the middle of the sky?" Prince Phillip's copper brows rose, his emerald eyes searched hers in delicate disbelief.

It was the first time he'd ever shown doubt about her abilities, and it pinched a knot in her stomach. "Yes, and they keep moving away from the mountain above the wasteland we just came from."

"If he was able to levitate both himself and Jane this whole time, why did he even bother climbing the mountain? Did he do it because he knew we were following and wanted to delay us here?" The knot inside Ash loosened. The tilt of Prince Phillip's head was inquisitive, but not accusing.

"I don't think so. Didn't you say before that you thought Sorcerer Tioroso might seek to escape to Ketskatoret? What if the place isn't in the mountain as we thought? What if it is next to it?" Ash rubbed her cold fingers together as she pulled her eyes from the prince to the wafting white mist spread thickly above, wishing her eyes could pierce through the haze.

"In the clouds?" Molly scoffed from behind her.

Ash had almost forgotten she was there. She turned to Molly and shrugged uneasily. "It's possible."

"How is that possible?" Molly's voice was shrill, her face red from more than overexertion.

Ash lifted her hands helplessly. "I don't know." Ash turned to the thick veil swirling white, then back to the prince. She grinned. "Let's go see. It shouldn't be too much higher before we reach where they crossed over into sky."

Prince Phillip's mouth opened a little in surprise. It twitched closed and he nodded. "We should at least try to find the entrance."

Molly's eyes were wide with horror. Brett flicked his gaze upward uneasily as everyone readjusted packs and continued up the mountain to find the door into the maze of Ketskatoret.

★★★

They found it just as the day turned to evening. The brisk air had dissipated briefly during the day, but as night drew in, cold gathered and hung in a wet chill. The path flattened out to a rock shelf like a natural stone stage. On the southeastern side of the mountain hidden from the earlier path, and bisecting the bumpy stone floor, a river of snow-melt cut through the rock, a blade of moving water that sliced through the stone and rocketed off the edge of the platform in chilly white ribbons through a haze of mist. The watery streamers fluttered and reached through the air as if trying to touch the rock archway sitting in the middle of the sky. It stood just beyond the spray's reach, framed by jutting toothlike pillars. Clouds surrounded the door. It looked like a madman's painting of a path connected to nothing, leading into darkness.

The soldiers gathered at the edge of the river just before the waterfall. Several made the sign to ward off evil as they gazed on the impossible sight of a doorway suspended by nothing more than mist. Ash shivered, unable to take her eyes from the empty space of air between the cliff's edge and the entrance. She felt a sinking sensation pull on her insides.

"How do we get to the door?"

Ash jumped guiltily at Prince Phillip's words. She turned to see him and Captain Forbs regarding her steadily, waiting for an answer she didn't know.

Her shoulders slumped. "I'm not sure. Give me time to think. We shouldn't attempt anything until the morning anyway. It's getting too dark." Prince Phillip inclined his head in a gesture that seemed too confident and too sure of Ash's competence. She felt wry amusement when Captain Forbs's mouth tightened, his eyes glaring suspiciously. At least she would live up to someone's expectations. The two men left her to stew in helpless thoughts as they prepared for sleep. Come morning, the party would expect a solution that she wasn't sure she could provide. Crouching at her pack, she retrieved her books and moved to one of the fires set up by the soldiers. She was determined to find an answer by the light of the flame, even if it took all night.

She drifted off with a book still open before her, the blaze snapping as it consumed the spindly wood until there was nothing but coals.

***

Her own shivering woke her at dawn. The fire was out, but someone had closed her book and draped her thin blanket around her sleeping form. Ash looked around at the lumps of sleeping bodies, wondering who had performed the kindness. Next to her lay Molly, and Ash smiled to think that with all the space available on the flat rock around the fire, she'd still chosen to sleep next to Ash. She wrapped the blanket around her pulled-up knees as she gazed contentedly at the river.

The sun reflected strangely off the water's farthest edges as it fell over the cliff face. Across the way, the path inside the floating door remained shadowed. As Ash watched, the glittering water almost looked like it framed a bridge spanning from the cliff to the door. She stood excitedly. The blanket fell forgotten to the ground as she rushed to the water's edge. Snapping and clicking the spell to see through illusion, she was relieved to see that her theory was correct. Above the water's roaring free fall, spanning the narrow river on both sides stood a bridge reaching across to Ketskatoret's entrance.

Ash hurried back to her books, looking for the spell words that would make the bridge discernible to more eyes than just hers. She was flipping through pages with no success, trying to think how to change the spell to an indicated number of people and the needed verb conjugation when someone above her cleared his throat. She looked up to see Prince Phillip blocking the sun behind him so that all she could see was the silhouette of a man with a blazing fiery halo.

"Did you find anything that could help us?" he asked.

"There is already a bridge in place. I just don't know how to make it visible to all of you. I thought I'd seen the correct wording for the spell somewhere in here before, but I might have to refer to the dictionary in order to change the spell I already know to something that will work for everyone. Though I'm hoping it's already a rote spell I can just memorize instead of having to hobble the wording together myself. Those hardly ever work as well. I just can't seem to find it." Ash blushed, realizing she'd babbled a much longer explanation than the prince could possibly have wanted.

Prince Phillip turned his head to look at the water plunging from the mountain, and the sun slid over his features, grazing his cheek with gold, bleaching the emerald of his eyes to a pale luminous green. She tore her gaze from the prince and turned back to her book, mumbling out loud to help herself focus on her book rather than the distracting silhouette of the prince's face. "I'm sure it must be near the spell that lets me see through illusions . . . hmm." She cursed very softly under her breath so the prince would not hear. "I don't see it here."

Prince Phillip leaned toward Ash to better read the words, his elbow brushing her shoulder.

"I can understand the explanation for the spell, but the spell itself is indecipherable. How do you read it?" He turned his head to look at her. The sun illuminated the curve of his inquisitive brow. His face leaned closer, and she felt flustered enough by his proximity to forget his question. Instead, she stared stupidly back at him, frozen. The golden glow lighting his cheek flushed with the red of sunrise, and he moved back. His retreat gave Ash enough time to gather her wits.

"I've memorized most of the pronunciations, so it's just a matter of matching the right sounds to the symbols, as well as getting conjugation and intonation correct," she said, directing her words to the book now lowered to her lap instead of to the price.

"Oh, uh, well, I'll let you get back to it then." He cleared his throat before straightening and quickly striding toward Captain Forbs.

Ash watched his swift, sure gait move across the solid shelf of rock. She tried to suppress the memory of disturbing delight at finding Prince Phillip's face so close to her own. Instead, she reminded herself that her reaction had made the prince so uncomfortable he'd fled. She felt a twang of embarrassment like a violin string plucked too hard, before turning her eyes back to look for a spell.

Dropping the book with a bit more force than was good for the binding, Ash stared at the way the mist swirled up and around the bridge almost outlining its edges. Of course! She'd been so set on finding the spell that would unmask illusions that she hadn't even thought about how she could just cast an exact illusion of the bridge right on top of its spell of invisibility. No one need know that they weren't seeing the real thing.

She stuffed her book back into the bag and strode to the edge of the bridge making the long vowel sounds, pops, and click-tock shush of the spell. An illusory bridge overlapped the hidden structure, becoming visible to all of the traveling party. Soldiers stopped and turned to regard the sudden structure. A few still made warding signs. Ash was beginning to recognize the soldiers most prone to touching their hand to ear and eye before throwing the evil behind them every time she did magic. But most of the soldiers seemed less bothered by her magic than with the sight of the bridge straddling the sky.

She had to admit the bridge was an intimidating sight. Though the base near the mountain was wide enough to span the water, it soon thinned to an arm's length in the middle, only broadening out slightly to connect to each end of Ketskatoret's entrance. There were no railings, nothing to stop someone who slipped from falling hundreds of feet to where the water crashed against huge sharp boulders below.

"Pack up, we're moving out!" Captain Forbs bellowed to be heard above the water's roar.

Soldiers began to move methodically, if a little slower than usual. When all the men had gathered at the foot of the bridge, Captain Forbs surveyed the group. He narrowed his eyes.

"Where's the other one?" He flicked his head crossly toward Ash, and at first she was unsure of what he meant. There was a general shuffle of confusion as everyone looked around to determine to whom Captain Forbs was referring.

Ash searched for those most familiar to her. Brett Johnson was standing among a group of other soldiers Ash had yet to meet individually. Prince Phillip stood next to the Captain, who was still glaring accusingly at Ash. It wasn't until she turned away from the bridge, back toward the dead fires of their abandoned camp that she noticed Molly still sitting on the ground where they'd slept, her arms crossed in a silent declaration.

"Get moving, woman. We're losing ground!" Forbs shouted to her.

"You've all lost your marbles. There is no way I'm crossing that bridge. I quit," Molly said shrilly.

The men glanced around at each other, then to Captain Forbs and the prince. Captain Forbs's jaw clenched in impatience, but when Ash turned to Prince Phillip to see his response, she found him gazing at her with a panicked expression. He looked away and strode to Molly.

"Please don't quit, Molly. We need you, and it would be dangerous to travel back down the mountain alone." Prince Phillip attempted to help Molly rise from her stubborn sitting position, but she refused to be moved, even by a prince.

"You don't need me. You need her." She flung her arm accusingly toward Ash. "I'm just here to keep things proper. Well, proper can hang. It's not worth my life. My father never would have sent me if he knew where you were going." Though the opportunity to put his daughter in the prince's sight had been slightly self-serving, Ash agreed that no caring father would wish his daughter to enter Ketskatoret, no matter whose company she would be keeping.

Prince Phillip stood helplessly above Molly. He shot another anguished glance Ash's way, but jerked his eyes back down when he saw Ash watching him. She walked over to join him next to Molly.

"It's all right, Your Highness. There is no need to force Miss Molly to travel with us. I'll still continue on without her. I appreciate your concern for my reputation, but we are entering a dangerous place. I also would not wish to risk Miss Molly's life just for the sake of propriety." Ash squatted down to look Molly in the eyes. "Thank you for traveling with me so far. Take your time climbing down the mountain. I've heard it can be trickier going down than coming up, so go slowly and rest often, all right?"

Molly looked down, color staining her cheeks, but Ash put her hand on her shoulder.

"There's no reason to feel guilty. Be safe." She stood and addressed Prince Phillip. "Is there any way one of the soldiers could stay with her? I realize that isn't proper either, but I would feel better knowing she isn't going down the mountain by herself."

Prince Phillip regarded Ash in silence. His eyebrows bunched, and his mouth opened, then shut, then opened as if he wanted to speak, but kept changing his mind. Finally, his warring features cleared. He nodded sharply and turned to the men.

"Once we enter Ketskatoret, there is no telling what magical challenges we may encounter. If there are any of you who feel that I am asking too much of you to enter, you may accompany Miss Molly back to the foot of the mountain and await our return there. I will not hold the choice against you, and no one is allowed to accuse those who stay behind of cowardice."

There was a rustling of feet as soldiers looked everywhere but at each other. Ash wondered if anyone would come forward. Brett took a baby step toward Molly, indecision clear in his pinched mouth and lowered brows. But despite what Prince Phillip said, the men's masculinity would be called into question if they didn't continue to stay and protect the prince.

When no one moved toward Molly, Captain Forbs finally assigned two men to stay with her. Both looked immensely relieved. Ash noted that they were men who'd made the sign against evil every time they'd seen Ash do magic. She was grateful to see them stay behind as well. Her opinion of Captain Forbs raised a notch.

After the matter was settled, it was decided that most of the men would cross first to scout out the area on the other side before Ash and Prince Phillip followed with a rear guard. The men looked fragile crossing one by one over hundreds of feet of air. Ash's stomach clenched just watching. When the signal was given and it was finally her turn to cross, she inched her way along the bridge, trying to look down at the path before her without letting her eyes stray to the drop below.

Her locked muscles, cold from prolonged tension, relaxed when she reached Ketskatoret's archway and traveled inward through the path's low ceilinged cave that smelled of stale, wet earth. Light dimly lit the passage, and Ash found it was because the rocky tunnel didn't last long before it opened up to where the soldiers waited. She gasped and flinched back toward the cave mouth. Across from her, a twenty-foot wave poised just at the breaking point. It took her a frightened second to realize that the wave was made of stone, forever frozen in place. It extended to the right and left of her in a continuous arch so far Ash couldn't see the end.

She turned around and saw that the entrance's cave was a tiny hole in an identical wave of stone opposite the first. Only about ten feet of sky showed through each crest. It looked as if the two waves would crash into each other at any moment. She lowered the arms she'd automatically lifted to brace for impact. Around her she noticed the soldiers nervously eying the stone's looming tips.

"Which way should we go?"

Ash jumped and turned to see Captain Forbs scowling at her. The man always seemed to be in such a foul mood, especially around her. It was like a bothersome itch that Ash really wanted to scratch. She longed to do something that would wipe the sour expression off his face, but there was no time for mischief. She sighed and clicked the spell to check on Jane's location.

"I'm afraid she's that way," Ash said, pointing directly opposite Ketskatoret's entrance into the stone wave.

"That's no help," he accused. "Which path will take us to her, the right or the left?" His foot tapped impatiently. Ash wanted to stomp it to stillness.

"I don't know. My spell doesn't work that way. It only tells me where she is now."

"Useless. Should have left you with Miss Molly." He threw his arms up in a sharp dismissing gesture.

Ash's opinion of Captain Forbs sank again, her own anger simmering in response.

"Such a quick judgment. I may not be very helpful now, but that doesn't mean you won't need me later." *You stupid, blind bat*, she added silently.

Prince Phillip approached, obviously having heard at least part of the conversation. "Please excuse Captain Forbs. This narrow canyon is making everyone jumpy, I think." He turned to Captain Forbs with a small calming smile. "We can direct our best trackers to look for clues on the ground to determine which direction to travel."

"The ground's solid rock, hardly any dirt anywhere to leave a track. You know that as well as I do. You're an excellent tracker yourself," Captain Forbs grumbled.

Prince Phillip nodded, giving Captain Forbs a rueful grin, as if aware that his flimsy distraction wouldn't work with the captain.

"We'll just have to choose one and hope for the best then. Let's go left. If I'm wrong, there's no one to blame but myself," Prince Phillip said amiably, but his eyes were fixed on Captain Forbs in silent command.

"Yes, Your Highness." Captain Forbs bowed stiffly and moved to direct his men to head north along the path.

The company continued on for half a day, heads bent instinctively, before the wave-like rock turned more normal in appearance. The rock stopped curving inward, and instead stretched straight up in streaks of gray, black, and burnt umber. Trees grew high above on the ridges. Ducked heads lifted, and everyone walked with wider, more confident steps until they came to a fork in the canyon. After consulting with Ash, Prince Phillip chose the path that seemed to lead closer to Jane's location, but when a three pronged fork appeared soon after, Ash saw Prince Phillip's confident veneer begin to crack.

"I can see now why they call it 'The Maze of Ketskatoret.'" Prince Phillip laughed, but it sounded false.

"So long as we keep track of which paths we take, we can always retrace our steps, Your Highness," Ash said.

"But how much time will be lost?" he burst out, his jovial mask breaking completely.

"I think we should worry about lost time only if we are forced to go back. For now, we should just keep moving forward." Ash wished she could pat his shoulder to comfort him, but didn't. It would be too awkward.

He took a deep breath and straightened his shoulders. "You're right. Let's take the second right, and see where that takes us."

Captain Forbs set a quick pace. The swift march did not stop the low-pitched murmurs from circling among the men as they walked. The indecipherable words jumbled together like skittering pebbles pushed off a dangerously steep path. Ash was relieved when the canyon they traveled through finally opened up into a valley. There were still rocky ridges enclosing the wide meadow, but the sight of open space and vegetation cheered her.

As they neared, Ash saw the whole valley was covered in beautiful white flowers unlike any she'd ever seen before. Long stems led to a head of graceful petals that wobbled in the tiny breeze as if nodding their heads. The flowers spread in a solid quilt of white and green impossible to walk around. Ash winced as she watched the soldiers trample through the flowers into the field.

A few feet in, as Ash followed in the wake of crushed beauty, the breeze dropped, and a hush fell. Even the sound of the soldiers trampling through the flowers seemed muted. Ahead, a green mist rose from the ground and hovered just above the flowers before them. Indistinct, ghostly shapes rose to the surface. They stretched, almost separating, then melded together and fell back into the mass. Ash thought she saw a wing rise and fall. A large face with squashed features popped up and then dropped back into the shifting surface.

Captain Forbs yelled for the men to fall back, an activity quite a few were already doing with alacrity. Sound washed from the mist in the same manner as the appearing and disappearing pieces of creatures. Ash heard the familiar consonants and click-pop of the language of sorcery before the roiling green mist sank back into the ground. As the fog sank, however, Ash and the prince's party rose. Men screamed as they found themselves hovering above the ground unable to go anywhere no matter how much they kicked and twisted. They were trapped in the air, weightless.

Chapter Thirteen

Unlike the men, Ash found the sensation of floating appealing. With the pressure of gravity gone, her whole body felt light. Stroking through the air experimentally didn't get her anywhere, but she was happy to note that although everyone was hovering out of the ground's reach, they were not rising any higher.

"Ash, is there anything you can do?" Prince Phillip shouted across the twisting men after they had calmed down enough to stop yelling. A few seemed to realize that their frantic squirming wasn't doing them any good. They stilled and floated in dejected slumps. Others still kicked around, refusing to give up. Small rocks from the ground and broken flowers had risen as well and hovered around the soldiers. The entire scene was surreal, and almost laughable. Strong, striking men suspended in the air with delicate flower petals floating around them like confetti.

"I think the spell was directed on this area rather than on us specifically. If that's the case, it's just a matter of moving beyond the affected ground."

"Can't you just undo it?" The prince swiveled his body, trying to face Ash but wasn't having much luck turning himself around, so he was forced to strain his neck to see her.

"No. It's too big." Ash pointed to the floating debris extending to the other end of the valley up until the pass leading out. There, the loose grass and pebbles stayed solidly on the ground. "We'll have to get over there somehow. Everyone protect your heads. With all the rocks hovering around us, this may not be a pleasant experience."

Ash spoke the spell for the most powerful breeze she could muster. Rocks and grass flew toward the passage, hitting the men as they passed like a mini tornado full of painful stings, but the barrage was soon over. The larger hovering people moved more slowly. The wind pushed Ash like a giant's fist, firm against her body. One by one the men reached the edge of the spelled area and dropped back to the ground, some more gracefully than others. Ash was disappointed to see Captain Forbs land in a crouch, one hand on the ground for balance. Ash's landing was less dignified than she would have liked. She was concentrating on making sure her spell would last long enough to get everyone across and forgot to pay attention to her own position. Her back hit the ground and she felt the breath whip out, leaving her gasping.

Sucking at the air produced no results until someone sat her up. Oxygen rushed in and she gulped and coughed. It took her another several breaths to realize that someone was patting her back. She looked over to see Prince Phillip crouched beside her.

"Thank you," Ash wheezed. She cleared her throat and tried again. "Did everyone make it?"

"Yes, but only just. The wind stopped as soon as you fell on your back."

Ash was embarrassed to know he had seen her graceless drop.

"I think we should move out of this valley as fast as possible. That mist might come back and do something else," Prince Phillip said. He kept his eyes averted from Ash's blushing cheeks as he stood and helped her up.

The soldiers practically ran out of the valley. The narrow passage soon opened to a forest of tall spindly trees. It felt as if the plants had grown up, but forgot to fill in, like a youth hit with an unexpected growth spurt, awkward and ungainly. The leaves on the trees looked brittle from lack of water. Many had fallen to the ground. They crackled loudly underfoot. Ash checked Jane's location and soon everyone was moving on a direct course to her. This bit of good news was tempered, however, by a new wariness in all as they wove through the forest's lanky tree trunks. Ash just hoped no more maze-like cliffs would bar their way. The air was dry and unseasonably warm, much warmer than the maze's canyons, as if it only took a few feet of space to change climates.

Ash thought she saw a creature with horns hop behind a pile of leaves, but it was so fast she wasn't sure if her eyes were playing tricks on her. When nothing untoward happened before it was time to make camp for the night, Ash felt herself relax a little. She heard a laugh from the campfire as she searched her bag for her meager meal, and she was glad for the comforting banter from the soldiers. The only sounds they'd made marching through the trees had been the crunch of leaves.

She slept at the edge of the camp. It was better for propriety's sake, but it still made her feel vulnerable. If anything attacked in the night, she would be the first to go. Though she slept fitfully, nothing bothered the camp. In the morning, a beautiful whistling trill woke her from her troubled sleep. She heard the tinkle of glass and was confused. Had she fallen asleep while helping Jenny clean the crystal? The crackle of leaves beneath her reminded her that she wasn't in the manor anymore. She wasn't even on earth, technically. For a moment, she lay with her eyes closed wondering how Jenny and the other servants of Trebruk manor were doing. Was her uncle still searching for her, or had he given up? She shivered and rubbed her eyes, wiping out the image of her uncle from her thoughts. The chime of glass sounded again. She sat up and looked into the trees to identify the source. A gasp burst from her mouth.

Perched in the branches sat a crystal bird. She would have thought it a spun glass creation if not for the fact that it hopped from a low limb to a higher one. Its wings flashed as they beat. She could see through the delicate wings as if they were glass. The body of the bird was more opaque, but still sparkled like a glacier in sunlight.

Throughout the morning she and the men marveled at the crystal birds whenever they were glimpsed in the trees. Prince Phillip came up beside her.

"Beautiful, aren't they?" he asked.

"Yes, Your Highness." Ash thought back to what she knew of the magical banishing. It wasn't much, only the things her father had mentioned, as well as what she'd learned from Lady Amelia that terrible day she'd discovered her father's illness. They'd had no books on the subject. Still, it was Prince Phillip's father who had ordered the banishment. Ash wasn't sure what Prince Phillip felt about the topic, so she tried to tread carefully. "It's hard to imagine that these small creatures could be at all dangerous." Ash's neck ached from looking up in the branches as she tried to keep the glittering birds in sight.

"It's a pity that when magical things were banished, the birds had to go as well," he said.

"The creatures that started all the fires were called Crystalicas, weren't they? My father told me a few stories of fires my mother had to put out because of Crystalicas. I wonder if these birds are the creatures of which he spoke. They don't seem to be doing any harm. Maybe it was a different magical species. Father said that the sorcerers only knew a spell to banish all magical things so even the good were forced to leave with the bad."

Prince Phillip's eyes dropped from the branches to Ash, but she kept her eyes searching through the parched leaves wrestling with the movement of the glass birds flying from one branch to another. Their flight dislodged yellow and brown foliage and the leaves fell like dirty snow to the ground. "Was your father a sorcerer, or did you just decide to learn sorcery on your own?"

"No, my mother was, but she died when I was born." Ash dropped her gaze.

"I'm sorry."

"Me too." She met his eyes and shrugged. "Tell me about life at the palace. What do you do all day?" Ash asked, eager to change the subject.

"Much of my time is spent in study of one kind or another. I am let out occasionally for an outing or two, but I'm often forced to take silly courtiers along to, as my father would say, 'develop relationships.'" His grin was sardonic.

"I suppose I don't envy you the last part, but I would love to have more time to study. To have a tutor would be heaven." Ash sighed wistfully.

"I don't think you would find it quite so heavenly if your father was the king. He is convinced that he is going to die at any moment so he's constantly testing me on my knowledge, assessing how well I've managed the courts on my days of duty, and pushing me to get married as quickly as possible so that he can, 'bask in the joys of being a grandparent.'" The last was said with an obvious imitation of someone else's voice.

Ash snickered, but cleared her throat and frowned seriously when the prince glanced at her. "I hope he isn't seriously ill."

"Not at all. The healers all say he is in perfect health. Honestly, I think he is pushing me to learn how to rule so that he can retire and go enjoy himself, leaving me to suffer instead." Prince Phillip winked.

Ash smirked. "I'd still love to have a tutor, at least as far as sorcery is concerned. Did you hear the spell the mist cast that made everyone float? I wish I could hear that repeated once or twice more. There were sounds in the spell that I've never heard before. I must have been deciphering some symbols wrong." Ash grinned in anticipation. She couldn't wait to try implementing some of the odd variations she'd heard in her spells. She was sure it would make a difference in their effectiveness.

Prince Phillip's eyes twinkled with amusement as he watched, but he didn't comment on her childish excitement. "What was that fog? It seemed as if creatures were rising out only to fall back inside," he asked.

"I've never read anything about it. I don't have that many books to refer to, and it's like wringing water from stone to get people who were alive during times of magic to talk about it. Aren't you the one with palace resources at your fingertips? Surely you learned something about the magic that used to be so prevalent during your history studies." She raised a brow in silent challenge.

Prince Phillip's red brow copied Ash's gesture in mocking rebuttal. "My tutor never seemed to get around to teaching about the magical aspect of our history. He mostly made me study the wars and reigns of kings and what they did during their reign, that sort of thing."

Prince Phillip cocked his head. "It's strange. My father has never encouraged me to learn that area of study either. It sounds extreme, but I think the magical banishment did more than just exile the creatures. It's as if it pushed away the very idea of magic. Don't you think it unusual how hard it is to get most people to speak of the time of magic? Since we entered Ketskatoret I've felt a difference in my own willingness to dwell on the subject. You'd be surprised how few courtiers ever asked to see Sorcerer Tioroso perform magic."

"That is an interesting theory, though I haven't noticed any change in myself. It might help explain why people hardly ever talk about magic even though the banishment was not that long ago. You didn't even sneak a peek at any of the magic encyclopedias? Hear stories of magical creatures? Anything?" Ash's teasing air vanished as she considered how odd his ignorance really was. She'd had only her mother's spell books to read, none of which covered more than magical language, but Prince Phillip had been surrounded by unlimited resources. Yet he hadn't used them. Maybe he was right. Perhaps there had been more to the banishment than simply expelling magical beings.

Prince Phillip flushed, snapping Ash back to their conversation. "When my required reading and lessons were over I was always so glad to be done I'd rush to escape outside. I didn't stay in the library any longer than absolutely necessary. I'm not sure if I can use that as evidence of my theory, however." He brightened. "I did talk to Sorcerer Tioroso sometimes, though. He told me a few things."

"Most of the soldiers in our party look younger than thirty-five, other than Captain Forbs. They would have been too little when magic was still around to remember much of anything, but I still think we should ask everyone what they know. We might be able to better prepare for what we encounter next."

"Their knowledge may not be reliable. When people actually do speak of magic, they have a tendency to exaggerate what really existed before in order to make a better tale," he said.

"We don't have many other resources at the moment." She felt her slow smile curve her lips, lift her cheekbones, and seep into her eyes. Prince Phillip watched her mouth as if watching a lion stretch: part fascination, part apprehension, and a bit of guilt.

"I'll speak with them to see what they know," he said quickly. He nodded and then strode ahead to consult with Captain Forbs. Ash watched him leave, confused at his sudden departure, but thought it best to follow up on her idea to pool the traveling party's knowledge.

She jogged to catch up with Brett so she could ask him what he might know, choosing the amiable young man because he seemed more openly curious about magic than the others. He strode through an open meadow. A thin veil of clouds dimmed the sun on his face. Before she reached him, he stopped and shielded his eyes, looking at something in the sky. She was struck by the oddity of shielding one's eyes when the sun was covered, but was distracted from her thought as other soldiers halted to stare upward as well. Ash followed their gaze, and saw a flock of crystal birds glittering in the cloud-muted sky.

There were thousands of them flying in a large cluster. They moved like a cloud of diamonds winking and flashing beautifully until the cloud blocking the sun moved.

All watching turned away as the sun hit thousands of crystal wings, magnifying the light to a blinding intensity. Squinting her eyes, Ash saw the light reflected from the birds fall on some bushes at the edge of the meadow near where she stood. A wisp of gray curled up from the leaves, and Ash smelled the stinging scent of smoke. There was a snap, and then a whoosh as the bush caught fire. It spread to the dead leaves littering the ground, and exploded into an instant inferno. Hot orange fingers scrabbled over the meadow's dry grass.

"Run!" someone yelled. Ash wasn't sure who it was. She was too busy trying to pump her legs as fast as her heavy pack would allow. She stopped a moment to catch her breath and snap the spell to levitate her pack, though it was still strapped to her back.

A soldier she didn't know grabbed her arm. "Come on!" he shouted over the increasing roar of the spreading fire. Her saber slapped and caught in the fabric of her split skirt, slowing her down. Smoke billowed around her in a suffocating wall of stench, burning her throat as she gasped for air. The soldier who'd grabbed her let go and began to draw ahead even with his pack still heavy on his back.

Ash looked over her shoulder and saw the flames spreading backwards the way they'd come through the forest. The thin spindly trees toppled like dominos. Fire nipped at her heels through the meadow, threatening to ignite her skirts. The only way to go was ahead, but it, too, was forest. They would soon be overtaken by the flames. The others ran, and she followed as closely as she could. As she entered the forest, Ash looked back one more time at the burning grasses and realized that no one else was behind her. The fire would take her first if she wasn't fast enough to keep in front of the swift-moving wall devouring the bushes and trees behind her.

Chapter Fourteen

Ash desperately looked around for a place to run to that would be protected from the flame's boiling fury, but she couldn't see anything past the trees. Creatures that resembled the animals Ash knew, but with odd differences that she didn't have time to examine, ran around her and up the slight rises in the land to the left and right. Ash followed those headed left. She'd lost track of the soldiers. The slight rise turned steep, the trees more sparse, but the consuming fire grew closer. She could see farther ahead as the trees became less dense, and aimed for where a rocky slope thinned the plant growth to sporadic patches.

Before she reached it, however, a mist rose from the ground. It roiled and shifted just as the fog in the valley had. An insubstantial arm was exposed before dropping back into the gauzy depths. Strange cylindrical leaves emerged and sank. The side of a head, an oddly elongated dog's muzzle appeared swiftly before being swallowed again. Despite the encroaching fire, Ash stopped, unwilling to enter the mist unless she had no other choice. The heat pushed at her back, so she stumbled forward until she stood an arm span from the cloud of swirling, half-formed creatures.

The familiar yet foreign pops, whistlings, and smackings that formed the sentences of a spell rumbled through her like an earthquake, vibrating through her bones. As it sounded, Ash recognized the meaning as it rolled over her. She glanced frantically around at the ground, ran to a body-length toppled log, and grabbed on tightly. The whoosh and crackle of the fire behind her was replaced by a thunder that steadily increased in volume to a crashing roar.

Ash turned her head toward the fire and watched a wall of water swallow the trees, snuffing the flaming forest as if it were an insubstantial match. She only had time to take a deep breath of air before the water engulfed her, sweeping up the log that she clung to with a blow that tried to steal her held breath.

She tumbled in the riptide of new water, eyes shut tight, legs wrapped around the log. Once, her log smacked into something solid before it was swept past, scraping Ash's hands in the process. Her saber caught, the blade twisting away with the log, tightening her belt in a bruising grip until the leather snapped and both saber and pistol spun away into the roiling depths. Ash felt her lungs tightening, straining for fresh air, but all she could do was hold on and hope that her log would lift her to the surface soon.

A back current hit, stopping the torrent's forward rush. Ash spun and almost lost her grip, but the water quickly calmed, and the log finally floated up to the surface. She gasped and coughed while trying to suck in air as quickly as she could without choking on water. Her whole body trembled. Ash was glad that she'd emerged on top of the log rather than underneath it. She didn't think she would have had the strength to pull herself atop otherwise.

For a long moment she just sprawled spread eagle on the tree trunk, her face pressed to the rough bark as she sucked in breath after breath. Never before had the decaying smell of sodden wood been so wonderful. When she'd calmed a little, she carefully sat up, looked around, and found herself at one end of a lake. At the edges, only the trees that had been highest up the slope were completely free of the water. Near Ash, the top branches of a tree were still exposed, but the trees that had been further down the slope were all completely hidden by the churned water's depths.

Ash paddled awkwardly past the barely exposed branch tops, past trees reaching higher and higher out of the water until she could clamber off the log and wade to dry ground. She dumped her soggy pack and sank to the earth, resting her palms against its comforting solidity. But the comfort of safety leached away. She was alone, and she was the only person in her traveling entourage who would have understood any part of the mist's spell. A knot of worry clenched her sore middle when she thought of where the others could be. A flash of Prince Phillip's green eyes appeared in her mind, and her heart flapped anxiously in her chest like a trapped bird flinging itself against a cage's bars. She clicked the tracking spell to find Prince Phillip and relaxed when she sensed him farther back on the slope, slightly higher up.

She searched for Brett Johnson and Captain Forbs, relieved to find them also above the water level and on her side of the new large lake. Even if she didn't like Captain Forbs, she didn't wish him harm. With an embarrassed sigh, she admitted to herself that she didn't know any of the other men well enough to search for them. She would just have to find those she could and figure the rest out later.

Feeling a bit shaky still, she opened her pack to assess the damage. Water had seeped through, but the oiled pack had done a better job than she'd hoped of keeping the contents from getting completely soaked. She took out her books, and upon finding the edges wet but the inside still dry, decided it would be better to find Prince Phillip and the others before taking the time to dry them out. She grabbed some damp jerky and repacked her books before shouldering the bag and searching for Prince Phillip.

When she found him, he was completely dry and pacing in the company of eight other soldiers. He spotted her and stilled. Their eyes met, and Ash saw his mouth form her name, though no sound came out. Her heart gave an uncomfortable jump and sped up as he strode purposefully toward her.

"I'm so glad you're here safe. I need your help to find everyone else." Ash's rapid heartbeat stuttered and slowed as she realized that Prince Phillip was only glad to have her skills returned, not her person.

"I. . ." She stopped to clear her throat. "I'm glad you are all safe as well. It seems you were fast enough to avoid the water entirely. Perhaps the others were also as fortunate."

"It appears that you were not," Prince Phillip said, looking her over.

Ash touched her wet hair self-consciously. Much of it had come free from her braid and been swirled into a knotted mess by the water. She looked down to see her maroon riding habit, no longer dripping, but muddy. Her assessing gaze rose back up to Prince Phillip. He was still watching.

Her lips twitched up, self-deprecating. "It seems I am the slowest runner."

Prince Phillip's smile mirrored hers. She looked away in order to stave off any bothersome heart palpitations.

"Captain Forbs is just a little farther over, if you'd like to go find him," she said. Prince Phillip glanced around at the soldiers watching and nodded, taking a step back.

"Lead the way."

Captain Forbs had most of the men with him. With Captain Forbs's help getting the soldier's names, Ash was able to locate the few remaining men still separated from the party. Only two others had been caught in the water when it hit. Unlike Ash, they'd been forced to abandon their packs in order to swim to the surface. One man had a nasty gash on his shoulder from striking the branches of a tree as he was whipped through the water. The other had been close to a firmly rooted trunk near the edge of the water. He'd been able to climb the submerged tree to the dry upper branches, and hang on till the water calmed and he could swim to shore.

The man who'd been hurt submitted distrustfully to Ash's spell of healing. He grunted in surprise and shrugged his shoulder experimentally before giving Ash a reluctant nod of thanks. By the time everyone was gathered and put in order, the sun was setting. They made camp above the new lake and left decisions of where to go next for the morning.

Ash was exhausted. She couldn't bring herself to care that despite the fact that everyone had suffered through the catastrophes together, the soldiers shot resentful glances her way as if she was the one responsible for all the magical mishaps that kept occurring in Ketskatoret's maze.

She ignored them and settled herself a few feet away from the group as she had the night before. Even as she tried to disregard the stares, she couldn't discount them fully and felt uncomfortable sleeping any closer. Before this disastrous day, she'd really thought that most of the soldiers were coming to accept her magic with, if not excitement, then at least equanimity. Their blame was like a needle's tip on skin just before it pierced. Ash tried to catch the eye of Anders, the soldier she'd just healed, but he avoided her glance. She turned away, stung, and pillowed her head with her pack.

The sounds of settling quieted as the men fell asleep, but Ash couldn't calm her mind enough to let sleepiness take over, despite her exhaustion. There was a soft rustle as someone settled to the ground behind her. She rolled over. Her eyes, which were finally drooping with weariness, popped fully open.

"Prince Phillip." She couldn't hide her shock.

"I've been known to go by that name." His mouth quirked up as he placed his pack in front of her.

"What are you doing here?" After she spoke, she realized how stupid her question was.

He smiled and gestured to the pack. "I was hoping you could help fix my pack. One of the strap's binding is unraveling."

"Are you sure that's wise?" Ash flicked her gaze to the soldiers farther away. All were unmoving lumps, and it was hard to tell if any had noticed where the prince had gone.

Prince Phillip laughed quietly. He followed her glance toward the sleeping soldiers but said, "I fail to see how fixing my pack so that we can travel could be considered unwise."

Ash scowled at his obvious attempt to dodge her meaning but then couldn't help but smile back. "That isn't what I was referring to, and you know it."

Prince Phillip's smile dropped. "Would it be better for me to avoid you completely, implying that I approve of laying the blame for our disastrous two days in Ketskatoret on you?"

"I know you don't." Ash looked down and awkwardly sat up. She reached for her own bag to get out the small sewing kit inside and pulled his pack closer.

"I'm the one who decided which direction to take in the canyon that looked like a wave after all." Prince Phillip wrapped his blanket around himself as he watched her retrieve needle and thread. "I thought you would do a spell to fuse it back together."

"Too tired to form the words correctly," Ash said absently as she focused her concentration on holding fatigued hands still enough to thread the needle. It took four tries before the thread went through the eye of the needle.

"You know, separating yourself from the group doesn't help."

Prince Phillip yawned and rearranged himself so that he was leaning on his propped hand.

Ash didn't look up from slowly weaving the thread through the strap. Her arms felt heavy, and each stab of the needle through cloth was difficult. She didn't think she had, or at least she hadn't tried to, but she wasn't as conditioned for hiking as the soldiers, and had often lagged behind.

"What else can I do?" she asked instead, avoiding pointing out the difficulties of his suggestion.

"Try getting to know them. You had to ask Captain Forbs for Anders's and Patterson's names so we could find them earlier. We've been traveling together for days now. Why didn't you know their names already?"

Ash felt a prick of guilt that turned quickly into annoyance. Her fingers stilled as she looked up.

"I have tried talking to them when I can catch up to them. It was about as effective as chasing a cat." She stopped, finally noticing how close Prince Phillip's lounging form was. She swallowed uncomfortably and wondered if she could somehow scoot back another foot without him noticing. Not likely. But even Ash, who wasn't one to care much for social etiquette, felt there was something decidedly improper in the way he leaned casually beside her.

"Cats are often standoffish at first but can become great companions with a little patience and diligence." His voice was soft, and Ash could not help but think he resembled the cat he spoke of, his voice a purr, his body relaxed with the loose grace of a feline at rest.

She quickly lowered her gaze back to her sewing. "I'll try, but there is only so much I can do with no reciprocity on their part." Even as she complained of their lack of effort, however, she remembered Brett's kindness. She also recalled that it had been Patterson who had urged her to run faster during the fire before they'd lost each other.

"I'll help out with that as much as I can." Prince Phillip yawned again, and Ash heard him adjusting his position, but she didn't look up.

"Thank you."

After that Prince Phillip was quiet. Concentrating on the in and out motion of her needle helped Ash forget he was near. Her head bobbed as she fought to stay awake and finish, but her fingers stalled their motion, and she slowly slipped down to the ground next to the bag. The earth was suddenly too soft and inviting to resist.

* * *

The rising sun and an aching back woke Ash. She opened her eyes to find Prince Phillip across from her, separated only by his bag between them. After her initial shock at finding him there so close, she studied him as he slept. The light freckles were more visible at this distance and made him look youthful, innocent. She watched as his chest moved evenly in and out, before a guilty feeling of voyeurism made her sit up and turn toward the soldiers to see if anyone had noticed she was sleeping next to the prince. With any luck she could move away before the others noticed.

She stopped mid-crouch. The soldiers were gone. When she spun, she saw that the lake was also missing. Where they'd been was only air. Prince Phillip and she lay only feet away from a jutting cliff's edge. They weren't completely trapped. Behind Ash, the slope where they'd lain the night before looked just as it had, leading off in a gradual descent. But before her, the earth had split and fallen away in the night without making a sound.

Her eyes scanned the scene, but her brain refused to acknowledge the surreal sight as truth. She sat frozen, uncomprehending for several seconds. "I must be dreaming." She heard her own voice as if from outside her body, but the sharp jab of a rock pushing through the fabric of her dress into her knee convinced her that she was not.

Adrenaline rushed through her, washing away her immobility, and Ash scuttled over to Prince Phillip to shake him, her motions jerky and panicked. He startled awake.

"Ow. What are you doing?" he asked, rubbing his shoulder as he glared at Ash in sleepy confusion.

"I think they might have fallen."

Prince Phillip's eyebrows bunched. "Are you feeling all right?" he asked slowly, his voice soft as if he were trying to calm a wild horse.

Ash didn't notice. She hurried to the edge of the cliff, careful to roll forward to hands and knees and crawl to where the land dropped away, checking each time she moved forward that the earth would not crumble beneath her. Behind her Prince Phillip cursed.

"What happened?" he asked.

She didn't answer, too intent on gazing over the drop-off to the undisturbed forest several hundred feet below. She slid back from the edge several feet before standing to face Prince Phillip.

"Are they . . . ?"

"No. They didn't fall. It's as if the land where we slept rose up several hundred feet and moved to a new location." Ash brushed the dirt of her split skirt to hide her shaking hands.

"Can you find them?" he asked.

"Oh, of course." She swallowed, her mouth dry. "Of course," she repeated more firmly before clicking the spell to find Captain Forbs and all the soldiers she knew.

"They're all still grouped together, but are miles and miles to the west. I can sense them moving, so I think they're all right." Ash sighed as she dropped the spell. She looked at where Prince Phillip paced in a tight two-step back-and-forth motion. As if he sensed her regard, he stopped and looked at her.

Ash shrugged and tried to laugh. The sound that emerged was nothing like laughter. "What should we do?" Another thought hit her. "What if they think I kidnapped you? You fell asleep next to me after everyone else was already sleeping."

"They won't," he said, but he didn't sound sure. "We'll go find them." Prince Phillip began pacing again.

"And Lady Jane?"

"We can only do one thing at a time, and I worry about my men being without even the meager protection you afford."

Ash stepped back, struck, a pang of hurt rising up from his thoughtless words. What stung the most was the revelation that Prince Phillip did indeed feel, at least partially as his soldiers had, that Ash was to blame for the magical happenings that they'd been forced to endure in Ketskatoret. If not directly, then indirectly because of her lack of sorcery skills.

Prince Phillip halted, his eyes widening as he realized what he'd said. "I didn't mean to imply . . ."

She turned away to shrug on her pack. Without looking at him, she marched past "His Royal Highness" down the slope. "It's true. I still have much to learn of sorcery." She paused, turned, and looked him in the eye. "But remember who it was who insisted that we follow Lady Jane and Sorcerer Tioroso into Ketskatoret." She turned her back and walked away.

He didn't let her get far before his stomping angry steps drew even with hers. "I didn't realize what we would face. So much about magic has been lost since the banning. How was I to know?"

"You've seen what Sorcerer Tioroso can do. You must have had some small idea of what it would be like here." Ash glared at the ground, her pace quickening.

"Please." Prince Phillip's laugh was harsh. "There is no comparison to what he can do and the destruction that ghastly mist creates or even the blasted birds. It's a hundred times more powerful."

"How soothing for you to divorce yourself from all responsibility by blaming me and my 'meager protection.' I suppose I should have known better than to believe your words last night when you said that you didn't blame me," Ash spat.

Prince Phillip grabbed her arm, jerking them both to a jarring halt. Ash narrowly avoided stepping in a muddy puddle. "I don't blame you," he said. She began to relax, her taut arm still in Prince Phillip's grip. "I just wish you . . . we knew more." Prince Phillip winced, and Ash jerked her arm free.

"Why you pompous . . ." Words failed her for a moment until an idea struck, and she felt an evil gleam light her soul that must have been reflected in her eyes.

Prince Phillip took a step back, hands raised as if to calm her. "Don't do anything rash."

Ash smiled the smile that every servant at Trebruk manor dreaded. She sauntered a step forward, head cocked invitingly. "What can I do, Prince Phillip? After all, my skills are so meager." Her voice dipped and rose with exaggerated humility.

Prince Phillip watched Ash like a moth fascinated by the sparkling flames of a fire despite the growing burn. "I was wrong to say that."

Ash waggled her finger. "No, no. No need to take it back. We both know the best I can do is only one thousandth of what this crazy land can. Ketskatoret can swallow us in tons of water to create a lake. All I can do is make you dirty." Ash clicked a spell. The water and mud from the puddle next to Ash and Prince Phillip rose into the air and hovered a split second, before dumping the whole muddy mess onto Prince Phillip's head.

The prince gasped and spit mud. He looked so shocked Ash couldn't help but laugh. His eyes shot to her and narrowed.

"Find that amusing, do you?" His tone warned Ash, and she took a hasty step away, but it didn't help. He dropped to the still muddy ground where the puddle had been, took a handful of muck and flung it. It hit her in the chest and splattered upward onto her face. She couldn't stop a surprised shriek from bursting forth.

Prince Phillip laughed. "It's not so funny when it's you covered in filth, is it?"

"Why you!" Ash scrabbled for the ground so she could lob another glob his way, but she was too slow. This time the smack of wet slimy earth hit her on the side of the head, getting in her hair. She reached the puddle and scraped up a big wet clump of earth, but Prince Phillip caught her hand. Crouched as they were, packs still on their backs, his movement threw them both off balance, tumbling them side-by-side into the sludge.

That didn't stop Ash from smearing her gooey contents onto Prince Phillip's already coated hair. "Ha!" she crowed before squeaking as Prince Phillip deftly caught both her hands with his own and held them in a surprisingly strong grip. She couldn't get purchase to wiggle free because her pack was wedged uncomfortably between her and the ground. Prince Phillip smiled wickedly as he transferred both her hands into one of his, reached down with the other to grab more mud, and smeared it into her hair. Cocking his head, he used his filthy fingers to paint a streak across her brow and both cheeks.

He leaned in close, conspiratorially. "You are not the only one with the power to get someone dirty."

A giggle erupted from Ash, and before she could stop herself she was laughing uncontrollably. Phillip chortled along with her. Ash was laughing so hard she felt short of breath and tried to roll over to her stomach so she could move from her awkward position under her pack and stand back up again. There was a pressure holding down her legs and arms. Prince Phillip still sprawled where he had tackled her as he laughed.

Ash's chuckles began to peter out as embarrassment replaced humor. As Ash's laugh faded, Prince Phillip calmed as well. The two looked at each other, still breathing hard, legs and arms tangled. A hint of red peeked through from under the cracking layer of mud on Prince Phillip's face.

"Uhh . . . I'm sorry." He tried to untangle himself, but his foot slipped on wet earth, and overbalanced by his pack, he instead fell on Ash's chest with a small oomph. Prince Phillip jerked up and rolled ungracefully to the side before kicking to his hands and knees and standing up.

Ash couldn't help it. She laughed again. He looked so silly, like a flopping fish on a bank, and she felt just the same as she tried to flip to her side so she could stand. Her guffaws were making it difficult, which just made her laugh harder.

Prince Phillip didn't join in, but he watched with an amused, partially exasperated smile for a moment before standing over her and offering a hand to pull her up. She grinned, standing before him with their hands still clasped. Her grin was a shield of good humor, but he kept holding her hand and looking at her with a strange expression. Ash felt her shield begin to slip.

"I've never met anyone like you," Prince Phillip said. His voice was too soft. She pulled away and turned to start walking.

"And you aren't likely to ever again," she called over her shoulder.

She kept ahead of Prince Phillip, needing space to let her tangled and unwanted emotions cool. It would take them at least a day and a half to reach Captain Forbs's men, and that was if there were no unexpected delays because of landscape changes, or disastrous events brought on by the mist. What was she going to do alone with Prince Phillip for so long? She had to admit to herself that the longer she spent in his company, the harder it was to remember that he was Jane's fiancée. It was wrong of her to feel a flutter when he held her hand or looked too long in her eyes. Impractical too.

The slope dipped into a tiny valley before ascending to a small grassy hill. The trees had dropped away as they descended, and the farther they walked, the more the landscape turned to open grasslands with mountains only far in the distance. Even the hills began to get smaller and smaller until they were walking on a flat plain. Prince Phillip seemed content to follow behind. The land rapidly transformed around them as if they were traveling on a miniature planet, fitting all types of topography.

Ash gazed ahead, marveling that the sudden flatness of the plain let her see so far. She squinted and stopped walking. A small green blotch rose up at the edge of what she could see on the plain. Prince Phillip paused beside her.

"Do you see . . . ?" Ash pointed to the smudge that was already falling back into the earth.

She heard Prince Phillip catch his breath. "Oh no."

"I can't hear what it did. It's too far away." Ash looked around helplessly. She wasn't sure what she was looking for, but all she saw was very flammable grass surrounding them on every side. There were no rocks for shelter, no logs for floating, and they didn't even know what was coming.

Prince Phillip gripped her shoulder, but his eyes were still focused on where the mist had appeared and disappeared. A thick dark haze stretched across the horizon.

"What is that?" Prince Phillip asked.

"It looks like a brown cloud."

"We may not need to worry since it's so far away," he said, but his eyes remained fixed on the mass as it seemed to separate into dots, some as small as a pin-prick, some as big as a thumbnail.

"We still have to travel that way." Ash watched the dots grow until the largest were as big as coins and the smaller had become the size of a small pearl. "It's getting closer."

"But what is it?" Prince Phillip leaned forward as if that would help him decipher the shapes.

Ash squinted and burr-snap-clacked the words of the spell to be able to see greater distances. She gasped.

Prince Phillip tore his eyes away from the speckles to look at Ash. "What is it? Your face has lost all color."

"They're boulders speeding through the air toward us. I can't tell proportions for sure, even with the spell, but some are at least as large as a cottage."

Prince Phillip frantically searched the ground around them, but Ash knew he'd find nothing more than she had. "We could run for the trees that we passed earlier," he suggested.

"I don't think we have time, and even if we reached the trees, it wouldn't be enough to save us. The boulders would smash the wood to splinters." Ash threw off her pack, ripped open the top, and yanked her books out, heedless of the rest of her supplies tumbling to the ground in her haste.

"Can you transform the rocks into something harmless?" Prince Phillip asked.

"I haven't mastered transforming things as dense as a rock, not to mention rocks as large as houses," Ash said as she flipped through the pages of her magic book.

"Then what are you going to do?"

"Figure out how."

"In the few minutes it takes for the rock storm to reach us?" Prince Phillip's voice was incredulous.

"That's the plan."

"Well, it's a terrible plan," Prince Phillip said loudly.

Ash's trembling fingers found the page she was looking for. She looked up. "Do you have a better one? No? Then be quiet so I can concentrate," she snapped, nerves getting the better of her.

She sounded out the spell that she'd never been able to master before. The sounds caught in her mouth, and no matter how many variations she tried to make for the snap noises, she knew she wasn't getting it right. Her shaking hands made it hard for her to follow the written line.

"This isn't going to work." Ash looked up. The largest rocks speeding toward them were the size of horses.

Prince Phillip dropped beside her and gripped her freezing fingers. "Look at me," he said when his grip failed to distract Ash from staring fixedly at the approaching deadly storm. She tore her eyes away from death to meet his, expecting to see accusation in their depths. Instead, they were intense, focused.

"You can do this. Is there any other way than transforming the rocks?" he asked.

"I . . . I don't know. Maybe." Ash glanced back at the rock storm. The boulders were floating even though they were moving at high speeds. She might be able to try something else. Ash yanked her hands out of Prince Phillip's and began flipping through pages again, looking for the levitation section. The green mist had actually helped her. Because she'd heard the spell's sounds of levitation in the meadow, she was certain she would be able to emulate them in order to make at least one stone drop to the ground. The question was how big of a boulder would she be able to drop. It needed to be large enough to shelter Prince Phillip and her from the rest of the onslaught.

She clicked the spell to levitate some dirt before her, and then carefully followed the word variation in the book that was meant to undo an even larger levitation. The dirt crashed to the ground with enough force to make a shallow crater. She turned to Prince Phillip.

"I have a plan, but it will go against instinct." She paused to gauge his reaction, and when he didn't flinch she continued, "We'll have to put ourselves directly in the path of one of the larger boulders, and wait until it is very close before I try undoing the rock's levitation spell. I've never done a spell this big before, even if it's just a spell of negation. There's a chance that it won't work. There won't be any time to get out of the way and try something else."

"It's our only hope." He nodded encouragingly at her.

The danger of the situation skittered through her stomach like spiders as she strained to think of an alternate solution.

"We could try to shovel out a hole with our hands and lie in it so the rocks would pass overhead," Ash suggested desperately. She looked at the hard packed earth, held even more firmly together by the dried yellow grasses' roots. Ahead, the boulders were the size of carriages and ponies. She thought about suggesting they dodge through the onslaught, but the rocks were too thick. As they neared, Ash could see even smaller fist-sized rocks within the mass. There was no clear path through, even if they tried weaving around the rocks.

In answer, Prince Phillip shoved Ash's things quickly into her pack. "I think we should head for that boulder there." He pointed to one of the largest rocks leading the storm.

"How about a slightly smaller one?" Ash asked as Prince Phillip helped her shrug on her pack and they began trotting to intercept the building-sized rock hurtling toward them.

"Anything smaller wouldn't be able to withstand the hundreds of similarly sized boulders pounding its rear once it's grounded. If we're going to die anyway, let's not make it because you succeeded in dropping a rock for shelter, but failed to make it big enough to resist rolling on top of us when it's hit by the other stones."

"Well, that's helpful. Now I feel so much better," Ash panted beside him.

"You can feel better after we live through this," Prince Phillip quipped. They stopped in the path of the house-sized boulder. Ash thought it was beginning to look more like a small castle. The stone was gray granite with one side sheared almost flat. The other sides curved in lumpy, uneven bulges like a poorly sculpted bear at rest. As she watched, the bottom edge of what could have been the bear's back paw hit a small rise in the ground. The lopsided weightless stone spun crazily.

"You have to do it now. Otherwise, even if it does drop to the ground it won't stop rolling before it gets to us," Prince Phillip watched the boulder warily.

Ash took a shaky breath and shoosh-snap-tocked the spell to release the levitation. In her nerves though, she stumbled on the complicated tock sound in the middle and had to start over. From the corner of her eye, Ash could see Prince Phillip open and close his mouth as if stopping himself from reprimanding her. His body was tense. She swallowed, looked away, and shut everything out as she concentrated fully on the sounds of the spell, focusing on speaking as clearly as she could and enunciating each sound with precision.

The spinning miniature mountain crashed to the ground so hard the plains shook. Ash and Prince Phillip stumbled to their knees but bolted up again despite the continuing tremors rolling like waves at their feet.

"We're too close. It's not going to stop rolling in time," Prince Phillip yelled over the rumbling thunder of the careening boulder. They clasped hands and ran as fast as they could. Prince Phillip tripped and, unable to catch himself in time, pulled Ash down with him. The roaring of crushed earth exploded behind them.

Ash struggled to stand, pulling on Prince Phillip's arm as she rose. "Get up."

"I can't. I think I broke my ankle." He shoved her hand away. "Get out of here."

"I won't." She dropped down to one knee so she could slip his arm around her shoulder and prop him up.

"That's an order from your prince." He tried pushing her off, but she gripped him harder.

"You can't order me to leave you," Ash said.

"Yes, I can. Now go." He kept trying to push her up instead of standing.

"No."

The groaning of stone on earth deafened them so that they couldn't even shout at each other. Prince Phillip used his arm already slung across Ash's shoulder to pull her in tight to him, trying to shelter her by will alone from the boulder that had the power to crush them both. The dirt they knelt on rose up and pushed them forward, but Prince Phillip held on tight.

Above, Ash felt the chill of the dark stone's shadow engulf them as the low rumble of its roll hummed in her ears and then stopped, the echo still ricocheting through her head. She lifted her face. The boulder loomed over them, its gray marbled with fissures containing the sparkle of quartz. Around the stone's rough and bubbled texture, a crack exposed white and purple crystals that stretched down inches from Prince Phillip's feet. She turned into Prince Phillip, hugging him exuberantly.

"We made it. We're alive."

Prince Phillip laughed and squeezed her back almost painfully. "I knew you could do it," he said over and over.

Ash shifted and heard a small oomph of pain. "Oh, I'm sorry, your ankle. Let me help you." She started to shift away. His pain also reminded Ash that hugging Prince Phillip was not appropriate, nor was it good for her already racing heart. His arms tightened for a moment before abruptly dropping as he repositioned his leg to let his ankle lie in a less painful position.

A boom sounded, and the boulder before them rocked a fraction before settling back.

"The rest of the rock storm is here. We need to get further away from this boulder in case one of the stones hitting it from behind it is big enough to make it roll again. It didn't land on the flat side, and that makes me worried," Ash said. She peppered the long- and short-voweled words with the proper clicks as she cast the healing spell to help the healing on his ankle, but from the look of the swelling, she knew that it would still be hard for him to walk on his right foot. "Use my shoulder as a crutch."

Prince Phillip stood shakily and allowed Ash to drape his right arm over her shoulders so they could walk out from under the shadow of their giant shield. A constant barrage of explosions boomed behind them as the rocks crashed and smashed against the rearing bear-like boulder. The smaller rocks disintegrated, and showered debris into the air. Rocks beyond the path of the downed boulder whizzed by on both sides. Prince Phillip and Ash ducked their heads forward to avoid any fragments that might ricochet over the boulder.

"You disobeyed my order. Not only am I your employer, but I'm also your prince," Prince Phillip yelled over the noise.

"What?" Ash was distracted by the giant monoliths flying past their boulder. A thrill of fear washed through her, and she had to think a moment to make sense of what Prince Phillip said.

"You are a citizen of this country, are you not? Then what on earth would possess you to defy me at such a moment?" Prince Phillip glared. With his arm draped over her shoulder, the heat of that gaze scorched her face.

Ash felt her cheeks warm. "I defied you precisely because you are the prince. Isn't it my duty to keep you safe no matter what? And I make it a point to disobey all irrational orders no matter who gives them."

"So I am to expect mutiny every time you don't agree with my decision?" They stopped walking. Ash was sure that if the boulder rolled again, they would still be safe. She tried to duck away from his arm, but his hold flexed like a rope, binding her to him.

"Only if your decisions are soft-witted." Ash smiled nervously at him, uncertain if she'd gone too far. He only stared back, his face unreadable. Her grin wavered, and Ash began to think that she probably shouldn't have teased him on this particular subject. Princes were used to being obeyed, and though Prince Phillip was nothing like her uncle, he might still have similar views when it came to obedience from his subjects. To think of her uncle now in connection with Prince Phillip made her feel sad and off balance.

"Thank you," Prince Phillip said.

Ash blinked, momentarily confused. "For disobeying you?"

"For saving my life." He grinned. "I suppose I can't complain about your disobedience this time either, considering that it kept me alive."

"It did not. The boulder stopped."

"So you're admitting that you should have obeyed me?" he asked, copper eyebrows arched.

Ash sighed, immeasurably relieved. So relieved it bothered her to think about it. She decided not to. Instead, she disguised the sigh by making it sound exasperated. "Obey an order to let my prince die? No one would do that."

"*Your* prince?" His brows waggled up and down suggestively, a huge grin lighting his face, making him look just as impish as Ash was sure she was wont to appear at her most mischievous moments.

Caught off guard, Ash couldn't hide the flush of heat burning her cheeks and staining them rouge. "Not *my* prince, of course," she stammered. "I just meant my next sovereign. You know, a very important person to the kingdom in the general sense of the word." Prince Phillip's smile grew as he listened to Ash's stumbled explanation. Ash was unhappy to note that the sound of rocks hitting the grounded boulder lessened as she and Prince Phillip limped further from its wall, making her inane chatter easier to hear.

"It sounded very personal to me." He had the audacity to wink.

Ash slipped quickly out from under Prince Phillip's arm before he could stop her, and let out a wordless frustrated growl.

A clarion boom came from behind their shielding crag. The earth groaned. She and Prince Phillip looked over to see the boulder shift and begin to topple toward them. The bear-like head rocked and began to tip forward hungrily. It looked longer than she'd thought, as if the stone bear's snout stretched out to dive for a tasty bite. Ash fretted about their distance. Were they far enough away to miss being flattened?

Prince Phillip snatched her hand and began hobble-hopping forward. She quickly stepped to his side and ducked back under his arm so they could move faster.

Ash looked up. The gray of granite loomed above, falling swiftly. They were close to the edge, but there was no time.

"Jump!" She grabbed the arm over her shoulder with one hand, and gripped Prince Phillip's side with the other, using painful force as she jumped forward and pulled. They leapt, fell, and rolled together, a tangle of arms, legs, and packs. The boulder hit with a deafening roar that shook the earth and made Ash and Prince Phillip roll one more time before coming to a stop, Ash on top of the prone prince.

She lifted her head. The dirt on Prince Phillip's face made his green eyes seem all the more brilliant. "That's too many close calls for one day," she said, and then to her great embarrassment, she fainted.

Chapter Fifteen

The first thing she was aware of was a sharp pain in her head that throbbed harshly when her eyes opened. She pinched them shut again and groaned.

"Try not to move." Though Prince Phillip's voice was soft, to Ash it rang painfully. She felt a wet, cool cloth placed gently on the side of her head and sighed as it suppressed the pounding drums in her skull. "You must have hit your head when we jumped out from under the edge of the boulder."

Ash couldn't summon the willpower to respond with more than an affirming, "Mmmm."

The cloth lost its coolness and was removed. She heard the splash of water before it was placed back on her head and braced herself to talk. "May need our water later," she whispered.

"That's true. But, then again, we may have a lake dumped on our heads at any minute." He tried to make his words sound light, but Ash could hear a bitter undertone.

The corners of Ash's mouth twitch up. She took several deep breaths to prepare herself. Slowly, painfully, she enunciated the vowels, snaps, and clicks of the healing spell through the sharp piercing in her brain. The pain eased considerably, though she still felt a slight headache. She sat up slowly, Prince Phillip aiding her, and reached a hand up to the now wet side of her head where she could still feel a small lump. It was frightening to think that even with her spell of a week's worth of healing, there was still a bump. A muted headache throbbed. How hard had she slammed her head during their fall?

Prince Phillip handed her a travel cup filled with water and Ash drank greedily, her hands unsteady. Out of the corner of her eye, she saw Prince Phillip reach out to help hold the cup, but he checked himself.

"Thank you," she said, handing the cup back to him. She looked around. The boulder loomed directly above, its shadow deepening as the sun behind the rock began to set.

"I suppose it's too late to keep moving today," she said.

"You need to rest, and if you don't, I do. It's been quite an eventful day," Prince Phillip said.

"Admit it. An unprince-like prince such as you loves this. You'll be sorry to go back to normal life again." Ash grinned at Prince Phillip kneeling beside her. He smiled ruefully as he poured another glass of water, but then he froze mid-pour, his smile vanishing as his copper eyebrows bunched in thought. He handed the cup to Ash half full.

"I thought you determined that I was only a very princely prince who wished he weren't," he said in a carefully casual voice. Ash was looking down, concentrating more on tenderly fingering the bump on her head than on their conversation.

"Well, I was hoping for something more shocking than simply escaping your guard to ride on your own. I suppose you can say you've done that now." She looked up to smile at him again, but then his words and her own response finally registered, and she realized what she'd done. She gasped.

"You!" he accused. "It *was* you at the ball. When you left and I found you again, I didn't really find you again, did I? That's when I found the real Lady Jane. Why did you impersonate her?"

Ash shrugged, chagrined. She also felt a spike of anxiety. "I suppose you could say that I was seeking an escape from my situation that night, if only for a few hours. I should think you would understand that. I hadn't intended to dance with anyone. Lady Amelia grabbed me and presented me to you as Lady Jane before I could escape."

Prince Phillip's face was hard to read. It looked like he couldn't decide on any single emotion but kept flipping through one after another, some that Ash could decipher, some that she could not.

"I really didn't mean to deceive you. It was just something I had to do," Ash said, quietly looking down at the cup in her lap.

"I have so many things I want to ask, I don't even know where to start. Something you 'just had to do'? One of these days your penchant for mischief is going to get you killed." Prince Phillip began to angrily shove things back into his bag. He stood and slung the pack over his shoulders as if to set out, even though the sun was setting behind the looming boulder above them.

"Are we walking farther today?" Ash began to stand but had to steady herself as her vision filled with black before expanding back into color. Prince Phillip took a step toward her as if to help but then stopped and turned away.

"I think we should make as much progress in the remaining light as we can," he said with his back to her.

Once out from under the shadow of the huge rock, Ash could see that the sun was still a finger's width from dropping below the ground. It was strange to think that it would really drop below Ketskatoret's floating landmass, lighting the earth underneath before finally disappearing behind the mountains. The plains were so flat here it was hard to remember that she was standing on a chunk of land hovering miles above a barren wasteland below.

She and Prince Phillip didn't travel far before the sun dipped out of sight. Prince Phillip's limp was more pronounced, and Ash tried to walk fluidly without bouncing so that her head wouldn't jar and pound louder in her skull.

In the dimming light, Ash trailed slowly behind him. He tripped and cursed when he was forced to put more weight on his injured leg to stop himself from falling. Ash stepped to his side as he glared down at his foot.

"I know you're angry with me, but I don't think we should travel any farther tonight, and as unappealing as the idea may be, I also think we should sleep close together. If we're too far apart, the land could shift between us," Ash said. She felt a surge of sadness mixed with a spark of embarrassing happiness that she and Prince Phillip would have to stay close.

Prince Phillip looked toward her in the deepening twilight. His face was shadowed so Ash could not read his expression. He said in a flat tone, "If we must." His indifferent words hurt. The forbidden thrill she'd felt snuffed out like damp tinder.

They shuffled around awkwardly in the dark as they retrieved their blankets, remaining silent as they settled next to each other, their backs nearly touching. Ash felt tense, and her head thrummed dully. Sleep seemed impossible. The miserable ache in her skull echoed her general feeling of unhappy sullenness. It was true: she'd impersonated her cousin. That had been a little ill-advised of her, but nothing to get really angry about. She hadn't harmed Prince Phillip in any way by doing so and had even inadvertently introduced him to his future bride. What right did he have to be so upset?

The thing that stung more, even as she grudgingly admitted it was probably for the best, was the fact that he never tried to find out why she had impersonated her cousin. He hadn't tried to discover anything about Ash. All he really knew about her was her nickname, never bothering to dig any deeper.

Beside her Prince Phillip shifted, his back brushing hers as he turned. She arched away from him to avoid all contact, feeling increasingly irritated by her thoughts and the headache that refused to recede. The sound of his movement paused.

"I'm not going to try anything untoward." His voice floated to her above the distant sound of crickets singing in the tall grasses. When Ash listened closely, she noticed the crickets' song had a strange vibrato, like a bow pulled unsurely across a violin's strings.

"You mean you'll refrain from punching me or otherwise physically punishing me for my presumptuous deceit at the ball?" Ash snorted.

There was a rustle, and Prince Phillip's hand tugged on her shoulder. She turned to see him sitting halfway up, torso supported by his bent arm as he peered down at her face. "I *am* angry about what you did, but it's understandable for a servant to covet the life of the aristocracy. But why Lady Jane, and why did you leave?"

Ash felt a twinge of indignation but kept her response simple. "It wouldn't be a good idea to stay, as I was pretending to be someone else. I told you I hadn't meant to dance with anyone." Ash swallowed, feeling his face was too close above her.

"I can understand that. Why Lady Jane? Do you envy her?" he asked again. Her nervous fluttering awareness of his nearness twisted into something less pleasant as she looked up to the dark outline of his face.

He was finally asking as she'd hoped, but she found herself having to brush off irritation rather than feeling pleasure that he was finally interested in knowing more about her.

"At the lake, did you see me check my wet and bedraggled appearance in the water's reflection? Have I ever demanded we stop our pursuit so that I can bathe and beautify myself? In all the time that we have traveled together, have I ever done anything to indicate to you that I am vain?"

Prince Phillip shifted back a fraction. "No, but even if you are doing your job well without unreasonable demands, it doesn't follow that you don't yearn for more."

Drat the man. He made it sound so believable that Ash should envy Jane, and if she were honest with herself, she had to admit that he was right, if not for the reasons that he assumed. She glared at him in silence.

Prince Phillip held up his free hand in a gesture of appeasement. "I can feel the heat of your stare, even if I can't see it well in the dark. If you did not desire Lady Jane's position, then why did you choose her?"

She wanted to correct his assumptions, to tell him everything, but her emotions were a tangle of resentment and hurt pride. She turned her face away, loathing herself for her cowardice and hypocrisy as she said, "You wouldn't understand." Her mutter was too quiet for him to hear. Louder she said, "Does there have to be a particular reason? I am very good at illusions. Her dress was most interesting."

"Hmm." He sounded unconvinced. She heard the rustle of cloth and the crackle of grass as he lay back down. "Try to sleep. We have a long day tomorrow. Good night, Ash."

"Good night," she replied, feeling a queasy certainty that she'd done another foolish thing.

When Ash finally did sleep, it was fitful. Even asleep she was unable to block out the throbbing in her head and the bite to the air. Her dreams reflected her discomfort by weaving stories with chill landscapes and unsolvable problems. A point of heat appeared within the thorny imaginings of her mind, radiating warmth that spread slowly through her body until she felt relaxed and free of pain, helping her to finally sink into a dream of being held in a gentle embrace.

***

Ash woke in the morning to a sudden whoosh of cool at her back. She shivered and reached to pull her blanket up surprised to find it already there. Her cheeks flushed as she remembered the dream, and who she'd imagined holding her. She turned her head to see Prince Phillip's back to her as he crouched over his pack, already stuffing his blanket back inside.

"We should get going. Can you check for Captain Forbs's location?" Prince Phillip asked, meticulously rearranging his pack. Ash rolled to a sitting position and pop-snapped the spell to find the captain. They were much closer to the west. The land must have moved them nearer during the night.

"We should reach them later today," Ash relayed.

Prince Phillip nodded, back turned away, and Ash sighed, figuring he was still angry with her after all.

"What about Lady Jane and Sorcerer Tioroso?" He shrugged on his pack. Ash got the hint and quickly rolled her blanket, stuffed it into her pack, and pulled the heavy bag on as she stood. She snapped the spell to locate Jane, paused, and clicked it one more time directed at Sorcerer Tioroso to be sure, feeling a strange mixture of anxiety, relief, and nervousness.

"They are between us and the soldiers. If we hurry, we could probably reach them by noon, but there will only be you and I to face Sorcerer Tioroso."

Prince Phillip finally turned to look at her then, gazing at her with intense green eyes, eyebrows drawn down in an indecipherable expression. Ash found his stare difficult to bear. She glanced away.

"We should go. Who knows what will happen next in here. It would be better to find them while we can," she said before walking away from him toward Jane.

Prince Phillip limped after her. Noticing, she slowed to let him catch up. "I wish I could heal you more thoroughly, but the spell can only be done to the same place every few days. I think, because the spell is incomplete, it prevents me from fully transforming a broken body to a whole one no matter how many times I try to increase the spell's effectiveness with repetition. My books hinted that there might be more that could be done, but I was never able to find any spell."

"I can endure it. How is your head?" he asked.

"It throbs a little, but is much better than last night." Ash thought ruefully that when she and Prince Phillip did come face to face with Sorcerer Tioroso they probably wouldn't be able to put up much of a fight.

As they walked, the plain turned to steeper hills, rising and dipping in a crazy patchwork of bumps and hollows too varying to be able to negotiate through only the low ground or the high. Soon the grasses of the plain gave way to large brindled bushes that snatched at clothing and left stinging scratches. Ash noted that their descents seemed to be aggravating Prince Phillip's ankle more than the climb. Their progress slowed as his limp became more pronounced, and Ash's headache grew from a dull background thrum to a pounding throb.

At the ridge of one of the hills, Ash stopped, cocking her head to listen.

"Does that sound like music to you?" she asked.

Prince Phillip mimicked Ash's pose. "It sounds like wind chimes."

"We're heading straight for it. Should we try to go around?" Ash took a hesitant step forward before pausing. So far Ketskatoret's surprises had not been kind, but to go around would delay them further and put extra strain on Prince Phillip's ankle.

"I think we should at least see what is there so we can better evaluate whether going around will even do us any good," Prince Phillip said.

Toward the top of the hill the clink and chime of notes like wind chimes became louder. Just to be safe, Ash and Prince Phillip crawled through the grass and bushes to peek over the edge into the next hollow only to see a valley of the strangest looking plants Ash had ever beheld. She couldn't decide if they looked more like squat trees or very tall bushes. They had odd cylindrical leaves. As the wind picked up, the leaves rattled against each other, clacking together with a hollow tong, and catching the wind through the lip of their empty shells to make soft feathered notes of long and short vowel sounds in harmonic ranges.

Ash's headache, which had been drumming relentlessly only minutes before, was completely gone. She reached up to touch her head. The lump wasn't there. In fact, the ache in her legs from walking and climbing all morning had also disappeared, as well as her cuts and bruises. The hand smoothing her hair didn't catch on cracked fingertips and she brought her hands in front of her face to examine them. The skin was smooth, her knuckles no longer swollen from years of washing laundry and scrubbing floors. Her fingers and palms were smooth and unblemished, free of scrapes and built up callouses. They were the hands of a lady.

"It's amazing," Prince Phillip whispered next to her. He slowly stood and Ash followed suit since there was no need to hide. She watched him swivel his foot back and forth before stomping the ground hard.

"All my pain just vanished, even the ache in my shoulder. I fell from a horse when I was young, and it sometimes still bothers me. But now, it's gone."

"I'm glad to know that there are wonderful magical things here in Ketskatoret. I was beginning to think that the soldiers who made the sign against evil every time they saw me do magic were right, that maybe all magical things, if not evil, were at least hostile," Ash said.

"My father once said that he felt tremendous guilt about banishing magic, even though he believed it to be the best choice for the kingdom. Though some of the sorcerers agreed to cast the spell after being paid handsomely, several had to be persuaded for many years that the negative aspects of magical creatures outweighed the positive before they finally agreed to help."

She and Prince Phillip wandered down the hillside to where the plants tinkled and hummed. The sound surrounded them in a harmonic orchestra of growing instruments. Ash touched one of the long rounded leaves, marveling at its smooth, thick texture.

"This is why I could never figure out a healing spell more complex than giving a week's worth of healing. It takes more than just getting the clicking sounds right. I'd have to mimic the pitch and harmony of the leaves' notes, something that would probably only be possible with more than one sorcerer."

Ash thought sorrowfully of her father. If she'd known then what to do, perhaps she could have saved him. She sighed, and it was almost a sob. It still wouldn't have been possible to save him alone. The only one who could have helped was out of the country at the time and was now ahead of them holding her cousin captive.

"We'll be able to make better time now," Ash said, reminded of the fact that she would soon see and have to confront Sorcerer Tioroso. Her stomach clenched as a pang of fear spiked through her. What could she possibly do against him, she, who had never even had a proper teacher?

"How far away are they?" he asked.

Ash checked. "About three miles."

"Lead the way." He gestured for her to precede him. Ash hesitated, still fingering a cylindrical leaf. Her hand tightened and pulled, snapping it from the branch. She plucked another smaller leaf as well.

A shrill screech drowned out the tinkle and hum of the healing plants. Ash brought up her hands still clutching the two plucked leaves to her ears, trying to block out the sound.

"What is that?" Prince Phillip shouted to be heard over the noise, eyes searching frantically, hands held firmly against his head.

"I don't know." Movement from the bush caught Ash's gaze.

Crawling on the branch to where milky sap leaked from the snapped leaves was a lizard with a white body and green jagged stripes. Sharp teeth threatened Ash as it screamed, and a red, feathered antenna extending from its head, like that of a luna moth, shook in fury. As its cry drowned out the healing song of the plants, small fissures opened on its back and began to bleed. The scream stopped. The creature panted as the healing balm of the plants' music healed the wounds. It screamed again, inching closer, legs crouched and ready to leap.

Ash backed away from the bush quickly, and as she did so the lizard settled back, silencing its cry.

Prince Phillip pulled her sleeve and whispered, "I think we'd better leave in case there are more of those creatures. We don't know what they might do to us if provoked."

"I agree." Ash trotted swiftly out of the healing bushes, Prince Phillip at her side. She didn't want to face Sorcerer Tioroso, but at least he was a human being. As little as that comfort afforded, it was still better than the completely unknown dangers of Ketskatoret's wildlife, at least she hoped.

The closer she and Prince Phillip came to Jane and her abductor, the tighter Ash held to the tracking spell focused on Sorcerer Tioroso. She felt an unreasonable conviction that if she let it drop even for an instant and lost track of him, she wouldn't be able to find him again, or he would discover her first.

On the downward side of a particularly high hill, Ash heard a faint click and whistle. She whirled to find the source, but the hill blocked her view. There was a loud crack. A deep groan reverberated through the air.

"Prince Phillip!" Ash snapped her hand out to grab his arm.

The ground underneath them shifted, moving downwards and sideways. Ash pulled Prince Phillip toward the stationary ridge of land rising higher as the earth they stood on sank and twisted.

"We're on the wrong side. If we stay here we'll be pulled away from Jane again. Grab onto the edge before it moves too high," Ash yelled, forgetting to use Jane's title in her distraction. She let him go in order to reach the rising chunk of land, already as high as her chest. He seemed to have no trouble lifting himself up. Though her arms were braced by her armpits, the ground below moved downward and to the side too quickly for her to push herself over the lip. She held on grimly, feet dangling, the weight of her pack dragging her backwards and eroding her grip as the ground she clung to crumbled beneath her.

Prince Phillip crouched in front of her and gripped her arms, hauling her up. His foot tripped backwards as he strained to lift her, and they tumbled next to each other on the ground, panting as the earth behind them rumbled and slid.

"We've got to stop ending up like this. What would people say?" Ash grinned across at Prince Phillip, relief bringing on a sudden fit of deviltry.

Prince Phillip smiled back, his copper brows arched in the expression that made Ash think of a child who'd eaten the hidden preserves and thought he'd gotten away with it. "How else can I convince you that I'm not as ordinary a prince as you'd supposed?"

"You'd rather me consider you a rake?"

"So long as you consider me," he quipped instantly. The implication of the words seemed to strike both Ash and Prince Phillip at the same time. Their grins dropped, and Prince Phillip looked away and rolled to his feet. "Forgive me. That was inappropriate."

Ash rose slowly, hating herself for wishing he hadn't withdrawn his words.

"Was the moving ground this loud the last time?" Ash asked to distract herself.

"I'm sure I'd have woken." Prince Phillip didn't look back as he responded, just started walking away from her toward where Jane awaited rescue.

He was soon blocked, however, by something that she and Prince Phillip had been too frantic to notice in their scramble to remain on the right portion of earth. Trees spread before them, so closely spaced it looked like a natural wall barring them from entry. But the trees looked anything but natural. Each trunk was a smooth wood of different colors. One was a deep burgundy, another golden yellow, followed by burnt orange, then royal purple. A teal trunk wove its branches with the forest green one beside it. All the trees had silvery blue foliage that grew in clusters like a flower, but with tapering points like the leaves of a beech tree. The whole effect reminded Ash of a rainbow in a cloudy sky.

She turned to explore the perimeter, looking for a space large enough to pass through. There were gaps she could peer into that showed a more normally spaced forest of rainbow-colored trees beyond the living wall of wood, but there was no place big enough for a person to squeeze past.

"Can you do anything?" Prince Phillip asked.

Ash eyed the weaving branches, thoughts flicking from one possibility to another. "I can transform wood." She glanced at the blue trunk in front of her dubiously. "If it is normal wood. But I've never tried to change a whole tree, and I always transformed the object into something of similar density." She shrugged. "I might as well try."

She knelt down to pull out her book in order to check that the conjugation and intonation she needed to use was correct, before packing it away and standing in front of the wall of trees.

She focused on one of the smaller saplings and sounded the words to the spell filled with short vowels, a consonant trill, several snap-tocks, and a long-voweled pop that should transform wood to water. The tree held its shape for a moment before the blue of the timber turned translucent. It trembled and broke, then crashed to the ground. Ash jumped back, but it was too late. Muddy water splashed upward, soaking the hem of her split skirt and covering her in a new layer of filth. The dress didn't even look maroon anymore.

She glanced over at a grinning Prince Phillip. "Do you want me to throw mud on you again? You probably couldn't get any dirtier, but if you keep laughing at me, I'll do it anyway."

Prince Phillip looked down at his dull brown shirt. At the beginning of their journey it had been cream. His sturdy waistcoat, once a rich emerald embroidered in gold, was a beat up murky swamp-green. His breeches were torn at the knee, his stockings detached and ragged, and his hair was a shade darker than its usual bright copper.

"I didn't laugh. I was simply smiling at a job well done," he said.

Ash harrumphed and took her pack off so she could turn sideways to squeeze through the narrow gap she'd created, pulling her bag through after.

Prince Phillip followed, his lips still quirked.

The trees beyond the trunks' barrier were tightly spaced at first. Ash had to haul her pack beside her through the slender openings. But as they moved farther in, the hindering colorful forest spread out enough for Prince Phillip and Ash to put their heavy bags back on.

A snap pulled Ash's eyes upward to the branches overhead. Yellow, slitted cat's eyes gazed at her through the silver and blue leaf clusters. It took her a moment to realize that the orange, black, and green dappled fur of the cat's face flowed into a body that looked like a cross between feline and chimpanzee. One of the creature's hands gripped an upward reaching sky-blue branch as its back paws rested on a thicker limb parallel to the ground. A velvety green tail hung down one side, twitching back and forth as the creature watched her. Ash stood very still, hoping motionlessness would keep it from doing anything more than stare.

"What is . . . ?" Prince Phillip began.

"Shh." Ash heard Prince Phillip stop beside her but didn't look away from the cat creature.

A rustle in the leaves of the next tree over had both cat and Ash glancing to the left. She saw the glitter of crystal wings. The cat-like creature leapt toward the shimmer. The trees were too far apart for a normal animal to span in a single jump, but Ash heard a hiss-kek-hum as it jumped and the creature disappeared mid-air. It reappeared in a pounce right on top of the crystal bird.

"That's worrying," Prince Phillip said beside her.

"And intriguing," Ash said, trying to see if she could duplicate the sounds the animal made. She feared the hum-like purr might be beyond her ability to mimic.

Prince Phillip tugged her arm, guiding her away from the strange monkey-cat when Ash didn't move. "Figuring out how that thing cast its spell is not worth chancing an attack against us."

"I suppose you're right," Ash said as she reluctantly allowed Prince Phillip to lead her away.

Chapter Sixteen

Ash kept her head craned upwards, searching through the trees for more of the strange monkey-cat creatures. She saw a flash of light reflected from another crystal bird, heard the rustle of leaves, but couldn't spot the orange, black, and green fur of the cat creature. With her eyes strained up, she missed seeing the branch in front of her feet and tripped forward, hands sinking into the muddy earth.

An explosion reverberated above Ash's head into the tree behind her. Prince Phillip grabbed her shoulders and pivoted her behind a wide trunk before Ash had time to straighten, much less realize what had happened. Through the silvery leaves raining down from above, Ash could see a large rock embedded in the still swaying purple tree across from where they crouched.

"Did the mist do that?" Prince Phillip asked.

"I don't think so. It's too small. Could it be Sorcerer Tioroso? But I thought he was still too far away," Ash said, stunned.

"Maybe he used the tracking spell on me." Prince Phillip peered around the tree. "I can't see him."

"I think we'll have to run from tree to tree in order to get close enough to see what caused this."

"You could have been killed." There was a hard edge to Prince Phillip's voice.

"We don't really know if Sorcerer Tioroso did it, but if he did, you're more likely to be the one tracked and targeted. I don't think he would even know to look for me. The rock was far enough away from you that he might have sent it as more of a warning than as something meant to harm you," Ash reasoned, hoping to calm Prince Phillip as much as herself.

"It does us no good to speculate. Let's find out." Prince Phillip held her hand and tugged her forward from their refuge to another wide trunk, but he soon let go as they both concentrated on darting from one cover to the next. When Prince Phillip began to veer off course, Ash took the lead, zigzagging from tree to tree, careful to keep the trunks between them and Sorcerer Tioroso.

No rocks sped past or into the bark around them, but Ash could sense through her tracking spell that Sorcerer Tioroso was moving away quickly, making it seem more likely that he had launched the rock.

"If we keep weaving, they're going to get too far ahead of us," Ash panted before abandoning the last tree's shelter to take a more direct path. Prince Phillip followed, and they sprinted to catch the sorcerer. His progress had slowed. Ash wondered if Jane was the reason. Even if she was running willingly, she'd led a very sedentary life and would not have the stamina to sprint for long. Even Ash, strengthened by years of forced hard labor, felt a jabbing pain in her side that warned she too would need to stop soon.

Ash sensed Sorcerer Tioroso halt. She and Prince Phillip burst through the trees into a clearing. Thirty feet away, at the opposite edge, stood Jane and Sorcerer Tioroso. For a moment everyone froze as the two opposing couples stared at each other, panting. Ash noted with a flash of wistful resignation that Jane looked beautiful, even though her clothes were rumpled and dirty and her hair mussed with stray hanging tendrils. She glowed like a winded wood sprite held motionless by fright.

Ash saw Sorcerer Tioroso's mouth move. He was too far away for her to hear what spell he spoke, but a large rock lifted from beside him and rocketed toward them. Pushing Prince Phillip down, Ash dove apart from him to the ground. The rock sailed harmlessly past, but Ash caught sight of another rising next to the sorcerer even as she landed in the dirt. Her mouth sped over the clicks and dips of the spell to launch her own boulder toward Sorcerer Tioroso even as she wondered why a sorcerer as knowledgeable as he was resorting to such a simple attack.

Ash sprang up as her rock sped toward Sorcerer Tioroso's. Mid-meadow the two rocks collided with a loud crack that Ash felt reverberate through her chest. Rubble rained through the air like a firework as dust and pebbles burst in every direction before falling to the ground. Sorcerer Tioroso seemed to be startled at the sight, before he pivoted, focusing his full attention on Ash. The sweat on her body turned cold, and she shivered as she looked into Sorcerer Tioroso's brown eyes. His face was so pretty, his lips full, his cheeks smooth above a sharp jawline. It was a kind face, but Ash's heart skipped a beat for a reason that had nothing to do with womanly admiration.

She stood like a cornered rabbit, watching as his lips moved while his gaze focused on her. A wall of fire sprang up from the grass at her feet. She jumped back and uttered a spell of transformation on instinct, converting the fire's increasingly destructive size into flame shaped water before it dropped to the ground in a puddle. When she could see again, she found herself facing not one, but many Sorcerer Tiorosos spread throughout the meadow. She looked for Jane but couldn't find her.

Ash started speaking the clicks and tocks for the spell to see through illusion. Before she could finish, a whir of sound prompted an instinct to duck. She whirled to look as something struck the tree behind her. It was another rock, this time hidden by illusion until the impact on the tree broke the spell.

Ash began the spell again. The water from the newly created puddle rose up and crashed into her, but Ash ignored the distraction so she could hold onto her concentration long enough to finish the spell. The many Sorcerer Tiorosos disappeared and left one Sorcerer Tioroso shielding Jane behind him. Before Ash could do anything to him, however, she saw his lips stop moving as he completed a spell. The puddle's water soaking her clothes and coating her body hardened to glass.

A moment of mind-numbing panic seized her as she felt her body freeze into a glittering statue, but she thrust the fear aside. The layer of water on her face was thin enough that when Ash jerked her head and forced her mouth to move, sparkling shards broke off and tinkled to the ground. She spat the spell to transform the glass back to water in quick snaps and burrs, feeling the cool of binding glass change back to the cold of wet. Without pausing for breath she continued to snap out the spell to launch a rock, then another, and another, hoping to keep him too busy to cast any offensive spells.

Sorcerer Tioroso transformed Ash's first rock to water just before it struck, making him almost as soaked as Ash, but she knew she wouldn't be able to try the same spell to trap him as he had her. He was able to dodge the second and third boulders easily. Ash worried that her distraction would not be enough to stop him from casting something else, but the shock of being imprisoned in glass had left her unable to think of anything more complicated than flinging stones.

Jane surged forward and tugged Sorcerer Tioroso's arm, speaking urgently to him. Sorcerer Tioroso shoved her to the side to dodge another of Ash's rocks even as he sent several wooden shards from the trees in a flurry of natural arrows showering toward Ash all at once. Jane pulled harder as Ash used the easier conversion of changing the sharp branches to something only slightly less dense. Fat flowers bounced off her body and dropped to the ground in a ring of bright blue.

Sorcerer Tioroso glanced at Jane as if startled. As he turned, one of Ash's smaller stones she'd launched behind the bigger rocks struck Sorcerer Tioroso on the head. Jane's ear-splitting scream filled the meadow as the sorcerer's head snapped back, followed by his body toppling to the ground. Jane dropped to the ground beside him only a moment after his fall.

Ash couldn't look away from Jane crouched at the still sorcerer's side. Prince Phillip turned Ash toward him, hands tight on each shoulder, and her gaze ripped from Jane like paper.

"Are you hurt?" he asked.

"What if he's dead?" Ash panted, unaware of Prince Phillip's question. Her body shook from the cold, and she couldn't seem to pull in a full breath. What had she done? She couldn't remember that the unmoving man on the ground had kidnapped her cousin or that he had tried to hurt her. All that flitted through her shattered thoughts was that she might be responsible for ending someone's life.

Prince Phillip finally looked away from examining Ash to where Jane knelt next to Sorcerer Tioroso. A slight frown formed and his forehead creased.

"I have to make sure." Ash broke from Prince Phillip's hold, knocking away his hands with flailing arms, and sprinted to Jane's side. "Is he . . . " She trailed off, hovering above Jane, afraid to kneel beside her.

Tears streamed down Jane's face as she replied, "He's breathing. I think he's only unconscious."

Ash let out the breath she'd been holding. Relief washed over her like a bucket of warm water. "Thank goodness. But what of you? Did he hurt you?"

Jane shook her head vigorously. "No, no." She looked up. "He . . ." Jane's eyes broke from Ash's and fixed on something beside her. Ash half turned to see Prince Phillip at her side. She felt a sour twinge tighten in her stomach as he and Jane regarded each other.

"I want to heal him as soon as possible just in case, but I think we should tie and gag him first," Ash said, unable to take the silence one moment more.

"Please . . .," Jane began.

Ash and Prince Phillip waited, but she didn't continue. When it was apparent that Jane was going to remain silent with her eyes down-cast, Prince Phillip searched through his pack for rope and cloth for a gag. When he was tied and healed as much as Ash could manage, Sorcerer Tioroso's long lashed eyes fluttered and opened slowly. After several groggy blinks he seemed to realize that his hands and mouth were bound. Tioroso's head snapped up, and his eyes darted around, wincing slits of movement, until he caught sight of Jane. Seeing her standing next to the prince, his alert pose crumpled and he sagged back to the ground.

"Why did you do such a thing, Sorcerer Tioroso?" Prince Phillip asked. "I thought we were friends."

Unable to answer, Sorcerer Tioroso slumped limply, head turned away. Prince Phillip looked down at him as if he wanted to kick the man. Instead, he turned to Ash. As his gaze caught hers, she saw some of the fury fade. She quirked her mouth up in an attempt to lighten his mood, and he smiled wryly in return for a moment before it was overtaken by a sad, brooding expression.

"We need to find Captain Forbs. Are they still close?" Prince Phillip asked.

"They haven't moved since the last time I checked," Ash replied after confirming the captain's location. "We should be able to reach them by evening if Sorcerer Tioroso will walk." Ash glanced dubiously at the sorcerer's inert body. He was turned away from Prince Phillip and Ash on his side in listless rebellion. "If he won't, my skills have improved since coming into Ketskatoret, so it is possible I could levitate him beside us."

"That isn't necessary," Jane said quietly, coming up next to Ash. Ash jumped. Jane had been so silent during the binding and healing of Sorcerer Tioroso that Ash had wondered if Jane was in too much shock to speak. Jane looked down at Sorcerer Tioroso's back. "Defiance at this point would be useless."

Ash watched Sorcerer Tioroso's body flinch inward before he rolled awkwardly forward. Unable to use the hands tied behind his back, he shouldered his way to his knees and stood up, head bowed. She expected his expression to be angry, defiant, but instead, his face scrunched in sorrow.

"What did you . . . ?" Ash trailed off, not sure what exactly she wanted to ask, but thinking that both Jane's and Sorcerer Tioroso's actions were unusual.

"Let's move quickly. I want to find Captain Forbs as soon as possible," Prince Phillip said before Ash could decide what she wanted to say.

Prince Phillip took the rear, marching Sorcerer Tioroso ahead of him while Ash led the way through the colorful trees toward Captain Forbs and Jane walked sedately beside her.

"Are you sure you are all right? He didn't try anything?" Ash asked Jane quietly so that the men would not hear.

"I'm fine. Sorcerer Tioroso is a gentleman."

Ash's brow rose in question, but Jane continued on before Ash could respond to the absurdity of referring to one's abductor as a gentleman, "But, Ashelandra, how did you come to be here? I never knew that you were a sorceress. How on earth did you have time to learn in spite of Father?"

Ash hesitated, unsure if she should explain, especially since Jane would be heading back to the manor and Lord Richard, but it seemed pointless to avoid the subject now. "Even if Lord Richard tried to hide the fact, you must have known my mother was a sorceress. She left me her books, and I hid them from him, practicing whenever I could find the time. You won't tell him, will you?" Ash asked, worried her part in Jane's rescue might be mentioned to Jane's father.

"Doesn't he already know? How else did the prince know to use you to find me?" she asked.

"He found me practicing on his way to visit you. It's possible Lord Richard didn't figure out I can do magic, and if he doesn't know, I prefer to keep it that way. At least until after I've reached my majority. I would appreciate it if you wouldn't mention that I was with the prince's rescue party. In fact, I would be forever in your debt if you don't mention me at all." Ash thought uneasily of the spell she had cast while escaping her uncle. If he'd heard her click the spell, he may have realized his stumble backwards had not been just from clumsiness. Still, she shrugged the worry aside; it would not matter if he knew or not. She didn't intend to come near her uncle again until she was safely twenty-one with the power to eject him from her home with force if necessary.

"You never call my father uncle," Jane said.

"He does not wish it, and I've no desire to do so either." Ash weaved her arm through Jane's. "But that doesn't mean I'm unhappy to have you as my cousin. I'm glad that you're safe. I've been so worried about you."

"There was no need to worry," Jane said.

"How could there be no need to worry?" Prince Phillip's voice asked from behind them. Ash jumped and pulled her arm free of Jane's, wondering how much of their conversation he had overheard. His expression, however, seemed filled with only concern and confusion about Jane's response.

Ash saw Sorcerer Tioroso, tethered to Prince Phillip like an obedient dog at heel, also watching Jane before he realized that Ash was watching him. His head dropped back down.

Jane turned shy, mumbling an apology before walking on again. Ash attempted to speak to Jane as they walked, but she seemed in no mood for talk, so Ash let her be. As they neared the soldiers, the gap between trees grew until they stopped altogether at a sight Ash found difficult to believe. Shells the size of buildings with a pearlescent glow sprawled next to each other in curving rows spiraling in graceful rounded bends before looping to a pointed tip. For a moment, Ash feared that a giant magical creature would emerge from each shell and present another situation capable of immense destruction that she would have to combat, but then she saw a person's face appear at an arched opening in the side of a shell near them.

The woman leaned out and shook a blanket, before drawing back inside. Ash noticed twisting coral-like fences surrounding each shell with vegetable and flower gardens lining the swirling walls.

"They're houses. People actually live here in Ketskatoret," Ash said in astonishment, hardly crediting her own observation.

"How is that possible?" Prince Phillip asked, coming to stand beside her with Sorcerer Tioroso following slowly behind as far as the rope would allow.

"This part of Ketskatoret is protected from the mist's constant spells. Sorcerer Tioroso told me that the barrier of trees we passed through has roots that extend down to the air beneath. It stops the mist from entering so that everything within the barrier stays stationary," Jane said without looking at anyone. "This area of Ketskatoret is where most of the sorcerers and magical creatures live."

Ash glanced back at Sorcerer Tioroso, who met her stare with an unreadable expression. Had the sorcerer planned to bring Jane here? And if so, why? Had the sorcerer, by chance, stolen Jane for more romantic than malicious reasons? Did he think that he might be able to convince Jane to love him if he had a place away from Prince Phillip's reach where he could woo her? Ash shook her head and looked away. Such fanciful speculations were pointless. She turned her attention back to the town.

"I'm fairly certain your men are in that strange shell village. I hope the natives are friendly," Ash said to Prince Phillip.

"Let's find out," he replied.

At the first swirling house, Ash noticed that the blue, green, and purple hues of the shell's exterior were dull with age, though still beautiful. Ash could see no doorway at first until she noticed a metal knob. Around the handle was the seam of the shell's door, perfectly matched with the rest of the structure. They walked past, toward the center of the village, where Ash sensed the captain. More and more frequently she noticed faces appearing at the curved windows of the shell houses as they passed. It made Ash nervous. If, as Jane had said, sorcerers and magical creatures lived here, Ash would be able to do little to protect herself, Jane, Prince Phillip, and their captive.

Her growing unease ceased in a wash of relief, however, when Ash spotted Brett Johnson slowly walking through the street as he concentrated on holding six loaves of bread without smashing them.

"Mr. Johnson!" Ash's profound relief at seeing the soldier made her call burst out in a shout. Startled, the young man almost lost hold of his bread before catching his balance to turn and see who'd hailed him. His mouth dropped open, and the rescued bread tumbled to the ground unheeded as he rushed forward to meet them.

"Prince Phillip, Miss Ash, we were so worried about you. Captain Forbs asked some of the sorcerers to help find you, but they said you were coming to us and that we should wait, so we waited even though it about killed the Captain to do so. But you did come just like they said you would, and you even found Lady Jane and the sorcerer! However did you manage that?" Brett spoke all in one breath. As his air ran out, however, he seemed to realize that he was babbling. He dropped his head in embarrassment before he whipped it toward the fallen bread abandoned in the dirt. "Oh no, the Captain's going to punish me for that." He couldn't seem to keep himself from adding.

"I'll make sure he doesn't. Why don't you pick them up? We'll brush them off as best we can and you can lead us to him," Prince Phillip said, smiling.

That done, the party set off, with Brett walking so quickly he was on the verge of trotting. Ash, Prince Phillip, Jane, and Sorcerer Tioroso were forced to walk in a quick march to keep up. The fast pace was short-lived, however. After passing six pearlescent houses, Ash spotted blue uniforms. The golden stripes across the shoulders were not as brilliant as when the soldiers first set out on their journey, but still eye catching nonetheless. Brett could contain his pace no longer. He sprinted forward past the few soldiers and into the house.

Ash, Prince Phillip, Jane, and Sorcerer Tioroso were nearly to the coral fence that surrounded the shell house when Brett reemerged followed by Captain Forbs. Brett's rush indoors had alerted the soldiers outside, so that by the time the Captain emerged to greet the prince, the soldiers had assembled in formation and knelt on one knee in front of Prince Phillip with bowed heads, and right fists on hearts. Despite the formality of the pose, most were unable to hide their relieved smiles. Captain Forbs strode to Prince Phillip and immediately followed their example, bowing even lower than his soldiers.

"I failed you, my prince. As soon as I have delivered you safely home, I will resign my post," he said, his voice sounding deeper than usual, as if his throat were coated in phlegm.

"You will not." Prince Phillip's voice cracked with the sting of a whip. Captain Forbs looked up in surprise, and Prince Phillip modulated his tone as he continued. "I brought us into Ketskatoret. You are not responsible for the ground separating us, and there's really nothing you could have done to prevent it. As it is, Ash and I made it safely back to you with Lady Jane and Sorcerer Tioroso, so our objective is accomplished. Are all of you well?" he asked, glancing around at the kneeling men. They watched him carefully, as if worried he might disappear if they looked away. "Here stand up. There's no reason to remain kneeling, though I do appreciate the gesture." Prince Phillip smiled, and caught the eyes of each soldier as they rose.

Captain Forbs rose from the ground slowly. He seemed reluctant to give up his position of penance.

"All are well, Sire. When we were separated from you and the land stopped moving, we found ourselves at the edge of the rainbow trees' border. A sorcerer named Shovaylan found us. He brought us within the trees' protection. I wanted to go after you immediately, but Sorcerer Shovaylan was too old to accompany us, and without a sorcerer's help, leaving here would have been disastrous. I've been trying to convince other sorcerers to go after you, but they were unwilling to risk their scrawny hides." Captain Forbs pierced the surrounding shell houses with an accusing stare before turning back to the prince.

Ash tried not to snort. She wasn't surprised that Captain Forbs had trouble convincing the sorcerers to help. He wasn't the most personable of men and seemed to dislike anyone he didn't already know.

"They could sense you were coming to us," he added grudgingly, his tone indicating how little he'd believed the sorcerers' word.

"Are there many sorcerers here?" Ash couldn't help herself from interrupting to ask. She felt her heart speed up in excited anticipation as she eyed the nearest pearlescent door longingly, imagining a sorcerer hiding behind its shimmery barrier.

"Yes," he said brusquely, glaring at Ash, proving that he was still no admirer. His eyes blasted blame. She couldn't stop herself from laughing. Meeting his gaze, she first gestured toward Prince Phillip, then Jane and Sorcerer Tioroso. His eyes pinched to slits, but he surprised Ash by nodding a reluctant recognition of her accomplishment in bringing the prince through Ketskatoret unharmed while still managing to capture Sorcerer Tioroso and rescue Jane.

The Captain turned his attention back to the prince. Prince Phillip had his hand up to his mouth in what Ash thought was a useless attempt to hide an amused smile.

Captain Forbs frowned. "We need to leave as quickly as possible, Your Highness. I discovered from the sorcerers that time in Ketskatoret passes strangely. There is no way to tell if, when we emerge, we will have been here for a week or several months. If it is the latter, the king will be anxious. I did manage to get one of the sorcerers to agree to take us to where the entrance lies, only two miles from the tree's border. If we leave now we can make it out of Ketskatoret today."

"Then find that sorcerer and we'll leave immediately." Prince Phillip turned to Jane. "Will you be able to continue traveling?" he asked.

Jane cast a quick glance toward Sorcerer Tioroso, who met her eyes before looking away. She looked back at Prince Phillip and nodded before fixing her eyes on the ground.

"Good." He placed his hand on her shoulder as if to give Jane strength and then turned to Ash. "And you?" he asked. Ash's heart twisted painfully. She wished she hadn't seen the gesture.

"I . . .," Ash began but then stopped as a torrent of thoughts swept through her. Was there really any reason for her to go back with the prince? If Captain Forbs was right, and time passed unpredictably in Ketskatoret, then her birthday could have come and gone already. If so, it would be safe to descend and claim her inheritance. But if only a week had passed, she would be homeless until her birthday arrived. In this village Ash finally had what she had always dreamed of—a plethora of possible sorcerer instructors surrounding her. Surely she could convince one of them to teach her what she'd only been able to use books to learn before.

And there was another very good reason for her to stay rather than join the prince's party back to the palace. Ash glanced at Jane standing beside Prince Phillip. Even dirty, the two complemented each other beautifully. Prince Phillip's firm form, bright red-gold hair, and green eyes accented Jane's slim figure, porcelain skin, and amber gaze. They would look like magical creatures themselves at their royal wedding. Ash preferred not to see it.

"I will stay here," she said.

"What?" Prince Phillip paled in surprise.

"You don't really need me anymore and there are sorcerers here. I've never had a teacher before, and I would like to learn. I have nowhere to live at the moment, so now is the perfect opportunity to take advantage of this chance. There is no good reason to return."

A beat of silence followed where Ash avoided meeting any eyes, though she felt Prince Phillip's stare pressing on her.

"You can't," he burst out and then continued more calmly, "You are still in my employ and you must act as a witness to Sorcerer Tioroso's attack and capture. None of the soldiers can since none were there."

"You were there, as was Lady Jane. You two can be the witnesses," Ash replied reasonably, her voice calm and even.

Prince Phillip's brow creased, and he glanced at Jane as if he'd forgotten that she too had been in the meadow during Sorcerer Tioroso's attack. Jane wilted under the group's sudden attention, pulling back slightly like a flower closing.

Prince Phillip raised his hand to Jane in a calming gesture but watched Ash. "You must see how cruel it would be to ask that of her. Would you really make her stand through the strain of a trial when she has already been through so much? I can't be the only witness, and we need a sorcerer with us as we travel back with Sorcerer Tioroso just in case something happens. We can't keep him gagged the whole time. He still has to eat. If he were to try anything we would need you there." Prince Phillip looked again at Jane, who was still poised like a frightened doe.

"And Lady Jane needs a female companion," he finished, smiling as if the last argument settled everything beyond question.

Ash squinted one eye and pursed her lips dubiously. Prince Phillip's points were valid, but the logic was as fragile as wet paper. Now that she'd seen a way to escape the discomfort of being near Prince Phillip while he fawned over his fiancé, she was loath to give it up.

"I don't see why you can't be the only witness. You are the prince. No one is going to doubt your word, and all you need to do with Sorcerer Tioroso is have him watched while he is eating. If he begins to cast a spell, just stop him before he can complete it. Molly is at the base of the mountain. She will be able to accompany Jane back to the palace to avoid any impropriety, though you have to admit it's a little ridiculous to be worrying about silly social standards at this point." Ash flinched and looked guiltily at Jane, silently apologizing for any pain or embarrassment her blunt words might have caused.

To Ash's surprise Jane looked more desperate than hurt. "Don't leave me, Ash," she burst out unexpectedly.

"I, but I . . ." Ash trailed off at a loss in the face of Jane's obvious distress.

"It's settled. We'll leave at once. Where is that sorcerer you said would escort us, Captain?" Prince Phillip asked, grinning, before he strode off with Captain Forbs as the soldiers scattered to ready for the journey. Two soldiers took charge of Sorcerer Tioroso, leading him away into the shell house and leaving Jane and Ash standing alone.

"You don't really need me, Jane. There is a woman at the foot of the mountain who will help keep at least some of the gossip that may arise from this situation at bay. Not that it matters much. You will be the future queen. Who in their right mind would choose to alienate themselves from you by spreading malicious gossip?"

"I don't think I can face father on my own," Jane said, voice small, her body folding in on itself.

"He can't blame you for being kidnapped. Even *he* is not so unreasonable." *And I certainly can't face him with you,* Ash added to herself silently.

Jane didn't respond, and the quiet soon became uncomfortable.

Finally, Ash sighed. "It would be unwise for me to see Lord Richard, at least not until I've turned twenty-one. We did not part on the best of terms." Ash decided it would be better to not mention the details of that last meeting. Jane was not completely ignorant of her father's desire to retain Trebruk Manor and all its assets, but Ash doubted Jane would believe the extent to which her father was willing to go to obtain that goal.

"So you're really not going back home?" Jane asked.

"Of course I am, as soon as I am able," Ash hedged.

"Would you at least stay with me until it's time to see Father?" Jane grabbed hold of Ash's hand. "Just for a while. I won't ask for anything else."

Ash glanced around at the village of shell houses. She'd yet to meet a single occupant and already she was expected to leave. What if she was never able to return to find a teacher? Jane's hand in hers was cold, her slim fingers squeezing Ash's tight. She met Jane's eyes.

"I will stay with you as long as I am able." The words emerged from Ash like tree roots pulled reluctantly from the earth.

"Thank you." Jane sighed and sagged in relief.

Prince Phillip and Captain Forbs soon returned with a lanky young man whose sudden growth had left him still unused to the length of his limbs. Ash watched him trip over air several times before she approached him on their march to the border. He nodded to her shyly.

"I hope you don't mind if I introduce myself. I'm Ashelandra, though everyone just calls me Ash. What's your name?" Ash asked with an encouraging smile.

The boy blushed. "I'm Jemorian. Everybody shortens my name too."

Ash gave Jemorian a conspiratorial wink. "Sorcerers' names do tend to be a mouthful at times. So, Jem, are you a full-fledged sorcerer already, or just training to be one like I am?" Ash asked him.

"I'm still training. Master Shovaylan asked me to escort you all on account of his joints aching." Jem bumped against Ash as he stumbled over a rock in the path.

Ash gripped his arm to steady him. "He should go to the valley of those healing plants. It's not far away, or at least it wasn't. I suppose it could be by now."

"You saw the Ootchink plants?" the young apprentice asked, excitedly jumping up and then stumbling over his own leap before catching himself. "I learned about them, but I'm not good enough with my spells to make a trip into Ketskatoret's maze, and Master Shovaylan said it's too much of a bother to navigate the maze just to cure a few aches. What did they sound like?"

"Like harmonizing wind chimes. Do you know if anyone in your village would be willing to take on another student? I have to leave with the prince now, but I hope to return. It would be so wonderful to learn sorcery from an actual person rather than books."

Jem stared at her, his mouth hanging open until he tripped on a pebble and was forced to concentrate on his footing. "You've been able to figure out spells just from the books? I've tried to go ahead of Master Shovaylan sometimes by reading the spell in the book, but I can never get the pronunciation right on my own. How much do you know?"

"Not much, unfortunately. I can transform things as solid as wood now but can't levitate anything heavier than about sixty pounds, although I guess I did make a levitating boulder the size of a house crash to the ground. Perhaps I could lift more now as well. My illusions can be detailed, but they still have problems at times. I lose the texture of the spell's appearance if I don't concentrate enough on the enunciation. Hearing the mist in the maze helped me quite a bit. I'm sure learning from an actual sorcerer would make a world of difference." Ash felt her words speed up in excitement. It was a heady feeling to finally speak with another person who shared her passion for magic.

"You heard the Mist?" Jem stumbled again in his excitement. "No wonder you look so ragged. I'm surprised you survived. Those close enough to hear the Mist don't often have time to counter the spell to save themselves."

Ash grinned ruefully, amused by Jem's lack of tact. "What was that mist anyway? When it was close, it was almost as if I could see creatures rising then dissipating as they melded back into the vapor."

"It's the source." He regarded her gravely, his tone almost reverent.

"The source? The source of what?" She stumbled as she tried to watch him and walk at the same time.

He laughed, whisking away his solemn expression. "Sorcery." Jem shrugged as if it was obvious.

Ash blew out in frustration. "I still don't understand."

"Master Shovaylan says nobody knows when or how it first came about, but the Mist is made up of the essence of all magical things. He says the mist is like a dust cloth that cleans the earth when things die, but sometimes pieces of the dust get caught in the rag and clump together. That's what you see and hear in the mist, leftover pieces of magical things already gone. It was from those bits that the language of sorcery was created."

"I'm not sure if I understand completely. Are you saying that the language of sorcery stems from the random mutterings of leftover parts of magical creature's souls?"

"Something like that. That's the theory anyway. Nobody knows for sure. We do know that is how the language of sorcery was first discovered. Though parts of sorcery could have been first learned from the magical creatures, the spells each kind of creature can do is usually really specific, and sometimes impossible for humans. I don't know how the first sorcerers stayed alive long enough to listen to the mist and figure out the more complicated stuff."

Ash had to agree. Jem's explanation made sense too since the words to spells were often different even though they were supposed to mean the same thing. It was never safe to just assume verb conjugations either. She'd always thought the language seemed like a cobbled together hodgepodge of several languages rather than just one.

"What's it like in the outside world?" Jem asked eagerly, too long legs tripping on a rock as he looked at her. He caught himself and a gentle blush spread from his neck to his forehead.

Ash looked away to give him a moment to recover his dignity and tried not to smile. "Much more boring than here, I'm sure. Sorcerer Tioroso and I are the only sorcerers left."

"Master Shovaylan says that the banishment spell made people without a really strong gift forget about magic, so most sorcerer families traveled here where the spell couldn't affect any children who might not be as talented in the language of sorcery." Jem looked at her with wide eyes, and Ash felt distinctly uncomfortable.

"But it's been fading for a while now. Have you noticed any difference in people's response to magic lately?" Jem asked, bouncing his next step in a skip.

Ash felt a note of alarm sizzle through her. "I am not really sure if I could tell you. I don't usually talk about magic with people." Ash belatedly remembered her uncommonly long conversation about magic with Lady Amelia and Miss Penelope several years ago. She had thought is strange at the time that the subject hadn't been turned more quickly. Come to think of it, the servants at Trebruk manor, who she'd been sure never took note of her magic before her father's death, had aided her in her studies during her time under her uncle's rule. Bill had even asked her to teach him a few simple spells.

Ash stopped moving. "Does that mean that all the magical creatures will start coming out of Ketskatoret?" she asked in alarm. Even the birds she'd thought so beautiful had ended up creating a disastrous fire. What other creatures were there, and what havoc might they create on a people who had forgotten about them?

Jem stopped too and laughed at her look of unease. "No, Master Shovaylan said that this is their natural habitat so not many of them will wander from Ketskatoret even after the spell has faded completely."

Ash did not feel completely relieved as she began walking again. "Not many" might still be too many to handle depending on the type of creatures that wandered out of Ketskatoret. She glanced over to Prince Phillip and saw him watching, eyebrows lowered in a grim look. He'd obviously overheard their conversation.

She wanted to ask Jem more and hear Prince Phillip's thoughts on the matter, but they had already come to the trees' thick interweaving wall. The young man pulled a set of door hinges out of his pocket and grinned at Ash.

"I can't do hinges yet. Too complicated," he said before he clicked-snapped several spells in quick succession. The two fat metal hinges in his hands shot forward toward the trees and stuck parallel to each other. There was a *thwunk*, and a split formed running up the trunk in line with the hinges, across to the next tree trunk, and down until it angled again to connect with the first split creating a rectangle of space.

The boy muttered another spell, and a wooden knot like a knob formed. He reached forward and heaved the thick wood toward him, opening the newly made door. The two trunks making up the door had melded together, and the inch wide space between it and the unaltered wood helped the door open smoothly, despite the wood's thickness. Ash peeked through and saw that they were at base of a hill. The group would have to climb to the top to see what lay beyond.

"Master Shovaylan can make a real fancy door with the hinges and everything, but I can't yet. To get back out of the maze you need to climb this hill and skirt the edges of the valley beyond it. That part of Ketskatoret doesn't shift either, so it's a straight journey to the gateway, but be really careful. That's where most of the more intelligent magical creatures live, and not all of them are very friendly. Try to stay out of sight of them if you can."

"What?" Ash felt her legs stiffen in alarm as she was about to step through the doorway. "What kind of creatures? What will they do?" Without realizing it, she'd gripped the young man's arm as she spoke.

He glanced bewildered down to her fingers grasping his sleeve. Prince Phillip stepped forward to place a comforting hand on Ash's shoulder while somehow moving her out of Jemorian's reach.

Ash's gaze swung from the apprentice to Prince Phillip and locked her anxious eyes on his two green pools of confident calm. "We have to go back. We should find a sorcerer to help us get out. Didn't you hear what Jem said earlier? The king will need some fully qualified sorcerers soon anyway to deal with the effects of the fading banishment spell," Ash said, easily resisting the pull of the prince's composure.

"Oh, you don't need to worry about that. Master Shovaylan said he would make a trip to the king soon to consult with him about the matter. I was to tell the prince to relay the message to King Ferdinand. He would have told the Captain to pass the message on, but Master Shovaylan didn't like him," Jem said, wrinkling his nose in silent agreement.

Ash tried not to chuckle as Captain Forbs aimed a fierce frown at the young man.

"Most of the things living out there won't bother you if you don't bother them," Jem continued, completely unaware of the captain's ire. "That's why you stay on the edge of the valley as you travel. So long as you don't go inside the valley, you should be fine."

Ash didn't find his words reassuring.

Chapter Seventeen

If you come back again, remember to always travel to the left. It will seem like you're going in circles, but it's actually the most direct route to the village," Jem added, looking back toward the shell houses as if the thrill of the strangers had already worn thin and he would rather get back to his normal routine.

"So to get out now we'll need to take right turns once we reach the canyon?" Prince Phillip asked, having somehow placed himself next to Jem, between Ash and the sorcerer apprentice.

"No, there are no turns. The passage to leave and the one to get here are different." He shrugged. "Master Shovaylan says it's not worth trying to come up with a logical explanation for Ketskatoret. It will only give you a headache."

Captain Forbs crossed through the door, followed by the soldiers. Brett Johnson courteously escorted Lady Jane through, holding her hand to help her step over the tree stumps while the rest of the soldiers pushed Sorcerer Tioroso through. They boxed him in a prison of people on every side. Ash lingered, frustrated and anxious. Why was no one else as worried as she was about Jem's vague warnings?

As Prince Phillip stepped through the door, Ash lingered. She held out her hand, and Jem shifted, a blush flushing his cheeks. She dipped to his side to retrieve his hand anyway, smiling conspiratorially. "Can't you come with us as a guide to the exit?" Ash asked.

Jem's gaze flickered to the shell village, though he didn't try to pull his hand free. "I wish I could help you, but Master Shovaylan just said I should lead you to the door. He will be expecting me back." When Ash dropped Jem's hand in disappointment, Jem gave her an apologetic shrug. "I hope to see you again soon, Ashelandra." The bashful crook of his smile broadened into a confident grin. Despite her dissatisfaction with his unwillingness to see them safely to the exit, Ash felt that she could have been friends with the young man. She wished that she could just stay, learn magic, and avoid the discomfort of her current situation.

"I also hope to return soon. There is so much I want to learn."

"You don't know the half of it," Jemorian said ruefully. "But you may not have to come back here if Master Shovaylan goes down to help the king. If he takes me with him, I'll come visit you," he added as Ash stepped through to the area unprotected from the more dangerous magical creatures of Ketskatoret. Jem waved once, then heaved the massive trunk door back into place. She heard a thunk and saw the door's cracks melt back together into two solid trees. She sighed.

"I'm surprised the boy didn't come with us after all that flirting. And anyway, I thought your name was just Ash," Prince Phillip said beside her, voice grumpy. Ash jumped, not realizing he'd stayed near her.

She scowled at him. "I wasn't flirting, not that it's any of your concern, and Ash is my nickname. Most people thought my full name too strange and long for polite society, so it was shortened to Ash. Only my father ever really called me by my full name, and even he chopped it short when I was being particularly mischievous." Ash grinned, anxious mood soothed as she remembered an especially sweet prank involving pudding and the manor cat that she'd played on her father and a vexing woman set on acquiring Baron Fredrick's wealth and lands. Though he'd grounded her for a week, Ash rather thought her father had been secretly glad to be rid of the meddlesome woman.

"That's too bad. It's a beautiful name. It suits you." Prince Phillip walked away to join Brett and Jane as they climbed the hill. Ash stood frozen for a moment, unnerved by how such simple words said in such a casual manner could affect her so much. She could feel the rhythmic tattoo of her heart tapping in her throat.

She swallowed it down and gripped the straps of her pack tightly as she marched forward to the valley.

At the crest of the hill, Ash looked down on a cluster of willow trees with swaying blue-green branches. Next to the umbrella woods, a stream meandered through a grassy open meadow where golden gazelle-like animals grazed. As she watched, a large patch of grass shifted and jumped at one gazelle. As the rest of its herd startled away, the gazelle's golden head twisted toward the green lump on its back and jabbed at the attacking creature with spiraled black horns. The bushy green animal sprang away from the gazelle and was immediately invisible to Ash among the grasses. The gazelle pranced nervously in place, golden coat flashing in the sun as its head swung around searching for the camouflaged attacker.

The gazelle turned, and the grass creature moved from behind, springing off the gazelle's hindquarters toward its golden neck. The gazelle shook its head, mouth open in a cry, though Ash was too far away to hear it. Blinding golden light emanated from the gazelle, and the grassy creature dropped to the ground, stunned. But it was too late. A garnet necklace of blood wreathed the gazelle's neck. Ash watched the gilded animal stumble to one knee as the grassy creature shivered like wind through unripe wheat as it shook itself and clamped onto the gazelle's already torn neck in a final death grip.

Ash glanced at the soldiers clustered around. Everyone was watching the scene with varying degrees of alarm.

A breath of air puffed out from Ash in a nervous laugh. This is what her countrymen might have to deal with soon? "Who knew sod could be so dangerous," she whispered to Jane beside her, trying to lessen her worry through humor. Trembling, Jane did not look away from the large lump of grass covering the downed gazelle, though Sorcerer Tioroso glared as if to say her joke was in bad taste. Her brow rose in a silent signal saying he was the last person who had the privilege to distribute censure.

Captain Forbs cleared his throat loudly to get everyone's attention, but then said quietly, "I suggest we stay alert to any moving grass, and do as the boy said by keeping as far to the edge of the valley as we can."

The soldiers surrounded Ash, Lady Jane, Prince Phillip, and Sorcerer Tioroso, though they kept the sorcerer separated from the prince. As they followed the crest of the hill along the gradually rising cliff face at the edge of the valley, everyone kept their eyes roving over the vegetation, looking for movement. Ash was happy to be surrounded rather than pushed to the front as she had been in the past. Though it most likely meant nothing, considering the prisoner was also protected by a barrier of soldiers, Ash felt more connected to Prince Phillip's guard than she ever had before, more committed to protecting the men who were, in turn, shielding her from harm. She scanned the area carefully, ready to launch rocks at anything that might attack.

They reached the group of willows Ash had seen from above. The trees clustered to their right as Ash and the others walked at the base of towering sheer rock on the left. Thick trunks were mostly veiled by hundreds of curved branches that swayed and knotted like tangled hair. Tiny blue-green leaves clung close to each bough like sharply pointed feathers, and the limbs' tips flicked toward them as if trying to breach the small gap of sky to reach where they walked beside the rock. Ash felt no breeze. The unexplained movement worried her, as well as the thought that there was nowhere to retreat if something emerged from the branches' shifting curtain.

Ash sighed when the willow forest began to thin. Evening was falling, and she didn't think it would be wise to make camp while still in Ketskatoret. Ash heard a hum under the clack of the striking branches. A flash of pale white in the swaying limbs caught her eye. She squinted, but the growing darkness blurred the trees' leaves to green fuzziness. Several branches swung apart, and Ash thought she saw a child sprint from the gap toward the more tangled section of tree. She rubbed her lids, sure her eyes were deceiving her, but soon the motion of the foliage parted to show large frightened eyes framed by tangled brown hair. The child hid her body behind hanging limbs but peeked around them to watch the prince's party.

"Blimy! It's a lass," the soldier beside her gasped. Ash thought his name was Barnes.

"Did she get lost from the sorcerer's village, do you think?" Prince Phillip asked, taking a step toward the girl.

"I don't know, but I think we should be cautious about approaching her." Captain Forbs put his arm across Prince Phillip's chest to stop his progress. "Barnes, Patterson, see if you can coax her out, but keep alert."

The two men nearest Ash nodded and slid slowly to the girl. Muffled noise behind her distracted Ash from watching the men's progress. She turned to see Sorcerer Tioroso widen his eyes and shake his head in an emphatic no.

Without even pausing to think Ash cried, "Wait!"

Barnes and Patterson hesitated, and the girl startled further into the willow's umbrella.

Patterson scowled back at Ash. "You've scared her," he accused.

"I'm sorry, but I'm not so sure we should . . . Look out," Ash yelled as several of the willow's limbs shot out and wrapped around the two men.

They screamed in pain as the branches' leaves sliced through cloth into their bodies. Ash clicked the transformation spell, and the strangling limbs pulling the men under the willow's umbrella burst into water. Barnes and Patterson dropped to the ground groaning.

"Run!" Prince Phillip yelled, pulling his sword free as he raced to help the men.

Captain Forbs passed the prince, commanding him curtly to stay back, but Prince Phillip didn't listen. As more branches snaked forward to grab Barnes, Prince Phillip slashed through the wood. The severed branch twitched on the ground like an earthworm in a puddle. Captain Forbs hacked at the branches reaching for Patterson as several other soldiers helped the two men move beyond the tree's reach. As soon as they were safe, Prince Phillip and Captain Forbs retreated as well.

Ash bent down to the two men to assess their wounds. The leaves had been as sharp as serrated knives. Jagged gashes ringed the men an inch deep. Ash snapped the words to the spell to heal, and the wounds closed, but the skin was still an angry red, the sealed skin fragile.

"I wish I could do more," Ash said helplessly to the two men. Barnes put his hand on hers, and Ash was so surprised she almost jerked away.

"You saved our lives. We couldn't ask for more than that," Barnes said, and next to him Patterson nodded agreement.

"The girl must have been an illusion. The sound I heard before the girl appeared must have been the tree casting an illusion spell, but the noise was too faint for me to make the connection," Ash said. She turned to look back at Sorcerer Tioroso, who watched her with such unwavering indifference she could hardly believe his warning earlier had been real.

"Now we know why Jemorian advised us to stay at the valley's edge.

I doubt any other creatures would venture through those trees to the cliff," Prince Phillip said as he helped Patterson to his feet.

Ash canceled her earlier expectant thoughts about becoming friends with Jem. At least no one would have to deal with these trees outside of Ketskatoret. Trees could not move from the maze, or at least, she fervently hoped not.

"I just wish the little idiot had been more specific about why we should stay at the edge," Ash replied as she put Barnes' arm over her shoulder to give him a boost up. Barnes snickered in her ear. Prince Phillip smiled grimly, and Ash thought it was a good thing the silly sorcerer's apprentice was not within Prince Phillip's reach at that moment.

"I think it would be best if we double time it to the canyon. The light is almost gone, and I don't want another disastrous encounter," Captain Forbs said.

Another soldier took Ash's place supporting Barnes, but he patted her shoulder before she moved away. The gesture warmed her more than she could say.

Much to Ash's surprise and relief, the party made it to the wave canyon and through the mile long passage without any incidents. Ash kept straining her ears for the sound of the mist casting its spells, sure the foggy green mass would appear at any moment and turn the stone waves into water, but the rock remained solidly looming.

The tunnel to the bridge was chill, but when a blockade of soldiers bottlenecked at the opening to the bridge, Ash understood why. Outside, the air was bitingly cold. The bridge was covered in a three-foot layer of snow. Though the water from the plunging river still flowed quickly, misting the air as it shot from the cliff to the rocks far below, the edges of the river were crusted in thick blocks of ice. White blanketed the mountain all around.

The sun seemed to be higher in the sky than when they were in Ketskatoret, and Ash was thankful for the little light remaining. It made crossing possible, if dangerous. The men got out what ropes there were and tied everyone together so that if one person fell, the rest would act as an anchor. Ash had to resist the urge to crawl across the narrow middle section of the bridge. Jane did drop down to hands and knees near the center portion, slowing the train of soldiers, and soaking the front of her dress. After safely crossing, a soldier loosed the rope around her waist, but she stayed sunk in the snow beyond the bridge, skirts wet both in front and at the hem as she shivered and waited for Ash to finish crossing. When Ash was safely on the other side, she grabbed her cousin's cold hands and rubbed them vigorously with her own.

Soldiers cleared away enough of the snow to set up two camp fires. The sun was almost gone, and no one had any coats. Their party had set out as summer was drawing to an end, just as the land began to cool from the summer's heat. Now the high mountain was frozen. Ash wondered how much time had passed in the outside world while they were in Ketskatoret. They were too high up to be able to determine if the icy grip to the air had recently taken hold or was loosening toward spring. Though they'd only been inside Ketskatoret for a few days, the constant barrage of events had made it seem longer.

When the two fires had been lit, Ash and Jane huddled close to the flame, sharing a blanket. Ash could feel Jane shivering next to her, and Ash worried that Jane's still-damp dress was making it impossible for Jane to warm up enough to fight the chill. Ash's own wet hem and soaked boots swaddled her in an icy cold wrapping that spread in a tight quiver through her whole body. Across from them on the other side of the fire, Prince Phillip strode to the edge of the campfire to warm himself. His blanket draped his shoulders. His eyes locked on to the flickering flames for several minutes. As if sensing her stare, he looked up and met Ash's eyes for a moment before they swiveled to Jane. In two quick strides, he'd circled the fire to stand at her side, draping his blanket on top of Ash's over the two girls.

"It's too cold to give up your blanket. You'll freeze in the night," Ash said.

"I can share with one of the soldiers. Is there anything magical you can do to help?" he asked.

"Perhaps. I can look in my books." Ash glanced over at the fire a few feet away where several soldiers guarded Sorcerer Tioroso. He was watching Jane. His long-lashed brown eyes filled with an emotion that Ash couldn't help but think was concern. Ash wished she could ask the sorcerer if he knew any spells that would help keep everyone warm.

She could guess at a possible wording to create the spell, but because the language of sorcery originated from a myriad of magical creatures, the wording could change. Thinking of Jem's explanation, she shook her head. No wonder the language had always seemed so random. She'd had terrible trouble pinning down all of its grammatical rules. It was a relief to know that her confusion hadn't stemmed from incompetence.

She glanced at the sorcerer again, doubting Prince Phillip would allow him to cast any spells, and it was too risky to trust him, despite his earlier help. He noticed Ash watching and jerked his head in a beckoning gesture.

Prince Phillip caught the exchange. "He would likely know something that could be done, but I'm not sure it would be wise to loose the gag to ask," he said.

Ash nodded absently, feeling Sorcerer Tioroso stare willing her to come talk to him. She stood, wrapping both blankets fully around Jane. "He has to eat anyway. I'll watch him closely, and ask if he knows what can be done. It's in his best interest to help since he also doesn't have a blanket of his own. If he tries to cast a spell, I'll stop him before he can finish."

Ash headed toward Sorcerer Tioroso, before stopping to consider. She turned back and retrieved her books from her bag, then strode to the sorcerer's fire. The soldier sitting beside Sorcerer Tioroso loosed the sorcerer's gag as another retied his hands in front of him so that he could eat. Eating would be awkward with his wrists stuck tightly together, but still manageable. When the food was handed to him, however, it sat unheeded in his lap.

Instead, he said, "There is a spell that can warm the air, but it won't do much good if there's nothing to keep the warmth in. You need to make a shelter so that the heat generated by the spell won't dissipate as quickly."

Ash looked around her as if to search for materials she could use to make a shelter. Night had fully fallen, and beyond the light of the fires the mountain was shrouded in darkness. Even blinded by the dark, she knew that there was nothing around other than rocks, river, and snow.

The roar of the rushing water beat in her ears, reminding her of the rolling thunder she'd heard before Ketskatoret's flood had swallowed her whole.

"You're not thinking like a sorcerer. Perhaps your uncle forcing you into the role of maid dulled your creativity." He let out a small huff of knowing laughter.

Ash froze as if keeping still would hold the moment still and keep Sorcerer Tioroso's subtle revelation from spreading to the soldier sitting beside them. Slowly, she met his eyes and then flicked her gaze to the soldier. The man seemed uninterested in Sorcerer Tioroso's words. She was sure they'd been too obscure to mean anything to him.

Ash narrowed her eyes in a hazel glare at the man, butter-toffee flecks surely sparking, but Sorcerer Tioroso continued without noticing.

"I know you have the capability to transform water to something at least as solid as glass. You changed glass back to water when we fought." Sorcerer Tioroso's mouth turned upward in a small and somewhat rueful smile. It turned his pretty face beautiful. Ash swallowed uncomfortably when she realized how quickly her face, tight with anxious suspicion, eased. It was hard for her to think of Sorcerer Tioroso as a criminal, in spite of what he'd done to Jane, and despite how Jane had obviously told him all about her situation.

"You seem to have a rudimentary knowledge of spells, though if Lady Jane hadn't informed me of who you were at the wrong moment, your skills would not have been enough. Still, something as simple as a small shelter should be possible." Sorcerer Tioroso glanced at the soldier sitting on alert beside him, ready to strike if the sorcerer began to speak a spell. "I would teach you the spell for warmth, but I'm afraid you'll have to look it up in your books." Though his words had been a little condescending, his expression was humble. His sheepish smile flashed again, and Ash had to stop herself from smiling in response.

"Thank you," she said stiffly to hide her confusion. It seemed a dangerous sort of thing to be unoffended and at ease around the sorcerer, especially when he knew who she really was.

As soon as Sorcerer Tioroso was done eating and had been gagged,

Ash took her books and stepped reluctantly away from the fire's warmth closer to the river's edge. She clicked the spell to levitate a large globe of water, much bigger than she'd ever managed to lift before. Her journey through the depths of Ketskatoret had at least taught her something. Moving the water closer to the two fires, she worded the spell to push the water from the middle outwards until it was in the form of a hollow dome hovering above. Many of the soldiers hunched closer to the fire as they watched the water above warily. A few others moved away from the fires out from under the dome. Ash couldn't really blame them. If she had mispronounced even a single word, everyone would be drenched in freezing water.

The words of her spell punched a small hole at the top of the globe to vent the fire's smoke, and lowered the water to the ground before transforming the liquid to wood. The light and people inside, visible through the watery wall a moment before, were now completely hidden by a giant curving bowl of pine. As the few soldiers who'd chosen to remain outside the water's reach walked around the wooden walls, looking for a door, Ash realized she'd forgotten to make one. She laughed, teeth chattering, as the icy chill in the air spread from her numb legs to her fingers and face, sapping her body's warmth. Rubbing her hands together, she spoke a spell to make an entrance and the soldiers and she hurried inside the odd dome shelter.

There was already a marked difference between the interior temperature and that of outside. The two fires did much to help as the smoke rose through her upper hole, but the snow on the ground around them would soon melt, leaving the party in mud. Ash directed the men to one side of the building so she could transform the snow already packed down from booted feet into a wooden floor. She then shooed everyone onto the new pine surface so she could transform the other side. The only area she left without floor was around the two fires. Surveying her creation, Ash felt the happy thrill she often experienced when mastering complicated spells. Though the building was odd by society's standards, Ash still felt it held its own strange charm.

Everyone settled down comfortably throughout the shelter once she'd declared the job finished. Ash was surprised to get several nods of acknowledgment and thanks from the soldiers as they moved to arrange their bedrolls. Patterson gave her a pat on the back in passing. Warmth spread through her. Even a small difference in the men's reaction to her magical display was an unexpected gift.

Ash flipped through her books looking for the spell that would keep the building warm through the night even if they let the fires die down. When she found it, she glanced at Sorcerer Tioroso again, wishing she could ask about the pronunciation of a difficult section. His head was bowed, the gag ringing his face, bound hands stretched behind his back. His form flowed in a graceful line of sadness and despair like a fallen angel whose wings had been clipped. Ash noticed him shiver, and she looked away, annoyed at herself for feeling pity. Her eyes moved to Jane, who huddled as close to the fire as she could, blankets wrapped tight around her, amber gaze locked to the flames. If the sorcerer resembled a fallen angel, the tint of blue to Jane's fine porcelain features colored by the cold, made her look like a frozen fairy trapped in the unforgiving land of man.

Brought back to task by seeing Jane's misery, Ash pronounced the words for the warmth spell, careful of the complicated trill in one of the words, but felt no difference. She tried several more times, varying the syllables and clicks to try to get the right sound. Out of the corner of her eye she could tell that Sorcerer Tioroso had turned his attention from the floor to watching her efforts. She didn't look up, finding the scrutiny of a trained sorcerer embarrassing. After about ten more tries she was finally able to find the right articulation. The room warmed immediately to that of a mild summer's day.

All around she saw blankets that had been used as coats drop to the ground. Conversation picked up. Prince Phillip walked through his soldiers, greeting and chatting with them. Occasionally, he patted their shoulders or shook their hands. He meandered through the soldiers, somehow still dropping by every member of the party. The men's dour expressions lightened, their eyes bent toward the prince as if he were the source of the warmth now enveloping the room.

The dimness of the firelight hid the brush of freckles on Prince Phillip's face and accented his high cheekbones and the aristocratic line of his jaw. His clothes' worn and dirty state could not camouflage the confident bearing of his shoulders, and it struck Ash anew that he was indeed a prince. One day he would be king. That daunting fact had faded somewhat during her time with him in Ketskatoret. He mingled easily with the men around him, putting everyone at ease as they settled down for the night. Even Captain Forbs cracked a small smile as Prince Phillip spoke to him.

Ash smiled wryly to herself, thinking that in one way he'd been correct to label himself as an unusual prince. Not all royals were able or willing to mix so well with commoners. He'd thought of Ash as a commoner the entire time she'd known him but had still treated her with respect. Rather than making him less like a prince, however, Ash felt that this quality made him truly royal. Though Ash would avoid court as much as possible once Jane and Prince Phillip were married, she was relieved to know that the responsibility of her country would one day be in his hands. It was better to dwell on that relief than on the sinking feeling in her stomach growing inside as his actions among the men reinforced the knowledge that her part in his life was finished. He had no more reason to devote any of his precious time to her.

Ash put her books away and came back to Jane, who, despite the warmth, sat close to the fire. She had loosened the blankets around her shoulders a little, and Ash was relieved to see that her face had lost its blue sheen. Jane smiled up at Ash and opened one side of the blanket in a gesture of invitation. Ash tucked herself in beside her cousin and stretched her still numb feet toward the fire.

"You really are quite amazing. I can't believe we've lived together all these years and I never knew. I should have guessed though. Father became increasingly clumsy after we moved to the manor." Jane paused for a moment, brows scrunched in thought. "Was that incident involving the cat practically climbing my father like a tree to get to the mouse in his clothes you?"

"I might have had something to do with that." Ash's grin was slow and inviting. Across the room, Prince Phillip's progress through his soldier's halted mid-step. His hand, reaching out to pat Brett Johnson, had stopped before it reached the young man's shoulder. Brett noticed the prince's distraction and followed Prince Phillip's gaze to Ash. The young man's cheeks flared red as he caught Ash's eye. Ash smiled wider and winked at the two men before turning back to Jane, content to leave them wondering about the women's topic of conversation.

"No wonder you always had such a hard time keeping still inside the house when you had such amazing things to explore beyond its confines," Jane said.

"I'm not sure if my natural restlessness can wholly be attributed to my desire to learn spells." Ash laughed. "Though my father did say my adventurous spirit came from my mother. Maybe it is a trait connected with being a sorcerer."

Jane sighed. "I envy you."

Ash was unsure what to say. "Soon you won't be living with Lord Richard anymore. You will be free to live your life as you like."

"You will be inheriting the manor soon. Father and James will have to come live at the palace as well. He doesn't think I know, but he had to sell our home in Durbinshire to pay the costs of a speculation that failed. We've been living on the stipend he is paid as your guardian."

"Ah." Ash shifted on the wood floor, uncomfortable. "Still, you will be the princess. You could give him a house as a gift."

"Even if that were possible, do you think I would so easily be free of his influence, his expectations?" Jane brushed a stray strand of hair out of her eyes behind her ear in a brisk jerking motion.

Ash agreed with her, but she was surprised to hear Jane speaking so frankly, even to the point of sounding uncharacteristically rebellious. As she contemplated a tactful response, a large yawn stretched her jaw, despite her effort to hold it back.

The corner of Jane's mouth crooked upwards, though her eyes were sad. "Let's sleep. Talking of these things is fruitless anyway." The two girls stretched themselves a little farther from the fire next to each other. Ash tentatively reached out and grasped Jane's hand. Jane squeezed back and held on tight until sleep loosened their clasped fingers.

Chapter Eighteen

In the morning, the party gathered their things. Several of the men cut slits in their blankets and wore them as parkas. Ash did the same for herself and Jane, using a bit of spare rope to tie the blankets at the waist. The cold of the outside air made Ash's lungs ache. Little needles of seeping chill pierced her hands and face.

Though the path down the mountain was at first broad, the party soon reached the narrower trail and found a wall of snow blocking the path. Ash moved to the front, levitated as much of the snow as she could, and dropped it to the side. Once there was only a thin layer, she changed the ice to wood, and the group progressed down the mountain at a slow, but constant pace on a dry, firm road of pine.

By the midday meal, however, Ash's tongue was cramped from hours of manipulating the complicated sounds of spells. Her throat felt dry, her lips chapped, and her cheeks ached. Prince Phillip approached her as she sat slumped on a large flat rock she'd swept clear of snow by hand rather than with a spell and offered her a canteen of water. She dropped her hands from massaging her cheeks and nodded thanks, loath to utter any sort of sound, and guzzled nearly half of the container.

"Should we stop here?" Prince Phillip asked.

Ash took one more drink before answering. "Let me rest an hour. I think I can continue after that." She lay down and curled herself tightly on the rock's chill surface.

"You should eat something first." Prince Phillip rocked her shoulder gently to prod her into sitting.

"Too tired. Rather sleep," Ash mumbled as she shrugged off his hand. Exhaustion sapped the surprise of discovering how much the constant concentration of speaking spell after spell had drained her. She'd never had an opportunity to discover that in the past.

"Sleep then, but don't forget to eat when you wake," she heard Prince Phillip say before she drifted into a cold and uncomfortable slumber.

Ash woke a half hour later stiff from the freezing chill of the air. The nap hadn't been very restful. The stinging slap of the cold overcame her body's desire for rest, but the short break helped enough for her to feel that she could continue.

"Awake already? I'm glad. I was a little worried. You wouldn't stop shivering and all the blankets are already being used by the soldiers." Ash turned to see Jane seated on the edge of Ash's rock. Her blanket was missing. Ash looked down and saw the extra blanket covering her. Jane's slim frame was shivering, though it looked as though she was trying to hide the fact.

"I'm sorry, Jane. You shouldn't have done this. You need the blanket for yourself." Ash pulled the woolen cloth off guiltily and resettled it around Jane.

"You really were starting to worry me. Your face went very pale and you were shaking so violently I'm not sure how you could sleep at all. Here, Prince Phillip asked me to make sure you ate these rations as soon as you woke." Jane offered her the food, and Ash glanced around as she took the nutty trail bread. Prince Phillip was talking to Captain Forbs with some of the other soldiers, but that didn't stop him from noticing Ash looking. He mimed bringing food to his lips and silently mouthed the word, "Eat."

She made a childish pouty face at him, even as her heart sped cheerfully, then took a big bite of the unappetizing trail food. He grinned and mouthed, "Good girl." Ash snuck a quick look to see if Jane or anyone else was looking, and when she saw that no one was paying attention, she stuck out her tongue at Prince Phillip.

He had to turn his laugh into a cough when Captain Forbs stopped speaking to glare at the prince indignantly. Ash saw him hold his hands up to Captain Forbs in a pacifying manner before he put one hand on Captain Forbs' back to genially turn and lead him to her.

"Are you able to continue on?" Prince Phillip asked when they were close.

"For a while, but we should look for a place where I can make a shelter by early evening. I'm afraid if we go too long, my tongue will spasm and I won't be able to help us with sleeping arrangements."

"I'm glad to hear that your tongue is functioning. A moment ago, I thought it was falling from your mouth," Prince Phillip muttered to Ash. She smiled innocently at him and took another big bite of bread.

At the trail, Ash found that the soldiers were shoveling snow from the path. They'd made a sizable dent, considering they only had a few travel shovels. It was much slower than using sorcery, but she appreciated the men's efforts anyway. She made sure to thank each person and find out their names as Prince Phillip had suggested days ago before circumstances had made getting acquainted with the soldiers impossible. She abandoned casting the spell to make the path wood, hoping to conserve energy, and walked forward slowly.

Sunlight shone weakly in the sky in the late afternoon when Ash opened her mouth to cast another spell of levitation only to find that her mouth would not cooperate. Her jaw opened slowly like a rusted lever, and her tongue felt like a slab of thick dead meat unable to produce words, much less the complicated clicks and snaps required in the language of sorcery. She rubbed circles on her cheeks to warm and loosen the muscles, but it was no use.

When Ash turned from the head of the path, she found Prince Phillip standing behind her. Too tired to speak, she shook her head.

He nodded. "I think we're almost to the overhang that sheltered us the night we climbed the mountain. We still have several hours of daylight. I think we can make it if we shovel the rest of the way."

She bobbed a weary acknowledgement, and stepped back to let the soldiers pass to the head of the trail. Three of the men whose names she'd recently learned inclined their head to her as they passed. The men switched off in shifts, clearing the snow to reach the overhang. Even Prince Phillip took a turn, despite Captain Forbs's protests. Hidden by the snow's obscuring blanket, the sweating soldiers almost bypassed the overhang, but once an entrance was shoveled, the snow's white wall served to shield them from some of the night's chill.

Ash tried to snap the spell to warm the interior, but stumbled over the phrasing. Her mouth still refused to work properly, so she gave it up. When the manor was hers again, and she was free to do as she liked, Ash planned to practice mastering more complex spells. If she could lift more snow at a time, her poor mouth wouldn't feel so abused. She supposed she could practice sooner than that as she wandered and waited for her birthday, but thinking of the manor brought an ache of longing. She wondered how Bill was faring in the stables. Had Ash's workload been foisted onto Jenny? Was Cook doing well? Had Henry finally stopped dithering and gathered the courage to propose to Annette? Ash pushed the contemplations aside. Worrying and wondering wouldn't answer her questions. She would have to wait until it was safe to find out how Trebruk's staff fared.

That night, Ash had another reason to be grateful for her cousin's presence. She and Jane huddled together back to back under their blankets, happy for the extra warmth body heat could provide. Despite the close huddle, however, Ash woke tired, bones brittle with cold. She jumped up and down and put her head as close to the fire as she could without getting burned to warm her face enough to continue casting spells.

***

The daylight seemed brighter as they slowly made their way down the mountain. The lower they descended, the less snow there was to clear, and there was a noticeable rise in temperature. It wasn't enough to make her feel warm, but her nose felt less like a block of ice that could be broken off if bumped, and more like a nose should, if still a little runny from the cold.

Just before Ash thought she would need to take a break for lunch to rest her tormented tongue, she saw something move at the side of the blockade of snow on the path. Pausing, she squinted ahead at the mountain's slope beside the blocked path, and saw a chunk of snow sail down the slope.

"Do you see that?" she asked, turning to ask Prince Phillip, but he wasn't beside her.

Captain Forbs regarded her, lips pressed together in the thin line they usually displayed, but without the downward curl that he'd so often given her in the past. Ash's eyes flicked away, searching, and found Prince Phillip farther up the path, holding Jane's arm, steadying and preventing her from slipping. Ash swallowed to wet her dry throat and turned back to Captain Forbs.

"I think someone might be digging out the trail from the other side," she said, unhappy with the rasp in her voice.

Captain Forbs nodded. "Finish removing the snow between us. My men will be ready just in case, but it's most likely a rescue party sent from the king." He signaled two soldiers following just behind him to join him by Ash as she clicked the spell that would remove the snow separating them from the section of the trail where she saw the snow tumble down the side of the mountain.

It took more than one spell to remove it all, but the blue of the army's uniforms was soon revealed. The soldiers held their shovels defensively, eyes wide with fear as they watched the large chunks of snow lift from the trail and drop to the side. One man dropped his shovel and reached for his pistol.

"Lower your weapon, Lieutenant Jackson. Prince Phillip would be displeased if you killed the sorceress," he said.

Ash stared at Captain Forbs, unsure of whether to feel grateful that he'd stopped the soldier from shooting her, or annoyed with the way his words made her sound like a mere possession of the prince's. At the sound of Captain Forbs's level command, however, Lieutenant Jackson dropped his pistol to his side in relief. The soldiers beside him also lowered their shovels.

"Captain, you're alive," Lieutenant Jackson said.

Prince Phillip squeezed between Captain Forbs and the soldier beside him. "We are all alive and well, Lieutenant. Thank you for clearing the trail. We'll make good time the rest of the way, thanks to you."

Lieutenant Jackson dropped to one knee in the slushy earth, head bowed, fist on heart. The two soldiers beside him followed. "It will only take a few hours to reach the foot of the mountain, Your Highness. A full company of soldiers awaits there. We've been taking turns clearing out the snow now that the winter storms are over."

"Please get up. So the storms have ended. What month is it exactly?" Prince Phillip asked.

"April, Your Majesty."

Ash's heart jumped in excitement. "What day in April?" she couldn't help asking, even though it wasn't proper to interrupt. Lieutenant

Jackson looked at her uncertainly and then glanced at the prince, obviously unsure if he should answer.

"Answer the lady's question. She is, after all, the hero of this rescue mission," Prince Phillip smiled slyly.

Upon hearing this strange declaration, Lieutenant Jackson's eyes widened and he looked at Ash with more interest. "It's the tenth of April, My Lady."

Ash grinned and after a stunned moment, the Lieutenant's mouth also curved upward as red blushed his cheeks. Only twelve days until her twenty-first birthday. Twelve more days and her uncle would have no more power over her. She clapped her hands together and squeezed through Captain Forbs and Brett Johnson to get to Jane, disregarding the confused delight of Lieutenant Jackson's answering smile, the disapproving frown of Captain Forbs, and the annoyed glare Prince Phillip was directing at the young lieutenant.

Ash grasped her cousin's hands when she'd reached Jane. She pulled her farther from the soldiers and whispered, "You're too far back to hear, but I just learned it is April tenth today."

"So much time passed? It was October when we entered Ketskatoret, and it seemed we were only in there a few days," Jane said, adopting Ash's hushed tone.

"I know. Isn't it amazing?" Ash exclaimed, volume rising in excitement. When she saw Patterson regarding her curiously from nearby, she lowered her voice. "I thought I would have to wander around for months, but I'm sure I'll be able to last for two more weeks."

"Was working as a servant really so horrible? I am sorry I was so impotent. I knew it was hard for you, but you seemed so strong, and I have little influence over my father. He isn't really a bad man, you know. He just doesn't know how to interact with someone like you." Jane's big amber eyes reminded Ash of a sad puppy.

One of Ash's eyebrows rose sardonically, but she decided to refrain from refuting her well-meaning cousin. "I just needed to share my excitement with someone. I'll soon be independent. But now I begin to think it poor taste on my part to say so to you. You'll be married soon, so you may be affected, but if you are still single by the time my birthday arrives, you're welcome to stay at the manor for as long as you wish. I might even let James stay if he behaves himself." Ash felt a guilty sort of hope that something would happen to stop Jane from marrying the prince at all.

"And Father?" Jane asked.

Ash's tone lost its excitement and grew grim. "As you said, we do not interact well with each other. After his treatment to me, I'm sure you can understand that I could never allow him to stay."

Jane nodded her head sadly, a sorrowing angel, but Ash was unmoved.

The men began moving down the trail. Jane and Ash followed, steps quick to keep up with the increased pace of the eager soldiers. Sorcerer Tioroso stumbled often, the lead rope pulling tight as he resisted keeping pace with his guards. His makeshift coat, fashioned from part of a blanket, was smaller than everyone else's. It barely covered his arms. Ash was glad that the weather warmed the lower they descended. The sight of Sorcerer Tioroso's constant shivering somehow made her feel guilty, though she tried to convince herself it was ridiculous to feel so.

Prince Phillip dropped back next to Ash and Jane. "You seem glad to have lost months of our life in a matter of days. Is there a reason?" he asked.

Ash saw no harm in telling him. "It's my birthday on the twenty-second."

"I find it puzzling that you are excited about your birthday after our previous conversation on this very subject concerning age and the effect of time on a young woman's marriageability."

Ash and Jane exchanged a look. The light caught the blond of Prince Phillip's copper eyebrow as it arched in question.

"Some birthdays are worth the cost of lost youth. And besides, technically I will always be six months younger than my age indicates thanks to Ketskatoret," Ash said, flipping a loose strand of hair behind her shoulder.

Prince Phillip looked like he wanted to press for a further explanation, but was distracted by the appearance of three more soldiers climbing the trail to meet their group. He left Jane and Ash to greet the soldiers who'd come to relieve Lieutenant Jackson and his companions of digging duty. Busy putting the new soldiers at ease, Prince Phillip did not come back.

It was dusk by the time everyone reached the foot of the mountain. A troop of soldiers moved about in organized chaos through the camp. Though the chill had thawed as they descended, the early evening sapped what meager heat hung in the air. Ash was grateful when she and Jane were escorted to a tent evacuated specially for the only two women present, Molly having traveled back home to her inn long ago.

In the tent, Ash spoke the spell to warm the interior, and she and Jane halfheartedly ate food rations from her pack. The soldiers outside most likely had a more appetizing meal prepared, but she was too exhausted to care, and Jane seemed equally disinclined to explore other options. After eating, the two girls arranged themselves on the extra blankets provided and slept soundly until morning.

Ash woke to the sound of dropping poles, the snap of canvas, and the rumble of men's voices as they broke down the camp. Apparently a day of rest was not to be forthcoming. Ash groaned and rolled slowly to her feet. She itched her head and wished for a bath as she combed her greasy hair before braiding it tightly down her back. At Jane's polite request, Ash handed over her brush. She noticed that the oil in Jane's hair only served to make the silvery golden braid she plaited shine in metallic splendor. Ash blew out a short powerful blast of air, irritated with constant reminders of Jane's perfection.

Her mood did not improve once out of the tent. A younger soldier ran up to greet Jane, bowing nervously, eyes wide with admiration as he drank in the sight of her.

"I'm to get you breakfast and help you with preparations to leave, My Lady," he said to her. His skinny frame didn't fill his uniform well, despite the fact that the king's uniforms were cut to flatter men, making their shoulders appear broader, their waists trim. It didn't work on the young man in front of Ash. He looked like a child playing dress up in his father's clothes. When his narrow face turned to look at Ash, his eyes widened, and his prominent Adam's apple wobbled as he swallowed nervously.

"Is it true what they say, that you captured the sorcerer all by yourself?" the young man asked, eyes open in an unflatteringly wide goggle.

"Prince Phillip was next to me at the time." Ash shrugged, uncomfortable with taking credit for Tioroso's capture, especially with Jane holding so carefully still beside her.

The young man nodded. "I heard the prince say you bested the sorcerer with magic. Wish I could have seen that," he gushed. Ash squirmed at the sight of his unexpected admiration and released him from his assistance as soon as he'd directed Jane and her to the horses they would be riding.

To her delight, Windrunner had stayed with the prince's mounts at the foot of the mountain through the winter in an encampment the king had ordered erected for those stationed to search for the prince. Windrunner stomped her foot in greeting and waffled Ash's hair as Ash stroked the horse's neck.

It was hard to leave the meager sunlight at the base of the mountain to pass through the dank gloom of the rocky wasteland beneath Ketskatoret. Though Ash knew it was unlikely the floating landmass would suddenly drop from the sky and smash them, she still felt the weight of the land above pressing in, making her feel as if the company traveled through a cave rather than above ground.

Some of the men stayed behind at the mountain to await Sorcerer Shovaylan's arrival and to make sure nothing else tried to slip out of the mountain past the wasteland and into the kingdom. Ash hoped the sorcerer wouldn't take too long to come speak with the king, but there was no way to tell when he might descend, since one day in Ketskatoret could equal months below.

Ash tried not to crouch down in her saddle as they traveled. To distract herself from the feeling of claustrophobia the thick clouds above inspired, she watched the soldiers. None made the sign against evil in her direction. In fact, she was getting so many glances of wide-eyed awe, nods, and shy smiles that she didn't know what to think. She wondered what on earth Prince Phillip had been telling everyone. Ash made a point of waving to the soldiers who'd traveled with her whenever they rode near and they were always good about waving back and joining her for a word or two now and then.

Though Prince Phillip did ride next to Jane and Ash occasionally, the conversation between the three was stilted and awkward. She felt like her presence was a contributing factor to that, but couldn't quite bring herself to ride farther ahead and leave the two alone, and Jane never tried to slip from Ash's side either. The prince never stayed long before finding some excuse to ride ahead with Captain Forbs. Ash ached for the lost ease between her and the prince.

The chill of the mountain's higher altitude was shared by the lower wasteland. Ketskatoret's cloud cover floated overhead, reinforcing Ash's image of traveling through an enormous dank cavern, ever cold and gloomy. Though the journey through the wasteland had taken three days travel on the way to the mountain, the size of the company, and treacherous footing of the rocks made quick return difficult. It took a full day longer to safely navigate the slippery rocks with so many people and horses. Ash was asked to heal four horses and one man by various members of her original traveling party. Each time, the soldiers gaped in wide-eyed wonder.

The night before they reached the first town beyond the wasteland, Ash sought out Sorcerer Tioroso. She hoped to speak with him at supper while his mouth was free from the gag, but the four soldiers all watching closely as he ate nodded to her politely, but would not allow her to talk with him. One ushered her away as the other three stood ready to pounce if he so much as smacked his lips suspiciously. The image of Sorcerer Tioroso's blank, hopeless face as he slowly chewed his food refused to leave her mind as she walked away.

The air warmed in a startling tingle of touch the moment the prince's party left the shadow of the wasteland behind, as if the sun spread soft fingers on Ash's skin. Spring fully gripped the land beyond Ketskatoret's looming cloud cover. The horses strained at their reins to rip the fragile looking clumps of grass lining the road. Unfurling leaves painted the stark tree branches with splashes of bright green. The road was muddy from a recent rainfall, but the storm had already passed, leaving the sky a crystal blue.

Ash noticed many of the soldiers looking up, drinking in the sight of a bright sky. She couldn't help but follow suit. It felt like being released after an extended imprisonment in a dank dungeon. The world seemed so much bigger, more open and full of possibilities.

That night, they stayed at an inn, and Jane and Ash were able to take a bath for the first time in more than a week. Despite Jane's protests, Ash let her use the water in the large wooden tub first. By the time Ash had a turn, the water was lukewarm and dirty. It hardly mattered. Scrubbing off the mud and grime that coated her was a relief. She felt like a snake sloughing off too-tight skin for the soft smooth scales underneath.

Prince Phillip bought two new split skirt riding habits for her and Jane. The longer of the two, which fit Jane's taller frame, was a light blue. Jane looked fragile and delicate as a porcelain doll. Ash's attire was mustard green. It made Ash look sallow. Jane tried to soothe her by saying that the fabric brought out the color of the butter-yellow and green in her eyes, but Ash was not fooled. Ash shrugged. It didn't really matter whether or not the clothes flattered her. She was just grateful to have something mended and clean.

Jane and she combed each other's wet hair and left it free to dry before the fireplace in their room. They sat in silence, and let the warmth of the fire seep in. Ash felt heavy and content as her eyelids drooped on the edge of sleep. When a demanding rap sounded on the door, Ash jumped and her heart sped.

"I suppose that's dinner, or maybe they wish us to go down and join them in the common room," Jane said as she deftly twisted her hair into a braid down her back. Ash was reaching up to do the same to her still damp locks when Jane began to open the door. She didn't get the chance to open it all the way. It was shoved inward, and Lord Richard barged through. Jane stepped back in surprise. Ash's fingers dropped and the few strands she'd woven together unraveled and fell around her face. He shoved the door closed, took two quick strides toward Ash, and clamped his hand over her mouth while using his other arm to bind her arms to her body in a manacle grip.

"Father, what are you doing?" Jane asked.

"Protecting myself. She's a sorceress. There is no knowing what she would do to me if she is allowed to speak," he replied. Ash jerked in surprise. She'd been hoping her uncle hadn't noticed the magic she used when escaping him, or at least not realized that it was her magic that had given her the advantage to run away. She slumped in Richard's grip as her mind raced. Lord Richard towered above Ash. His thick arms encased her in an inflexible lock. She needed a distraction to help her escape. Ash's eyes flicked to Jane in desperation, and her stare seemed to compel the usually obedient daughter to speak.

"Ash wouldn't do anything to you. Please let her go. And why are you here? Does the prince know?" Ash watched Jane's hands fidget in the folds of her dress helplessly.

"No, and you are not to tell him." Ash used Jane's distraction to twist in Lord Richard's grip and bite his hand. Lord Richard grunted in pain. "Go back to the palace with him. If he asks about his pet sorceress, tell him that she had a pressing matter to attend to and found herself unable to accompany him back to the palace." Lord Richard commanded Jane in short staccato phrases with pauses as he pushed his palm into her mouth until her jaw creaked and biting was impossible.

"How did you know that I was here at this inn, and that Ash would be with me?" Jane asked, echoing Ash's own silent question. She paused in her twisting struggle to relax her uncle's guard as she listened for the answer.

"When the mountain's pass snowed in, the king felt that I should know what had happened to you. The soldiers from Prince Phillip's company that were left at the base of the mountain explained how a sorcerer girl named Ash tracked you and your kidnapper to Spirit Mountain. To request a pigeon be sent to me the moment you came back was only natural. I sent the pigeon back telling how James was too sick for us to be able to meet you until you reached the palace. No one will know I was here." Lord Richard's last words woke Ash into a frenzy of kicking and twisting. She tried to make herself boneless so that she would slip out of Lord Richard's grip, but he lifted her much shorter body off the ground easily as he hauled her toward the door.

"Where are you taking her? What are you going to do?" Jane's voice was unusually shrill.

"You don't need to worry. I'm just taking her home. I am responsible for her after all." His voice was soothing, but the effect was lessened by his curse at the end when Ash elbowed him in the stomach. He rearranged his grip to squeeze tighter, trapping her arms.

"Not for long. She's almost twenty-one, and the prince asked her to go to the palace. He will be angry if she does not." Ash heard the quaver in Jane's soft voice as if she couldn't believe she was talking back to her father. Ash could hardly believe it herself.

"Jane," he said in a one-word command. Her mouth snapped shut, and she hunched inward in defeat. "Do what I tell you. If Ashelandra is able to inherit the manor and all her lands, then you will not be able to marry the prince. You don't have to worry. I'll keep her in a safe place, and once you are wed, she will be free to go." Ash let out a muffled grunt of disbelief and thrashed again, but Lord Richard's constricting grip was unbreakable, and it was tightening. She sucked in from her nose, but the vise on her ribs would not allow her to breathe deeply. There wasn't enough air. The room was going fuzzy and dark as Ash pulled what little air she could in and out of her partially obstructed nose.

"Considering all the circumstances, perhaps it would be better if I didn't marry the prince." Jane's words were almost too quiet to hear over the sound of Ash's struggle to breathe.

"You must. You will not disappoint me, Jane. I will come see you at the palace soon." As Lord Richard paused to ensure his words were understood, the arm surrounding Ash's ribs loosed enough to make the black dots in Ash's vision fade. "Open the door for me and make sure no one is in the hallway so I can take her out."

Jane wouldn't meet Ash's eyes as she slowly opened the door and looked out to see if anyone was in the hallway. She swung it wider to let her father and Ash through. Ash glared at her, but Jane never looked up to see it.

Lord Richard took a back stairway of which Ash had been unaware. It led to the kitchens. Inside a woman chopped vegetables, facing away from the hall. The rhythmic *thunk thunk* sound of the knife slicing through potatoes to the cutting board was barely discernible over the muted roar of the common room chatter and music seeping through the door to the right. Ash tried to yell through the hand clamped painfully tight against her mouth, but her uncle slipped her through the opposite door, leading her outside before the woman even had the chance to turn around.

James waited outside, holding the reins of three saddled horses. Like Jane, James avoided meeting Ash's eyes as he helped his father sling her belly down across the horse's back as if she were a sack of grain. She made tying her as difficult as she could, squirming and kicking as she tried to slide back to the ground.

The moment her mouth was free, Ash yelled as loud as she could. "Prince Phillip!"

Lord Richard's fist crashed into her skull and her cry was cut short by a tide of pain.

"Gag her before she recovers enough to get someone's attention or cast a spell. Tie her feet and hands to the saddle as well so she can't keep flailing around. I don't want her to even be able to wiggle," Lord Richard ordered James.

James stuffed a wad of cloth in Ash's mouth. He ran another strip across her open lips to hold the wad in. It cut at the corners of her mouth as it stretched to tie in the back. While Ash was dazed from the sting of her uncle's blow, James was able to finish gagging her and tying her hands before she remembered to kick and struggle for freedom.

Wham. A thunderbolt of pain struck her back near the shoulder blade. Even through the muffling cloth, her scream was piercing. Before the pain had a chance to subside, her legs were tied together to one side of the saddle, her hands to the other, immobilizing her like a bug pinned to a board. Lord Richard held the lead rope to her horse as he mounted his own, and spurred the animal to a gallop. Ash's horse followed. Each time its hooves struck earth, the saddle punched into her stomach, and her newly injured back zinged with pain.

Time seemed to stretch out interminably as they traveled the whole night long. The horse's flanks became sweaty, and Ash's face itched and burned from where it pressed against the mare's chestnut hair. She maneuvered an arm in between the mount's body and her face to create a cushion of space, and she felt the heat of the horse increase through the night's long exertion, warming and soaking her arm in a silent warning of the horse's exhaustion.

Only when the animal's breathing became ragged with foam slipping from its mouth did Lord Richard finally slow to a walk.

By then, light crept into the forest as the morning's sun overpowered the dimness of the moon. When Ash turned her head to look at the land around her, she could tell, even from her awkward angle, that the frenzied pace Lord Richard set had carried them to her forest. It took almost two days of travel to track Jane from this point to the edge of the wasteland when Ash had traveled with Prince Phillip, but a company of soldiers was much slower than three galloping horses pushed to the limit of their endurance. She was almost home. The prospect failed to cheer her.

Lord Richard halted his mare at the edge of the trees.

"Go ahead to the stables and manor and tell everyone they have the day off to visit family. Make sure they leave before you come back to get me," Lord Richard said.

James nodded and left Ash alone with her uncle. The horse was too tired to even fidget. As she lay like a dead man across the horse's withers, Ash considered trying to slither free of her ropes, but the chafing bindings had very little give. Her body ached. Even if she could somehow free herself from the rope, it was likely that she would land in an awkward heap and be unable to recover in time to flee. So she waited, hoping a better opportunity for escape would occur before freedom became impossible. Thinking back to the conversation with her uncle before she'd fled, she remembered his threat of marriage to James and what he planned to do to keep her complacent. Or had Lord Richard planned to marry her himself? It would cause less talk if two cousins were to marry rather than a niece and her uncle. She wondered if her uncle would have her marry before or after he reduced her to a simpleton.

Ash thought it would most likely be before, considering any number of things could go wrong when trying to beat someone just enough to make them permanently impaired mentally without actually killing them.

James returned just as Ash was building herself up into a panic. She heaved backwards to slide off the horse but didn't budge at all. Inside the stables, Lord Richard untied Ash from her horse and flung her to the hay-strewn floor. Ash crumpled. One tied foot twisted painfully as it hit before her knees struck the floor and lessened the tension on her bound feet. Still unbalanced, she fell forward onto one shoulder. Dust and hay puffed into the air filling her nose with the musky smell of the stable. She coughed into her gag as her eyes watered.

A gentle grip lifted her from the floor back to her knees. Ash looked up through her tearing eyes to see James's hand on her shoulders. When he saw her seeking his gaze, however, he jerked his arms away as if burned. She continued to stare, willing him to meet her eyes. Surely James could not be happy with his father's arrangement, no matter the benefit it would have to their family as a whole. If she was indeed to marry James, Lord Richard was dooming his son to a loveless marriage with a soon to be witless wife.

"Let's carry her inside," Lord Richard ordered. James's shoulders slumped.

"When does the priest arrive?" James's nose crinkled as he asked, as if smelling something bad.

"This afternoon." Lord Richard gripped his son's shoulders and met his eyes with an intensity that made Ash shiver. "We must secure things for the good of the family as quickly as possible. You understand why this sacrifice is necessary right now. As soon as Jane is wed to the prince, it will be possible to take care of things here so that you can marry whatever woman you wish."

Ash felt a little bubble of hysterical laughter building, but it was locked behind the gag in her mouth. James glanced at her for a brief moment, guilt etched in the creases of his brow. Lord Richard turned his son back to face him.

"To follow through with the hard decisions takes strength. Show me your worth." Lord Richard's voice rang with command.

James's creases of guilt smoothed into an expression of determination, his desire to please his father apparently outweighing his reservations. The water would not stop streaming from Ash's eyes despite the fact that the dust had long since settled back to the ground as the hopelessness of her situation seeped into her like poison spreading through her veins.

Chapter Nineteen

They put Ash in the small linen closet off the main hallway. It was only large enough for her to sit up with her legs tucked to her chest, hands retied behind her and pressing uncomfortably into her back. A sliver of light leaked through the crack at the bottom of the door, highlighting the curve of the folded lavender-scented sheets stacked neatly on the shelves.

Despite her distress, Ash dozed in dispirited discomfort until the sound of voices roused her.

"Don't try to back out now, Diakon Percival. I've already paid handsomely to keep your little indiscretion with the church coffers a permanent secret, and as my late wife's brother, you would also benefit by having my daughter as the future queen." Ash heard Richard's words rumble through the door. He was not pleased.

"You didn't tell me that it was *her* daughter," Ash heard a wobbling tenor voice say.

"What does it matter whose daughter she is? I told you it was my niece. You knew my brother married *that* woman. I thought you were smart enough to put two and two together. I should think you would be glad to exact a small revenge on the child of the woman who rejected you." Richard's deep growl bellowed with exasperation. "Didn't you join the church in a pathetic attempt to make the shrew regret her choice not to be with you? It didn't work. She forgot you and married my brother."

"I didn't give up the world to make her remorseful. I did it so Lady Rorinala wouldn't feel burdened by the feelings I couldn't hide. But that is long since in the past. I am a priest for better reasons now." The man's tenor voice faltered, and Ash thought it lacked conviction.

"Gave up the world, did you? Forgive me if I don't believe in your pious sacrifice after settling your gambling debts and replacing the church's money. You're lucky no one noticed." Lord Richard's roar dropped to a low rumble that Ash had to strain to hear through the door. "So you will marry my son to that woman's daughter and make sure there is never any question about her willingness or I will make you long for a permanent escape from this world."

Ash was leaning into the door to listen, so when it pulled open, she tumbled forward to land on her already sore shoulder. Lord Richard yanked her to her feet. Next to him stood a man not much taller than Ash in the long black robe, black pants, and braided red rope collar of a Diakon priest. On his thin face perched a pair of round spectacles on a small pointed nose. His hair was receding and neatly trimmed on the sides. He'd had the good sense not to comb over what hair remained over the middle bald portion. Looking at his well-kept appearance, Ash found it difficult to imagine the older man having a gambling problem, but people were not always what they seemed. She still had trouble thinking of Sorcerer Tioroso as a kidnapper.

Diakon Percival's eyes widened when he saw Ash. He pushed up his glasses with quick jerky fingers in a nervous habit that would be death to a gambler. He surveyed her loose hair, tangled like a rat's nest from her recent indecorous journey. Her mouth, wrists, and ankles were still tied tight, the rope on her legs catching her dress so that she looked like a sacked and trussed animal ready for the pot.

"You're Lady Rorinala's daughter?" He sounded incredulous.

She would have replied that the resemblance was much more apparent when her eyes weren't ringed with the blue under-shadow of exhaustion and pain and her hair was combed, but her mouth was full of saliva-soaked cloth. Instead, she straightened and stared at the man with fierce pleading determination, hoping to stir a feeling of shame for what he intended to do to the daughter of the woman he once claimed to love.

"Ah, I do see you have her eyes," Diakon Percival stammered before looking away.

Lord Richard bent to cut the rope at Ash's feet while still holding her arm in a tight meaty grip. She tensed. The rope snapped free from her ankles. Ash kicked up toward her uncle's head with all her might, wrenching her arm free at the same moment and bolting to the side. Lord Richard twisted so that the kick landed on his shoulder, but she still managed to slip free of his grip. She watched him as she sprinted away and so was unprepared when she crashed into a soft, but solid wall.

Ash looked up into James's eyes, his expression carefully blank.

"I'm sorry, Ashelandra. I can't let you go. I don't have a choice," he whispered so that only she could hear.

Ash shook her head at him frantically, but his grip on her arms only tightened as he turned her to march her back toward his father.

"Coward!" she screamed through the gag. Her word was understood by no one but herself. How did her uncle keep such a hold on his children? Why did they allow themselves to be so ruled? She twisted and tried to kick him, but he evaded her blows and entrenched his fingers deep into her flesh. Lord Richard grabbed her other side and the two frog-marched her to the manor's tiny chapel. Diakon Percival trailed behind, pausing, then hurrying to catch up, then pausing, and then tripping forward to trot at Lord Richard and James's heels.

Afternoon sunlight flowed through the tiny chapel's one stained-glass window, bathing the pulpit and benches beyond in a rainbow of blue, yellow, purple, green, and red light. When she was little, Ash loved to visit the chapel and hop from one section of colored light to the next, watching her arms turn the colors of the rainbow.

Trapped on both sides, she waded through the tinted light toward the pulpit as if receiving one last kiss of sweetness before her burial in the dark hopelessness of the future. The aisle was so narrow with both Lord Richard and James at her sides, Diakon Percival was unable to pass. He coughed nervously, and Lord Richard shoved Ash sideways to make way. Standing on the raised step, the Diakon's bald crown was coated in red light, casting a sinister glow on the otherwise unintimidating man. He reached into the pocket of his robe and pulled out a rolled piece of paper, which he slowly stretched flat.

Diakon Percival cleared his throat nervously. "Lord Richard, I'm sure it just slipped your mind, but do you have anyone else that can be here to witness the marriage? To be legally binding there needs to be at least two to sign this marriage certificate."

"You can act as the second witness." Lord Richard's voice held steely command.

Diakon Percival shifted, bathing his head in yellow. "I must sign as the priest. I can't sign in two places."

"Is it really necessary?" Lord Richard growled.

"If you want to avoid any legality questions in the future." Diakon Percival moved back to the red light. As he did so his gaze flicked to Ash before the rouge glow reflected off his glasses, hiding his eyes.

Lord Richard's grip tightened on Ash's arm as if he wanted to squeeze out his frustration by crushing bone. Ash could not help the whimper that emerged from the back of her throat and traveled through her muffled mouth. "I will sign as the second witness using another name. We can't afford to involve anyone else in this. I have neither the time nor the money to ensure anyone else's silence. Just start the ceremony."

"What about Willie?" James asked.

"Willie began to be under the mistaken impression that he could control me after all the help he gave in the past." Lord Richard met his son's eye with a message that said more than his next simple words. "I had to let him go."

Ash shivered, sure that the slimy Willie would not be seeking new employment ever again. She'd always suspected her uncle was capable of murder.

"I will be the second witness," Lord Richard said firmly.

The priest jerked his fingers to his glasses, almost stabbing his eyes under the spectacles as he pushed them up the bridge of his nose. "As you wish," he stammered.

Ash twisted against James's and Lord Richard's hold as Diakon Percival cleared his throat and began droning the long complicated, archaic verses traditionally used in only the most formal of wedding ceremonies. The hand holding Ash's arm twisted. Lord Richard shifted his weight, his arm muscles flexing as he anchored Ash in place. On her other side, James's grip twitched loose, then tightened as he struggled to hold her still. He switched hands and rubbed the freed one on his shirt to wipe his sweaty palm dry.

"Is this really necessary?" Lord Richard interrupted. "Just get to the exchanging of vows."

"Since there won't be much of an exchange," Diakon Percival glanced meaningfully at Ash's gagged mouth. "I thought I should make it as close to legitimate as I could by at least following the traditional wedding sermon."

"Fine, but hurry it up." Lord Richard moved his leg to avoid Ash's foot stomp. He backhanded her across the face with his free hand, and the world darkened and swirled around her. She sagged into their grip, a dead weight, as the priest stuttered over the verses. Ash struggled to see through churning black. The thrum of her heartbeat was loud in her ears. When a resounding bang rang from behind, Ash didn't realize the sound wasn't the blood rushing in her ears until both her uncle and cousin turned toward the rear of the chapel. Their movement twisted her arms painfully.

Ash craned her head to see through the receding black. A blurry image of blue light bathed the face of a man. For a moment he held still. The light washing his hair and skin of its original color made him look like a marbled statue. Ash's vision crystallized, the details sharpening. The man moved forward into a yellow swatch of sun, and Ash could finally see through the golden glow haloing copper hair that it was Prince Phillip.

Her heart jumped and picked up speed, bumping madly in her ears. He met her gaze and his jaw tightened.

"Let her go." Prince Phillip's commanding voice rang through the small chapel.

For the first time since Ash had met her uncle, Lord Richard looked disconcerted. He glanced at his hand still holding Ash's arm tight, then back at the prince. Her uncle's eyes cleared.

"Your Highness, I know this may look bad to you at the moment, but I am only doing what I must in order to secure your future happiness." Lord Richard softened his bear's growl to a convincing croon.

"And how could this"—Prince Phillip stretched his hand out to encompass Lord Richard and James gripping Ash's bound figure and the priest standing behind her at the altar—"possibly accomplish that?"

"This must be done to right a wrong and make it possible for you to marry Jane." Lord Richard's grip tightened with conviction. Ash winced, and Prince Phillip's eyes narrowed.

"Forgive me if I find it hard to believe that such actions could ever right any sort of wrong." Prince Phillip took another step forward. James jumped, twisting Ash's arm. The unexpected pain surprised Ash into a muffled squeak. Prince Phillip stopped, his face washed in green light, making him look like an enigmatic woodland creature.

"You have to understand. This girl's mother was a sorceress." Lord Richard spat the word as if to even say *sorceress* was to taste poison. "She ensorcelled my elder brother. Not only did she bewitch him into marrying her, she made sure that he would pass the lands on to her child, even though it was a girl and the land should have gone to the closest male relative." He spewed the word *girl* with almost as much venom as sorceress. "And not only is she a girl, she is just like her mother, a sorceress. She is bound and gagged for our own safety, Your Highness."

"So you want to marry her to Lord James so that he can share her lands. And then what? Do you plan to keep her muffled and imprisoned for the rest of her life?" Prince Phillip's face was expressionless, his tone neutral, but his muscles were tight as he leaned forward. His whole body seemed to radiate compressed energy like a loaded spring held in place by only a flimsy hook. Ash dimly registered shock that he knew that Trebruk was hers. She wished she could ask him how.

James looked like he was going to be sick all over the chapel's floors, but Lord Richard gazed steadily back at Prince Phillip as he said in a calm, reasonable voice, "Of course not, Your Highness. She will be treated as she deserves. You don't need to worry over the details. I will take care of everything so that you and Jane can be happy together. I promise to make it so no one will be able to find fault with you marrying her."

Prince Phillip's eyes narrowed, but his voice was calm. "If the reason you feel compelled to take this action is to ensure that Lady Jane is legally qualified to marry me, then there is no need to continue. Hand Lady Ashelandra over to me." Prince Phillip stretched out his hand in cool command. Ash blinked in surprise to hear the unfamiliar sound of Prince Phillip's voice using her full name.

Lord Richard's fingers dug in to Ash's already-forming bruises. The pain of his grip was becoming unbearable.

"Of course we must continue. This must be done for you to be able

259

to wed Jane. The law requires it." Lord Richard's rumbling voice held a hint of fanaticism.

"That's enough." Prince Phillip's order echoed through the small chapel. "It makes no difference whether the law requires it or not. Give Ash to me now or I will arrest you on charges of abduction, abuse, and fraud with the intent to deceive the crown." Prince Phillip drew his saber as he stepped forward into another swath of yellow light. It tipped his red hair in golden flame.

"I am doing this for you and Jane," Lord Richard roared.

Prince Phillip stepped close enough to hold the tip of his sword at Lord Richard's throat. "I doubt very much that you were only thinking of my happiness, or that of Lady Jane's, especially since she informed me she does not wish to marry me. She never did. She only agreed to my proposal because her father ordered her to."

Ash felt a cold flood of pity wash through her for Prince Phillip. Within that flood, however, she could not help the warm flush of relief that heated the torrent within.

"Let. Her. Go." Prince Phillip enunciated every word like a jab from his saber. Angry red suffused Lord Richard's face, but a trickle of sweat trailed down his brow, and he held very still so the sword would not nick his throat.

James dropped Ash's arm as if burned and backed away. When Prince Phillip saw James swift retreat, he leaned back and lowered his sword tip slightly to allow Lord Richard to do the same. Lord Richard growled and pushed Ash toward the blade as he stepped back to draw his own sword. Prince Phillip pulled his arm back as quickly as he could, but the tip still sliced her sleeve and slit the surface of her skin.

Prince Phillip froze, a horrified look on his face as he watched a thin trickle of blood stain Ash's yellow-green sleeve bright red.

"I had hoped to save you from her before she had a chance to use her foul arts on you, but it seems I was too late. You've been bewitched by this girl just as my brother was ensnared by her mother. There is only one way to save you now."

Lord Richard leapt toward Ash, saber extended, aiming for her heart. For a moment, time slowed. Ash watched, unable to move as the sharp tip of the sword thrust forward with the force of her uncle's rage. Prince Phillip shouldered her out of the way, and the clang of metal striking metal pierced the silence as he blocked her uncle's sword. Time snapped back into motion as Prince Phillip parried another swing.

Ash stumbled away to give him more room to counter her uncle's relentless blows. Lord Richard's sword flicked through the air with fluid efficiency, and Ash could see that Prince Phillip struggled to counter the added weight wielded behind each blow.

After having watched many practice sessions between her uncle and James over the years, she knew her uncle was a formidable opponent, showing little mercy even during practice bouts. Prince Phillip's skills were obviously impressive as well, but a manic frenzy fueled Lord Richard's strokes that made Prince Phillip's counter strikes seem feeble and hesitant in comparison. Ash bit down hard on the fabric in her mouth, her eyes glued to the fight as if the power of her stare could somehow make her uncle stumble, or help Prince Phillip's blade strike through Lord Richard's defense.

"Yield. You are only making things worse for yourself by fighting me," Prince Phillip said as his sword clashed and pushed against Lord Richard's. They broke away. Lord Richard tried to circle past, but Prince Phillip was careful to keep Lord Richard from slipping through the aisle around him to where Ash stood.

"Once she is gone, you will see. You'll be yourself again and will reward me for saving you. When I heard the sorceress was pretending to help you find Jane, I knew you would need my aide." Lord Richard maneuvered around a bench as he tried to sneak around Prince Phillip toward Ash. Prince Phillip countered the action, blocking him. "I made sure a messenger would be dispatched to me as soon as you reached the rescue party at the foot of the mountain. I came as quickly as I could to save you from her." Lord Richard struck Prince Phillip's sword near the hilt and jammed his shoulder with his own, knocking the prince into the pew. He struck the bench at an awkward angle and rolled sideways to the ground.

While he fell, Lord Richard rushed toward Ash. His face was red with sweat dripping freely to the collar of his shirt. A vein bulged out at his temple, and his slit eyes focused on Ash with an intensity that burned. Ash ran toward the door that led out of the chapel to the outside. Lord Richard slashed at her legs and the sword caught in the fabric of her skirt, tripping her. She stumbled forward and fell into a pair of arms that caught and steadied her before moving her to the side.

Strange consonants and clicking sounds of a spell rolled through the church. It caught and swept Lord Richard into the air. He yelled and kicked, slashing his sword into space, but he succeeded only in looking like a hooked fish flapping ineffectually from a fishing pole. Spell finished, Sorcerer Tioroso looked over at Ash, a small smile playing across his pretty face. She stood dumbfounded, not sure if she was saved or in more trouble now than before.

Prince Phillip limped toward them, sword loose at his side.

"I assume Lady Jane sent you," he said.

"She thought you might want some help," Sorcerer Tioroso replied in his soft baritone.

Prince Phillip nodded. "It was good of you, considering . . .," he trailed off.

Sorcerer Tioroso inclined his head. "Neither of us handled things very well." The two men locked gazes for a moment before Prince Phillip limped the rest of the way around Ash to untie her bound hands. Once free, Ash tried to release the cloth's knot at the back of her head, but found her fingers too numb to manipulate it. She rubbed her wrists to get the circulation moving and stared up at her uncle warily. He was silent now, his eyes boring into hers. Prince Phillip untied her gag, and Ash spit out the cloth, opening and closing her mouth to loosen her jaw.

"It was foolish to let you live all these years just so I could save on the cost of paying a servant. I failed to realize how dangerous you truly are. But soon all will see and thank me," Lord Richard spat. He pulled back his saber, holding it like a spear, and threw.

Chapter Twenty

APRIL 15, 1751

It flew forward straight toward Ash's chest. As the weapon hurtled toward her, an arm wrapped around her body and jerked Ash back and to the side. She tripped on her heels, and behind her, Prince Phillip lost his footing. He crashed to the ground with Ash falling backward on top of him as the saber clattered across the stone floor beside them. Ash's head hit Prince Phillip's jaw. She gasped in pain and heard an echoing grunt from Prince Phillip.

"I'm sorry," she said as she rolled off him and got to her knees.

He winced. "There we go again. If I didn't get bruises every time I come in contact with you, I'd almost think you liked me," he said, sitting up and rubbing his jaw, a smile pulling at his lips.

Ash gingerly touched her head, her answering smile painful. "I can't take all the credit. You acquire injuries quite well on your own."

"I received them while trying to save you, so . . ." He shrugged and grinned in victory.

Ash's smile dropped, and she regarded Prince Phillip with steady, serious eyes. "Thank you for saving me."

"I would like to point out that I was really the one to save you in the end," Sorcerer Tioroso quipped from behind.

Ash looked up. "But why? How are you even here? Aren't you under arrest?"

"Not anymore." Sorcerer Tioroso turned and helped Prince Phillip to his feet. "More importantly, what should we do with Lord Richard and those two over there?" Sorcerer Tioroso asked, pointing to the back of the chapel.

Ash looked over to see James fidgeting near the wall as if he would like to slip past the gathered group and out the door. Diakon Percival still stood at the front of the chapel, hands clenched on the edge of the pulpit. When he saw everyone looking at him, he released his grip and came up the aisle, careful to duck down as far as possible while traveling under Lord Richard, until he stood before Prince Phillip.

The priest dropped to the ground. "I will submit to whatever punishment you decide, Your Highness. I am a weak man and have let my weakness rule me and lead me to actions of which I am deeply ashamed." He looked up and met Ash's eyes. "I hope one day you will forgive me also, My Lady."

Ash felt uncomfortable. She thought that Diakon Percival might have been trying to help her by making the ceremony as long as possible, but he still hadn't refused to marry her to James. Ash gave him a tight nod indicating, if not acceptance, then that she would at least think about it.

There was a clattering outside the door that led back into the manor, and Ash turned to see Captain Forbs followed by five of the soldiers that had traveled with her to Ketskatoret. Brett Johnson smiled wide when he took in the hanging man from the ceiling, James cowering in the corner, and Diakon Percival on his knees before Prince Phillip. Even Captain Forbs's mouth curled upward for a moment in a look of satisfaction before he ordered his men into action. Diakon Percival and James were bound, and Sorcerer Tioroso removed the levitation spell with little finesse. Lord Richard dropped painfully to the ground. He had no time to gather himself to run before he too was bound.

"What took you so long?" Prince Phillip asked Captain Forbs. He gestured in an exaggerated manner as if irritated, but the smile pulling at his lips revealed that he was teasing the Captain.

"I would like to point out, Sire, that you did not inform us where to go, or even impart to us the full details of the situation." Captain Forbs eyed Sorcerer Tioroso with narrow-eyed distrust. "You only insisted that Sorcerer Tioroso be released, and that all charges be dropped due to a misunderstanding. Then you ran off, claiming you had to *rescue* Ash."

Prince Phillip flushed a little at the word rescue. His eyes flicked to Ash and away in embarrassment.

"Sorcerer Tioroso took a horse and followed you before anyone could object, and it wasn't until Mr. Johnson suggested we ask Lady Jane if she knew anything that we discovered where we should go. However, she would not let us press for details as to why Ash was at Lady Jane's manor in need of help. She would only say that we should follow you as quickly as possible. So here we are. And what in the blazes is happening?" Captain Forbs finished in a huff. It was the most flustered Ash had ever seen the man, and the most she'd ever heard him speak at one time. His face reddened, and he hastily added, "Your Highness."

"Lady Jane and Sorcerer Tioroso are in love. He didn't kidnap her as we thought. They were running away together to escape Lady Jane's father, who demanded that she marry me." Prince Phillip shrugged a little as if to show that it didn't really matter that he hadn't been loved by the woman he wanted to marry, but Ash saw him wince. She wanted to feel angry at her cousin, but couldn't quite bring herself to do so. Even if Jane had hurt Prince Phillip by pretending to love him, she'd been pressured by her father, and had even run away to avoid living a lie. Still, Ash ached for Prince Phillip. And though she didn't want to admit it, knowing that he still must hold some love for Jane made Ash ache a little for herself as well.

"Not only did Jane not wish to marry me, she did not have the requisite lands to legally do so. We were led to believe that this manor belonged to Lord Richard when, in fact, it doesn't. It belongs to his niece, Lady Ashelandra," he said, gesturing to Ash. "She will inherit everything fully and have no need of a guardian in a week when she turns twenty-one. Lord Richard wanted to prevent that from happening by marrying her to her cousin Lord James, then he planned to keep her out of the way." Ash wondered if she should reveal that her uncle had planned to do more than just keep her imprisoned. Prince Phillip saw her wry look and added, "Or maybe more than that." She nodded, and his expression darkened.

Brett's eyebrows bunched in confusion and he blurted, "But I thought you were a servant." His eyes went wide with mortification as all heads turned to him, and he mumbled an apology.

Ash smiled at him. "For the past three years I have been. When I wouldn't do everything my uncle wanted exactly as he ordered, he decided that being a servant would keep me from rebelling." Ash's smile faltered and her hands curled into fists. She looked down and released her fingers one by one until they fell loose at her sides. "It didn't work." She gave Brett a wicked little grin and winked. He smiled back, blushing. When Brett looked over at Prince Phillip, the smile vanished abruptly and Brett ducked his head. Ash turned her head to see why and saw Prince Phillip glowering at the young man.

"Sire, please. Can't you see? She's bewitched you all. I tried to save you," Lord Richard's said, his voice cracking. Two guards stood over him. His upturned face blazed earnestness and he knelt as if in fervent prayer. The posture was so alien to her uncle that Ash felt a shiver run down her spine. Lord Richard was so altered from the neatly pressed, always-in-control man that she knew. His clothes were rumpled and torn. His eyes glinted with a hint of desperate insanity. It was more frightening than when he had thrown her down on the floor of her ballroom to furiously declare she was to be a maid in her own home.

Prince Phillip redirected his scowl to settle on Lord Richard. "If she was able to cast a spell of bewitchment, why didn't she cast one on you years ago to save herself the pain of your abuse?"

When Lord Richard's mouth flapped wordlessly, Prince Phillip blew out his breath in disgust.

"Take him away to await trial," Prince Phillip ordered.

Seeing his last chance to convince Prince Phillip slip from his grasp as the soldiers propelled him out the door, Lord Richard yelled, "Wait. We are related by blood. That's why she can't ensorcell me. You can't punish me. The law is wrong. I was righting an injustice!" His shouting grew muffled as Captain Forbs and the soldiers herded the priest, James, and Lord Richard outside.

Sorcerer Tioroso, Prince Phillip, and Ash watched them go until they went around the corner out of sight. Prince Phillip turned to Sorcerer Tioroso and cleared his throat.

"Perhaps you should go with them to make sure nothing happens along the way. I'm sure Jane has made it back to the palace by now. The king will need to hear both your explanations," Prince Phillip suggested.

Ash caught the sorcerer's sleeve before he could follow Captain Forbs. "Wait. I'm still not exactly sure what happened here. I understand that Jane and you are in love, but how is that possible? When did you meet? For Jane to even consider running away from her father seems unbelievable."

Sorcerer Tioroso smiled, his eyes going distant in memory. "I first met Jane at the ball. She'd hidden herself away in the side chamber to escape her father's expectations for a moment of peace. I was hiding from the courtiers demanding I perform magic, and we began talking."

"Are you sure you were speaking to Jane?" Ash asked. Prince Phillip snorted, and Sorcerer Tioroso's eyes narrowed in a glare. Ash shrugged. "It was a masked ball after all."

The sorcerer's pinched lips relaxed and curved up. "I caught her at a weak moment. She'd just had a particularly vexing encounter with a young man her father wanted her to encourage." Tioroso's eyes hardened in anger. "I later made sure he would never bother Jane again." His expression cleared and he focused on Ash again. "I couldn't even see her face, but I loved her at once. She had to go back in to the main ballroom before the unmasking so that her father would not be angry with her, and that is when Prince Phillip snatched her away."

Prince Phillip's mouth opened as if he wished to object to the sorcerer's wording, but he closed it again and gestured for Sorcerer Tioroso to continue.

"I went to her house the next day. She was reluctant to see me at first since I wasn't calling on her in the proper way. More than her reputation was at stake if her father ever found me talking with her in her room, but she would not send me away and I could not make myself leave her alone. There was no way her father would ever let us marry, even if I did formally call on her. The prince was courting Jane, and Jane told me of her father's unreasonable hatred of sorcerers. I couldn't bear to see her forced into a marriage she did not want in order to satisfy such a tyrannical man, so I convinced her to run away with me." Sorcerer Tioroso shrugged. "It was the only thing we could do."

Ash patted the sorcerer's arm. "For you to convince my mild-mannered cousin to rebel and actually run away with you means she must really love you." Ash glanced at Prince Phillip, unsure, a question in her eyes. "I hope there is nothing to prevent you from marrying Jane in a proper chapel now."

Prince Phillip held up his hands in surrender. "Sorcerer Tioroso and Lady Jane are free to do as they like. I would not stop them."

"But why didn't you say this to Prince Phillip and me when we were in Ketskatoret?" Ash asked, baffled.

Tioroso raised a brow. "You do remember that I was gagged at all times except when eating, don't you?"

His shoulders sagged and Tioroso's cheeks flushed in embarrassment. "But I probably could have told the prince if I'd really tried. I didn't because of something I overheard Prince Phillip say long before I met Lady Jane. He'd just observed a case where one man had run off with another's wife. Prince Phillip's father decreed that the husband and wife divorce, but the man was so grieved at losing his wife that he pleaded with the king to take back the ruling and arrest the adulterer instead so the husband could have his wife back. Later, when Prince Phillip was alone with the king, I heard him insist the adulterer receive life imprisonment."

Sorcerer Tioroso shrugged as Prince Phillip opened his mouth to retort, but the sorcerer continued before the prince could say anything, "Jane and I felt we were in a losing situation no matter what we did. Prince Phillip, usually so calm in his judgments, seemed to be less forgiving about matters of the heart. Since I had become like that adulterer, in a way, I reasoned it would be better to take all the blame rather than include Jane in the prince's censure."

Prince Phillip spluttered for a moment. "You . . .," he began, but stopped. "I . . .," he tried again. "What a mess. I can't believe you thought so poorly of me. You must not have known about the whole case. It was found the man who ran off with the wife killed the couple's only child and then used her grieving as a means to woo her away from her husband. If that isn't worthy of life imprisonment, I don't know what is," Prince Phillip huffed.

Sorcerer Tioroso's eyes widened as red rushed to his face. He knelt on one knee before Prince Phillip and bowed his head. "I am truly sorry, Your Highness. I have wronged you, in more ways than one. I do not deserve it, but I beg that you will forgive me someday."

Prince Phillip looked distinctly uncomfortable. He tugged on Tioroso's arm to make him stand. "Do get up. I'm the one who should ask for your forgiveness if my behavior led you to believe that you could not trust me. I hope I can rectify that by helping to clear any misunderstandings I may have caused by in turn maligning your name."

Sorcerer Tioroso bowed in gratitude. "I too am sorry for not trusting you and would appreciate your help." Sorcerer Tioroso looked from the prince to Ash, and she was surprised to see a small smile playing around his lips. "As soon as you are able."

After another slight bow, Sorcerer Tioroso turned to lope out of the chapel toward Captain Forbs and his men.

Silence engulfed the small, hallowed hall. The sound of Ash scuffing her foot on the floor rang overly loud to her ears. The sun had moved, bathing her and Prince Phillip in golden light as they stood in the aisle.

"Uh, I know it's inadequate, but I can't thank you enough," Ash said again, trying not to be distracted by the way the yellow glow cast by the window lit Prince Phillip's hair in a halo and gilded the contours of his face in gold. Metallic skin made his eyes appear all the more green, and Ash found herself unable to stop staring.

"You have nothing to thank me for. I've been so blind." His voice was soft, but filled with venomous self-reproach.

"No, you haven't. It isn't your fault Sorcerer Tioroso didn't trust you enough to explain himself. For that matter, my cousin should have been more honest with you about her feelings, even if it meant facing Lord Richard's displeasure." Ash's ire faded a little at that thought. "Though I hope you will one day forgive her being unwilling to face her father's wrath. He is not a kind man." Ash shivered.

Prince Phillip's jade eyes darkened to the green of a deep forest. "He will face justice, Ash." Prince Phillip shifted. He glanced away, and back, eyes light again. "But you misunderstood me. I am not angry with Jane for what she did. What happened was as much my fault as it was hers. You see, I was under the mistaken impression that she was you."

"I beg your pardon?" Ash wrinkled her brow in confusion.

"I think I should start from three years ago when I encountered a spirited young woman galloping alone through the forest. She was wild and free, with brown and blonde streaked hair in wet curls down her back. I had to be sure that she was real, so I followed her only to have her disappear like a wood nymph just as she caught my heart with a mischievous smile."

Instantly Ash remembered that day when she urged Windrunner on as the sky pelted her face with stinging rain. She listened in stunned silence to Prince Phillip, unaware that her mouth hung open until he reached out a gentle hand and put a finger under her chin to close it. A corner of his mouth lifted as he continued.

"For three years I couldn't get that wild, beautiful creature out of my mind, even though I was half convinced that she was nothing more than a figment of my imagination. Finally, at the ball, a woman sparked my interest. She was mysterious, intriguing, and fun. When the masks were lowered and her face revealed, I wished for one face, but when I found another, I decided that it was time to put my fantasy aside and move on. Lady Jane had proved herself interesting. She was pretty, and my father was pressuring me to choose a suitable companion, so I thought she was as good a choice as any. But she never revealed that spark of amusing antics again. It was as if she'd shown me a glimpse of the pearl that lay within only to close her shell tight ever after." Prince Phillip absently played with a strand of Ash's hair as he talked, and Ash stood frozen, afraid to move in case he realized what he was doing and stopped. "And then I found you again, and you were real. I convinced myself that finally discovering you were an actual person would make it possible to put the fantasy of you behind me. So I continued to pursue Lady Jane, hoping that she would eventually trust me enough to show me her true self again. And though I never saw another hint of that spunk, she was genuinely sweet, and I felt that a life with her would not be a bad sort of existence." Prince Phillip's finger traced Ash's jawline. She held her breath, afraid even the slightest puff of breeze would blow his feathered touch from her face.

"I proposed, only to run into you in the woods afterward. You slipped a thorn of doubt back into my heart. Still, I convinced myself that my regard for Lady Jane was a more practical, lasting sort of affection, and when Lady Jane was kidnapped, I was genuinely distressed."

Prince Phillip edged even closer to Ash, trailing his fingers from her face, down her arms to gather her hands in his. "I didn't realize how shallow that affection was until I traveled with you to save her and fell utterly and hopelessly in love with you. Your uncle was partially right. You have bewitched me, but it wasn't with magic.

"It happened when I discovered your strength of will, your love of mischief, your bravery and self-sacrifice. It happened because of you. Even when I thought I could live my life with Jane, I was still hoping she'd show that witty spirit I first saw in her. But it wasn't her at all. It never had been. It was really you. It's always been you."

Prince Phillip drew her hands up to his face and kissed them. Even in his gentle grip, Ash's fingers trembled. Her heart burned with wonderful spreading warmth as it beat faster than a hummingbird's wings. Her shocked body slowly unfroze as the warmth trickled upward, and she felt her cheeks lift and her lips curl up in a wide, stretching smile.

Seeing it, Prince Phillip's slightly anxious expression relaxed. He mirrored her foolish grin. "So, what do you say? Will you forgive me for being a blind fool and marry me?" he asked.

She lifted her brow in an arch, though her grin refused to drop. "That depends. Are you sure you can marry a sorceress? Society might frown upon it."

"Society can hang, and did you not notice how my soldiers have come to admire you? Your deeds of heroism are already spreading far and wide. Soon the people will insist that I marry you," he said as he reached one arm around to pull her against him.

She frowned at him but didn't stop him from pulling her closer. "What mischief have you been up to?" she demanded.

He smiled the mysterious lazy smile of a cat that had just caught a mouse, but didn't answer. Her fingers rested on his chest as his other hand cupped her head and drew her lips to his. His mouth was soft and warm and his kiss sent shivers of happiness through her.

He drew away slightly, face inches from hers. "You still haven't answered, you know." His lips curved up, but his eyes looked worried.

Ash smiled the slow mischievous grin that she knew lit up her eyes. Prince Phillip's mouth dropped open, and a small puff of air escaped.

"Of course. Even if your devious methods don't work to sway the people in our favor, it could be a lot of fun convincing them," Ash said.

Prince Phillip laughed, a sound that somehow conveyed both admiration and exasperation. "Ash, I'm not so sure your method of convincing people would work in our favor."

"It seems to have worked on you," Ash said with a saucy look that couldn't completely hide the new shy happiness bubbling up from within.

"Heaven help me," he said as his lips were inexorably drawn back down to hers.

Epilogue

She hadn't returned to the manor at once, since the king had required a full explanation from everyone involved in the kidnapping fiasco. The prince's party all shuffled in to the king's study, which surprised Ash. She'd thought they would report to the king in the throne room. He stood from a desk piled with loosely organized paper, and Ash saw that he was as tall as Phillip. His clothes hung just a little too loose, as though he often forgot to eat. But when he strode forward and hugged his son fiercely, Ash could see the strength of his grip. Any false assumptions of weakness were further rebutted when he then pulled away from his son to whack the backside of his head.

Prince Phillip winced and rubbed his tender skull as his father sighed and walked back to sit at his desk. He gestured to Prince Phillip. "I've already received some reports, but you'd better tell me everything anyway." His keen eyes moved from his son to Captain Forbs, swiveled to Jane and Tioroso standing slightly behind the prince as if they wished to avoid his notice, and then finally stopped on Ash. She felt the weight of his assessment and wondered what exactly he already knew.

As Prince Phillip began the tale, the king steepled his fingers together and watched the five participants of the story carefully without interrupting. Ash felt herself flushing several times as Prince Phillip described her involvement in saving the two of them from the floating boulders and capturing Sorcerer Tioroso. She felt herself go even hotter when the prince announced that he intended to marry Ash at the end of the long recitation.

The king unfolded his fingers and leaned forward, face unreadable. Everyone held their breath as they waited for his verdict. "As there was no crime committed other than that of young stupidity, there is really nothing for me to do about the matter. Your foolhardy rampage into Ketskatoret did prove useful in one way. I am glad to hear that my old friend Sorcerer Shovaylan is still alive and will be visiting soon to help us as the banishment spell fades. Though I'd hoped it would last, there appear to be a few drawbacks to the spell we hadn't foreseen. We'll have to plan how best to deal with the consequences as they come."

He sat back and Ash thought he was finished speaking when he added, almost as if it were an afterthought. "It will be handy to have a sorceress in the family." He caught Ash's eye and gave her a sly smile that looked startlingly like the cat-in-the-cream expression Prince Phillip had given her in her family's chapel when he'd boasted the people would soon beg him to marry her.

"Though I won't be of much use to you as I'm not much longer for this world," he added, his grin growing.

Prince Phillip huffed in happy exasperation. "You can't retire from being king no matter how many times you hint about it, father."

King Ferdinand just shrugged. "We'll see."

***

"Hold still," Jenny admonished as she sewed on another pearl that had come loose on Ashelandra's gown.

"Is that really necessary? This dress has so many pearls sewn all over no one will miss one." Jenny didn't bother to respond as Ash regarded herself in the full-length mirror in the newly remodeled master bedroom of her manor.

As soon as she'd turned twenty-one, Ash and the recovered Mr. Thursley went to work tidying any legal loose ends in regard to her inheritance. There really hadn't been that much to do. Mr. Thursley's burns had healed without complications, though the skin on his left arm would always have a tight shiny sheen. Despite Lord Richard's efforts, Mr. Thursley had made sure that Ash's uncle was never in possession of more money than was required to run the household. In fact, the lawyer had managed her business ventures so well that she'd acquired a small fortune. Money would never be a worry. Ash made him a full business partner, and raised the salary of everyone in the manor to three times what it had been before, adding two extra half days and another full day off every week in addition to the one full day of rest that they usually received. She also offered to help them start their own household if they wished to leave. No one had wanted to.

Ash shifted so that the light caught on the hundreds of pearls sewn onto the white satin dress, making it glow like moonlight on snow. Jenny grunted a warning, and Ash stilled her fidgeting. She sighed, but it wasn't a big sigh. The corset of the elaborately decorated wedding gown did not allow for deep breathing. The twining pattern of the pearl-laden dress swirled over the corset and down the full skirt, becoming larger looping shapes as the pearls descended to the dress's gigantic train. Dragging the heavy trailing fabric was a chore, but the royal wedding planner nearly had a nervous breakdown when Ash suggested they leave it off completely. She'd finally talked her down from a ten-foot train to a six-foot one, but that was as far as the surprisingly tyrannical coordinator would compromise.

In the mirror, a stranger looked back at Ash. Annette had styled her hair so that it swept softly off her face in fat curls, looping at the top. Several perfect curlicues fell artfully down the back. Small pearl strings were woven through the locks, and a tasteful tiara of diamonds and pearls rested at the crown of her head.

"There. Yer done. Ye'd better hurry. Bill's wait'n with the coach." To her surprise, Jenny sniffed, rubbing an impatient hand under her eye to rid herself of a tear. "Ye deserve this. I wish ye happiness."

Ash smiled. "Thank you, Jenny. You've been a wonderful friend. I wish you happiness too."

Jenny nodded curtly and busied herself gathering up the heavy satin of Ash's train so that they could descend the stairs to the carriage outside. It would carry her through a people-gawking procession to the palace.

Bill stood holding Windrunner's connecting reins at the head of the carriage. Three other gray horses were hitched to the shining white open coach, prancing nervously, ready to move. Bill's gaze fixed on Ash in a sad sort of awe, and Ash felt a pang of sympathy for him. She knew what it felt like to yearn for someone that you shouldn't. She noticed Jenny darting wistful looks Bill's way, and her lips curved as her eyebrows rose.

Bill left the horses and came to the carriage's door to help Ash ascend. Her gloved hand left his at the first step, leaving Jenny standing awkwardly behind her beside Bill. Ash clicked a spell. Arms full of satin, Jenny was unable to stop herself from falling into Bill's arms when she suddenly lost her footing.

Jenny and Bill shared twin blossoms of red on their cheeks as he carefully set her back on her feet, both stuttering apologies. They smiled shyly at each other as Ash finished climbing into the carriage. She was careful to keep her face, with its accompanying smile of satisfaction, turned away. It took a bit of arranging to make her dress fall neatly in flowing folds across the red leather seats. When it was done, Ash sighed, glad to be sitting alone at last.

"Where is Captain Forbs? Isn't he escorting me?" Ash asked no one in particular. The clop of horse hooves on dirt drowned out her question as Captain Forbs rounded the corner into her courtyard, dressed in his formal dress uniform of blue and gold. Behind him trailed ten men, all of whom had journeyed on Prince Phillip's rescue mission. She'd made a point of staying involved in their lives after returning home, visiting the barracks often when she was at the palace to see Prince Phillip.

She waved cheerfully at them now. Brett Johnson gave a small low-down wave in return. Newly married himself to Molly, he seemed in a state of constant moony-eyed happiness. Molly had shocked Ash at their wedding by hugging her tightly after the ceremony.

All the other soldiers approaching, except Captain Forbs, smiled in greeting. Forbs just frowned and gave her a pointed look for her lack of decorum. She made an especially unrefined face to irk him and then grinned as he shook his head in exasperation. The soldiers arranged themselves so that five rode before her and six trailed behind as they all proceeded slowly to the palace. People gathered loosely at the side of the road when she was still far from the city, but the nearer her entourage got to the palace, the more crowded the roadside became.

Ash smiled and waved. Prince Phillip's plan to sway people's opinion in her favor had worked more than even he had predicted. Due to loose tongues among soldiers and servants, her role in helping Prince Phillip, and his rescue of her from her uncle had spread like seeds in the wind among the people. The tale burrowed deep and shot forth tender unfurling leaves of exaggeration, until Ash's story was so embellished and romanticized she became firmly planted as a hero of the people.

The lower classes especially loved to hear about her time as a servant when she was treated worse than a slave. A queen on the throne who knew what it was like to work hard every day gave them hope. Surely, they said, she would help their lives improve someday too. The magic she'd used to help the prince just added to the story's allure and soothed concerns about what the kingdom would do if any magical creatures wandered down from Ketskatoret.

The heralds announced the prince's bride as Ashelandra Enando Camery of Trebruk, but the people didn't call her that. To them, she was simply the Ash princess. Some of the more superstitious people started carrying little vials of hearth ash in their pockets for luck. Ash was uncomfortable when she'd heard of the trend, but Prince Phillip had just laughed and kissed her cheek.

"I don't blame them for wanting a symbol of you with them, so long as I get to have the real Ash to myself," he'd said, pulling her to him in an embrace.

It was a hot summer's day, and the carriage moved at a crawl. Ash clicked little puffs of breeze into existence as they drew closer to the palace so that she wouldn't melt. She longed to strip off her elbow length gloves, but she contented herself with sticking to unnoticeable spells that would help keep her cool.

Prince Phillip and she had decided to have the wedding ceremony at the top of the wide curving staircase at the entrance to the palace with chairs arranged in the courtyard below for the nobles. That way they could seat as many as wished to come and avoid offending anyone.

Prince Phillip's promenade preceded hers. Ash was relieved to see him waiting at the top of the wide curving staircases next to his father when she finally reached the palace and was helped down from the carriage. King Ferdinand had put on a little more weight since the first time she'd seen him and finally fit his clothes. He smiled at Ash as her train was put in order, and she grinned back. She'd gotten to know him better since her first stressful meeting and liked him immensely.

The seated nobles turned to watch as Ash walked down the aisle. It was difficult to gracefully glide while dragging her long train behind, and impossible to keep from falling if she allowed herself to look up at Prince Phillip, so Ash resigned herself to glancing at the guests. She was surprised to recognize Lady Vivian, the lady she'd seen picnicking with Prince Phillip so many years ago, by the fluffy plumed hat she wore. One of the large feathers bobbed in the face of the man beside her, and Ash had to stifle a laugh at the sight of his annoyed expression.

On the other side of the isle, Ash recognized Miss Penelope in a dress exploding with pastel yellow ruffles. She watched Ash with a pinched, disapproving expression, though Ash could not imagine why. Most likely, she disapproved of the length of Ash's train. Next to Miss Penelope, Lady Amelia met Ash's eyes and inclined her head in a gesture of both acknowledgment and approval. Ash grinned back in response.

Beyond Miss Penelope and Lady Amelia, closer to the front row, sat Lady Jane and Sorcerer Tioroso. Jane's smile was bright with happy tears. She gave Ash a little wave with the hand holding her damp tissue. Sorcerer Tioroso patted her shoulder comfortingly, used to his wife's recent bouts of emotional upheaval. Ash smiled back at the two newlyweds in greeting, thinking it an amusing irony that pregnancy could transform the very quiet and reserved Jane into someone who could cry or laugh at any moment.

Ash suspected that the metamorphosis was connected to more than just hormones. With Lord Richard sentenced to life imprisonment after it was proved he killed Willie and orchestrated the death of several court officials, Jane no longer had to bend to her father's expectations. That, combined with Sorcerer Tioroso's unconditional acceptance, did much to help Jane break free of her reserved shell. Her surprisingly impassioned plea on her brother's behalf at his and Lord Richard's trial was the deciding factor that reduced James's sentence from ten years to just one.

Ash ascended the stairs slowly, careful to lift the front of her dress just enough to avoid tripping and crashing back down again. The royal wedding planner had insisted she practice the climb with an equally heavy layered dress, and as Ash climbed, she silently thanked the annoying woman's compulsive need to oversee and plan for every possible eventuality. Ash glanced up and caught Prince Phillip's eyes, and her heart jumped. She knew her cheeks would ache later, but she couldn't stop the wide smile stretching her face.

He grinned back, and broke tradition by bouncing down the few remaining steps to meet her and help Ash the rest of the way to the landing.

"Planning to run?" he asked playfully.

"Absolutely not. I wouldn't put up with a thirty-pound dress that is slowly squeezing the life out of me just to give up before receiving the prize," she whispered back.

"I'm not sure how I should feel about that statement. Should I be happy to be considered a prize or displeased at being objectified?"

Ash barely managed to stop her laugh from wedging through her corseted lungs and out of her mouth.

"I love you. I tried so hard not to love you, but I couldn't stop myself." Ash squeezed his hand holding hers.

"Good." Prince Phillip's voice was low and intense. "Don't ever stop, because I will never stop loving you."

At the top, they faced each other, holding hands at the landing's railing so that everyone below would have a clear view as the priest intoned the same long invocation that Diakon Percival had used as a tactic to delay Ash's marriage to James. Then, she'd been grateful that the long indecipherable speech had lengthened the process long enough for rescue to arrive. Now, she wished the priest would hurry.

Prince Phillip noticed her shifting back and forth and stepped closer so that he could whisper to her under the booming voice of the priest.

"I hope you're not reconsidering."

Ash grinned and tried not to laugh as she shook her head no.

The priest loudly cleared his throat, the rasp of phlegm somehow conveying both resignation and annoyance. Prince Phillip and Ash jumped, and the two couldn't completely suppress guilty giggles, sounding like kids caught red-handed who still hope they might escape punishment by playing down the situation with a laugh.

The priest stared pointedly at Prince Phillip, and he recited the vows the he had been required to memorize. When he was done, Ash delivered her portion, hoping she remembered all the words correctly. Ash trembled as she held out her hand for Prince Phillip to place the ring on her finger. The diamond winked in the sunlight as he placed it on her hand.

When Ash and Prince Phillip were finally allowed to kiss, a cheer rose up from the guests. Prince Phillip pulled back a little, arms wrapped around her waist.

"You're stuck now," he said as he grinned down on her.

"I'll try to endure." She arched her eyebrow and made sure her smile went devilishly crooked. "And when things get dull, I can always make life a little more interesting." Ash clicked and snapped in a complicated combination. Dust whirled up from the ground and transformed into thousands of tiny white petals raining down over the heads of the guests in the courtyard below. Some swirled up to Prince Phillip and Ash, sprinkling and catching in their hair.

Below, the guests ooed and ahhed, clearly thinking the display a planned part of the wedding ceremony, though Ash caught a glimpse of the wedding planner racing around frantically, trying to find the culprit of the sudden snow of flowers.

Prince Phillip reached forward to brush a petal free of Ash's cheek. "I doubt that life with you will ever be dull." He pulled her closer. "But I wouldn't have it any other way," he added before bending down for another kiss.

About the Author

Alicia Buck was born in Salt Lake City, Utah, on a cold November day, and has hated the cold ever since. Luckily, she lives in the desert now with her husband, Jason, and three children. Though writing is her greatest dream, she also likes to dabble in making jewelry, singing, and working on finishing a 5K with a time that isn't so embarrassing. Alicia loves to read, and goes through book-craze phases where she reads at least a book a day until guilt kicks in and she tries to do something productive, like get back to work writing and fix the disaster her home has become. She graduated from Brigham Young University with a bachelor's in English and had to constantly defend her major when she had absolutely no desire to teach. *Out of the Ashes* is Alicia's second novel.